GIVING

A SATURN'S DAUGHTER NOVEL

Jamie Quaid

OTHER BOOK VIEW CAFÉ BOOKS BY PATRICIA RICE

MYSTERIES:
EVIL GENIUS, *A FAMILY GENIUS MYSTERY*, VOL 1
UNDERCOVER GENIUS, *A FAMILY GENIUS MYSTERY*, VOL 2

HISTORICAL ROMANCE:
NOTORIOUS ATHERTON, *THE REBELLIOUS SONS*, VOLUME 3
THE MARQUESS, *REGENCY NOBLES*, VOLUME 1
ENGLISH HEIRESS, *REGENCY NOBLES*, VOLUME 2
IRISH DUCHESS, *REGENCY NOBLES*, VOLUME 3

PARANORMAL ROMANCE:
TROUBLE WITH AIR AND MAGIC, *THE CALIFORNIA MALCOLMS*
THE RISK OF LOVE AND MAGIC, *THE CALIFORNIA MALCOLMS*

GIVING HIM HELL

Jamie Quaid

ooo

Published by Rice Enterprises, Dana Point, CA, an affiliate of Book View Café Publishing Cooperative

Publication team: Beta reader: Mindy Klasky

Proofreader: Phyllis Irene Radford

Formatter: Vonda McIntyre

Cover design by Killion Group

Book View Café Publishing Cooperative

P.O. Box 1624, Cedar Crest, NM 87008-1624

http://bookviewcafe.com

ISBN 978-1-61138-419-2 ebook

ISBN 978-1-61138-420-8 print

One

MY FIRST December in the Zone, and I simply hoped for peace on Edgewater Street.

Forget peace on earth. The industrially blighted outpost of south Baltimore that I called home had become so damned complicated that I yearned to just walk down the hill for a little normal Christmas shopping. After the horrors of this past year, I *deserved* a Currier-and-Ives holiday.

In my office, watching the snow fall in greeting card prettiness through the big plate glass window, I abandoned my desk to grab my coat. For the first time in my entire history, I had money in my pocket, and I could do what I wanted.

Through my office doorway, I watched my six-foot-five quarterback assistant catch a buzzing fly against the glass door in the front lobby. I held my breath while he eyed the insect like an appetizer. Then he opened the door to let in a client, and I sighed in relief as he sheepishly flung the fly out the door. Ned was a trifle self-conscious about his former life as an amphibian.

It had been a brief episode in Ned's thuggish career, and I wasn't certain how much of it he remembered, but it pained me every time Ned pounced on an insect. I held myself responsible for his condition and used him as a chronic reminder not to misuse my weird abilities.

Hi, my name is Justine Clancy, and I'm a freak of nature. Or Saturn's Daughter, according to my mother and grandmother, but they're not in the picture much anymore. Mom was hiding in an isolated Peruvian village, and Themis... I wasn't totally certain she wasn't communicating from the Beyond. Since a few months after my twenty-sixth birthday, when I learned I could damn my boyfriend to hell and get rewarded for it, I'd been without a rulebook. I had no idea what would happen the next time I damned someone. So I tried very hard to keep my vocabulary polite.

"C'mon, Clancy, It's lunchtime. Let's find something to eat." The client who had just entered dropped ominous envelopes from the city on my desk.

Most people called me Tina. He was just being obnoxious.

Andre Legrande could have walked out of my favorite old-fashioned cowboy movie, the kind where the slick gentleman gambler wears a frock coat and silk ruffles and vest. Today, under his shoulder-hugging leather blazer, he wore a blue silk shirt that emphasized taut abs and wide pecs. Combine all that hunkiness with thick black hair, and curious blue-green eyes and a smile that could melt bones, and Andre was the most dangerous man on this side of Baltimore. He knew it, too, and his arrogance was another reason, despite our past history, I wasn't going to bed with him.

Mostly, it's unethical for a lawyer to sleep with her clients, and Andre's business paid over half my bills. The amoral cad liked to kick me in my principles.

"It's almost Christmas," I reminded him. "I'm going shopping."

Andre helped me pull on my leather biker jacket. The proximity to his spicy aftershave had me drooling, so I had to counterbalance with snideness. I tapped the stack of letters he'd just dropped on me. "Don't beat up any of those building inspectors or you'll end up paying twice."

"The city is after us because of all the damned tourists," Andre grumbled. "You'd think the idiots would have the sense to stay out of an environmental hazard zone. Acme used to keep the city off our backs and the tourists off the street. You're the one who took Acme's management out of commission. You do something about it."

Acme is our neighborhood chemical factory and unhealthy for our environment in so many ways— but people have to work.

"Tourists are profitable," I argued, half-heartedly. I pulled on my gloves, striving not to admire Andre's conquistador profile.

"Not for the tourists," he warned. "I'm suing the moron who shit his pants when one of the Dumpsters got in his way. The damned fool shot at a frigging Dumpster and *missed.*"

Among other things, the chemicals permeating the Zone's ground have given theoretically inanimate objects the ability to move. Waltzing Dumpsters used to scare me too. It would only be a matter of time before the media realized the Zone wasn't just a drunken hallucination or a new kind of theme park but the real deal.

"That bullet took out the bar window and the arm of one of my bartenders. Just give me one good excuse, and I'll sue Acme too," Andre grumbled.

"Gun control laws should involve intelligence tests," I muttered as Andre accompanied me to the outer lobby. "But Acme has no responsibility for keeping out tourists or idiots."

"Someone has to keep them out. The Zone isn't normal and Acme is the reason!" he protested, as if he weren't preaching to the choir. "Imbeciles are going to be trouble if we don't find some way to move them along."

I didn't have an answer to that. He was right. The Zone with its dangerous idiosyncrasies was no place to play. It was a worse place to live, but once infused with the chemicals that permeated the area, some of us had little choice.

My assistant, wearing a pink shirt, rose-colored tie, and a pink quartz earring, held the door open for us—as if he hadn't been hunting more flies in the window.

I worried about Ned's other froggy friends and whether they'd ever returned to normal. They'd been Acme thugs and the world was probably better off without them, but my over-developed conscience didn't like condemning people without a real trial. Consequences inevitably sucked. I wanted a rule book that promised I wouldn't go to hell for condemning people without due process.

Outside, a cold wind rushed down the hill, promising heavier snow than the pretty flakes falling now. My office was in an old storefront across the street from the row of Victorian houses where Andre and I lived. Andre probably owned the whole street, but our apartments were in separate buildings.

Below us, in the Zone proper, I could see bums warming their hands over steaming manholes, unbothered by the traffic creeping around them. I knew manholes could steam in the cold, but this steam had an oddly red tint to it. Given that sidewalks here turned to green mud and the buildings glowed neon blue, a little steam wasn't worth questioning.

"No wailing sirens, no gaseous clouds, no chemical waste lines exploding." I recited my litany of gratitude every time I saw this peaceful scene. "May Saturn be praised."

I was being facetious. So far, no one had told me if my Saturn was a planet or an antique god, but astrology and ancient gods made as much sense as anything else.

Andre snorted. "If you think killing off Gloria Vanderventer means the Zone will stay peaceful, you haven't lived here long enough. Something's stewing. It just hasn't broken out yet."

I knew that. Gloria and her grandson Dane had once owned Acme Chemical. They had been evil personified, as far as I could determine. I'd damned them both to hell and been rewarded for my good deeds. I had no other way of verifying that they were actually gone. I worried sometimes, because I'd seen them writhing in flames and cursing me.

But they hadn't succeeded in destroying my home, and it was the season of peace. I wanted—needed—to celebrate my new security for a while. After a lifetime of wandering, I finally had a home, friends, and a new career. That was worth a revel or two before life started tossing fireballs at me again.

"Are the Christmas lights on the streetlamps supposed to be pink and orange?" I asked cautiously, still admiring the view as we strolled down the hill. "Because they kind of clash with the red wreaths." The day was gray enough for the twinkling lights to sparkle nicely.

Andre jammed his hands into his pockets and studied the holiday scene below. "No one here paid for decorations. That must be the DG's work."

The DG, otherwise known as Dedicated to Good Inc. or the *Do-Gooders* in local lingo, had been inexplicably attempting to clean up the Zone these last weeks. They were mundanes from outside the Zone. For whatever reason, we'd become the nonprofit's charitable cause, whether we wanted it or not.

"Cheap bulbs from China," I suggested. Or the Zone's pollution was already eating at them. It happened.

"Don't go getting happy ideas about this spell of quiet," Andre warned as we headed down.

I grimaced. "It's Christmas, Legrande. Be merry. We'll worry about calamity in the new year." I walked faster, eager for my shopping trip.

The orange and pink bulbs below exploded into little flames that ate the red wreaths and produced colorful circles of hellish flames on all the lampposts.

Then the manhole covers blew off.

I hated it when Andre was right.

Two

ANDRE and I watched the flaming scene in awe and horror.

To add to the Zone freakishness, a blue blob the shape of the Pillsbury doughboy crawled out of one of the exploding manholes and sauntered toward an alley, away from the flames and in the direction of the polluted harbor.

Could blue blobs cause exploding wreaths?

The Do-Gooders in their knit hats and gloves frantically screamed and jumped up and down, trying to douse fiery wreaths by ineffectively waving their hands in panic. I wasn't at all certain they noticed the blob. People tend not to see what doesn't make sense to them.

I, on the other hand, started to wonder if the city really shouldn't shut down the Zone, as they'd been threatening recently. The Zone had never actually *created* an object before. That we knew of.

"You saw that, right?" I asked as we hurried toward our so-called business district.

"Nothing a little cataract surgery won't solve," he muttered.

"Cataracts aren't blue. That was *blue*. As in Cookie Monster blue." Even my deprived childhood had included Sesame Street.

That neither Andre or I raced to douse burning Christmas wreaths said a *lot* about the Zone. Instead, we cautiously scanned the street for any more dangerous phenomena, leaving the mundanes to deal with normal occurrences like fire.

Mostly, after realizing they couldn't spit out a blazing wreath, the DG people stared in helpless astonishment as their fiery ornaments disintegrated. They apparently hadn't even completed putting them up. The guy holding the last wreath dropped it and backed away.

One of the homeless guys lay sprawled on the street, kayoed by a flying manhole cover just outside Discreet Detection Agency, where Cora Isabel worked. As the agency's receptionist, Cora appeared in the doorway to check out the confusion. She wore her tight curls cut short to accentuate the glory of her razor-sharp cheekbones and rich coffee au lait coloring. Despite her irritating beauty queen glamor, Cora has her own set of weirdnesses. I still counted her as the kind of friend I'd never thought to have. Seeing us, she leaned against the jamb and waved.

People began emerging with fire extinguishers to spray down the wreaths. I sincerely hoped these were normal electrical fires. In the Zone, the alternative could mean anything from more chemical floods to hell's demons emerging.

I wasn't exaggerating. Much.

"Does anyone have a clue what kind of fires those are so they aren't blowing them up with the wrong chemicals?" I asked with reasonable trepidation.

"We don't all have college degrees," Andre said scornfully as one of the sprayed wreaths exploded—as I'd feared. "We learn by doing."

"Ow, that's gotta hurt." I watched one of Chesty's regulars dance up and down and beat at his flaming sleeves after the fire extinguisher he'd been holding turned into a torch. "Maybe we could start a Zone school and offer common sense degrees."

"And enroll Leibowitz," Andre said with a resigned sigh, nodding in our neighborhood flatfoot's direction and punching the buttons on his phone at the same time. There was no guarantee emergency services would bother with his call or even that the Zone would let the call go out, but I let him handle the outside world.

My urge was to follow the Cookie Monster dough boy, but Leibowitz seemed to be writing a ticket to the DG's who'd been installing the holiday décor. He'd no doubt fine the stunned bum and the would-be fireman for littering the street. Authority should be useful, but Leibowitz worked with a different dictionary than me.

And I had this unholy obsession about serving justice.

"If there were any fairness in this world, petty-minded officialdom would be illegal," I muttered, wishing for a good excuse to send Leibowitz to another dimension.

Even knowing my dangerous propensities, Andre looked only vaguely alarmed as he cut off his phone and tried 911 again. "He's one of us. Maybe he'll learn." He returned his attention to reporting a fire. At least he'd finally got through. Whether the fire department responded was another question. Officialdom didn't like having their tires melted on our polluted blacktop.

"Or maybe we could isolate those who lack the imagination to see the bigger picture and ship them to Nebraska," I snarled, knowing he wasn't listening.

Andre would have had the sense to look alarmed if he'd heard me, because I could do exactly that. I preferred visualizing baddies to other places or into other things. It just seemed less permanent and safer than sending them to hell without a trial. Nebraska sounded about right.

I sauntered toward the cop. Leibowitz hated me on general principles. There was no point in wasting a good hate.

Only last spring, I used to hide from Leibowitz and most of the rest of the world. I'd been small, crippled, and invisible, and carried a big grudge. These days, thanks to insanity or Saturn, whichever you'd like to believe, I had straight legs, great eyesight, pretty teeth, and my hair belonged on a shampoo model. And I now had my law license— but that was mostly thanks to me and no heavenly entities.

"Leibowitz!" I shouted. "Call the damned ambulance! If you ticket an injured man, I'll sue your fat pants off."

This was how I'd built my clientele so quickly. I stood up for the little guys, and there were *waaaaay* more of them than there were rich fat cats around the Zone. Couldn't say that I always won in court, but I had other methods.

"He's not injured," Leibowitz said with suspicion, looking at the shocked Do-Gooder. "He tried to set the place on fire. So, go ahead, sue me."

"*China* tried to set the place on fire." I gestured at the burnt wires hanging from the lamp poles. "We're suing the manufacturer. Call the ambulance for the real injured parties here."

Since sirens were finally screaming in the distance, I knew Andre had succeeded in reaching 911, but it was always good to give Leibowitz a task he understood.

Sure enough, he was distracted enough to tuck away his ticket book and wander over to look at the homeless guy struggling to sit up. He didn't help the bum, mind you, but he did pull out his phone.

I glanced warily at the nearest alley. Had the Cookie Monster really been invisible to everyone else? A gnawing in my gut told me I needed to investigate, but did I really want to know if I was nuts or the Zone had upped the ante?

Fortunately, I didn't have to answer that question yet. People came first.

"Thanks," the DG I'd just saved from a ticket said, rubbing his head and staring at the wires. "They all went up in flames at once. How is that possible?"

He was young and lanky, with sandy hair, but he looked intelligent enough to want to dissect the wiring. *So* not a good idea.

"If you accept the impossible, you'll fare better down here," I suggested, holding out my hand to distract him from live wires. "Tina Clancy. And you?"

"Rob Hanks, scout leader for Dedicated to Good's ninth division, pleased to meet you Ms. Clancy. And I have to accept responsibility for the faulty wiring. I just want to know how it happened so I can file a report." He studied the dangling wire, but it still looked too hot to handle. "Thank you for talking the officer out of a ticket. Our funds don't cover fines."

"Leibowitz is a decent guy with a few frayed ethics I'm trying to clean up. It's possible to change people, but not the Zone, Mr. Hanks. In case you haven't noticed, technology has problems down here. There's a reason we only accept cash and not credit cards, and even cash isn't safe. I'm sure there are far more appreciative neighborhoods than ours, and gangs are less hazardous to your health than an environmental disaster zone. You really should take your folks elsewhere."

He looked at me with puzzlement. "Senator Vanderventer has given us a grant to help clean up this area. He's set up a foundation in his late grandmother's name just for this purpose. He wouldn't send us anywhere dangerous."

Rage nearly blew off my lid. I smothered it before I did something rash like send Max to hell for a second time. It had been only a fluke getting him back the first time around, and he'd not been the same since he woke up inside his cousin—the wretched senator.

Granny Vanderventer was probably torching Christmas wreaths from hell to voice her objections to Max using her money for charity. I held the senator's grandmother directly responsible for the chemical flood that had warped the Zone and its inhabitants.

Rob didn't deserve my wrath. Max and his Do-Gooder soul did. I was taking me down one stupid senator. Around here, we lived with blue blobs and fiery manholes, for pity's sake! Sending innocents in was the kind of idealistic stupidity that had got him killed once already.

"Take the money and run," I advised the overgrown Boy Scout. "Because Vanderventer and his interfering lunacy will be withdrawing his offer shortly."

A fire truck screamed down the road and pulled up short at the manhole.

I opened my phone and walked toward Cora, who was admiring the scurrying of Do-Gooders and tourists as they beat out fiery wreaths and occasionally threw punches when they got in each other's way.

Since the gas cloud earlier in the fall, casual violence had become chronic. Occasional bouts of benevolence erupted as well, but mostly they went unheralded—just like in the real world.

I reached Max's—Senator Vanderventer's—voice mail. "You flaming moron," I shouted at the phone. "Do you want to get these nice people killed? Pull your Do-Gooders out of here *now,* before your grandmother starts crisping them!"

I wished I had enough money to fling phones at the wall to express my frustration, but I'm not that rich. I clicked OFF and shoved the cell into my pocket. Lawyers probably shouldn't throw tantrums anyway.

"Grandmother?" Cora asked, crossing her arms and letting the snake wrapped around her biceps sink back into her tattoo. Once upon a time, Cora had been a prostitute working the streets in the Zone. Weirdly, the chemical flood had given her tattooed snakes a life. That was just how the Zone worked. "Were we talking to the good senator? Must be nice to have private congressional phone numbers."

"Dane's a tool meant to be used," I muttered.

Granny Vanderventer had been evil, as in demonically impaired. She and her real son, Senator Dane Vanderventer, had my boyfriend Max killed and had done their best to kill me.

Except Max's Do-Gooder soul now resided in his cousin Dane's senator body, which was a source of constant confusion. Don't make me explain.

"And what does our good senator have to do with flaming wreaths?" Cora asked with interest, as the fireman attempted to find a hydrant. I winced as a hose melted before they could hook it up.

"Dane's formed a foundation with granny's money to improve the Zone that she polluted." I should have known he'd do that. I'd threatened him with mayhem if he dared close down Acme, because mass unemployment was as toxic as chemicals in this industrial backwater. The DGs were his retaliation. "I'm sure he didn't order flaming wreaths, though. Do you think there's a gas leak?"

Cora gazed at the pole outside the office with interest. "They were gas lamps once, but they quit working a gazillion years ago. The city wired them for electricity back before the chemical spill, but they've been blowing out lately. Maybe they've reached their expiration dates."

I didn't have to turn to recognize the snort of derision behind me as Andre's.

"They call it infrastructure deterioration," he said, pocketing his own cell now that the posse had arrived. "Our sewers and water mains are leaking, the underground wires are corroding, and the gas lines are decaying. And until recently, we didn't have enough tax base to be worth the city's time. The good senator has apparently been pulling strings to finally get inspectors down here." He didn't say that with appreciation.

I wasn't so certain that bad wiring was at fault, but Andre hadn't seen Granny's face screaming at him from a gas flame. Max and I had, though, and we knew there were stranger things between heaven and earth than even Hamlet knew about. After all, Max had lived in the outer rings of hell—or another dimension—for a while.

"And here come the infrastructure police." I nodded at a yellow truck covered in ladders and spitting out men in hard hats and orange vests. "That was mighty quick."

The fire department's tanker truck arrived at the same time. Amazing. Two trucks at once—Max had really been leaning on the city. Usually, they just waited for us to burn down. This bunch intelligently hooked hoses to the tank instead of hunting non-working hydrants.

Andre ignored the wreaths and firemen and focused on the utility guys. "That was one of the notices I gave you this morning," he said, his usual insouciance barely hiding his irritation. "For whatever reason, we're to be inundated with line crews covering every damned utility at once. I predict power outages and gas shut-offs in our future."

I shivered, but not just from the chilly wind. I didn't need to walk between dimensions as Andre did to predict the future. I had an overabundance of common sense and disaster expertise to calculate the odds of the city approving of sidewalks that turned to mud and stoplights that flashed rainbows. Or manholes containing sentient Cookie Monster blobs. Trepidation escalated to flashing amber alert.

"Let's go shopping," I told Cora as a white hard hat walked our way. "I don't want to be here for this."

"Frank has our computer cable wired outside the Zone," Cora said. "But I'll have to shut the machines down if they're turning off the electricity. We can't risk frying the equipment."

Frank was the shadowy owner of Discreet Detection. He'd been helpful in the past, but I wouldn't want to dig too deeply into his business or his abilities. Right now, the sign above his agency was flashing a collage of unsavory mug shots—including the mayor's. There'd been a time when my photo had been up there.

So much for normal. Resigned to hunting down new monsters instead of holiday shopping, I waited for the hardhat guy to finish flipping through his clipboard of papers. In the TV ads, guys with hardhats had six-pack abs and cleft chins. This guy was bundled up to his ears in a down jacket and wore a wool scarf muffling everything above the jacket. Management, I concluded, not acclimated to working outside.

"We're gonna have to shut down the electricity for a few hours, folks," Hard Hat informed us, handing over a printed memo.

"This can't wait until after the holidays?" I asked, covering my half frozen nose with my gloved hand. "This is the busiest time of year for the shops around here."

Well, for the clubs and bars, anyway. The florist shop and a minimart up the road was as close to legitimate businesses as it came.

"Won't be busy if they burn to the ground," Hard Hat said laconically, nodding at the flaming lampposts that the fire hoses hadn't doused. He walked off without further pleasantries.

"Crap." I shoved my hands into the pockets of my jacket as Cora ran back in to turn off the computers, and Andre headed for Bill's Biker Bar to set his own office in order.

Down the block, Ernesto, manager of Chesty's Bar and Grill, shouted his rage and shook his fat fists at another utility worker. Chesty's is a bar and restaurant with pole dancers that caters to the industrial workers from the plants to the north. Andre owns it, but Ernesto was apparently furious at having to turn out his lunch crowd.

I studied the fizzling wreaths with disgruntlement. "If that's you, Gloria," I told the post, "I'm sending your bony ass straight to the deepest bowels of hell, so you'd better think twice about messing with me, lady."

The wire shot sparks.

See, this was where superstition started. I could believe Granny had heard me, or I could figure the wiring was faulty. Except in my case, it was almost always the supernatural and not natural physics at work. My life was such an *interesting* balance of the impossible and the improbable.

That was Granny in there all right, doing her best to destroy us. Her last goal in life had been to shut down the Zone so Acme could take it over. I didn't know why and cared less. She was gone. I wasn't. I would not let her have a second chance to destroy my home from the Other World—if I had to hunt blue monsters to prove it.

Three

I CONSIDERED hunting my sisters in Saturn—I had their useless web page so I knew they existed in some form—but I had a notion that ones with experience in evil electrical wiring were thin on the ground. Besides, I had been handling problems on my own practically since infancy, so I had no good mechanism for saying *help me,* even if I had a way of contacting them, which I didn't.

With a sigh of regret at missing my personal holiday celebration , I shoved my hands deeper into my pockets and stalked down the nearest alley. If Cookie Monsters and fried utilities had any relation, I needed to slay me a monster.

Reaching the dead man's land between the Zone buildings and the harbor, I could see no blue blobs. The usual assortment of vagrants camped on the chemically polluted ground, undisturbed by the Zone's peculiarity. Of course, some of the tent people were as peculiar as the Zone.

Avoiding a lackadaisical fist fight just outside the fenced-off harbor, I turned back up the next alley—not a blue blob in sight. I headed home without a clue of how to stop Gloria. I shuddered at the possibility that the answer was—blow up the Zone.

My fancy new phone rang the "Star-Spangled Banner," jarring me from my funk. The Zone has a warped sense of humor I'd hoped to shut out when I'd bought the not-so-smart phone. I had not programmed in the song, but I knew who it was.

I punched a button without bothering to check ID. "Max, if Granny doesn't set your ass on fire, I will. You had—"

"She's already tried," Max/Dane said with weariness. "My condo went up in flames about three this morning. Don't you ever listen to the news?"

"Oh crap." I picked up my pace. "I work, remember? Listening to the news is for retired people. What happened? Are you all right?"

I didn't much care if his ultra-wealthy neighbors lost their Guccis and Rolexes, but I still cared about Max. Learning how to retrieve him from a hellish dimension had been an education I'll never forget.

"I had my gas turned off, but the lines burst next door. We have good fire walls and smoke detectors and everyone escaped, but flames went through the roof and both units are total losses. If Gloria is causing trouble in the Zone, too, then she's on a rampage."

"We have no proof," I offered tentatively. "It could be coincidence. Mercury retrograde maybe. We just got flaming wreaths and steaming manholes down here."

He almost chuckled. "Dump steaming shit down them and see what happens."

"Love to, but now we have inspectors crawling all over the place and dumping shit on them probably won't improve their humor. And your damned Do-Gooders are in danger of going to hell with the rest of us. Call them off, Max. They don't deserve this."

I shoved my key in the front door lock and yelled a greeting to Mrs. Bodine, my landlady, to let her know it was just me before tramping up the boarding house stairs.

"No one deserves this. We have to stop whatever's happening in the Zone, Justy," Max said, back to weariness again.

Max was the only one who got to call me Justy.

"Now that Paddy has some control over Acme," he continued, "we have to clean up the environmental disaster the plant's created."

Paddy is Dane's father, Max's uncle, and theoretically a stockholder in Acme. He either plays his hand close or he's missing a lot of marbles, take your choice. Sadly, a mad scientist might be our only link to sanity and responsibility at Acme.

"You can't clean up the Zone by frying the innocent," I warned, unlocking both locks on my door. Caution-is-me. "I'll deal with Granny and Acme, if I have to, but not Do-Gooders going up in flame."

"I'll call the agency and tell them to pull back until we've determined if the area is safe," he agreed. "But I don't guarantee the Zone will ever be safe. If Granny Gloria can still rampage after she's dead, you need to go somewhere she can't find you, like Alaska."

"I'm freezing my buns off in bloody Baltimore!" I cried, wiggling out of my jacket as I hit the warmth of my rooms. "No way. This is my home now, and I'm not running from Dane's grandmother." Having spent most of my childhood traveling with my wayfaring mother, I had home issues. I wanted roots.

Putting down roots in polluted soil made no sense to normal people. It apparently did for me. I blamed it on my contaminated gene pool. "Gloria is going down, and I'm taking her there. Where are you now?"

"I have a driver running me over to Hell's Mansion. I'd rather Granny burned it down than my neighbors," he said dryly.

Ah, that explained his weariness. Max had hated his cousin Dane and Dane's grandmother Gloria when they'd been alive. He had reason to hate their mansion, the one Acme had built on blood money, where Gloria had died so spectacularly. Despite his distaste, it belonged to Dane/Max now. Max's soul lived a life of irony these days.

And Granny's house was sitting on wide open land well above the rest of the neighbors. It could go boom and Baltimore would simply admire the fireworks.

"Ruxton is a pretty far hike from D.C.," I argued. "Find a fancy hotel and forget the mansion."

"I have to decide what to do with it sometime. Congress is closed for winter break, so I might as well look around now."

"Merry Christmas," I muttered, sitting on the floor and taking Milo in my lap. Milo was a tailless, tufted manx who looked like a baby bobcat. In the Zone, it was hard to say what he really was, but he never hurt anyone unless they tried to hurt me. His purrs soothed my troubled soul. "Did Papa MacNeill invite you for a fun family dinner over the holiday or are you on your own?"

The MacNeills were Max's real family. They thought he was dead and didn't know his soul had moved into his cousin's body after Dane had abandoned it—probably in embarrassment at getting caught trying to kill me. Middle class families were merely dysfunctional. Max's family was rich and powerful and had thus acquired a higher degree of impairment.

"I could invite myself, if I was interested." Max didn't sound interested. "What are you doing for the holiday?"

"Updating case files, filing petitions, the usual thing." Hunting for my invisible and possibly dead grandmother Themis, looking for other Daughters of Saturn, and gunning for Gloria's evil soul, but I'd rather sound busy than nuts.

"I have tickets to a D.C. gala this weekend. Go with me," he said impulsively.

That was my old Harley-riding rebel Max speaking. I scratched Milo behind the ears and shook my head. "Not happening, babe," I said regretfully. "You're everything I oppose these days. Bad bad karma."

"You'll look gorgeous, no one will know who you are, and we can both get bombed on pricey drinks we don't have to pay for. It's a holiday, celebrate!"

I'd never looked gorgeous. Thanks to my weird ancestry, I have a naturally tan middle-eastern complexion, and thanks to Saturn Daddy granting my wishes, I now have good hair and straight teeth, but the bus stops there. "You're sounding a little desperate, Maxie. Take one of Dane's dollies to the party and boff her silly after. You'll be fine." I hated saying that, but the truth was, as lovely as Dane's body was, I wasn't attracted to it.

I wasn't even certain I'd loved Max while he was alive. I'd learned he was a lying shit just like most men. I might occasionally be desperate but never stupid enough to make the same mistake twice.

But dressing up and getting plastered had its appeal. And it had been a damned long time since I'd had sex. I had to admit to temptation.

"Maybe I will. Anything is better than staying in this place," he said gloomily. "The car just reached the gate. I'll buzz the DGs and call off the kids. Stay safe, Justy."

I don't know how he did it. I wanted to rip him a new one for bringing the nutwings down on us, but I ended up feeling sorry for him. Hanging up, I cuddled Milo. "It's you and me, babe. Simpler that way."

I called up Fat Chick in Canada's blog, another Saturn's Daughter. She's not really fat but Viking goddess beautiful. We'd been e-mailing occasionally, enough for me to learn that she'd been crippled when she'd gone looking for a car thief to execute because she wanted to ask Saturn Daddy for a new car. *Really* bad karma. Thieves are redeemable, especially the young ones, and killing them isn't justified. So Saturn put her in a set of wheels of his choice.

Our super-abilities came with a rough downside if we didn't carry out justice correctly.

Does anyone know anything about evil and hell's dimensions? I typed under her public comments, not knowing what else to ask. I mean, how do you phrase conundrums like that? No wonder we had communication problems. I kept hoping there was a Saturn's Daughter out there who could at least intelligently discuss my questions, but Fat Chick knew about as much as I did.

"You could give your daughters an instruction book!" I told Saturn while fixing my sandwich. As usual, he didn't answer. Not that I knew if he was an actual entity or just a genetic flaw. No instruction book, remember. All I had was the name. My own family couldn't tell me more. I liked the astrology aspect of Saturn better than the astronomy one though. I was pretty sure I hadn't been born on the planet Saturn, but I was a December baby. I'm actually a Sagittarius, but Capricorn/Saturn *might* be considered part of my astrological identity. Maybe my mother lied about my birth date.

To pacify my shopping urge and keep the holiday mood before returning to monster hunting, I cruised some on-line sites and ordered a few presents. I still didn't have a credit card, but I had sufficient cash now to fund a Paypal account.

It was easy to order for my more human friends, but what did one buy for a former thug and frog turned gay assistant? Or amoral Andre, who had everything except a soul, apparently.

Not expecting any immediate replies from Fat Chick—we hadn't exchanged real names and exchanging phone numbers with a murderous Amazon gave even me a creepy feeling—I hugged Milo and ordered him to be my guard cat. I still had normal work to do. As long as the Zone was simply shut down by normal utility workers and not in danger of blowing up, hunting Gloria and blue blobs had to come under after-hours tasks.

I dashed across the street to my office. The snow was falling harder. Brushing off my discontent with the snowflakes, I took some satisfaction from entering my very own law office. Being a lawyer with my own space gave me a warm tingle of accomplishment that was almost as good as sex. Almost.

The Do-Gooder, Rob Hanks, and Ned looked up at my entrance. Uh-oh. I dragged my fingers through my uncut mane to remove ice particles and narrowed my eyes at them.

"I thought you'd be gone by now," I said rudely. Rob reminded me of myself in college, when I'd egged the provost's office in protest against his fraudulent practices. At the time, I probably should have been locked up for my own safety. Rob had that same look of determined idealism.

"They're forcing the homeless off the harbor," he said indignantly, all fiery-eyed and waving the invisible flag of justice.

Damn, I wondered if Saturn had sons.

"The harbor isn't healthy," I countered.

"Where else can they go?" Rob argued. "The shelters are full or won't take addicts. At the harbor, they've got tents and barrels for fire and they look out for each other. Where in heck does the city expect them to live?"

Heck. The guy actually said *heck.* I'd pray for him if I believed in prayer. "And I suppose you want me to sue the city to stop them?"

He got all steely-eyed and resolute. "Yes."

"And I suppose you want me to do it for nothing?"

More fiery idealism. "Yes. Lawyers do *pro bono.*"

"Established lawyers. With real clients and lots of money," I reminded him. "Do you have any idea how much it costs to heat this place?" I gestured at the twenty-foot pressed-tin ceiling.

He looked a little more desperate. "They're *old* people. Army vets. They deserve better."

He almost had me there. I'd once feared my psychic grandmother was living in the camp. Still wasn't sure that she wasn't. Of course, I wasn't even sure she was alive. And Max and his friends were vets. I wasn't immune to idealism. I'd just had to learn practicality.

"The harbor is polluted. It's *dangerous,*" I repeated. And could be sitting on Granny and fire-making blobs. "Find them a city park, an empty building, and I'll do what I can, but fighting to let them kill themselves with chemical beds is not on my agenda."

His eyes lit with new enthusiasm. "This area is crammed with empty buildings! They'd be better off inside for the winter. Will you help us hold off the cops if we trespass?"

I knew this wouldn't end well, but I sympathized with his cause. The homeless at the harbor were mostly homeless because they couldn't take care of themselves within the strictures of a so-called *civilized* society. If we found them a building, one of them would eventually burn it down or stab someone for a better corner or another bottle of whiskey.

In my jaded mind, those animal survival techniques weren't a whole lot different from white-collar workers using more socially acceptable tactics to rob and steal each other blind. And it wasn't as if our guys would ruin the neighborhood by moving in.

And every once in a while, I knew, someone could be saved with a helping hand—and that's where my bleeding heart kicked in.

"I'll do what I can," I agreed with a sigh of resignation. "But Andre probably owns most of the buildings on Edgewater, and he doesn't always recognize the law."

"I'll talk to him," Rob said gallantly. "He can't hope to rent out those wrecks."

Well, yeah, he could and he had, but Rob was heading out the door and there was no point in hindering his progress.

Ned leaned back in the massive sixties' orange desk chair we'd dug out of the rubble of the warehouse next door. "Lawyers don't encourage crime," he said disapprovingly.

"Define crime," I said. "Leaving those old guys out in the snow is a crime in my book."

Which was kind of where I got myself into trouble. Law books existed for a reason, but I had this really bad habit of wanting actual *justice.*

Justice would be making Acme pay for the damage they'd done. Justice would be allowing the denizens of the Zone control over their destinies. And their electricity. And when I got feeling irritable about the lack of justice around me, people ended up in hell.

Four

IT WAS still snowing when I left the office after dark. Intent on avoiding confrontation with Gloria and hell before dinner, I sloshed through several inches of wet stuff on my way to Chesty's. And then the walk turned dry.

Amazed that anyone had bothered shoveling sidewalks, I checked the building I was passing to see who this energetic person might be. The boarded-up windows looked like every other empty storefront on the street as far as I could tell. Odd.

I reached the first intersection—and the road had been plowed. The city *never* plowed down here.

The reason for the clear intersection became apparent as I crossed—the street was *hot*.

Swearing, I hurried to the other side. I could feel the heat even through my heavy-duty Uggs. Hot streets, that was just plain scary given my fear of Gloria and hell's dimensions.

I pressed onward, keeping an eye open for any more dangerous anomalies. That didn't take long. A red-hatted garden gnome statue relaxed and splashed his little feet in a gutter of gushing melted snow that steamed like a hot bath. Shit, this couldn't be good.

I pretended not to see him as I spun around and marched back home to fix my own dinner. At least the Victorians were on a hill out of the Zone—or Gloria's—reach. I hoped.

Gloria's goons had once blown up Andre's warehouse next to my office, but she was dead now. If I kept telling myself that long enough, I might learn to relax and enjoy floating garden gnomes.

After feeding Milo and nuking a meal, I concluded I couldn't relax until I'd investigated the Zone's anomalies, but I could attempt it from a relatively safe location. If I wanted to know what was under the Zone, I could start by investigating the bowels of my office building. Maybe I could determine the extent of the danger.

I went in search of mole clothes. I dredged out ancient corduroys and a sweatshirt and a hoodie.

"Want to go for a walk?" I asked Milo as I loaded up a tote with flashlights and batteries and other useful equipment.

He washed his whiskers and eyed me with suspicion. Then, head held high, he trotted to the door. Milo is one very spooky cat. I could swear he understood me. Worse yet, he had a tendency to follow me when I was heading for trouble. His escort wasn't exactly a good sign.

I hadn't anticipated any other company, but emerging onto the porch, I almost fell over Sarah Jones, currently a waitress at Chesty's. Sarah and I had a peculiar relationship based on the fact that we wore identical scales-of-justice tattoos on our backs, presumably making us both Saturn's daughters.

Except Sarah took her justice powers to some pretty weird extremes in attempts to beautify herself, and I avoided sending tools to the devil in exchange for wishes. Not that I hadn't done it, mind you, but I'm trying harder not to these days in fear for my eternal soul. Or wheelchairs. Or pointy boobs like Sarah's.

She sat on the snow-covered front step looking as if someone had just run over her best friend. Crap.

I sat down beside her. "Something up?"

"I've got elves swimming in the birdbath," she muttered. "I don't believe in Santa but I got elves. What's next, reindeer?"

This was a huge conversation for Sarah. When I'd first met her, she'd jump at a car door slam and turn into a chimp if a man looked at her. Sarah's not real clear on how she did it, but she had admitted to killing her abusive husband. I was thinking she'd damned him to hell, and Saturn had obliged by giving her a chimp's strength to send him there. Just my guess.

"Reindeer—or the devil," I suggested experimentally, to see if her late mother had passed on information that mine hadn't.

She shrugged. "Life is hell. That makes sense. Elves don't make sense."

"Neither do dancing Dumpsters." If garden gnomes were her only problem, I had better things to do than freeze my ass off. I got up and brushed snow off my corduroys. "I'm going exploring. Want to come?" I asked, hoping she wouldn't.

"Dumpsters don't dance," she argued, following me across the street.

Sarah's company was dangerously unpredictable, but I had no good reason to tell her to get lost.

The pavement up here wasn't as hot as the Zone's and the road was getting slick. I hoped that meant I wouldn't be descending directly to Gloria's den—yet.

"The Dumpsters just roll around," she continued. "I figure it's earthquakes or the ground settling."

Everyone lives in their separate states of denial. I shrugged. "If you believe that, then believe garden gnomes are rolling around in your bird bath."

"You mean those weird little statues people put on their lawns? We don't get those down here. We don't have grass." She waited for me to open my office door without any expression of curiosity.

I categorized Sarah as a classic sociopath. Raised by a serial killer mother and abused by her husband, she was what life had made her. I had hopes the Zone would morph her into a better person, eventually. It had already improved her social skills.

I had no good reason to damn a coward with extreme reactions to fear, but I stayed clear of her when possible.

"Maybe your elves are escaping the heat of hell," I suggested, flicking on a flashlight. I didn't want Andre seeing lights and coming over to get in my way. It was time I learned the Zone's secrets. I knew tunnels existed up here on the hill. I didn't know if they connected with the main drag.

Milo trotted ahead of the light beam. Sarah simply shoved her hands in her baggy coat pockets and followed.

"Demons instead of elves?" she asked. "Mama said demons walked this earth, but I don't think I've ever met one, unless it was my husband."

I didn't want to believe in a superstitious, Bible-thumping hell, much less demons on earth, but events had forced me to at least accept string theory and hypothesize that hell was another dimension. And with my luck, it existed beneath my feet.

"Maybe she meant metaphorical demons." Even as I said it, I knew that comment went right past her head. Sarah isn't the most educated member of our community.

"How many kinds of demons are there?" she asked grumpily. "And can you point them out so I can kill them?"

I rolled my eyes. Sarah didn't want to kill demons because they were dangerous, but because she wanted to wish for a reward from Saturn Daddy. I bit my tongue.

"Andre still won't look at me," she continued, proving my point. "My legs aren't long enough."

Legs weren't her problem. Andre knew she was a killer. Okay, with Andre, maybe lumpy ankles made the difference.

"Andre has a lot of problems on his mind right now," I suggested. "Why don't you try for Ernesto? He has a steady job." As the creepy manager of Chesty's pole-dancing bar, Ernesto ought to be right up Sarah's alley.

I made my way through the unused warren of offices behind my front lobby. The building had been abandoned long ago for lack of elevators, lack of air-conditioning, and a general lack of anything new over the last fifty years. My rent was cheap.

Discussing Sarah's boyfriend troubles distracted me from fretting over what I might find in the tunnels below the building. The likelihood of spiders and rats I could handle. But after encountering Gloria's demonic bats in Hell's Mansion, I had kept my exploratory nature in check—until steam started emerging from the street. Self-preservation trumped squeamishness.

"Ernesto is creepy," Sarah protested.

And a girl who turned into a chimp wasn't? "He's getting better. He even says *hi* and *bye* occasionally now."

I unlocked the battered wooden door Andre had once shown me. The harbor just east of here had been the site of Civil War shenanigans, and the area was permeated with old tunnels. Andre had turned the one under his warehouse into a bomb shelter, then the warehouse had been bombed. Life is just a jiggling bowl of irony.

A blast of musty air hit us when I opened the door, but that was nothing unexpected from an unused basement. The air might be a tad warmer than I'd anticipated, but for all I knew, heat goes down instead of up here.

That open-mind thing I was acquiring necessitated an Alice-in-Wonderland mentality. I might be heading down a rabbit hole, but I'd avoid anything in a bottle labeled Drink Me.

The stairs were totally dark. I should have invested in a new LED flashlight. The dim beam on this old one revealed a wood step, relatively intact. I flipped an ancient light switch but nothing happened. I didn't even know where the bulbs were to check them. Using my feeble light, I tested each step with my boot before putting my weight on it. Milo trotted down without hesitation.

A vaguely damp concrete cellar greeted us at the bottom. I couldn't find another switch. I swung the flashlight along the ceiling and found one of those bulbs with a chain hanging next to it. I tugged that and the bulb briefly illuminated, then exploded. Par for the course.

Milo sniffed along the concrete block walls. A cat really needed a tail to express itself, but Milo didn't appear concerned about his lack.

He tagged my flashlight beam, leaping on it as we crossed the cellar.

"You should start a bar down here, call it The Cellar." Sarah studied some old abandoned doors leaning against the wall. "You could make tables of these."

"The neighbors probably wouldn't appreciate it," I said, "but there might be more cellars like this nearer the harbor. You can have the doors."

"I don't have the money." She dragged one of the doors to the side and pointed to a shadow behind the others. "Is this what you're looking for?"

Crafty, Andre, hiding the door behind a stack of doors. We hauled the stack to one side and examined the cracked and peeling panel in the wall beneath. The last time I'd opened a cellar door, I'd been hit by a flock of demonic bats. But Hell's Mansion was a long drive from here.

"You go first," Sarah said, not as dumb as she seemed.

Don't say I didn't learn from experience. I removed an umbrella from my tote of tools. A cloud of bats wouldn't catch me unprepared again. Milo clawed at the door and left scratches in the mold or algae or whatever coated it. Opening the umbrella, I twisted the door latch.

It resisted. I rattled and tugged and the latch fell off in my hands, leaving me with no knob to turn. Sarah giggled.

I might be small, but I'm persistent. Like a mosquito.

I folded up the umbrella and removed a hammer from my bag of tricks. I whacked the door hardware a good one. This time I was rewarded with a click, except I had no handle for dragging the warped panel open. So I kept hammering until the latch hardware fell out on the other side, leaving a hole. One learned interesting things when traveling the country and living in shacks.

One also learned to don gloves before sticking hands in dark corners. I pulled on my leather ones, grabbed the latch hole, and tugged. The warped wood scraped the rough floor.

No bats flew out, but an unholy sewer stench washed over us. Gagging, I flashed my light around on the far side. Ancient crumbling brick walls. I eased past the door and into the tunnel itself. Showing definite signs of intelligence, Sarah stayed safely in the cellar. Milo, the damned cat, slipped between my legs and trotted into the darkness beyond my light.

The floor was hard-packed dirt. I followed the tunnel downward, in the direction of the harbor. I didn't see hell, demons, fire, or feel extreme heat. Choking on the stench, I started worrying about plumbing.

I ran the light over the ceiling and winced when it appeared to be rough-hewn *logs*—under a street carrying two ton cars. Not healthy.

I apparently had a Civil War tunnel under my office. It might make a good escape route if I trusted the ceiling. I didn't. Unless I inherited a fortune to pour cement to support the tunnel, it looked like I'd have to find another path under the Zone. I headed back.

"No gold?" Sarah asked in disappointment as I reappeared.

"I doubt it. You're free to look if you don't mind two-hundred-year-old timbers over your head." I dusted my hair but didn't detect any spiders. Shouldn't there have been spider webs?

"Milo!" I yelled into the tunnel, listening to it echo faintly. "Get your rear end back here!"

A ghostly shriek responded, followed by the scurrying of rat feet, a flapping of large black wings, and my curses.

I dashed the last few feet of the tunnel into the cellar, shoved Sarah to one side, and flattened us both against the cellar wall. Unearthly large shadows flitted along the ceiling. I swallowed my fear, flashed my light upward, and wished I hadn't. I could swear, a dozen red laser beams glared back at me. The wings swooped at our hair. Sarah screamed and held her head.

My most favorite Saturn talent is visualizing my enemies into anything harmless that appeared in my fevered mind at moments of panic. That's how Ned became a frog—he'd been shooting at me. I had no idea if it worked on demonic bats.

Closing my eyes, I frantically visualized the shadows converting to confetti. If I went to hell for killing bats and rodents, so be it.

Black snow pelted our shoulders and hair. The shriek from the tunnel escalated in volume into a mournful howl, drowning out Sarah's screams. Milo fled past us, scampering for the stairs.

That did it. Milo wasn't frightened of anything. In any other situation that wail could have been the howl of the wind—except there was no wind.

With a mighty shove, I slammed the now knobless, lockless tunnel door. I was hot on Sarah's heels a second later.

Five

GIVEN my life lately, I half expected my office to blow up.

We frantically ran our hands through our hair and brushed black *confetti* from our clothes as we ran up the stairs. Black bat innards for all I knew.

I could almost sense a *presence* in that wail. I shivered at the eerie howl creeping up and down my spine.

I glanced at Milo with suspicion, but he wasn't much given to wailing, and he was racing faster than us for the escape hatch.

We gasped for breath, still madly beating at our clothes as we fell into the upstairs hall. I slammed the cellar door and threw the bolt while Sarah raced ahead of me. I no longer smelled the sewer stench, but my neck crawled. I wanted a hot shower.

The wail stopped. Just like that—frozen, ghostly silence.

By the time I reached the quiet lobby, I felt like an old-fashioned jackass for fleeing from nothing but rats and a few bats and red laser beams.

I tried to gauge the eerie silence and realized *that* was what was truly alarming. On a quiet night, the Zone blasted music, Harley engines, ambulance sirens, and drunken laughter.

I heard *nothing*. It was as if the building had been enveloped in a smothering quilt—or transported to another planet.

Milo fled into the cold the instant I opened the front door. Smart cat. With the door open, all the noise returned. I even heard a tug tooting in the harbor.

"Okay, I'm getting out. After you." I gestured politely for Sarah to go ahead of me.

She hesitated. After what we'd been through, she actually *hesitated*. I frowned and waited.

"Could I stay here, please?" she whispered.

I blinked and groped for all the reasons that was so very wrong. All I got out was "Why?"

She shrugged and held up her hands. "I didn't turn into a chimp."

Oooohkay, that was a notch above all my reasons. Scary, but a logical point. She'd been frightened but her usual response hadn't happened. She'd screamed like a normal person.

"The wail and the bats don't scare you?" Maybe I was the only one who heard them? Nah, Milo had run too.

She shrugged. "I won't go into the basement. They didn't follow us up, did they?"

For all I knew, she didn't realize the black ash on her clothes was bat remains. I wasn't the one to tell her. "It's cold in here. There are no beds or covers or anything," I pointed out.

"There are elves swimming in my birdbath," she argued back. "And it's warmer here than in my house. You have an old couch in that back room."

It made me really uneasy to have Sarah camping out in my office, and not just because of the basement adventure. I glanced at the door to my file room. So far, I hadn't accumulated enough files for me to bother worrying about the expense of building a locked vault.

I couldn't imagine that Sarah had any interest in the civil complaints in the drawers. So I had no *logical* reason to say no. I asked hesitantly, "You think the Zone turns you into a chimp?"

"It's where I work and live. That's all I know." She tried to look defiant, but she had orange hair and pointy boobs and short, plump legs and mostly she looked like a truculent orangutan. Okay, so I don't know my primates well.

"Write a note saying you won't sue me if you freeze to death. We'll figure out something better in the morning." I was so kicking myself for agreeing, but I was spooked and wanted to make certain Milo was all right. And yeah, I wanted out of there.

She offered a tentative smile. "I'll try not to scare Ned."

I hoped she hadn't set her heart on my good-looking assistant because she realio, trulio, wasn't his type. Or preferred gender. I just nodded, stepped out, and locked the door. I took a moment to inspect the noisy street at the bottom of the snow-covered hill, watch my breath smoke the air, and gather my shattered nerves. I needed to plot my next move.

Maybe tomorrow I'd get to the bottom of hell. Humor, ho, ho.

I woke up the next morning with Milo on my pillow. I knew I had to be exaggerating what had happened in the cellar last night, but I still checked my hair for bat remains after I got up. I prayed I wasn't rewarded or punished for turning flying rodents into confetti. That had been self-defense and not a judgment call. I was still pretty amazed that it had worked.

I'd showered the night before and had no excuse to do so again, so I aimed for the closet. Much as I'd like to be a free-loading superhero, I had real clients who paid real money and expected me to sit in a real office working if I wanted real food in my belly. What I did after hours—was likely to get me killed. So I focused on normal.

I liked wearing a classic tailored look for my office—made me feel lawyerly and less like the outcast I'd been all my life. But now that I had nice straight legs to show off, I favored short skirts and funky tights with my shirts and blazers. I checked out the window to see if I could make a quick run across the street without freezing.

Fuzzy gray fog clung to the glass, obliterating all sight of the world outside.

Hot and cold air make fog, and we had some real weather clashes happening out there. I told myself fog was better than crazy gas, and hell wasn't changing the weather.

Not knowing whether I'd be walking into a sauna or a snowstorm, I sauntered from my hidey-hole just before nine. I let Milo decide whether he wanted to follow. He took one look at the fog and curled up on the window seat cushion. Not dumb, my cat.

The fog was clammy and clinging but not as cold as it could be. Yesterday's snow had mostly melted away in the strange warmth. Street noise was oddly muffled, but nothing like the dead silence of last night. I had an only-woman-on-the-planet moment as I crossed the street with zero visibility.

I had my key out, prepared to unlock my office, before I realized the door had been jimmied. My cautious nature took over, and I froze—until I heard a scream.

Sarah! Sarah had been in there overnight.

Caution be damned. I shouldered the door open, preparing mental whammies.

A shot flew over my head, and I ducked and rolled for the gloom behind the door.

The spooky gray light through the front windows didn't help me see. Using the open front door as a shield, I peered out to locate the muffled struggle.

Sarah had stopped screaming. That was bad.

A man's voice cut the silence. "What the f—" the word was severed by a male shriek. Then even the shriek died.

More muffled struggling. Hunting my phone and scanning the darkness, I finally detected two shadows rolling across the floor of the back hall. My lobby was too huge to see across clearly in the darkness. I had to hope that one of the figures was Sarah, but the hall was too distant to tell.

Probably because Sarah in her chimp form wasn't an obvious shape. I hesitated over punching 911.

"Sarah, don't kill him," I shouted, panicking when I finally realized her inner chimp was in the process of throttling an intruder.

Chimps are not cuddly stuffed animals. They're mean and strong and unpredictable.

The chimp kneed the perp into prostration. I swung the light of my phone in her direction. That provided enough illumination to see that the chimp sat on the intruder's chest, pounding his head into the wood floor. She glanced up at my shout and let go of her victim's throat long enough to put her really flexible foot on his chin while she groped around the floor.

I wasn't certain of the Saturnian etiquette here. The jerkwad had apparently attacked Sarah, so I figured he was hers to deal with. But unlike my preference for visualization, she liked to kill.

Her long chimp arms swept an object off the floor, and before I had the wits to react, she blew the guy away at close range.

Damn, but cleaning blood and brains off my floors was not the way I wanted to start the day. Double *ewwwww*. I'm a lawyer, not a badass superhero. I fought the urge to upchuck.

Taking a deep breath, I forced down the need to regurgitate my egg burrito. Then I donned my lawyer stoicism and punched my phone to begin the process of legal clean-up.

I didn't dare leave Sarah alone while she came down off Cloud Chimp. And I wasn't calling 911 to arrest a chimp. I needed my hero, Lieutenant Schwartz, my across-the-hall neighbor. While I wondered if a chimp had the mental capacity to ask Saturn Daddy for long legs, he answered my ring.

"Put your pants on, big boy, and meet me in my office," I told him. "I'm pretty certain Sarah just blew away an intruder."

Studly-Do-Right said a bad word and hung up. I rang Andre next. This was his building.

My assistant arrived for work about the same time as Andre and Schwartz ran across the street. Dark and indiscernible little ol' me was hiding cross-legged behind the door when all the big manly men rushed in and right past me.

They saw Sarah first. Schwartz flipped on the overhead. The fluorescent beam added a cold gray-blue illumination that didn't prettify the bloody sight at all. I turned away.

Ned choked and ran back outside to barf.

Schwartz held out his arm to prevent Andre from contaminating the crime scene while Sarah's big dark chimp eyes watched him.

Andre searched the shadows until he found me on the floor, staring at my fancy phone. He grabbed my elbows and hauled me up and shoved me out the door with Ned.

I didn't even pretend I wanted to stay. I held up the text screen to him.

HAPPY BIRTHDAY, JUSTINE!–THEMIS

Six

THEMIS was my invisible grandmother. *I'd* never seen her, anyway. She just left me messed-up messages in seriously weird ways. I had to wonder whose phone she'd stolen to text, or if she'd psychically invaded the air waves because the only number attached was zeroes.

I'd forgotten today was my birthday. I was twenty-seven, one year short of attaining my full Saturn powers, if I wanted to believe Themis. And Sarah. Apparently the planet rotated the sun approximately every twenty-eight years. I still viewed astrology as superstition but astronomy made even less sense in this scenario.

I cast a guilty look over my shoulder at the office, but Schwartz blocked any view. Ned had stopped barfing and gone back inside. He'd been a big bad bodyguard once, but I guess since his days of frogdom he was a bit too sensitive for the tough guy gig.

After glancing at my text, Andre half-dragged me across the foggy street in the direction of his house, wearing his grim, clenched-jaw expression. I protested, but not heartily. My fine legal mind still didn't grasp murderous primates and invisible grandmothers and dangerous birthdays.

"Schwartz won't arrest a chimp, will he?" I asked anxiously as we reached the steps. "It was self-defense. The goon was probably gunning for me."

"Stop thinking about it. Visualize a happy place and go there," he ordered. "I'll send you a birthday cake."

Andre was probably just trying to stop me from blowing up his building with rage, but I was more than willing to disconnect from reality. "Will you pop out of it, naked?" I asked.

"Dream on." But he almost sounded amused as he opened his door. "You're in shock. What was Sarah doing in your office?"

"Sleeping." I shrugged. "Or not sleeping. That couch isn't conducive to rest."

Andre's father—my silent partner Julius—met us at the front door. He has a brilliant legal mind, but he quit leaving the house to care for his wife. When I was the only lawyer in the world who would defend Andre against a murder charge, Julius had agreed to give an inexperienced newly-hatched lawyer like me advice. Civil cases are much more my style, though.

Despite the rugged sweater, Julius still possessed an elegant old world look. Maybe it was the thick shock of white hair or the dark Spanish eyes and high cheekbones. Hard to say. Andre would look like him some day.

"I'll pour some brandy. Sit down," Julius ordered. He took my other arm as if I were a cripple and pushed me onto Andre's plush leather sofa.

"Coffee," I demanded, coming down from my silly place and finally leaping to the angry conclusions that Andre was trying to steer me away from. "Someone needs to investigate why Acme's goons are gunning for me again. This is *not* Sarah's fault."

"Clancy's back," Andre said wryly, halting in the doorway instead of fetching coffee. "Find a rope and I'll tie her up until the boys in blue are done."

"If Schwartz is calling his squad, I can't abandon Sarah." I was up out of the sofa before Julius could stop me.

Andre scooped me up by the waist and flung me back. "Sit. Stay. Let Schwartz handle this. Keep your mouth out of it, got that?"

That was so not fair, using my size against me. Besides, I detested being patronized.

I jumped up again and rammed my heel into Andre's instep when he tried to repeat his maneuver. "*Do you have any idea what Sarah can do to Schwartz and his men if they frighten her?*" I shouted.

Andre backed off warily. "What can Sarah do?"

"What, you're not omniscient?" I mocked. "She can *damn them all to hell!* Don't you get that yet?"

Andre remained motionless, processing that admonition long enough for me to run out the front door. I heard sirens in the distance and cursed.

Andre was right behind me as I returned to the office. Ned was cradling a terrified Sarah—in person, not chimp form. Ned glanced up at my arrival, a picture of male bewilderment.

Sarah's usually kinky orange hair now fell in long, shimmery copper curls to the floor, covering her mostly bare assets. That was some hair, topping my Saturn-granted shampoo-model mop by a mile. I hadn't even known she was a natural redhead.

Sarah had offed a bad guy, and Daddy Saturn—or Satan, which I was starting to believe was the correct designation—had rewarded her with Lady Godiva hair.

Ned and Schwartz must have watched Sarah morph from chimp back to human. The Zone bred peculiarities, but Sarah's handicap pretty much topped them all. She would be embarrassed out of her mind, and they were politely trying to ignore it.

Schwartz read from his little notebook. "Your assistant says the victim, one Harry Bellamy, worked for Acme and the Vanderventers but lost his job after Mrs. Vanderventer's demise. Bellamy had to take a job with the electric company. He had his tools from the utility truck with him. Ned has no idea why the victim would blame you, but vengeance could be his motive for breaking and entering."

Maybe he sought vengeance because I turned granny's bodyguards into frogs a few months back. I glanced at Ned again. His froggy form had licked magic pink particles and turned out good. The other goons... I'd need our resident mad scientist to explain the results of Acme's nasty experiments, but if our intruder was any example, it looked as if the frogs had returned to human form. Had Harry been planning on blowing up my electricity?

Ned set Sarah on her feet. "I think maybe Miss Jones should lie down for a bit. She's had a bad shock," he said disapprovingly.

Oops. He was right. Sarah needed comfort far more than I did. It's just hard to think about protecting murderous chimps. "Put her in my office. Sarah, want coffee or brandy?"

"Green tea," she whispered, clinging to Ned's arm. Her hair, honest-to-Saturn, fell to her knees. Good thing, because the chimp had only been wearing her tank top and undies, and they were a bloody mess.

"We can leave out the chimp part, can't we?" I asked Schwartz with resignation, observing the grim line of his mouth. Our good cop looked like a Viking. He even had dimples when he was mad. "Just say she got the gun away, and it was self-defense?"

"Hallucinations don't look good on my record," he agreed obliquely. "And you have no idea why this crud was gunning for you?"

Andre just watched, arms crossed and smirking. He knew about the frogs.

"I may have told a few of the DGs that I'd help the homeless, even if it meant closing Edgewater." Which was a lie of such convoluted proportions that even I didn't know what it meant. "Since the utility company is working down there, maybe Bellamy was afraid he'd lose his job again if the street closed."

I might be more likely to believe in Daddy Saturn if he'd slap me for lying.

Schwartz drilled me with a look that said I'd better come up with a better one.

"He's one of the same goons who stalked me a few months ago," I protested helplessly. "Maybe they're fixated."

Ned rode to the rescue, posing in my office doorway with one hand against the jamb and his hip cocked. "They're all obsessed," he confirmed. "They kept calling me for a while, trying to find out Miss Clancy's schedule. After she got Andre off on the murder rap, they think she's jinxed them. They blame her for their divorces, for losing their jobs, for some weird stuff that's happening in their heads. I blame Acme. There's no telling what was in the air over there."

"Divorces?" I asked with interest, happy to have the subject diverted.

"Yeah, both George and Harry vanished for weeks after that chemist...Bergdorff?... killed himself," Ned said with a wave of disgust. "Their wives figured they were out playing around. So when they finally went home, their families booted them. They've been griping ever since."

Bergdorff had been the head chemist at Acme until I'd sent him to hell. Harry and George had *vanished*, as in hopped around my office eating flies until Papa Saturn poofed them back to human. I'd never had the opportunity to watch. The frogs had just drifted away. I'd quit worrying about them once Ned showed up. I assumed they had the power to fix themselves as Ned had, but apparently Ned in his froggy state had lapped up the pink particles from Acme's last gas blast and the others hadn't. Acme's cancer-curing, coma-causing mystery element had good and bad sides. Ned had been fortunate. The other two—not so much, apparently.

So, yeah, maybe I was guilty of something.

"Besides George and Harry, how many more of them are there?" I asked warily.

Ned shrugged. "I don't talk to them much anymore, so I don't know how many are still griping. There were several squads of us. Besides George and Harry, Ben and Arnold were also there the night Bergdorff took a flying leap. They were single, so they didn't lose wives, at least. Maybe they found better jobs. Shall I go for coffee? And tea?"

I reached for my tote, but Andre pulled out his wallet first, handing over a wad of cash. "Buy a coffeemaker and donuts. I have a feeling this place will be needing them regularly. Schwartz, would you be a good guy and see if Sarah left clothes in the back office?"

I couldn't even look at the blood-spattered back hall much less crawl over a corpse to look for Sarah's clothes. I really wanted a wall between me and the gore. My office would have to suffice. It was in the front, off to one side of the lobby, so the door overlooked Ned's desk, the front door, and nothing else.

The sirens screamed to a halt outside, and I retreated to my inner sanctum.

Sarah had wrapped her arms around her knees and was rocking my rickety office chair back and forth. She cast me a nervous glance, then went back to staring at her bare feet.

No tears. Classic sociopath. She was probably calculating if she could earn longer legs by offing a policeman.

I rummaged in my tote and found my faithful compact. I'd bought a new one since beaning a senator with the old one. Never knew when I might need to kill another politician.

I opened to the mirror and handed it to her.

She barely looked at it, at first. Then apparently catching a glimpse of the Godiva tresses, she snatched the mirror and tried to study herself in the limited view. Her eyes widened, and she began tugging her curls in front of her face so she could see them.

"I thought Papa waited until after midnight to bless us," I said with sarcasm. That's how it had worked for me. Sarah must be special.

"That creep must have been really bad," she whispered uncertainly. "I never get anything pretty like this when I kill people. And my ex deserved to die a whole lot more than most people."

So did her serial killer mother, but that was probably one of those things best not said aloud. I usually just damned people and they died in some freak manner and I got my wishes. Sarah simply killed them outright, but I had to assume the result was still damnation if she was rewarded. It's not as if I meant to descend to hell to find out. I was still telling myself that Saturn was a good guy, but it made more sense that the devil rewarded us for sending him more souls. Ambivalence is me.

Maybe creative marketing over the eons had turned Satan's Daughters into Saturn's Daughters. *That* almost made sense.

"You killed your ex for yourself," I reminded Sarah. "Maybe it's because you killed the goon out there to protect me that you got prettier hair." I'm a lawyer. I'm pretty imaginative at coming up with theories without proof.

She dangled a silken curl in front of her nose until her eyes crossed. "I should kill for others?" she asked blankly. "How do I do that?"

"Become a police woman," I said cheerily, listening to the cops in the other room. "Join the army. I bet there are a whole lot of justice-makers there."

"Not ones who turn to chimps," she reminded me.

Well, yeah, there was that. A Zone occupation was the only one that would suit her—one of the many reasons I couldn't let the bad guys take it down.

Schwartz arrived with a handful of clothes, threw them on the desk and hastily departed. I turned my back as Sarah began to strip.

My phone rang—saved by the bell. I groped through my tote and checked ID but didn't immediately recognize the name.

"Clancy here," I answered in my clipped business tone.

"Miss Clancy?" a vaguely familiar voice said. "This is Rob Hanks. You said you'd help us with the vagrants if we found them a healthy place to stay."

I kneaded my brow as a uniformed police officer loomed in the doorway, notebook in hand. He was straining to see over my shoulder. I hoped Sarah had dressed quickly. "Yes, Mr. Hanks, but this isn't a good time. Have you found a building?"

"There's an old insurance office on the corner across from Chesty's that's in pretty good condition. Some of them stayed there last night."

I had a feeling he wasn't calling me to brag. I held up a finger at the officer, who scowled impatiently. "And?"

"And there's a man out here with a ton of security guards claiming it's his property and he wants us out. They've got guns."

Seven

"ANDRE, we have a situation," I shouted past the cop blocking my office.

With his great sense of timing, Ned chose that moment to enter the front door bearing a spaceship-sized coffee urn. It looked like he'd just bought out the entire coffee stand at the mini-mart down the block.

The delicious aroma of fresh-fried donuts permeated the air, and all gazes followed his shopping bag. Not a plastic grocery bag, mind you. He'd apparently used Andre's funds to purchase an environmentally friendly sparkly tote to carry all the donuts and coffee makings. In the *Zone*. He wanted to save the Zone's environment?

"I'll have this ready in a trice, gentlemen," he sing-songed, well aware he was the current center of attention. My ex-jock assistant was finally releasing his inner rainbow.

Andre appropriated one of the donut bags from the tote and approached my personal dragon, offering up the contents and slipping past when the cop was distracted choosing a fritter.

After seeing splattered brain decorating my lobby, I figured I'd never eat again. I was suffering flashbacks to the time I'd seen Max crisped. Lawyers shouldn't puke in front of clients. I shook my head at the greasy sack. Sarah had no queasy stomach problem. She took two fritters. At least she was half way decently garbed now in jeans and long-sleeved shirt.

"The DGs have occupied the old Morgan building," I told Andre as the others ate. "That's one of yours, isn't it?"

"Do-Gooders are *occupying* my building?" he asked, narrowing his gaze. "Why?"

"Housing the vagrants," I said without mentioning my part in the suggestion. "That's not the situation. Someone is down there with security guards and guns, trying to heave them out."

"Out of *my* building? Not on my request!" He already had his phone out, punching buttons. "Hurry up here. I'll have your partner pull deeds on that property and have their sorry asses thrown out for trespassing."

My partner—his brilliant father. He was protecting his parents' privacy.

"Better find out whose sorry asses you're tossing." I glanced at the donut-eater's nametag. "We may need your help down the hill, Officer Tallent. Could you take my statement on the way down there?"

"I need to talk to Miss..." He glanced at his notebook. "Miss Jones, first. I'll get you next, Miss Clancy, if you'll wait outside." He gestured at the brain-spattered lobby I didn't want to see.

I'd wait outside, all right. Way outside. I glanced at Sarah, who was eyeing the officer with curiosity. *Sarah is not my client,* I told myself. Conflict of interest.

I just had to hope she didn't have any more energy to unleash if she didn't like the tone of Tallent's questions. As I'd just proved, it's not as if I could stop her from killing or damning anyone. It was depressing developing the maturity to know I couldn't save the world.

Andre escorted me to the lobby as if obeying the cop's wishes. We were out the front door before anyone looked up from playing with our fancy new coffeepot.

The fog hadn't lifted much. Luckily it wasn't cold, because all I had was my second-hand wool blazer.

But through the gray wisps of moisture, we could distinguish a mob gathering in the center of Edgewater. Traffic up to the chemical plants had to perform U-turns and attempt alleys. The Dumpsters didn't like their alleys disturbed. If they weren't already rattled and blockading them, they would be soon. Wouldn't the tourists love that?

"How did the DGs get into the building?" Andre asked, studying the situation as we hurried down the hill.

"That's not as important as the identity of armed storm troopers," I pointed out. A ring of khaki uniforms was holding back the crowd with what appeared to be automatic weapons. Automatic weapons in the Zone! I shuddered to think what could happen.

"I've paid the taxes on that place for years. It's mine," he said grimly. "If anyone is doing the throwing out, it's me. And I don't need Nazis or Uzis."

Cora hurried up the street to meet us. Bill, the bartender for the Biker Bar, lumbered after her. Bill was a quiet bear of a man, usually peaceable, but he wasn't smiling now.

"What's with the goon squad?" Cora demanded as soon as she reached us. "And why are the police up here instead of down there?" She lifted her chin to indicate the black-and-whites all around my office.

"Sarah killed an intruder," Andre snapped bluntly. "And since the cops want Clancy for questioning, they'll follow us down soon enough."

Thanks, Andre, I thought grimly. *Pin it all on me.*

Before Cora could question, we'd reached the outskirts of the crowd. I recognized some Zone residents, but the majority of the mob was young and outraged and probably part of the DGs that Max/Dane was supposed to call off. Saving the world apparently meant ignoring United States senators.

My rebellious student self would have pumped my fist in solidarity. Lawyer Tina only saw trouble. What a drag it is, getting old.

The Morgan insurance building was a boring three-story brick edifice much like my office. The windows had been boarded for as long as I'd known it. Most of the businesses down here had closed after the chemical flood. *Sensible* people feared a contaminated harbor and fled.

Did no one have any common sense anymore?

A couple of tourists in the crowd were pointing out the grinning gargoyles on the building's roof. One of the stone carvings waved a ribbed wing, and the tourists gasped, then laughed and took a picture as if they were seeing a Disney special effect.

Nope. No common sense here.

Until recently, Acme had scared off the tourists, often with goons like Ned had been. Only the locals had learned that the weirdnesses were real. These last weeks since Gloria's demise had been...interesting, in a creepy sort of way.

I waded into the fray after Andre. People stepped aside for us until we reached the armed guards with ugly automatic weapons across their chests. You see this kind of thing on the news in photos of third world countries. It's not the kind of sight you want in your own front yard.

"You're trespassing and causing a disturbance of the peace," I announced loudly to the uniform in front of me. I might not be the tallest person around, but I have an excellent courtroom voice.

The crowd grew silent as if watching their favorite cop show.

The security guards didn't even acknowledge my existence. Like the royal guards, they glared straight over my head.

Andre strode up, picked a uniform taller and wider than he was, and swung his fist at the guard's nose. In the same motion, he yanked the automatic from the jerkwad's arms, and slammed the stock into his groin.

The guard bent in half with a groan, holding his nose and his man parts at the same time. Before the other guards could find someone to tell them what to do, we'd broke past the circle and sprinted for the door.

"Assault and battery," I murmured in Andre's ear. I couldn't let him know his lawyer approved of his behavior.

Cora and Bill were right behind us, protecting our backs. The Do-Gooder crowd spilled through the break in the ranks faster than the armed guards could react.

Sometimes, it just took one person to bring down fascists.

Of course, I had enough experience to know we had about ten minutes before men in riot gear arrived, but triumph felt good as we surged past the bewildered creeps.

Bill held the door just long enough for Andre, Cora, and me to enter, then slammed it before anyone else could follow. He leaned his bulk against the wood and threw the latches, leaving the DGs to block the outside.

Tall, sleek and stylish in her fitted jacket and leggings, Cora hid her snakes well. I didn't know if she'd released them from their tattooed form yet. She merely glanced around as if sizing up the room for potential décor.

Smarter than the students in the ways of the world, the vagrants had apparently already fled. The shabby DGs sat cross-legged on the floor, refusing to budge. Men in khaki were hauling them by their arms and physically heaving them out the back door.

Fists on hips, Cora took an Amazonian stand over a female protester, and defied anyone to haul the kid away. Now that I knew to look, I could see an asp flicker defiantly from her coat sleeve and another above her neckline. Shades of Cleopatra.

Andre and I zeroed in on the silver fox in a tailored suit overseeing the proceedings with a smug air of satisfaction. Always go for the fat cat is my motto.

I yanked out my phone, hit speed dial, and said loudly. "Officer Leibowitz, we'll need help clearing trespassers. Assault and battery charges are likely, along with disturbing the peace. There may be some connection to the shooting Schwartz is handling, so call in as many cars as are available."

In reality, I was talking to a Chinese restaurant—in China.

Crossing his arms, Andre entered into a stare-down with Silver Fox, apparently leaving me to be his mouthpiece.

Silver Fox had a head full of expensively highlighted salt-and-pepper hair, a beaked nose, a sardonic smile, and his tailored suit coat needed padding to disguise his sloping shoulders. Well-groomed and weak was my totally unbiased conclusion.

"You'll have to remove your men from the premises," I said authoritatively. "Mr. Legrande has not authorized the use of force in removing the occupants."

"The property is mine and I don't allow squatters." He held out his hand. "Graham Young, CEO of Medical Science Inc. And you?"

I didn't accept his hand. Color me less than impressed. "Justine Clancy, attorney for Legrande Enterprises. There has apparently been some mistake. Mr. Legrande owns this property." And most of the others on the street, but I didn't like revealing all my cards.

I heard frantic knocking at the front door but left Bill to deal with it. Cora was smiling coldly at a uniform, daring him to approach her asp, one of which was now wrapped around her coat sleeve and hissing. Andre had balled his fingers into fists. The tension escalated like steam in a balloon.

If I wanted to avoid Andre's knuckle-swapping methods, I really needed the deeds Julius was looking up. I didn't know how long I could delay before the inevitable explosion.

"I'm sure you believe your boss owns the land," Mr. Smug said, "but MSI has acquired the rights to all the property along the harbor, which includes every building on Edgewater. They're scheduled for demolition as soon as we have the final paperwork, and we don't want vagrants taking up residence." He continued to look amused as he spoke to me and ignored Andre.

Demolition! Even if I didn't believe a word of this spiel, he was blithely talking of demolishing the homes and jobs of Zone inhabitants as if we were inconsequential termites! I was seriously considering damning him to hell just because I couldn't stomach his arrogance. If Saturn was testing my temper, he'd picked the wrong damned day to it.

Happy birthday, Tina, indeed.

Andre had raised his dangerous fists when I regained the sense to grab his arm, throwing him off balance enough to stop his swing. Andre normally tried not to get his hands dirty, but some smirks were simply meant to be swiped.

Bill opened the door. I could feel the rush of cold air, but I didn't hear him greeting anyone. I was praying for deeds or Schwartz or someone useful but my luck didn't run that way.

The whole Zone? This character thought he *owned* the Zone? This was such seriously bad shit that I was having difficulty coping.

My tongue finally caught up and by-passed my panic. "I suggest we agree to meet at the courthouse records office," I said as Andre ripped his muscled arm from my puny grip. "Mr. Legrande has at no time sold part or all of any holdings in this area."

Something poked me in the back. I swatted at the air behind me and encountered paper. Neither Andre nor Mr. Smug seemed to notice. I glanced over my shoulder and saw no one.

Tim. Whenever I saw no one, I could count on it being Invisible Boy. I grasped the thick folder he was shoving at me and tugged. He let it go. Anything Tim held disappeared with him, until he released it. I didn't think it wise to produce papers out of thin air, so I faked removing them from my tote.

"I'm sure you'll find my documents are in order," Young said, while I flipped through the copies of deeds.

I found the one with the Morgan building address and skimmed through it. All perfectly legitimate. Andre had bought the property at a tax auction sale. I assumed he'd acquired the others the same way after all the respectable citizens abandoned the area.

I held up the deed for inspection. "All seems to be in order. The property is owned by Legrande Enterprises, as noted in the deed."

Silver Fox didn't even bother looking but gestured dismissively. "Those are no longer valid. The EPA is condemning the entire area by eminent domain in the interest of public health. We'll dig out the polluted land and build a much needed medical facility here."

I stepped in front of Andre before he could fling another punch.

We knew who had been trying to grab this land for years.

Acme. Acme and their mysterious cancer-curing, coma-inducing pink and green particles were behind this. Mr. Smug, Acme, and the mysterious MSI were threatening my home and my adopted family and grating nerves already frayed by the dead body in my office. *Eminent domain!* That abominable law had to have been invented by Satan.

Listening avidly, the DGs started chanting *Nazis, go home*.

While I struggled to smother my rage, one of the uniforms smacked a particularly loud Do-Gooder. The kid cried out in pain.

Cora seized the abusive snot's arm to prevent another blow. Violence seethed while my friends waited for my reaction.

A second storm trooper rushed up to jerk Cora around. Her snakes hissed.

My restraint snapped. I would not tolerate more shooting, splattered brains, or risk snake poisoning. Uniformed Nazis did not belong on my turf, yanking my friends around. The red rage for justice started smoking my mind, rendering logic invalid.

Maybe my crazed brain truly believed I was saving the uniform from an asp fastening its fangs into his wrist. Or my subconscious could have been hoping to prevent a full-scale riot. Given that Bill was unlocking the door to let in a mob, that was a very real, very explosive possibility with all the guns in here and outside.

Whatever. In full blown Saturn mode, I never operated lucidly. Instead, my warped imagination visualized Smug and Company as garden gnomes with pointy red hats and ugly grins.

Startled, Cora was suddenly shaking off a concrete garden ornament, while the Do-Gooders screeched in appalled horror. Bill swung around to study the dozen foot-high gun-toting gnomes where uniformed guards had been, and re-locked the door.

Andre stared down at a miniature silver-haired statue with raised fist—and started to chortle.

It was no laughing matter. I'd just converted live people into garden statuary in front of an audience.

Admittedly, the gnome's shocked expression was priceless.

Eight

"OUT," I yelled at my startled audience, in the same urgent tone as one would shout "fire." I pointed at the back door.

Not stupid, the student protesters fled the office, leaving scattered garden gnomes rolling about the filthy floor. My handiwork seldom resembled my creative imagination. These were damned mean looking elves. I wondered what was happening to the half dozen or so guards outside.

Stifling his laughter, Andre studied the fallen statues, crossed the room, and locked the back door after the last fleeing student. Then he turned and regarded me. "Now what?"

"Umm, we take them to Acme and set them on the conference table while we discuss the eminent domain suit that we were never told about?" I suggested. "Tim, are you still here?"

Invisible Boy popped into view, managing to look sheepish and shocked at the same time. He'd grown a few inches since I'd last taken him Goodwill hunting. His jeans barely covered his ankles, and his suede boots had holes in the sides. He needed a haircut. He looked like a shaggy character in a Scooby-Doo cartoon.

"I was just hanging out to see if you needed me," he said.

"Impolite to hang out when no one knows you're around," I corrected in big sister mode. "It's like eavesdropping. Find some newspapers and wrap up the statues and let's box them up. We'll let Paddy deal with them."

Andre was chuckling again as he toed one of the little monsters. "Can we keep them? What if we built shelves for them on the walls at Chesty's?"

"Seriously, Andre? You've just learned the EPA is in the process of condemning everything you own, and you want to dance with garden ornaments?" I had my phone out, punching numbers again.

"Would anyone care to explain what just happened here?" Cora asked in righteous bewilderment. "Am I losing my mind or is this a mass hallucination?"

Cora knew I was peculiar but hadn't actually witnessed my earlier weirdnesses. Neither had Bill, but he remained a stoic observer. Andre just left me to explain, as usual.

"We're fine," I said curtly, "The Zone is just fucked. Let me speak to Padraig Vanderventer, please," I said to the receptionist answering my call.

I had a lot of experience in bad vibes, and I was quaking with them now. Andre had to unlock the back door for Tim to slip out in search of newspapers. I followed on his heels. We still had a situation back at my office and cops would be hauling me into jail if I didn't put in an appearance soon.

I didn't bother checking the mob out front to see if the guards still held them at bay or if the tourists were taking home garden gnome souvenirs.

"*Mr.* Vanderventer," I said in my snottiest voice when Paddy answered. He used to wander the Zone like a homeless bum, scrounging meals from Chesty's kitchen, until I'd got him to start talking to his nephew/son, Max/Dane. Now he was a trustee on Acme's board and had a real lab to play in.

"To what do I owe the honor, Miss Clancy?" he asked warily.

"To the visit of one Graham Young, CEO of MSI and apparently new owner of the Zone. Know anything about that?"

"Owner of the Zone? Since when?" He sounded genuinely puzzled.

"Probably since MacNeill sold us down the river," I said with a sigh. MacNeill was the real Max's dad. Max's mom owned half of Acme, but she let hubby run things.

I'd hoped Paddy hadn't joined the forces of evil after returning to work. But he wasn't much interested in the politics of a corporate board, so his offense was that of ignorance and neglect.

"You might try attending a meeting or two occasionally," I told Paddy. "I don't suppose you recall hearing anything at all about this Medical Science Inc.?"

I was half way up the hill with Andre hot on my heels. Cora and Bill must have obediently scattered in search of newspapers and boxes with Tim. They still didn't know for sure that I'd done the dirty deed, but a few more episodes, and they'd work it out.

"MacNeill has been dealing with MSI," Paddy confirmed. "They have some kind of grant from the university to research our formerly comatose patients. We probably should have shot those med students before they spread the word about the miracle cures."

I snorted. "Thanks, Padraig. I'll keep that in mind next time Acme poisons the town, and we need medical help. Shoot the doctors."

"Shoot MacNeill." He hung up. Paddy lacked a sense of humor.

He probably meant it. Former senator Mike MacNeill was a felonious asshat who had been booted from his senatorial office for nefarious dealings years ago.

I had to shift gears when I arrived at my office just as the coroner's office was rolling a body out on a gurney. I offered up a good thought or two for the goon's family, then cringed, wondering how many families I'd just affected with stone statuary.

Maybe the fascist guards would take up gardening once they came back around. It wasn't as if Saturn had given me a rule book. I simply didn't know.

Officer Tallent didn't look any too happy about my departure. Since he hadn't bothered coming to look for me after I'd requested his help, he didn't get any sympathy. I told him clearly and concisely what very little I knew. He threatened to take me downtown when I refused to repeat myself. I retaliated by telling him Julius was my lawyer, and he could direct any further questions to him. He shut up and left me alone. I sought Sarah in my office.

She wasn't there, naturally.

Ned carried in a cup of coffee, which I gratefully accepted.

"I've hired a clean-up crew one of the officers recommended," he said. "We probably should close for the day."

"You've earned a day off," I acknowledged. "This is good coffee. Where did you find the urn so quickly?"

"Malik at the mini-mart had just ordered new ones and hadn't set them up yet. He was more than happy to make a profit on one. We may have to charge by the cup to pay back Mr. Legrande."

"We'll just call it part of his capital improvements in the building." I dismissed his concern for Andre's money. We had bigger problems on the line. "You go on and I'll lock up in a few minutes."

As soon as Ned left, I called Jane the journalist and my access to the latest local news. She only worked for an online rag and had to supplement her income by asking people if they wanted their order supersized, but she was no slacker.

"I'm on my way out," she said breathlessly in answer to my call. I could hear her toddler yelling in the background. "Have you got something interesting?"

"Eminent domain in the Zone. Fancy new medical clinic by a company called Medical Sciences Inc. Ring any bells?"

"A filthy rich sheik just awarded the university with a few fortunes for saving his son's life. Medical Sciences is a spin-off. Don't know more than that. Eminent domain?" She whistled.

"Exactly. Keep me posted on anything you find, and I'll do the same."

"Start riots and I'll be on top of the story. Fires, death, action," she prompted.

"I'm trying to *prevent* those," I reminded her. "Sometimes, the news ought to warn people before the fact."

"Doesn't sell papers. Will do what I can."

She rang off. Cynicism bites.

I decided I could make these calls just as easily from my front room with my cat on my lap to keep my tension levels below electric wire proportions. Doing my best not to look toward the dark back of the lobby, I locked up and crossed the street. The fog was finally lifting.

My cell rang before I made it up the stairs. "Wassup?" I asked wearily and unprofessionally, recognizing Max's ringtone.

"Happy birthday, Tina," he said in the same weary tone. "The gas lines erupted two streets from Hell's Mansion."

Rich people going without heat didn't roll my wheels as much as poor ones. I chose to smile that he remembered my birthday instead of fretting over what I couldn't control. I unlocked my locks and welcomed Milo's cry of greeting.

"Can you get solar panels?" I asked frivolously. "And what do you know about Acme condemning the Zone with eminent domain?"

"They can't do that, can they?" he asked, diverted from his own predicament. "I mean, I'm all for it. The place should have been condemned ten years ago. Andre will walk away with a lot more than he put into the place. But Acme can't do a thing. The state has to condemn the property for a public purpose, like a highway."

"Or a medical research clinic?" I wasn't going into the argument about people giving up their homes and lives, yadda yadda. We'd had it before. Max had grown up rich and privileged. His family probably owned half a dozen houses. They had country clubs, private schools, and ivy league colleges for networking.

Those of us in the Zone were lucky to have one hovel apiece. We hung on to our jobs by our knuckles. We used the street for playground, community, and education. Taking away our neighborhood would take away more than just our homes and livelihood—it robbed us of the village we needed for support.

"Nonprofit research, for the public good, maybe," Max said

dubiously. "But Acme's never been a nonprofit."

"We have a Graham Young down here declaring he's building a tribute to medical science on our land. MSI just got a grant for a bundle of money from the university. You really, really do not want normal people down here. And if they condemn our homes, I'm sending everyone in the Zone up to Hell's Mansion to live with you."

"So the place can blow up faster. Good thinking, Justy. I don't understand why you defend that disaster zone."

Sitting on my window seat in the front bay window with Milo on my lap, I watched Tim carrying a box of stone gnomes up to my office door and leave it on my step. If I was really lucky, Graham Young with his smug arrogance was freezing his butt off in that box. And Max wanted to know why I defended the Zone.

"You'd have to live here to understand. And if Granny blows up her mansion, you might just end up living with us and find out. Should we call in a priest to exorcise her?"

"Couldn't hurt," he agreed wearily, giving up the Zone argument. "A posse of them maybe."

I knew I should be worried and horrified. Except, after living through the time with Max in hell's outer dimensions and gas attacks that left my friends comatose, I couldn't get too riled by exploding grannies. I was still striving for normal. "Can I watch?"

"Sure. Bring the Mormon tabernacle choir and we'll have the film at ten."

I giggled. On a day like this, I giggled. That was my old Max talking, the man I missed, who'd once ridden a Harley, fixed car engines, and made crazy mad love to me.

"Benedictine nuns," I suggested. "They're closer."

"I'll give you a date," he agreed. "Thanks, Justy. And I'll look into the eminent domain thing. Christmas at the mansion doesn't offer better entertainment."

I heard a boom in the distance. Max cursed, letting me know he was still alive.

"I'll get back to you—if I don't blow up," he promised.

I suspected people would pay more attention if pricey Ruxton blew up than if the Zone did, but we didn't need attention. We needed supernatural help. I was learning that came with a steep price—and it looked like I was the one to pay it.

Nine

THE accumulating stacks of gnome boxes had nearly blocked my office door by lunch time. I clung to the hope that meant Tim and company had wrapped each one in lots of padding and that I hadn't petrified an army. It was only just sinking in that Sarah had killed a man in my office, a man presumably looking for *me*—while carrying a gun. An army of Nazi gnomes with guns didn't relieve my nervous anxiety.

I spent the rest of my morning hiding in my room, responding to a few cursory birthday messages on Facebook. Because I'm cautious and always plan ahead, I also started a search for affordable housing. So far, I hadn't found any homes available for nothing upfront and next to nothing a month.

About the time my stomach finally realized it hadn't been fed, my door rattled, and Schwartz shouted, "You have to come out sometime, Tina. Ernesto said his new cook is testing pot roast on the lunch crowd."

"I don't eat pot roast, Schwartz." But I was tired of my own company. I offered Milo a ride in my tote, and he accepted. That probably meant trouble, but what else was new?

I was still wearing my lawyer clothes, so I was at least respectable. I was a walking target any way I looked at it. If someone else wanted to rub me out, I might as well look decent for the morgue.

I opened the door and handed the heavy tote to Schwartz. He looked startled, exchanged glares with my cat, then shouldered the burden.

"There's some kind of new soup, too," he said. "Crowds are picking up with these tourists, so they're expanding the menu."

Why tourists? Why now? What idiot was advertising the Zone as a safe place to visit? Maybe I should be looking into that instead of exploding wreaths.

I really ought to take Schwartz to bed and forget my problems for a few hours. I wasn't sure if I was saving myself or saving Schwartz for a better opportunity. The inclination just wasn't there.

"Soup is good," I agreed. "Any more impending riots I should be aware of?"

"After the garden gnome incident, the place cleared out. Want to explain that sometime?" With old-fashioned etiquette, he opened the downstairs door for me.

"Why do you think I can explain anything any better than Andre? The Zone doesn't like being attacked. End of story." So, I lie. Professional hazard.

"You think the Zone is some kind of sentient being that plans these things?" he asked incredulously.

"I don't think anything. I just like to stay the hell out of the way. Although if you want to believe in the power of prayer or the power of a group mind, you could be onto something. We wished them gone, and poof, the Nazis disappeared."

"Stone gnomes are strange souvenirs to leave behind," he said grumpily. "It's gonna be tough to explain to the precinct when the missing persons reports are filed, although the lot that went missing from Acme eventually showed up. Maybe you're on to something."

Outside, we met with no snow, no fog, just the usual blue glimmer of the buildings below, faintly visible in the gray day. I'd approve, except I was now seeing an eerie red glow around the manhole covers and through cracks in the street. Really, maybe we *ought* to be scouting new locations.

"Group mind," Schwartz snorted, slowly following my earlier suggestion. "If all the brains around here were put in one pot, it might make one whole. New theory needed."

"Provide your own, Schwartz. My head has retired for the day. I would simply like some hot soup with some of those yummy oat rolls Jimmy made last week and no one shooting at me. I don't think that's too much to ask."

No snow and no steaming gutters distracted me as we walked down the hill. It was almost a normal, crisp December day. We lacked Christmas lights, but who needed them when the sewers blazed red? Wonder what it would take to get a little green around here?

Given our environmental disaster problem, going green was a joke.

Loud music poured from Chesty's even before we opened the door. It's hard keeping the music pumping when the Zone messed with electronics, but apparently we'd expended enough bad energy today and the good vibes flowed, even though it was only afternoon. I was already feeling cheerier and humming to the beat when we entered.

"*Surprise!*"

The music kicked into a painful birthday rock song. Balloons dropped and the crowd shouted and screamed "*Happy birthday!*"

I almost fell on my face. I grabbed my chest, certain my ticker had stopped ticking.

Andre swung me off the floor and planted a smooth, rich one smack on my mouth. Before I could start drooling, he slid me down his front, allowing full access to the whole package before he gestured for a glass of champagne.

I detest champagne, but I was too totally stunned to notice the taste. And I couldn't say for certain if that was due to Andre's kiss or the surprise party. I tingled in places that hadn't tingled for a long time, my eyes moistened, and a strange emotion ballooned in my chest that I thought might be joy. I wasn't sure because it had been so long since I'd known true exhilaration. The sensation was more dizzying than the champagne.

A man had died this morning. Fascists had threatened us with condemnation. But the Zone partied. I got that. But to go to all this trouble for *me...*

I'd never had a birthday party. I caught a balloon and hugged it and batted back tears. "I love you guys," I muttered, leaning back against Andre and letting him hold me while I appreciated the truly admirable chaos.

Chesty's walls were decorated with naked mural figures that, like the Zone's statues, had developed a life of their own. They were rocking hard, pumping their fists and gyrating the way they'd never done before. Ernesto's pole dancers wore their finest feathers and cheered to the stupid birthday song as they writhed. Cora was twisting and swaying with Bill, while her boss tossed one of the waitresses in some fancy swing move. Sarah, with her Godiva hair rippling, was shyly sitting at the bar and listening to Ernesto.

Milo leaped out of the tote and went in search of mice in the kitchen.

All was right in my world for this one moment. This was why we needed the Zone. I might wonder about Max in his lonely haunted mansion, but this was my world, my people, not his. I wiped a tear from my eye, handed my champagne and balloon to Schwartz, and rocked into the crowd, with Andre hot on my tail.

"Unless somebody can produce no-see-um magic to disguise our existence, I vote we talk to the environmental agencies and whoever else is prying around," I proposed over a bowl of scrumptious kale soup. My empty stomach had finally demanded feeding while the party partied on. Given Ernesto's tightwad tendencies, this wasn't exactly a private celebration. Some of the hard hats had taken up stools at the bar, and a scattering of tourists had stared for a while before joining us on the dance floor.

Schwartz, being the only mundane among the Zone crowd, snorted skeptically at my premise. "The feds only have to walk down the street and watch the snow melt to figure we're hot. Expect evacuation shortly."

He meant *hot*, as in radioactive. I didn't think that was our problem, but telling him my paranoid theory about sitting over hell—possibly with Gloria smoldering beneath our feet—wasn't conducive to a rational discussion. If word got out, we'd have every freakin' religious idjit in the state marching through Chesty's.

Glancing at the dancing naked people murals, I almost giggled at the image of sour-faced fanatics cruising through, falling all over each other in shock.

"We could keep the bums warm this winter by letting them put up tents over the steaming manholes," I said brightly.

"Not if the EPA bulldozes us," Andre retaliated, swiping my beer.

"All right, let's just find out who's doing what and why and go from there," I suggested, giving up on optimism. "Make Acme gather a town meeting and include the feds. Let's lay it all on the table instead of speculating. I'll try studying up on eminent domain law."

Andre's expressive eyebrows rose. "No hiding in shadows anymore, huh?" he asked enigmatically.

Damn right, but I wasn't letting him draw me out. Tim kind of shrank up in fear at the thought of newcomers, but Schwartz looked interested. He was all about law and order, and my proposal was far more sane than what I actually intended to do.

After I revitalized with food, I let Andre claim a slow dance. I didn't know who'd planned this gig, but Andre had been the one to see Themis's message. He had to have been the one who'd passed the word about my birthday.

I was feeling extremely friendly toward Andre for a change.

Extremely friendly. His hands were on my ass, and we swayed pretty damned well together. He kissed behind my ear, and I felt electricity shoot up and down my spine. Maybe I would fire Andre as my client, and my twenty-seventh birthday would break my long dry spell.

I was humming along with the song and the memory of all the nice things Andre had done for me. Yeah, he could be a mysterious bastard who liked to have his own way, but he *understood* me in ways no one else ever would.

"What did you mean, that Sarah could damn us all to hell?" he whispered in my ear.

"That's a mood breaker," I growled back.

"Communication makes or breaks a relationship. I read that in Cosmo," he said solemnly.

I wanted to smack him, but his arms felt too good. I rested my head on his shoulder and rotated my hips against his so he'd know what he wasn't getting later. "Saturn's daughter, remember?" I'd once tried explaining some of my weirdness to Andre. "It's all theory. I don't know anything. But you did notice her hair, didn't you? She kills her abusive husband, and she gets big boobs. She kills a goon, and she gets good hair."

"So you think she's damning them to hell and Satan is rewarding her?" he asked incredulously. "And that's how you got your hair? Not the Zone?"

"Theory," I reminded him, belching a little beer. "Satan, Saturn, who knows? My mother and grandmother just keep telling me to use my Saturn justice wisely. Sarah's mother said go forth and kill. I think she likes killing. I don't know if she can simply damn them to hell like I can because she's never tried."

"The way that you damned Max," he said warily.

I traced a seductive finger down his throat. "Like I can damn you," I agreed.

"And Saturn's daughters are born every twenty-eight years when Saturn comes around or something?" He didn't loosen his grip or miss a step, but his head had obviously taken a leap I didn't want to follow.

"So I've been told. I probably get really dangerous next year. Ain't life grand?" I was too bombed on beer and hormones to care what I was saying, but I was feeling just a little bit sorry for myself.

"And if this daughter thing is genetic but only kicks in when the planet Saturn reaches some point near Earth on your birthday, that means you'd have to have a kid before your twenty-eighth birthday if you're to pass on Saturn magic?"

I dug my fingernails into his earlobes to stop his dancing in the middle of the dance floor. Then I placed my hands on his chest to shove him away and glare at him. "You've jumped from sex to kids to bad genetics as my birthday gift? Do you have any idea how close I am to damning you right now?"

"But you're Justine, my goddess of justice, and you won't," he said soothingly, pulling me back into the dance.

But it wasn't the same. How good could birth control be when weird planets or gods were involved? And did I really want to find out?

I didn't even dare express my dismay with a *damn*. Talk about your lust-busters, I didn't even need a cold shower now.

The party began breaking up early. Evening gloom had settled in, and it was time to think of supper. I'd had enough of Chesty's fare, so I rounded up Milo, and judged this a birthday well spent, if I didn't count the morning's disasters or my fight with Andre.

Schwartz followed me to the door. He lived in the same building, so his escort made sense, even if it was too early for the drunks to be out.

One of the utility workers who'd spent the afternoon at the bar instead of working turned and watched us go. The hair at my nape rose, but I figured that was just Ned's warning raising old fears about his ex-friends.

Outside, the snow had turned into an unusual December blizzard—which *steamed* on the city street. Schwartz and I stopped to admire the effect.

"Maybe we've invented a new product for snow removal," I murmured. "Figure out how it works and we can make a million."

"Nah, the EPA is right, we're sitting on hell. Maybe they can shovel out the chemicals." Schwartz sounded resigned as he stuck his hands in his pockets and started up the street.

"You believe in hell?" I asked with interest, hurrying to keep up with his long-legged strides.

"Spend Friday night in the lock-up, and you'll know hell exists right here on earth. What I want to believe in is a wrathful God and justice." He gazed at the burned-out wiring still dangling from a lamp post. "Not happening."

"If hell is here on earth, then so is justice," I pointed out. "The good guys just don't do as good a job as the baddies in making themselves known. Most people keep waiting for someone else to do something." And there I went again, espousing vigilante justice. I had to stop that.

"So, what do we do about the creep who followed us out?" Schwartz asked, surprisingly. "He's carrying concealed. Want me to arrest him?"

Shit crap. I had been hoping our tag-along was just a drunk on his way home. The plant had closed down at five and traffic had died to a crawl by now. I wandered out in the street to examine a steaming manhole and caught a glimpse of our unfriendly utility worker slipping into the shadows of an alley. Definitely not a sign of good intentions.

Milo leaped from the tote and stalked off to investigate the alley. A chill ran down my spine, but not from the cold.

We were standing in the middle of a blizzard, and I was warm enough to remove my jacket. The snow fell silently on a street simply waiting for me to do something.

"I'm going to find my cat," I said.

"You're a nutcase, Clancy, but you're not stupid. The cat will find its own way back." Schwartz hunched his shoulders and placed his big body between me and where we'd last seen the thug. "C'mon, let's move on. He can't gun us down in the middle of the street."

"Well, yeah, he could, if so inclined. And I'm not leading him home or letting him shoot Milo. You go on up. I'll be right after you." I'm small and dark and good at vanishing into shadows. I hurried after Milo, concealing myself out of the neon-blue glow of the buildings.

Schwartz, however, wouldn't leave my side. He was one of the good guys, and I really didn't want him hurt. "Okay, big boy, have it your way," I murmured, patting his arm.

Then I darted down the nearest dark alley, took a flying leap from a garbage can over a fence, and dropped into the harbor zone. I was out of sight before Schwartz could climb the can. Make size work for you, I say. His large frame was a disadvantage against my slightness.

I saw Milo's tailless hind end running along the fence. I followed.

The homeless hovered by their fires near the water, ignoring me or too stoned to care what they saw. The snow was thicker on this side of the fence—where the pollution was supposed to be worse. Interesting. Schwartz could follow my footsteps in the snow, if he were so inclined. But if he was smart, he was heading back for the street— which was where the thug would have to go if he wanted to see where we were.

Milo vanished through a missing section of the chain link. Pushing the metal aside, I returned to the long harbor alley running parallel to the main commercial district. I couldn't see Milo, but we think a lot alike sometimes. I found a pussy print in a patch of snow and turned in the same direction, walking past Chesty's and toward Acme, north of where we'd last seen the utility guy.

Apparently the utility work had allowed us to keep our lights on for a while longer.

The blue neon coating the buildings glowed brighter on this end of town, presumably because it was closer to Acme and got hit with more of the chemical spills. Bill's Bar was down this way, but Bill was as uptight about little ol' me wandering loose in dark streets as Schwartz was. Really, I might not be large-boned, but I more than make up for it with attitude. I'd survived a lot of tough places, and besides my martial arts training, I had a secret weapon. I was stupidly confident that I didn't need protection—just like Milo.

Maybe Milo was heading to Bill's for a fish treat. I didn't think so, though.

Following Milo's tracks, I turned between two buildings and emerged on Edgewater. A block to the south, in the direction of Chesty's and my home, the utility thug stalked toward the alley where I'd disappeared. I couldn't see Milo, but I recognized the worker's big, bulky build and nylon down jacket from the morning of the burning wreaths—the management guy who didn't like cold. Intent on his search in the wrong direction, he didn't see me.

Spotting Milo's shadow darting into the street behind the armed utility guy, my insides clenched and I raced to rescue my idiot cat.

Milo was swelling into super-feline, prepared to leap on the thug's back and take an ear off.

"Milo, don't!" I yelled, panicking that my cat might not take bullets as well as he bit ears.

Utility Thug swung and fired—at me.

Ten

"DAMNA—" I bit off the dangerous curse that might jeopardize my eternal soul and dived for the gutter. I registered a stinging sensation in my arm and considered reinstating the epithet.

"Take that Saturn Daddy," I muttered, proud that I'd learned to temper my fury and not kill anyone without knowing my enemy. "I'm not joining Gloria in hell for bigger boobs." That was my main reason for fearing eternal damnation—the rewards I'd seen for sending souls to the devil had been mostly superficial. I wasn't believing a righteous entity would hand out pretty teeth in exchange for a soul.

Of course, I'm a lawyer. I wasn't really believing in hell and the devil either.

Holding my arm, I glanced up in time to see Milo leaping for the gunman again.

Before the jerkwad could take aim at my cat, I visualized the image of the garden gnome I'd conjured earlier in the day. *Villainous utility worker, you're a gnome until I say otherwise.*

Fat Jacket fired at me again.

Crapshitfuck, my secret weapon hadn't worked! The slug hit wide, splattering asphalt.

Milo's mighty leap caught the thug's arm and forced it upward. The next bullet hit the sky and the utility worker howled in rage.

I huddled in the street in a state of fear and genuine shock. I couldn't visualize anymore? What had happened? Frantically, I called up images of stone statues and frogs, then began imagining him in Antarctica. How long could Milo hang on? I didn't want him shooting my cat! Or me.

Fat Jacket remained stolidly alive and functioning and trying to throttle Milo while aiming at me.

I nursed my injured arm and stared at the battle in horror. Did I risk my eternal soul by damning him to hell?

Would he go?

Lawyers aren't the best people to react during a murderous attack.

Schwartz, bless his heart, dashed to the rescue. Coming up from behind the furious utility worker, he walloped Fat Jacket on the crown with his trusty truncheon. Not one to waste bullets was our Viking cop.

Milo leapt free and trotted back to me, mysteriously returning to normal cat size—although for him, that was still pretty large. I cuddled him against my chest. Swearing under my breath that a bullet had creased my beloved biker jacket, disgruntled at my spectacular failure, I crawled out of the gutter holding my cat, and shaking violently.

What the hell had just happened? A baddie had *shot* at me. I was allowed justice. I'd turned men into frogs for less than that. Well, not much less. Shivering in confusion, horror, and pain, I held my injured arm and my cat and trotted over to join Schwartz and the devil's minion.

Schwartz was reciting the guy's rights and handcuffing him. The gunshot apparently hadn't registered inside the booming din of Chesty's. Only a few drunks staggered out to their cars, paying us no mind.

"Are you hit?" Studly Do-Right asked, throwing me a look of mixed exasperation and concern.

"Grazed—he dinged my jacket! What is *wrong* with people?" Furious and terrified, I kicked the asshat's shins when Schwartz hauled him around. Milo purred his approval. "What did I ever do to you?" I shouted when Fat Jacket winced. My kick couldn't have hurt that much. I was only half his size.

Half his size. Like I was half Ned's. Recognition set in. How many huge hunks normally roamed the Zone's streets? Bill and Schwartz, I knew. The only others I remembered had been out to stifle me one way or another—Ned's ex friends.

I yanked off my assailant's bulky muffler and recognized the square cleft jaw that Gloria favored in her guards.

Déjà vu all over again. Facing my old enemies took the wind out of my sails. Did Gloria control them from hell?

Schwartz dragged his prisoner out of my reach. "Go get your arm bandaged. I'll do the questioning."

"No, you won't. He looks like one of Granny's crazy gang, and you don't even know where to start questioning with that lot. He'll be out on the street again in the morning, still gunning for me, and I'll never know why." Just like the guy Sarah had murdered. Not knowing what they wanted frustrated the crap out of me.

I was already furious and beyond irritated at my spectacular failure. I wanted him to be a garden gnome like the others. Why wasn't he? Had I worn out my visualization for the week? The year? Forever?

"Granny's gang?" Schwartz asked warily.

"The ones who almost sent Andre up for killing Old Lady Vanderventer. Remember the guys following me last fall? Them."

"The ones you blew the wheels out from under?" He'd been there to catch that particularly satisfying event.

"Yeah, them. But I'm still telling you, the Zone did that, not me." That was probably a lie, but I didn't need Schwartz to go twitchy around me.

"I don't know what she's talking about," Utility Guy finally muttered. "I thought I was being mugged."

Even Studly Do-Right rolled his eyes at that bit of hokum. "She called her cat. You always shoot at people who shout?"

Stupid didn't respond, just glared.

"If Ace Associates is on his resume," I said, while using my aching arm to shove my self-satisfied cat back into his tote, "I want him locked away for assault and battery, attempted murder, illegal wire-tapping, and I'll think of a few more things before the night is over. And I want his bond at a few million. Tell the prosecutor he might even be responsible for Mrs. Vanderventer's death. Throw the book at him and keep him off the streets until we know what's going down."

"Yes, ma'am," Schwartz said with a chuckle. "Anything else, ma'am?"

"Shut up, Schwartz. I've never been shot before, and I don't want it happening again. If he's got a license for concealed carry, he needs it taken away." I scowled at the evil perpetrator. "You don't shoot cats or people down here for *any* reason, got it?"

"You're all a nest of weirdoes, and you're going down," Stupid shouted. "I'm just getting my own back, that's all."

Until recently, no one but Granny's henchman had noticed or cared that the Zone was a little off balance. We liked it that way. I had a feeling our peace had ended.

The goon tried to wrench from Schwartz's hold, but that was a waste of time. Even with one hand around a phone, Schwartz had a powerful grip. He shoved jerkwad to his knees. Apparently the bad green particles had rotted this thug's brain—or testicles. Nest of weirdoes—he was a fine one to talk.

I pulled out my new toy phone and buzzed Andre, just for fun.

People didn't threaten my posse without consequence.

Andre strolled out of Chesty's a few seconds later. He actually wore a full-length cashmere coat that would have made him look like Cary Grant in a forties flick, except he was more an Antonio Banderas type. I shot him a stare of disbelief. This wasn't Hollywood but the muddy streets of Baltimore. Not a good place for cashmere.

"Here's your chance to ask about our inundation of utility types," I suggested.

Andre waited expectantly for an explanation.

Schwartz hung up on his call and let his prisoner stand again so Andre could examine him. "He shot at Tina. She thinks he's one of the security guards from the Vanderventer estate."

The guards who had killed Granny, then pointed an accusing finger at Andre, and disappeared—because I'd turned them into frogs for trying to kill us. Andre was not predisposed to be kind to them.

Andre studied Stupid's snarling visage and shrugged. "Morons all look alike to me. Can't tell. You can ask Ned to identify him in the morning. But the coroner ruled Gloria's death accidental, so you can't hold him on that. You shot at Tina?"

Without any more warning than that, Andre drove a swift uppercut into Stupid's jaw. Schwartz's prisoner slumped like a dead weight.

"You could have broken your knuckles," I protested in awe, watching the guy go down and not come back up. I sooo wanted to be able to do that.

"Not if you know where to hit them. Besides, it keeps you from standing here badgering him anymore. C'mon, let's get you home." He shouldered Milo's tote, clamped my uninjured arm, and began dragging me uphill.

Schwartz saluted his actions in appreciation.

I wasn't so appreciative, but my arm stung, and I was still recovering from the surprise of that blow. Andre had bruised his knuckles for *me*. I had to admit, that was some kind of impressive.

"We'd better let my mother look at that scratch, Clancy. It apparently took out your tongue."

I shook my head to clear the cobwebs. "Will this place ever make sense? Or is it a law of the Universe that the cards get shuffled every time I figure out the game?" I was remembering my botched curses but Andre didn't know that.

"Survival of the species requires adaptation to change," he said with a shrug. "We're survivors. Anyone else would be dead meat."

That was painfully true, given my recent experiences. "Let's not distract from the moment. Why would one of Gloria's thugs be gunning for me?"

"Do you know for certain that he's one of her men?" he asked with interest.

"Who else would it be? Two in one day is no coincidence. What I don't understand is *why*. Granny's gone and Acme is under control again. I'm not bothering anyone."

"Yet," he added in grim amusement. "Maybe they're gunning for you before you start something."

I grew up watching old westerns, but I wasn't buying the black hats shooting the sheriff *before* they robbed the bank. Besides, I wasn't the sheriff.

The blood leaking down my arm probably bled my brains, too. "I think we're standing on hell, Legrande," I said wearily. "And I think the ground between us is melting."

"There's always that possibility," he agreed, humoring me as he dragged me up the stairs to his home. "Or else, you just bring out the devil in people."

When I think of the world being full of possibilities, those were two I'd rather not consider. Chemically polluted ground—yes. Biblical fire—not so much.

I followed Andre inside. Milo stuck his head out, shook snowflakes out of his fur, and settled into his tote to lick himself dry.

Andre had taken the ground floor apartment during his mother's illness, leaving her undisturbed in the attic they'd converted into a hospital. Julius, his father, lived on the floor in between.

Acme's mystery element had cured Andre's mother of cancer ten years ago, only to send her into a coma for the past decade. Another gaseous experiment a few weeks ago had created monsters, but had also mysteriously returned Katerina Montoya from the near-dead. Once a proud, beautiful woman, she hadn't appeared in public since her recovery.

Since Katerina still couldn't get around on her own, they'd not changed the household arrangement a lot. Julius stayed by her side, rendering him the most silent partner a lawyer could hope to have. Because Julius Montoya is a well-respected and beloved attorney, and Andre is a lying manipulative cad most of the time, Andre protects his parents by generously not polluting his father's good name.

Andre led me upstairs to join them.

Since her recovery a few weeks ago, Katerina and I had both been too busy to do much more than wave across the street at each other. I'd first met her as a raven-haired Sleeping Beauty who hadn't aged in ten years. But we'd never really talked since she'd woken.

She was sitting in her wheelchair in the kitchen, chopping peppers, when we came up the stairs. She was still beautiful, although dark circles rimmed her brilliantly green eyes. She smiled genuinely at our arrival.

"Ah, the mysterious Tina, at last we meet properly! I enjoy the way my son grits his teeth when he says your name."

How could anyone not like a woman like that? I grinned and shrugged off Andre's hold on my arm. "Now that he has you back to keep him honest, I'm trying to avoid being a thorn in his side, but he's just so *easy*."

Andre began prying my coat off my back. "Easy is not a word I'd apply to you," he said snarkily. "Tina's just got herself shot by baiting an idiot."

Concern creased Katerina's face, and she rang a buzzer that brought Julius hurrying in.

"We'll need a first aid kit, if not a paramedic," she said in the same dry tone as Andre often used.

Julius Montoya had a photographic memory, a formidable legal mind, and the patience of a saint. He merely lifted his expressive brow at sight of my bloody sleeve and hurried off to find bandages.

"Andre, bring her one of my shirts so we can remove this one, and then have the decency to disappear instead of hovering," Katerina commanded.

To my surprise, supercilious Andre obeyed without questioning.

"Smart man," I murmured in amusement, taking the kitchen chair indicated. "He knows when he's outgunned." I forced myself to look at the stinging arm. The bullet had burned through the sleeve of my black Lauren tailored shirt, one of my favorite Goodwill finds.

"If I knew how to sew, I'd turn it into a sleeveless," I said with more carelessness than I felt. I grabbed the fabric with my good hand and ripped off the sleeve. The seams had been giving out anyway.

"Antiseptic," Katerina insisted, examining the wound I'd revealed. "Something to keep dirt from it for a while. But I agree, you won't die. Do you know who did this?"

"Schwartz has him. We'll find out. It's the *why* that worries me. I don't think I've even riled Paddy lately." Well, I'd turned a CEO into stone, but who knew that?

"We haven't seen Padraig around recently. Perhaps it's time we ask him over and discover what is happening at Acme." Katerina took the washcloth and soap I soaked for her and began dabbing at the scratch.

Julius returned with the first aid kit in time to hear us. "I think Paddy is caving under pressure. He's a scientist, not an administrator. The MacNeills are running the show. But they have no reason to shoot Tina."

Andre entered with a sexy red silk blouse that was so not me. He could keep on wishing. I glared, and he got the picture pretty fast, tossing the garment over the back of a chair. "You'll have to pull your senator's strings, Clancy. Make Vanderventer find out what's going down."

There were so many ways that wasn't happening, and most of them I couldn't explain. So I shrugged. "Until I know this wasn't some kind of personal grudge, I'm voting that we go for a town meeting with Acme. Who wants to be neighborhood representative and speak for us?"

To my utter shock, Katerina spoke up. "I do."

Eleven

WITH my arm taped up, I left Andre and Julius shouting at each other—because they'd never shout at Katerina. I was liking the idea of Katerina acting as unofficial mayor of Whoville.

The night was young yet. Refusing to let anyone think I'd been intimidated by a thug with a gun, I locked Milo in the apartment, and headed right back to Chesty's. With the Saturn legacy hanging over my head, I wasn't thinking about getting lucky, but I could get drunk. What I really wanted was answers.

As I walked down the hill, the almost spectral appearance of the dark, foggy street lined with utility trucks weirded me out. I had good reason to be uneasy. Unless there was an emergency, utility workers had no business lingering after business hours. They should take their big yellow trucks and orange cones and go home to the kiddies.

I didn't see the workers. Had they gone down the steaming red manholes?

Acknowledging the danger of my stubbornness in returning to the scene of the crime, I slipped down a cross street in the direction of the harbor. Over the years of keeping my head down, I'd learned all the hidden shortcuts and twists the Zone created. The harbor alley took me behind the buildings on Edgewater.

The clang, drag of a Dumpster echoed against brick walls. I didn't glance back to see if it followed or guarded me. Garbage cans shouldn't *move,* no matter what the case. I wanted to accept that the ground here was so polluted that it gave life to inanimate objects. I just had the uneasy fear that was too simple a solution.

Fires flickered in the homeless camp on the far side of the chain link, out by the water. For a moment, I thought I saw a blue blur. I took a step toward the fence, and the blur dissolved. Maybe Andre was right. We had cataracts. Blue ones. That's what happened when our local neighborhood chemical company gassed us.

I wanted to believe that with Gloria gone, the bad days were over and rationality had returned, but hot streets and exploding wreaths proved otherwise.

These back streets weren't as hot as the main one, so I had to be careful not to slip on ice or puddles. I safely entered Chesty's through the rear door. I used to work here, and I waved at the cooks as I skirted the kitchen. In relief at the normality, I offered weather reports to the dancers and waitresses in the passage to the front.

Chesty's is the only place to find any food besides fries and burgers after five, so everyone in the Zone stops by here in the evening. I noted a few nylon-coated utility workers still getting a buzz on at the bar and a few tourists surreptitiously checking out the naked murals decorating the walls. I took my favorite booth behind the pole dancers.

Schwartz and Andre slid in shortly after. That they'd known I'd be back and had followed me down couldn't be good.

"Merry Christmas," I said brightly, flashing a fake smile. "Don't give me any bad news until I have my spaghetti."

"If you would read the crap I bring you instead of lecturing me, you'd already know the bad news," Andre said unkindly. Even at day's end, he looked sexy and unrumpled. Better, he had that five o'clock shadow thing happening.

But I was staring at the possibility of being celibate for another year if I didn't want to bring any more paranoid Saturn's Daughters into the world. Even if Andre wasn't still my client, which he was, I couldn't do sexy—maybe not for another year.

"They can't condemn your buildings if you're making repairs." I waved at Diane, and the waitress nodded, knowing my order without being told. I'm not a dead cow aficionado, and Chesty's menu was limited. I came here because I got a thrill at being recognized after all the years of invisibility. So, call me shallow.

"The EPA has inspectors testing the soil any place that isn't paved," Schwartz said, unrelentingly.

"*Not until I have my spaghetti,*" I warned, accepting the beer Diane brought over.

Andre ignored my protest. Naturally. "Clancy, we need *you* to breathe fire down the EPA's back. My mother calling a nice meeting won't do it." He waited expectantly for the spark of justice to light my fire.

Not damning anyone, I promised myself. Sighing, I set down my beer. "Me fighting the EPA isn't David versus Goliath, it's *Toy Story* versus the Universe. Not happening except in the comic books."

"It's *Vanderventer* trying to shut us down," Andre reported.

In the bad old days, Vanderventers wouldn't have been involved for altruistic reasons. Unfortunately, Max's new regime of power-to-the-people was just as much a nuisance. I wasn't certain that being socially conscious was any better if it had the same result—shutting down my home.

"I told the senator to back off." I swigged more beer, self-medicating the pain in my arm. "He's pulling out the Do-Gooders. And there's nothing wrong with changing the world. It damned well needs it."

"You haven't lived here long enough to get a vote," Andre scoffed.

"You don't get to play lord over me, Legrande," I warned. "Max has nothing to do with us. It's the city who governs the Zone. *No one's* getting a vote unless you want to start a recall election and overthrow city government. So stifle it."

"If the EPA condemns the Zone, they have to offer recompense for the property, don't they?" Schwartz asked pragmatically.

That did not enhance our gloom. It wasn't about the money. It was about the community. Even Invisible Tim got that—maybe more than the rest of us. Andre with his PTSD, and me with my justice problem, might not do well in the outside world, but we could pass as normal. Tim was a gay teen with cowardice issues who blinked out when confronted. He'd never survive elsewhere. If he stayed here, with people who accepted him, he could grow up in one piece and have time to develop confidence.

I ordered another beer. My birthday wasn't over, and they were harshing my parade.

"We need exorcists," I said drunkenly as Andre and Schwartz steered me up the street around midnight. No more utility thugs appeared to shoot at me.

"Exorcists ought to do it," Andre agreed, obviously appeasing me. "A few voodoo priestesses while we're at it."

I wasn't that drunk. "Not to exorcise the Zone, dumquat." I thought about that. "Okay, maybe for the Zone, too. But for Hell's Mansion. Know any priests?"

"Hell's Mansion?" Schwartz had obviously come along to protect my virtue from Andre's marauding hands. He didn't know how to follow my drunken rambling.

Andre did. "Dane has demons?" he asked in amusement. "I'd pay to watch that."

"I'll tell him you'll pay the cover charge for the priests," I said. Max would probably kill me for mentioning any of this to Andre, but now that it looked like Max and I would never get it on again, I was still worried about my ex. "I'm thinking Benedictine nuns. No sane devil could hang around when they sing like heaven's angels."

"We could hold the meeting about Acme and eminent domain at Dane's place," Andre suggested, possibly with tongue in cheek. "The Zone's newly self-appointed representative used to love visiting the mansion. With priests and nuns around, no one might get killed."

His mother wanted to be the town rep, I remembered hazily. I could hope that Katerina might be more stable than Andre. "If Gloria doesn't burn the house down around us," I agreed, revealing what shouldn't be revealed.

"Gloria?" Schwartz asked in puzzlement.

"Clancy's drunk, Schwartz. She has nightmares. You gonna take her upstairs or shall I?" Covering for my lapse, Andre propped me up on the bottom step of my boarding house.

"Taking myself up. Tell Katerina if she knows priests, we'll exorcize the mansion. We'll make Max..." Even I wasn't that drunk. I corrected myself. "We'll make *Dane* see what we're up against."

If Andre narrowed his eyes suspiciously, I didn't notice. I just stumbled to the door, let Schwartz open it, and proudly hauled my own carcass upstairs.

Since he lived in the apartment across from me, Schwartz followed to keep me from toppling backward.

Pinned to my door was a pink ribbon and a pencil message in a familiar scrawl:

Hell has many dimensions, aziz. *So does time. Don't risk them.*

Themis, my mysterious Iranian grandmother—whom I've never met. She's the only one who speaks Persian to me. I unpinned the ribbon and message and crushed them against my chest. My birthday present.

Hell exists and my grandmother is reading my blog messages to Fat Chick. Swell.

Schwartz was studying me with bewilderment, as well he might. In theory, no one can enter the boarding house without a key and our landlady can't climb the stairs. Messages appearing from nowhere are a trifle unsettling, as I should know.

I unlocked my locks, then stood on my toes and kissed the good lieutenant's rough cheek. He smelled of beer and Old Spice. I hiccupped and kissed him again. "Night, Schwartz." I hastily opened my door and shut it between us.

With any luck, the kiss ought to distract him from weird messages. I was in no shape to explain invisible grandmothers who spoke foreign languages. I'd looked it up. *Aziz* is Persian for *dear*. My very own Mesopotamian grandmamma—except she used the English alphabet.

Twelve

BY THE next day, the police had taken down the crime scene tape, and Ned's clean-up crew had scrubbed my office lobby to a pristine brilliance it hadn't seen in fifty years.

Nursing a dull headache, I began shoving the boxes of gnomes inside, mostly using my feet instead of my injured arm. It was Saturday. I didn't have office hours on weekends. Even the Do-Gooders had taken the day off.

Unless I learned otherwise, I might have an entire lonely year of celibacy ahead. I could fill my working hours fighting eminent domain. But for relaxation, I'd better find a hobby—one safer than ticking off thugs and exploring under the Zone. I wasn't sure exorcising Gloria was healthier, but she and Dane were the only demons I knew who might set wreaths on fire and blow up gas lines.

I'd rather tackle Gloria than go wandering under the Zone again. For all I knew, the utility workers had gone bonkers from walking through the Zone's underground pollution.

I just didn't know how to hunt a dead person in the hellish dimensions that my granny said I shouldn't risk.

I shoved a box of gnomes to an empty office and studied the situation. I wasn't accustomed to idleness. I needed activity before I went looking for trouble.

Andre had a huge building here. The wiring was ancient and wouldn't support modern electronic offices. He'd had cable run in from a safe neighborhood behind us for my computer. So far, the Zone hadn't grown tentacles this far up the hill.

That didn't mean the building was secure or comfortable. But it was empty, had four walls, and a roof. It had possibilities—if one ignored bats, stenches, and mysterious wails in the cellar. I'd lived with partying college students, screaming sirens, and rodents and been homeless the better part of my life. Now that I had a place of my own, I couldn't let the Zone's idiosyncrasies scare me. Sarah and corpses had put me off yesterday, but I needed to do something about sealing up the cellar.

I carted a few boxes of gnomes to the cellar door to block it—until my arm ached worse than my head. I kicked a few more over to reinforce the barricade. The Force could wail all it liked, but it would have a lot of concrete to deal with if it tried to get out.

I had an insane dream of a little community of enterprises in this big empty space. I liked having people around me. I needed the human interaction to get outside the weirdnesses in my head.

So when Sarah showed up later and asked if she could rent a room, I didn't automatically yell *hell no*.

Logically, I knew I should. No kitchen, right? Limited toilets. And she *had* eventually turned into a chimp.

But she'd been severely provoked, so maybe that didn't count as much. The fact remained that Sarah thought she was steadier up here.

Justice was a bitch to deal with.

"Just a room for sleeping in?" I asked warily, leading her around the maze of hallways. "It's probably not good to have cosmetics stacked up in the bathroom of a professional office."

"You don't use the upstairs," she pointed out, taking the stairs in question to the second floor. "I could put in an air mattress in the office next to the restroom up here. I eat at Chesty's anyway. I don't need much."

That was pretty sad, but really, not my problem. "You were nearly mugged by an intruder the one night you slept here. Why would you want to live here?"

"But I *killed* him," she said with relish. "And I got great hair. The way you attract trouble, you'll probably have more intruders. I can kill them, too. I'll be your guard dog."

Ah, now I got it. Silly me. Sociopath at work. But instead of hiring the fictional Dexter, I would be renting space to a black widow spider. Swell.

I thought of the stoned Nazis in the office downstairs. What if they started coming back to life as the frogs had? Sarah would call them intruders and kill them.

Really, I think too much. "I can't have the police out here all the time," I said sternly. "If that's your only reason for renting, then forget it. No more violence."

"Okay, okay." She gestured dismissively and studied an office suite that overlooked my apartment and Andre's. "I just want to get over this chimp stuff and change my life around like you have. Living outside the Zone could be my chance."

When she put it that way... I still didn't believe it. But I'd laid out my rules, and I couldn't argue if she wanted to stalk Andre. "I'm thinking the Zone makes us better if we *behave* better, if we *try* to fit in," I warned. "If you want to try, have at it. There's a back exit you can use so you don't disturb my office. I'll get a key made."

That's how Sarah and I ended up spending the weekend painting my office slate blue and her room a pale pink. I hate pink, but that was her choice. She'd probably install a cute white princess bed next.

Milo prowled the halls, occasionally bringing me gifts of mice. As long as they weren't bats, I was okay with that. I decided a smaller coffeepot was more practical than an urn and installed a two-buck Goodwill one in my private office off the lobby. I admired the blue walls and white trim and added a navy blue and maroon silk sash above the window for color. I bought—paid full price, mind you—a shade to fit the window so I could work when it was dark without the world seeing me.

I found a fireproof safe on Craigslist and sent a friend with a truck over to get it. If Sarah was living in my office, I needed a place to lock up sensitive records.

Deciding that if Sarah could live with the Force in the cellar without a qualm, that I could, too, I unpacked a few of the gnome boxes still sitting by the front door. The statues were easier to lift one at a time. I distributed them around the building in dark corners. I patted them on their gnarly heads and called them my guardian angels and prayed like crazy they'd wake up and run away and never return.

The Graham Young gnome I put on the building's flat roof and hoped he'd fall over the edge if he woke up. He needed to know what it was like to live with the elements, like the vagrants he'd tried to toss into the cold.

Sunday evening, Andre arrived with a Christmas tree.

"The mayor is throwing this out," he announced, apparently promoting his mother to a higher rank than neighborhood representative. He looked almost defensive when I stared in amazement at the seven-foot fake monstrosity. "Julius and I have been using it, but she wants a real one."

"That makes sense," I agreed, studying plastic branches with built-in lights. I was pretty sure the lights were pink and purple. "Thank you, I think. The place could use a little holiday décor."

"We've called a meeting at the mansion for nine tomorrow." He dropped the heavy tree in a corner near the front lobby window, then looked for a place to plug it in. "Paddy and MacNeill will be there representing Acme, plus Dane and the doctor behind MSI." He shot me an evil glare. "For some odd reason, they can't find MSI's chief executive."

Because he was languishing on my roof. I shrugged, not even bothering to play innocent. "And someone from the EPA, I hope?"

Andre scowled. "Your boyfriend pulled the strings, so yeah, the feds will be there. You're invited, of course, along with our new Zone representative."

"The senator is not my boyfriend," I said reflexively. "You probably know Dane better than I do." Of course, I knew Max better than Andre did, but the mix that was the senator was a puzzlement I couldn't intelligently discuss. "I don't want to be there, but given Hell's Mansion, I probably ought to be."

"Right. They may need a few more garden gnomes," he said with his usual sarcasm. Then he plugged in the Christmas lights and glared at me. "I don't want Katerina involved. She just doesn't realize what's happened to the Zone since she went comatose."

"I can't make your mother stay home, Andre. She has to make a new life for herself. And she isn't dumb. She's spent some time in a different dimension and has to know the world is more than what we see in front of us. You just have to decide at what point you're going to tell her that the Zone is cracked, and she's defending monsters."

He ran his hand through his glossy black hair and glared at the blinking pink and purple tree lights. "Maybe the EPA is right. Maybe they should raze the place and dig out the dirt."

"What color are the manholes tonight?" I asked cynically. "You want to send innocent workers down those hellholes? You want construction people crushed by angry Dumpsters or suffer heart attacks when the statues throw darts? What if displaced gargoyles move uptown? And then you want some smug fascist to build a medical clinic on that ground to experiment with the dangerous chemicals that *started* all this?"

"Thanks for making it clear, Clancy," he snarled, advancing on me. "You do have a way with words."

I wanted him to hold me too badly. I put up a hand to stop him. "Maybe Papa Saturn will give us a solution for Christmas. I'll see you tomorrow morning."

He studied me for a minute, letting the tension smolder. He knew I wouldn't protest too hard if he applied his moves on me. But he probably remembered Friday night's discussion better than I did. "Merry Christmas, Clancy." He strode out.

I needed to turn *myself* into stone.

***

Monday morning, I rode the Harley out to Ruxton. Yeah, I know it's unprofessional to arrive wearing leather pants, knee-high boots, and Max's biker jacket—since mine was being mended. So, sue me. Nothing good had ever come of a visit to the Mansion. This time, I came prepared.

Besides, I needed an edge to deal with silver foxes in suits. They needed to know I wasn't one of them, even if I am a full-fledged, card-carrying lawyer. And Max's soul needed to see the rebel Justine, not the white-collar female in his Senator Dane fantasy.

It was kind of cool boldly roaring up to that guard booth where my swarthy self hadn't been welcome when Gloria was alive. The guy at the gate simply waved me through.

The circular drive was lined with limos and expensive sedans. Heaven forbid that they share a car.

If I was polite, I'd have to find an empty place in the north outer forty and freeze my tush off walking up the drive. Instead, I parked the bike near the pretentious portico, among the azaleas.

Pulling off my helmet and letting my shampoo-model hair swing free, I held up my ID to the guard at the door. He looked disapproving, but in my experience, that's the normal face of authority. He ushered me in.

I followed the sound of voices and the trail of armed security guards across the three-story atrium where Gloria had so ignominiously popped her head like a pumpkin. I avoided looking at the marble tile where she'd briefly turned into a demon before she gave up her rotten soul. The memory was seared firmly in my neurons without any reminder, thank you very much.

I entered the ginormous dining hall on the right side of atrium.

Picture this: Shrimpy me in black biker leather, mink shampoo-ad hair swinging in all its glory, helmet under my arm, and Milo peering out of my newly-acquired black leather backpack as I posed in the doorway. And a luxurious, chandeliered room full of silver foxes in tailored suits and designer ties, all hobnobbing and rubbing elbows—falling silent and staring.

Even Katerina in her wheel chair, wearing a silk bow on her navy blouse, her gorgeous blue-black hair pinned into a chignon, turned and stared. I smiled and waved at her. She almost smiled back.

Max/Dane looked a little stunned. Senator Dane Vanderventer

was a hunk and a half—his thick chestnut hair framed a strong jaw, cleft chin, and deep blue eyes gleaming with interest. His broad shoulders filled his suit nicely. He towered almost a foot over me. But Max's soul glowed from those eyes, and I could see his appreciation. That's what I'd been aiming for.

"Hi, I'm Justine Clancy, unofficial attorney for the Zone neighborhood association until we have time to petition for representation on the city council." I let that bombshell sink in while I chose a chair at the table beside Katerina. I glanced at Andre, who was playing it cool, as if he'd known I'd drop a bomb. He took a chair across from us. "Has everyone been introduced but me? Then let's settle in, gentlemen. I don't have all day to waste."

Every person in there was older, richer, and more powerful than me. I figured that gave me leverage to be rude.

"You're supposed to play nice, Tina," Katerina whispered as the others began jockeying for position.

"*They* don't," I reminded her. "Every damned one of them is here to throw his weight around. I don't have weight. I'm here to keep them unbalanced."

She gazed at me approvingly. "Times really have changed. I'll keep that maneuver in mind."

Two women against a table full of men. I wiggled my fingers at Andre and made him scowl.

Senator Dane stood at the head of the table and made official introductions once everyone settled in. Dr. Abdul Bakir, MSI's representative, had positioned himself at Dane's right hand. Brown, bald, and bearded, wearing an unflattering gray suit, he didn't look comfortable, but his dark eyes glowed with determination. He'd obviously drunk the Kool-Aid and meant to save the world.

Paddy, our neighborhood mad scientist and also Dane's father, looked decidedly uncomfortable in his rumpled suit, but at least he'd had his hair cut and had bothered to shave. He'd be a silver fox if I hadn't seen him with food in his beard.

Former Senator Michael MacNeill had apparently elected to represent Acme's board of trustees. He'd helped me get my law license, and he was Max's father, but he'd been involved in shady dealings that had got him ousted from office, and Max hadn't trusted him, so I didn't. The man was more weasel than fox.

The EPA rep looked like a lawyer. He practically snarled at me as he produced a briefcase just spilling over with documents. From a legal standpoint, I couldn't blame the man, so I just smiled at him, too. That startled the shit out of him. He dropped a file folder and had to scoop up the contents. Let him be as conflicted as I was.

"Ladies, gentlemen," Dane said, silencing the rattling papers and murmurs. "For good or ill, I'm here to represent the heritage my grandparents left to me. I've established the Gloria Vanderventer Foundation to make restitution for the damage done to the environment by that heritage."

Nice, Max. He'd been using me to spy on Acme and the Zone when he was still alive. Now he had it all in the palm of Dane's hand, with the power to crush every peon who disagreed with him. I waited.

Gloria didn't.

The smell of gas flashed through the glittering room seconds before the crystal chandelier flamed on and the windows blew out.

Thirteen

I WOULDN'T have been surprised if the flaming chandelier had cackled.

I grabbed Katerina's wheelchair and shoved her for the door while she grimly clung to the chair arms, and the room erupted in chaos.

On my own, I might have stayed to watch the show, but Katerina had suffered enough at the hands of the Vanderventers. I needed to remove her from Gloria's malevolence.

Andre vaulted over the enormous shiny dining table, seized his mother in his arms, and ran faster than I could push.

"Welcome to the Zone!" I shouted at the elegant men brushing embers from their hair, their belongings, or their burning suits. I grabbed Paddy's arm to keep him from standing there, studying the phenomenon, and pelted after Andre as more fiery debris spewed from the ceiling.

No fire erupted in the vast foyer. Dane was shouting orders at his security guards and already had a fire extinguisher in hand. That was my Max, always prepared, even wearing a senator's suit.

Torn, I had to release Paddy to grab the extinguisher from the senator. I shoved the canister into a guard's hands, swatted Dane's muscled shoulder, and pointed toward the door. "She's after you, remember? Get your ass out of here before the whole place comes down around our heads."

The safety of others would appeal to Dane's inner Max faster than his own safety. Proving he was still my guy, he caught my arm and practically dragged me outside to prevent all Gloria from breaking loose.

Once we were on the lawn, I could see that Katerina had insisted on being returned to her feet rather than lugged around like a sack of potatoes. She was leaning heavily on Andre, but she was fine and observing the scene with acute interest. She had every right to be entertained by watching our opponents prance about patting out their charred clothes or just generally cursing.

Many of the curses were directed at us. The foxes had apparently decided the Zone representatives had perpetrated a magic trick to scare them. I understood their problem with our reality.

Paddy wasn't on the lawn. He hadn't followed us out. I sighed and shook off Dane's grip. "Your father is probably inspecting the chandelier to see how you did that. I'll go get him. You...*stay here.*" I met his frown, forcing him to recognize what I couldn't repeat again in a crowd.

The good senator glared, but he was far from dumb. He found another use for his energy by ordering his security guards to call the fire chief and electricians.

This had once been Paddy's home. He'd grown up here with his insane mother. I could hardly blame him for turning out weird. I did blame him for leaving his son Dane behind for Gloria to raise.

Inside, one of the men holding a fire extinguisher reported the fire was out—for now. If Gloria had learned to inhabit electric wires, then the Mansion wasn't long for this world. Neither was Max, if he stayed.

Leather doesn't burn well, so my clothing had emerged relatively unscathed for a change. My hair smelled, so I assumed it had been charred. I trotted back inside, ordered one of the guards to take the wheelchair out to Katerina, and found Paddy staring at the blackened ceiling.

"I could have sworn I saw my mother in those flames," he said. "Maybe I should retire."

"You did see your mother." I didn't add that he might have seen his son as well. He still thought the Dane outside was his son with a new and improved conscience. I didn't want to disillusion him. "She's been haunting Dane since her death. That's why his condo burned. But usually she inhabits gas lines."

Paddy looked briefly startled, then a little grayer, a little more wrinkled, until his formidable mind kicked in, and he straightened. He's a pretty tall guy, if not as powerfully built as Dane. He could be impressive when he wanted. He studied the hole where the chandelier had been.

"Gas lines? This is an old house. It had gas lighting at the turn of the century. There are probably still lines in there. We'd better get out before the whole place blows." He started for the door. Unlike his son, he didn't grab my arm and drag me with him.

I tagged along anyway. "I think she's trying to kill Dane. And maybe Andre. I doubt she'll expend any energy when they're not in range."

"That's not physically possible, you realize," he admonished, ever the practical scientist.

"Neither is blue neon without electricity or snakes materializing from tattoos," I reminded him as we reached the portico. "I think we're dealing with a different dimension."

When in doubt, hand a scientist string theory. They lap it right up. Paddy's expression revealed instant absorption in this new idea.

Of course, Andre joining us just as we approached Dane spoiled my trip into reality land. Andre handed Dane a neat computer printout. "Exorcists," he said curtly. "Also a voodoo priest, a witch, and a warlock."

I almost choked on laughter as the good senator and his scientist father stared at the list in equal parts horror and fascination.

"I want the Benedictines," I insisted, fighting a grin. One really shouldn't grin when confronted with the devil, but despite flaming chandeliers and blown glass, I just couldn't cope with believing in the tenants of hell.

As far as I was concerned, Schwartz was right. Hell was right here on earth—or in a dimension we could cross into under the right conditions.

"When have you ever seen a nun?" Andre asked, rightfully so since I probably look more Muslim than Christian to him. Color blindness doesn't exist.

"In the hospital, after one of my leg surgeries. The nuns sang Christmas songs in the chapel. That's as close to heaven as I've ever been." I wasn't ashamed to admit it. I really don't have a spiritual side. I'm a lawyer, after all. But those nuns were beyond awesome.

"You're not serious?" Paddy asked, staring at the list. "An exorcism?"

"Think of it in terms of closing any holes into another dimension," I said encouragingly.

"If that were physically possible," Paddy mused, going into one of his fugue states, "chances are good the holes would blow open elsewhere. The quantum pressure..."

I left him to it. Men were checking their watches and heading for their cars. We hadn't settled anything. I needed to do something drastic to protect my adopted home and friends.

"Gentlemen," I shouted, moving away from Dane so it didn't look as if I had his permission to speak.

"We came here to inform you that we're not helpless," I shouted once I had their attention, "that the Zone *will* fight eminent domain if it's taken for the benefit of a profit-hungry, environmentally unfriendly organization like Acme. That is not the purpose of eminent domain. We are open to any studies the EPA would care to conduct and any improvements they might suggest, but you cannot steal our property and shut us down. Not without a fight."

Dane clamped a heavy hand on my shoulder, through Max's bomber jacket. "What Miss Clancy means is that we still need to work together to do what's best for the Zone neighborhood. I apologize for the interruption. My secretary will call you, and we'll organize another meeting somewhere a little less explosive next time."

"Nice, Maxie," I said under my breath. "You'll be a politician in no time."

"And you never will be, Justy," he agreed in a low voice, reminding me with the nickname that really was Max inside the suit and tie. "Let's get Andre's damned circus in motion and put an end to Gloria's stalking while I'm still alive to appreciate it."

I might not believe in a superstitious, Bible-thumping fiery pit, but I'd spent some of the worst weeks of my life bringing Max back from what we called hell's outer circles. I wasn't letting him go again so easily. I left him to answer a question from his security people and caught up with the EPA rep before he could reach his car.

"I meant what I said," I told him. "We'll help however we can to clear up the harbor pollution, but it's ten years too late for the people living there. Eminent domain is out of the question."

This gray-haired fed wasn't as slick as the others. He had bags under his eyes and an air of infinite weariness. "Says the mouthpiece working for the wealthy scoundrel who owns the land," he said with a shrug.

Mouthpiece. Nice. Not. "That shows how little you understand." I nodded in Andre and Katerina's direction. "If she should tell him the land is a menace and to get rid of it, he'd sell us all out to the highest bidder. That's not the point. You do *not* want a medical clinic in an environmental hazard zone next to the chemical company that caused that hazard. Clean the harbor up if you like, but keep Acme and their cohorts out of the picture. They are not upstanding citizens."

He looked at me with a little more interest. "I'm with the federal government. The state controls eminent domain. Without state involvement, nothing's happening."

"Then let nothing happen. Don't let them sell you on eminent domain for the sake of cleaning up the hazard. Andre may be a slumlord, but he isn't the villain in this picture." I handed him my card and walked away.

I didn't know if I'd accomplished anything, but I felt better for having tried. Of course, I wasn't helping any when I walked straight toward Katerina and Andre.

"The circus is on," I blithely said under Andre's glower. "Let's round them up, head 'em out."

I picked a charred piece of plaster from Katerina's blazer. "Do you need a tour of a senator's home," I asked her, "or are you ready to head back?"

She brushed my hair with her hand and handed me a burned chunk. "I think I want to be able to escape on my own legs before I go back in there," she said dryly. "Gloria and I used to work together on volunteer committees. I had no idea that she had let the place run to rack and ruin. That's not like her."

"She wasn't herself those last years," Andre said consolingly.

I politely didn't snort and moved the subject forward. "I want to be part of the circus when it happens, please."

"You bring the nuns, I'll bring the clowns. What's the big guy gonna do?" He jerked his chin in the direction of Dane, who was back-patting and schmoozing the lawyers.

"Bring the flame thrower," I said with a shrug.

I took the Harley back to the Zone and my new slate-blue office. Stupidly, I decided to stop at Chesty's for lunch first. Running scared apparently makes me hungry. I should have asked Schwartz if my would-be murderer was out on the streets yet, but I had this itching for normal. I just wanted to be a lawyer stopping for a bite to eat.

As soon as I parked, Tim came running from the florist shop across the street, waving a paper as if he'd been waiting for me.

"The city has condemned the shop!" he shouted, nearly in tears. "The plants will all die. We just got a new succulent shipment!"

Nancy Rose, the owner of the florist shop, was Tim's second mother. His first was a drug addict who OD'd a year or more ago. Tim would do anything for anybody who helped him. He worshipped Nancy.

This was what a lawyer did, I reminded myself. I snatched the letter from his hand and skimmed it as I crossed Edgewater in the direction of the florist shop.

It was still December. It was still cold. And the pavement still felt like Savannah in July. We could probably grow plants out here—for all I knew succulents were flesh-eating greenery—but I didn't mention the street heat to Tim. He was a teenager and a bit impervious to any oddity but his own—as a gay teen with a tendency to literally vanish, he had a *lot* to cope with.

Nancy Rose was a short, plump, fiftyish, grandmotherly sort with dark graying hair she didn't bother dying or styling. Wearing khaki slacks and denim shirt, she looked up when the bell over the door rang, then returned to potting.

"I probably should retire anyway," she said with resignation. "Business is bad. I just don't know what else to do with myself."

The shop was a veritable jungle of plants. I wasn't a nurturing type and had never bothered growing even a spider plant, so I didn't know the names of most of the inventory. But there were towering trees and tiny blooming bundles of flowers and the place smelled like a forest. I had a suspicion Nancy had a hidden weirdness involving green things. No one grew jungles like this in Baltimore, much less in an environmental disaster zone.

Amid the greenery I spotted a familiar shape. I pushed away a large fern frond and came face to face with a garden gnome. Someone had placed a red felt elf cap on its ugly head and turned the automatic pistol into a Christmas tree.

"Tim," I said warningly, nodding at the statue.

"He was cute," he said defensively. "I didn't think it would hurt to keep him warm in here."

"In the Zone, Tim? Really?"

"I broke the gun," he argued. "And glued the greenery onto the stock. I can glue his feet to the shelf."

"Timmy has a talent for decoration," Nancy acknowledged. "He did all the fairy lights in here."

The entire ceiling glittered with tiny white lights. They adorned the taller trees, along with jolly red bows. "Very festive." For a second, I almost smelled live evergreens.

My mother didn't believe in Christmas. My heart kind of craved the Dickens' specials I'd seen on TV, with peaceful villages, big fluffy trees, pretty lights, and drifting snow. I didn't need the presents and bows, just the serenity of the glass globe fantasy. Tim had created a lovely peek at my dream.

I didn't kid myself into believing a jungle in the Zone qualified as a Dickens' village, but it was worth defending. I waved the condemnation notice. "We're fighting these," I told Nancy. "If you want to join the coalition, let me or Andre know. We may have to secede from the city and create our own town."

"Our own town?" Nancy looked up from her potting. She was wearing little round spectacles just like Mrs. Claus should. "None of us has that kind of money. Even if we did, it would mean more taxes."

"Has your heat bill gone down lately?" I asked, raising my eyebrows pointedly.

She looked surprised. "I guess it has. We keep it kind of tropical in here, but I haven't had to turn up the thermostat this winter."

"Use the money you saved on heat to buy some live Christmas trees. See if they don't bring in a profit. Use that profit to pay into the town fund. We just have to use our heads to figure out how to make this work."

"We already have ribbon," Tim said eagerly. "I could sell holiday bows."

"See? The money part is easy when we put our heads together. It's dealing with the monsters that's a little harder. But we're trying." I studied the gnome in the greenery and wondered if he had been a monster or just an underpaid flunky.

"It will take a whole lot more money than a few bows and trees will make," Nancy said skeptically.

"Not when you have lawyers willing to work for free. It's all just paperwork."

She actually started to look a little hopeful, and that made me very afraid. But I was a hard worker and learned fast, plus we had Julius's brilliant legal mind on our side. Maybe, as long as the research company's CEO was a gremlin on my roof, we stood a chance.

"Anything can happen," I warned. "Because it always does. Just don't buy a retirement cottage in Florida yet."

Tim hugged me. He actually hugged me. And it felt good.

I left them cheerfully discussing Christmas plans. In the street, the manholes glowed brighter, and a couple of Do-Gooders were hanging *real* wreaths where the burned out lights had once been. I could smell pine.

Smiling, I inhaled the scent.

And smelled gas.

Fourteen

THE gargoyles had alerted us to our last emergency, when the chemical plant had exploded with green and pink gas that left half the inhabitants of the Zone comatose or violent. I glanced up at the two stone creatures on the florist shop. They looked back at me, bored.

Complacence is dangerous anywhere, but particularly in the Zone.

"Gas, fellows?" I asked. "Smell anything dangerous?"

One actually sniffed the air, then settled his wings more comfortably and closed his eyes for a nap.

Edgewater needed a real warning siren. Like a tornado siren, it would mean run for cover when Acme spreads its chemical clouds—or gas leaks from the sewers.

I just wasn't sure where cover was.

Since no one else was panicking, I called the gas company and reported a leak, like any normal citizen might do. Infrastructure deterioration, I reminded myself.

Then I calmly walked down to Bill's Biker Bar, which does a booming beer business at noon, leaned in, and shouted, "Anyone smell gas?"

A few of the guys looked around, sniffed, and shrugged. Hulking Bill emerged from behind his shiny mahogany bar, drying a mug, and strode into the street. "Nope, nothing. You been working too hard? Come in and have a fish cake and a beer. What did you do to your hair?"

I'd forgotten about the burned bits. I needed a mirror. "Playing with fire," was all I told him, tugging to see if any more came off.

Silent Bill had been talking more lately. He was probably more brute than brains, but he was a solid guy to have behind you. Trying to calm my jittery nerves, I followed him back to the bar and let him fuss over me.

"How's Milo?" he asked, delivering a well-seasoned fish burger.

"I left him at the office guarding Sarah and Ned," I admitted. "I probably ought to get back and see if anyone survived."

Bill snorted. "Well, bring him down here for fish sometime." He wandered off to deal with another customer.

I loved the Zone and the people in it. There was potential here. How could I live with myself if I let everyone down? How did I know who to fight when all I had to work with was hot streets? My Gloria theory was all I had.

Munching my sandwich, I called and found the Benedictine nuns first because they were easiest. For a generous donation they happily agreed to sing for a holiday benefit at Senator Vanderventer's home.

Learning about eminent domain would take more time. I didn't know how much time we had, but at least the law was familiar territory, and I knew my enemies. I needed experts on my team. I ran a few searches on my cell and had a list by the time I finished lunch.

I really didn't have to investigate everything myself, I concluded as I walked back to the street. I'd spent a lot of money to work my way into a white collar job where I didn't have to get my hands dirty, right? Let the gas company handle leaking pipes. I did *not* have to go under the street—especially if I couldn't visualize weirdoes out of my space anymore.

Outside, a truck advertising Jacuzzis was parked near an empty storefront. People with the time and money to indulge in a sauna or whirlpool bath didn't live on this end of town. It was worth a side trip to check out the anomaly. Keeping my hands clean didn't mean my curiosity was dead.

Two guys in coveralls stepped out of the van carrying pipes and assorted equipment. Ignoring me, they dragged their dollies down an alley toward the cordoned off harbor. I followed.

They were setting up a spa on one of the steaming manholes in the back lane near the fenced off area.

"Not enough hot water in your part of town?" I asked. I knew better than to question, but I could never help myself.

They scarcely gave me a second glance. I hadn't felt that invisible in a long time.

"Hot springs have healthy minerals," one of them finally replied. He had a jackhammer in hand. A jackhammer. In the Zone.

One more anomaly to investigate. Had Acme sold this land around the old plant?

Most of the city thought the EPA had cordoned off the chemical hazard caused by the old plant's explosion and the ensuing chemical flood ten years ago. Apparently the city had short term memories or believed the harbor had magically cleaned itself. No one but the people who lived here fully understood the Zone's real eccentricity... but *hot springs!* Infinitely delusional. One hoped they knew better than to drink the bathwater.

Ignoring an itchy feeling, I roared the Harley back up the hill. I wanted to bag some eminent domain lawyers before I ran into any more interruptions.

Schwartz and the DG guy, Hanks, were waiting for me outside the office. I didn't like leaving my bike out where anyone could help themselves, so I unlocked the office door and rolled the bike in with me.

Schwartz shook his head and Hanks stared, but heck, I was still wearing my biker leather and burned hair. Let them make of it what they would. I was more concerned about why Ned hadn't let them in.

"To what do I owe the honor, gentlemen?" I asked, parking the bike at the back of the lobby. Ned's desk was empty. Milo didn't run out to greet me. In my world, silence was not only creepy, but dangerous. It took all my focus sometimes to keep a handle on my paranoia.

Schwartz spoke first. "I just stopped by to let you know that your friendly mugger got out on bail this morning. Rob here mentioned housing vagrants, and we got to talking." Schwartz propped the heavy bike more securely.

I rolled my eyes. My life was a thrill a minute. "And the two of you decided jail was a nice warm place for the homeless while crazed utility shooters stalk the streets?" I asked, while listening for some evidence that Ned and Sarah and Milo hadn't killed each other.

"Kaminski has been ordered to stay clear of the Zone as part of his bond," Schwartz said stiffly.

"But Dedicated to Good has agreed to spend some of their grant money on renting the Morgan building," Hanks said excitedly. "We need to know if Mr. Legrande still has legal ownership, and if he'll rent it out for a minimal sum if we fix things up. Lt. Schwartz said he'd see what he could do about finding off-duty policemen as security."

Oh crap, uptown cops in the Zone was a disaster in the making. I gave Schwartz the evil eye. "What, you think Leibowitz will work off duty?"

"After the eminent domain protest and all the missing person reports were filed on MSI's security guards, the honchos think we need more feet on the ground," he said nonchalantly, with his official face on.

I translated—*Acme complained.* Which meant Max's father, ex-Senator MacNeill, had reported Graham Young's disappearance, because Paddy wouldn't notice unless the plant blew up in his face.

And with his substantial assets locked up in a blind trust, Dane didn't get a say in anything.

Filling the town with Do-Gooders and cops couldn't possibly be safe. Realizing how that sounded inside my head, I rubbed my brow and tried to remember which side I was on.

"Okay, fine, I'll talk to Andre. Eminent domain talks are currently at a standstill. I make no promises that we can hold them off," I warned Hanks, who'd broken into a big smile.

"Thank you! Here's my phone number. Just let me know what Mr. Legrande says, and I'll have the crew down here immediately to start cleaning up the building." He handed me a scrap of paper.

I stuck it in my pocket and watched them depart before I started an office search for my cat. Ned and Sarah could take care of themselves.

Milo had parked himself on the far side of the hall from the cellar door. The gnome boxes still blocked access. His ear tufts stood on end, and he growled when I came in sight. Take my word for it, my cat growls. Think lion. I studied the door worriedly, but I couldn't see anything.

"What is it, killer? Did the evil monster come visiting?" That wail had been almost physical and still gave me cold shivers. And it had been in my damned basement. With huge red-eyed bats.

I didn't want hell—or Gloria—to be under my floor.

One of these days, Milo would learn to speak. As it was, he gave me a glare of disdain and trotted toward the back entrance where I'd left his food.

Stupidly, I put a hand to my cellar door. It was hot.

I should have barricaded that tunnel. With my luck, it probably provided a direct passage to the Zone, and zombies would come parading up one of these days.

They'd have to wait in line. If my mojo wasn't working anymore, I was not about to tackle demons with a law book.

Sarah was free to come or go, so I refused to worry about her. Hoping Ned was just out to lunch, I returned to my office, fired up my fancy new computer, and began contacting eminent domain specialists. This was what I'd trained to do.

I was nicely into my comfort zone when the front door blew in with a cold blast of wintry wind and the fresh scent of pine. I'd left my office door open so I could see anyone entering. I saw a sideways-moving evergreen tree. With feet.

Tim followed the tree, carrying Ned's glittery tote bag spilling with packages. He waved at me and set about dismantling Andre's ugly electric monstrosity.

"Ned, we had *clients* standing outside," I shouted at the footed tree.

"I'm allowed a lunch hour," he caroled back. "And that bike in here is really bad feng shui."

I shut my door.

I'd found a specialist willing to consult with me and was up to my ears in the intricacies of fighting city hall when Andre rapped on my office window. I'd forgotten to pull the shade. At least he'd warned me before he sauntered in, carrying the icy scent of winter and a draft of pine. In the lobby beyond, I caught the glitter of a proper Christmas tree—although a little on the bent side if my eyes did not deceive.

"Not into pink and purple and artificial, I see," he commented, nodding at the lobby. "Why is Ned standing on his desk?"

"He saw a mouse? Do I really want to know?"

Andre peered around the doorjamb again. "Nope, you probably don't." He shut the door and dropped into the chair. "Got your nuns?"

"I do. Got your exorcist?" I countered.

Damn, but he looked good occupying that chair. I wished he wasn't paying my bills. If he wasn't my client, all we would need was a fireplace and hot toddies and I'd forget all his faults and mine and jump his bones.

Except I wasn't jumping anyone's bones these days. I'd fired off questions to my mother, in hopes she'd actually read her email sometime in the near future, but until I knew what genetics I was dealing with, I wasn't producing any more Rosemary's babies.

"I've lined up an exorcist, a witch, and a voodoo priest, as promised," Andre replied. "And we have a date with Hell tomorrow. Dane says he has the gas company turning off the lines to that neighborhood at three."

"The nuns said they would send whoever was available when we need them. They think they're doing a benefit. Let's try not to scare them. We won't have them arrive until what...four?"

"Three-thirty so they can sing our souls to heaven after we've blown up the place," Andre said cynically.

"You don't have to be there," I pointed out. Saying it was damned dangerous for him to go would only convince Andre not to miss the show. I was starting to believe his Special Forces training required a suicidal mentality—especially since he'd *been* suicidal at one point. The experimental Acme pharmaceuticals he'd taken had sent him tripping into other worlds not so long ago. Now, he had hallucinogenic flashbacks when stressed.

"Neither do you," he pointed out, reasonably enough. "But you're going aren't you? Want to enjoy our last night on earth?"

"Some of us have to work," I reminded him, conceding his point without argument. No way was I letting Max do this himself. "The DG's want to rent your insurance building for a minimal sum, and the cops are sending back-up patrols to harass the vagrants and tourists. Cora just called to report the utilities are shutting us down again tomorrow, and that there's a bulldozer on the harbor grounds. There's no joy in Whoville yet."

"I received an offer on my property from MSI that would pay us to retire to Hawaii," he said with amazing composure.

Excrement meet oscillator. I clicked off the computer and clenched my fingers in my lap, waiting to see if Andre meant to sell out the Zone.

It would make perfect, logical sense to do so, even I could see that.

He raised his eyebrows and watched me with interest. "What, no comment? A year ago you would have said good riddance."

"A year ago, my only goal was to pass finals. There's a little more at stake than my grades these days." I tried to sound as nonchalant as he did.

This was a big friggin' deal. Andre owed nothing to the Zone inhabitants. They were mostly freaks who had lived pathetic lives until they'd stumbled on an area no one wanted to live in. Over the last ten years, they'd made something of themselves. Mostly.

Chances were pretty good they couldn't carry those talents into the real world, but Andre didn't have to care. He owned the Zone. My assumption was that he'd bought everything on back taxes with the intent of blowing the place up. Only he could decide what he wanted. I waited.

He shrugged and stood up. "I don't have to decide immediately. Don't tell Katerina what we have planned for tomorrow. Today was the first day she's been outside the house in ten years. Instead of being terrified, she has Julius drawing up papers asking for Zone representation on the city council. It's good to have her back."

He walked out, leaving my door open to blinking Christmas lights and the forest smell of pine.

Andre would never in a million years admit a weakness, but he would protect his parents with his life. If Katerina wanted to represent a hellhole, he wouldn't sell. If Katerina was endangered by her persistence at fighting eminent domain, Andre would burn down the town and everyone in it.

Not totally reassuring, but I finally understood his priorities.

After making a few more phone calls, I gave up for the day and wandered out to Ned's version of Santa Claus Land.

The Christmas tree twinkled in white and gold lights and glittered with plastic stars. Silver and gold swags adorned the tin ceiling. In the center of the swags was... I studied the greenery-studded object dangling from a ribbon over Ned's desk. It had mistletoe tucked into the end. Digging into my deranged memory banks, I came up with... a kissing ball?

"Tim, you're jailbait," I shouted at the floppy brown hair on the far side of the tree.

He stuck his head around a branch and blinked in puzzlement. "What?"

"Just clearing the air." I found Ned on a ladder adding the final swag to the back of the lobby. He stuck his tongue out at me and returned to fussing with ribbons. Maybe he was just being a gay big brother. I was the one with trust issues.

"Okay," I announced in apology, "since this may be my last night on earth, I'm making white bean chili and spice cake. You're both invited if you don't have other plans. And I'd suggest you don't tell Sarah what that giant ball represents."

This was the Zone, and they were male. They heard *food* and ignored the rest.

So did Milo. He trotted into the room as Ned and Tim erupted in a chorus of *Bring me figgy pudding*.

Of course, Milo could have been responding to my prediction of the apocalypse. One never knew with cats.

Fifteen

TUESDAY morning, still stuffed full of my favorite cake and chili, and warmed by the carefree laughter of Ned and Tim from last night, I cleared my desk of all Andre's pesky problems. Most of them would have been simpler if the Zone was actually its own town, and I could become the town's official attorney. Utilities listened to communities, not individuals.

I doubted that Baltimore would be interested in letting us secede. That didn't mean I couldn't try. For now, I just called myself the attorney for the neighborhood association when I yelled at the morons at the utilities trying to shut us down.

Of course, all I managed was to limit the hours of utility cut-offs and annoy the hell out of the EPA. I could see the temptation of using Saturn justice and visualizing them all into obedient robots who only took my commands.

Some days, I'm my own worst enemy.

By noon, the electricity was off at the bottom of the hill, and utility workers had all of Edgewater closed. From the reports I was receiving, bulldozers were digging up the contaminated harbor and hauling it away. I wondered what the deranged sauna guys thought about that, but I worked through lunch and didn't stop to find out.

I needed time to hit the hairdresser and get my newly-shaggy hair cut, but it wouldn't be today.

My sugar high had worn off by the time I had to drive out to Hell's Mansion for Max's version of Christmas entertainment. Planning my own possible demise took the fun out of the holidays.

Out of sheer meanness, I drove my rusty Miata convertible and filled the back seat with Andre's pink and purple artificial tree. If Gloria meant to burn me or my friends down, I wanted her to take out the ugly first.

I arrived early. By the time I putt-putted past the guardhouse and up the drive, Max/Dane was waiting on the portico. He lifted Dane's elegant eyebrow at my offering and trotted down the steps to relieve me of the gaudy ornament.

"Is this what the fashionable set brings to an exorcism these days?" he asked.

That was pure Max. Didn't make me any less uptight, however.

"I've never summoned the devil before," I retorted. "I thought I'd offer a worthy pagan sacrifice."

"Yourself?" he chortled at his own witticism and carried the hideosity into the towering, empty foyer. "Think this is a suitable setting for Gloria's last stand?" He gestured at the layered rotunda of balconies.

It had been *live* Gloria's last stand. I winced at the reminder.

"If it's large enough to hold a priest, a witch, and a voodoo doctor, sure, the rotunda works. I'm just going to find a comfortable chair and whistle Dixie. Are you offering refreshments?"

"Catering firm left punch and sandwiches in the kitchen." Flipping back a brass plate in the floor, he plugged in the five-foot, plastic tree. "Gloria used to have a twenty-foot fir imported every year. This piece of shit ought to summon her if nothing else does."

"Then for pity's sake, unplug it until everyone else arrives." Men, the ultimate in testosterone stupid. I headed for the back of the foyer and the kitchen.

Mostly, I was avoiding listening to Max's words coming out of Dane's mouth. The confusion was too harsh while my stomach was tied in knots. I really didn't want to die or go to hell or take anyone with me. I didn't have to be here. But I couldn't let Andre and Max do this without me. Okay, so women get to be stupid, too.

I warily cracked open the swing door and checked the kitchen for bats before entering. "You nailed that basement door shut, right?" I asked as Max/Dane held the door and followed me in.

Instead of answering, Max/Dane stopped behind me, wrapped an arm around my business-like blazer, bent over and kissed me upside-down.

I melted. He could always make me melt. If I didn't have to look at Dane, I could taste Max. I could smell him and hear him. And his kiss was so damned familiar...

I trod on his instep and jerked away. "Not doing this, Max. It's Christmas and we're scared but still not doing this."

To give him credit, he let me go.

"Nothing wrong with comfort sex," he argued, as only non-charming, Motorcycle Max would do.

He helped himself to a sandwich and a cup of punch while I studied the lock on the gateway holding back demonic furballs.

"Oh yeah there is something way wrong if comfort sex results in another Saturn's Daughter on my time. Not happening, babe."

Assured the locks on the basement were strong, I helped myself to his punch and returned to the foyer, hoping a priest would show up real soon.

Max was smart. He didn't need explanations.

Celibate. For a year—until the planet Saturn cycled safely out of earthly reach again. Ugly, but it certainly solved some personal confusion. Didn't make me any less horny. How safe was safe sex when planet gods were involved? My mother still hadn't replied to my email. My tree-hugging mother wasn't averse to conflict, but maternal, she was not.

Hearing a car pull up outside, I pushed the kitchen door open again. "Company coming. I suggest you stay out of sight if you want to preserve your professional image."

Not being the center of attention would tick off both Max *and* Dane. Served him right for stirring up my hormones.

Andre arrived in his sporty Mercedes with what I assumed was the voodoo doctor beside him. Even I managed to twitch an eyebrow upward as a seven-foot tall scarecrow pried himself out of the tiny car. It was below freezing and spitting snow and this character bared his gleaming ebony torso with a red cotton wrap around his hips and a multitude of scary-looking necklaces on a chest so lean I could count his ribs. He wore bones in his braids and carried a painted gourd under his arm.

"Planning on terrifying the ghosts?" I asked dryly as the two of them loped up the impressive stairs.

The giant looked down on me with amusement. "Bad juju needs good voodoo."

Andre just gave me a disgruntled look. "Dr. Pierre Nganga, meet Annoying Lawyer Tina Clancy."

I didn't offer my hand because the doctor's appeared to be coated in magic dust. "No chickens will die for this?" I asked in suspicion, looking at the greasy white coating on his palms.

"They already have," he said solemnly, cruising past me to inspect the foyer. He pointed at the plastic tree. "*Very* bad juju. We will need this space to trap the spirits."

I was pretty sure he was pulling my strings by using ridiculous slang and talking down to me. Or he was a fake doctor.

I crossed my arms and defied the skinny equivalent of Shaq O'Neal. "Believe me when I tell you that I'd rather sacrifice that tree to the spirits than anything else around here."

Andre rolled his eyes and began hauling chairs from the dining room. The professor circled me menacingly, looking me up and down while idly shaking his maraca. I had every right to feel intimidated. As usual, only irritation surfaced.

"Unusual mojo," he declared a minute later with puzzlement. "The spirits speak to you?"

I wasn't much interested in answering that. The explanations would be lengthy, irrelevant, and I wasn't entirely certain that demons weren't involved.

Pragmatic Andre saved the day by slamming a chair down in a curved niche under one of the staircases in the three-story foyer. "Where's our lord and master?" He checked the protective ceiling above the chairs and scooted them more toward the wall.

"I thought it wiser to limit the explosives available," I said dryly.

He shot me a look of curiosity but nodded, as if accepting that.

I hoped Max had gone up the servants' stairs to someplace safe, but I knew him better than that. He was more likely sitting in the shadows on the next level up, prepared to bungee jump over the railing if necessary. And gritting his teeth in frustration at not being able to interrogate the professor. Or heave out Andre. I could practically feel his steam.

But United States senators did not attend exorcisms involving chicken guts and witches.

An engine with a missing piston rattled up the drive. I returned to the door to watch an ancient VW beetle gasp a dying breath as it pulled up behind Andre's Mercedes. A short, stout woman wearing a ragbag of shawls, ponchos, long skirts, and—I swear—an apron, wiggled out from behind the wheel and emerged examining her bag of tricks. She didn't once look at the imposing mansion or me in the doorway.

The professor had been creating a perimeter in the center of the rotunda by scattering fairy dust from one of the many packages hanging around his neck. He stopped to look over my shoulder and snort in disgust. "Not Hagatha. The woman has beans for brains."

"You really need to develop a better dialect and use fewer clichés," I said idly, watching the witch check under the hood, presumably for bat's ears and toad spittle. She added more vials to her apron and bag.

"Eh, mon, dat loco is no mambo, *bwahaha*." His cackle lacked style.

It was like dealing with competitive six-year-olds—or Andre and

Dane in the same room.

While the professor returned to muttering chants under his breath and poisoning any silverfish in the walls, I jogged down the stairs to help the witch carry her heavy load.

"Hi, I'm Tina Clancy. Welcome to Mad Mansion." I slipped the striped cloth bag over my shoulder and accepted two canning jars of pickled pigs' feet or worse that she shoved at me.

"Evil," she muttered. "The house radiates evil. We'll need..." She rummaged in the crowded baggage space and produced a dusty plastic carton. "Still not safe. I'll need to get busy."

Okay, without introductions, I'd call her Hagatha, too. I climbed the stairs behind her in case she toppled backward under the weight of the boxes she carried.

Andre arrived to relieve her of the burden, but she wouldn't release the boxes. On level ground now, she bent forward, and propelled by the weight, trundled onward to drop the stack on one of the chairs.

"Whew." She wiped her brow with the back of her sleeve, checked her stash for stability, and then finally, turned to look around her. "Agatha Wimple," she said, nodding at us and then glancing up at the three-story ceiling. "Bad, bad vibes."

Agatha Wimple and Pierre Nganga, I got it now. They were stage names. Don't tell the spirits your real name and all that. I ought to come up with a superhero name of my own. Terrible Tina sounded right.

As our witch and voodoo doctor painted their spells on the terrazzo floor, pointedly ignoring each other, I leaned against the wall beside Andre. "Why do I get the feeling that this is just a Vegas magic show?"

"I'm trying to remember why I'm here at all." He scanned the next balcony up, but I'd already done that. It was impossible to see over the railings into unlit corridors.

"You brought the guests," I reminded him. "It's only fair that you stay for the show. There's food and drink in the kitchen. I've already checked for bats."

He eyed the balcony where we both knew Max/Dane lurked, looked down at me with a smoldering glare that lit my tinder, then, choosing the wiser path, walked away.

Andre had actually helped bring Max's soul back to Dane's body, even if he didn't fully realize what he'd done. But no matter how he felt about that, he didn't get to kill a senator just for existing. And defying Max by putting the moves on me would send our good senator straight over that railing. I knew they admired my brains, but I had self-esteem issues with my looks, so I didn't think that out of vanity. For all they cared, I could be an ox with a ring in my nose. They were both just competitive asses.

I didn't hear our next guest's car arrive. He politely knocked on the open door, and I had to hurry over to greet him.

I'd left the door open so the winter air could disguise some of the rancid odor emanating from the weird potions now decorating the entry. With the gas heat off, the inside was just as cold as outside. I still wore my coat and scarf. The priest was wearing a long overcoat and homburg. He didn't take them off as he surveyed the increasingly weird setting.

The professor shook his maraca around the unplugged Christmas tree and hung hoodoo dolls from the branches. Hagatha had drawn an enormous pentagram in chalk on the terrazzo, with the tree in its center. She was currently anointing the points of the star with the contents of one of her boxes. Another of the boxes appeared to be rattling.

I thought guiltily of frogs. Both witch and professor frowned in my direction. Bad, bad mojo if they could hear my thoughts. Or pick up my vibrations.

"Unusual," the priest acknowledged, removing his wire-rimmed spectacles and polishing them. "Am I here to exorcise evil or insanity?"

"Excellent question and one I can't answer. I'm Tina Clancy." This time, I held out my hand and the priest accepted it. He'd removed his gloves and his hands were warm.

"Father Ryan Morrison, good to meet you, Miss Clancy. Is Senator Vanderventer here?" He stuffed his fur-lined leather gloves inside his coat pockets and studied the balconies with curiosity.

"He doesn't approve of witchcraft," I said solemnly. Heck, I was a lawyer, one step removed from a politician. I knew the drill. "But the servants believe the late Mrs. Vanderventer's spirit walks uneasily after her tragic death, and the senator wishes to reassure them."

"I see." As the others had, he studied me with interest.

I was getting a creepy feeling about the way these weirdness experts kept looking at me.

"Well, I'd like to believe I'm as broad-minded as the next person. I

don't suppose it hurts to have assistance in summoning lost souls."
Father Morrison produced a small Bible and a vial of what I assumed
was holy water from his inside pocket.

I hesitated, but I couldn't send this mild priest into the fray
without warning. "Umm, the servants believe the spirit that lingers
is...demonic."

He raised his eyebrows to a fine point. "Ah good, then you
understand what we face. In her last years, Gloria Vanderventer was
possessed by evil incarnate," he said.

Sixteen

I *SOOO* didn't want to hear about demonic possession from a religious authority. I was just getting used to sort of believing in a maybe scientific hellish dimension. I knew Gloria had warped into something ugly at the time of her death, and so had the bats in her cellar. I just didn't want a perfectly normal person, a priest yet, verifying that the cause was anything other than chemical pollution.

"You understand that I'm a lawyer, and I really don't believe any of this?" I asked as nonchalantly as possible.

Father Morrison shrugged, set his Bible and vial on a chair, and removed his coat. "You don't have to believe. After you've been in this business as long as I have, demons are still hard to credit. I would like to blame mass hallucination. But those of us cursed with the ability to communicate with the Other World have no choice but to believe."

Oh crap. Did that make me some kind of hoodoo woodoo priestess? I had certainly communicated with Max when he'd been Down Under.

"You could see Gloria's demons?" I asked dubiously.

"Not visually, but spiritually," the priest said without blinking an eyelash. "Her soul was polluted. It may exist now in limbo and that is the reason for the haunting reports."

Limbo! A whole new theory to deal with, shudder.

When in denial— "Would you like anything to eat or drink before we begin?"

"Not a good idea," the priest admonished, just as Andre reappeared bearing a platter of sandwiches and a bottle of Max's beer. "Save it for later."

"The gang's all here," I called cheerfully to the room at large. "Shall I plug in the Christmas tree?"

All three of our guests sent me identical frowns of disapproval. Okay, I'm Saturn's Daughter. I get to have my own pagan rituals.

Andre took the tray into the fire-damaged dining room and helped himself to a sandwich. Apparently, when in doubt, Andre eats. Not so very long ago, he'd wig out under emotional strain, so food was an improvement. With everyone paused and waiting, he shrugged, and set down his sub. Crossing the wide foyer, he plugged in the tree.

It glowed red.

Happy Zone to you, too, Gloria.

Andre shoved me back against a wall and stood protectively in front of me as the tree buzzed, crackled, and grew brighter. I drilled my thumbs into his kidneys, but he wouldn't budge. Feeling kind of safe behind his muscle, I satisfied myself with peering around him to watch the show.

The ebony scarecrow giant began to dance to the rhythm of his maracas. I kind of wanted a drum to join him. His hair bones rattled, and I thought I saw one of Cora's snakes writhing in his necklace.

Hagatha had candles burning in each point of her pentagram. Chanting, she went about anointing the flames with herbs that sparked and smoked. She intoned incomprehensible gibberish in a rhythm that oddly mimicked Pierre's rattles.

The priest murmured in Latin and made signs of the cross.

Outside, the snow cloud darkened what remained of the day, and sleet pelted the windows.

The tree began emanating waves of heat in the chilly foyer.

"Good floor show. Need more naked women," Andre muttered under his breath.

I poked his kidneys again. I needed the touch of solid reality because I could *feel* the bad vibrations our resident witch doctors were raising.

I wanted out of there. If the Force started wailing and sending bat shadows, I had my exit plan ready. I checked to be certain we'd left the front door open. That was best. The staircase to the next floor was beside us, but I didn't know if I could find outside exits up there. The kitchen door was furthest, but it led to the cellar I already associated with hell.

This damned well better work. I had no clue what an exorcism entailed. I just wanted Gloria and Dane's evil souls gone.

Nervously, I watched the devil tree flicker and glow hotter.

The priest's Latin phrases grew increasingly insistent and louder. Pierre started shouting, leaping, and flinging his bony arms into the air. Hagatha adopted a yoga pose on the floor with her palms turned heavenward while she spoke in garbled verse. The stench of her candles and herbs swept the room on the winter wind.

I didn't realize I was clutching Andre's jacket until I crushed his cell phone beneath my fingers. He had a special lining sewn into his pocket for his damned phone.

Pierre's curses reached a crescendo. Hagatha shouted something resembling "Thou Wilt be Done!"

The priest splashed his holy water on the gleaming red tree.

All hell broke loose. Literally.

The tree burst into flame and shot upward as if rocket propelled. I swore I saw Gloria's cackling demonic face in the fiery trail. Steam rolled out of the flames, fogging the foyer.

Andre flung me toward the front door and ran back to haul Hagatha's dumpy form off the floor.

Max bungee-jumped—men are so damned predictable—from the railing into the back of the hall—

Just in time for the kitchen to explode through the swinging doors.

I was pretty sure I was shrieking. Andre thrust Hagatha at Pierre and ran for the senator, whose clothes had caught fire from the kitchen blast.

I couldn't think. As flames licked their way up the wall separating us from the kitchen, I couldn't even summon red rage and damn someone to hell. For all practical purposes, Gloria was already there. I grabbed the stunned priest and pushed and elbowed him toward the door until his feet began moving of their own volition.

Heat couldn't melt terrazzo, but I had the awful notion that the beams and flooring beneath it could internally combust. My boots felt like they were melting as I ran to where Andre was rolling Max on the floor, using his jacket as a blanket to smother the flames.

I threw my leather jacket onto the last of the sparks. Andre looked at me then, through eyes so deep and dark, I could have sworn they reflected another dimension. Or one of his nasty predictions. "I was afraid this would happen, sorry," he said.

And then the blast vacuumed air backward, and we were sucked into the kitchen inferno.

Maybe I blacked out. Maybe my brain couldn't accept whatever took place. I just didn't have a clear memory of what happened between the foyer and when I opened my eyes next.

It was damned dark and hot wherever I had landed. I couldn't see a thing and wondered if I'd gone blind. I took stock of my surroundings as best as I could with muffled senses.

I wasn't experiencing any pain. The flames that had shot through the foyer must have blasted themselves out. I didn't appear to be on fire.

I wasn't certain I appeared at all.

"Justy?" A hand groped my breasts and I sighed in relief that I could feel *something,* even if it seemed more memory and sensation than physical contact. In the dark, I could pretend this was Max and not Dane.

I scooted closer, groping his thigh. At least, I thought it was his thigh. I wasn't entirely certain that I felt my own hand. "I'm feeling kinda insubstantial here, Max," I whispered. "Where are we?"

"Hate to say this, babe, but it seems familiar." He wrapped his arm around me and continued to knead my breast.

My horniness level escalated. So did my fear. Strange combination and maybe a factor of this dimension or hell or whatever was happening here. I wasn't pushing off his hand anyway. "You went up in flames again, Max. You should be in pain."

"Not feeling a thing but you." He rolled my nipple until it stood at attention. "You feel good, but you're right, a trifle insubstantial."

"Not liking this, Max." Well, I liked what he was doing, but coherency wasn't happening in these circumstances. "Where's Andre?"

"Montoya!" Max shouted into the darkness. "I owe you. You'd better be alive."

Huh. I hadn't known Max knew Andre's real name. *Dane* had. They'd gone to school together. Maybe Max had gained access to some of Dane's memory cells. I shivered despite the heat.

Andre didn't answer.

I started to get up. Max held me down.

"Don't, babe. If we're back in hell, he doesn't need to be here. *You* don't need to be here. I just don't know how to send you back." He lifted me into his lap and began massaging my belly. If I was wearing anything, I couldn't tell. His fingers were hot and knew what I liked.

"Hell? Hell is nothingness?" I arched into his caress. It had been a damned long time...

"Listen."

I listened as much as I was able while his magic hands performed the feats for which he was known, and my insides unknotted and opened. There was a reason I'd put up with Max for months beyond his useful life.

But then I listened, and shuddered. I heard maracas. And chanting. Or maybe praying.

"Our bodies are back there and apparently still breathing," he suggested. "Gloria's finally sucked our souls down with her."

So not liking that theory. I explored his chest. Had the fire burned off our clothes? "No bodies? Then what the hell are we doing now? Soul petting?"

I could *feel* a fully aroused Max beneath me. His hands were doing all the things my breasts liked best. I was open and ready for him. More than ready. This was beyond insane and well into the world of nightmare. Or wet dream. I was shuddering with need.

"Souls are pure essence, babe. We're still us. We still need each other. And this is how we're used to expressing that need."

"Not making sense, Max. I'm wearing clothes, aren't I?" I couldn't tell, that's how insubstantial I felt. *I was a ghost?*

"No body parts, no clothes." He flipped me on my back.

I knew there was dirt below me, but I wasn't really touching it. I was sensing Max's thoughts? His arousal? I was feeling his whole damned *essence*. And it was all powerful male and more sensational than Max in human form. And with no bodies...why not?

I reached out and his essence was abruptly inside of me and around me and holding me as I desperately needed to be held, and I was steaming hot and ready.

I understand the romance books crow about the blending of two souls during sex, but all I'd ever experienced was purely physical. This...this was incomprehensible. I felt the need that drove Max, recognized his humanity and how it matched the craving in my own heart and soul. It was like our vibrations hummed in synch, creating a more powerful reality. I opened. I blossomed. The whole world rocked.

Even if everything else felt insubstantial on a mortal level, the ensuing orgasm shook my spiritual world.

Max thrust, shuddered, and cried out at the same time. I could sense an ethereal blending of our...essences? Incredible, potent, and just a little frightening as I felt Max inside and out. I really didn't need to be in his head when he was doing me, but...

Man, I'd needed that. Soul sex. What a concept. I gave a shuddering sigh of gratification.

"Wow, maybe we belong in hell," he muttered. "I didn't see that coming."

I snickered. Okay, so in real life, I'm a soulless lawyer. I only get mystical experiences while in hell, and I can't handle it. So I revert to cerebral and snicker.

"Dirty mind, Justy." He rolled over and tugged me...my essence...with him. "Hope that cleared the air so we can think again."

Now that my mind had returned...I pondered that. "I can't think clearly when I go all red ragey and damn people. Is this some other weird magic? We get all sexed up and mindless after we're damned?"

I ought to be terrified. But I wasn't. That was weird in itself. I just felt satiated and pleased with myself, with just a little tremor at the unknown. I know—stupid. Sex makes people stupid.

"I don't know about me," Max said, holding me. My essence. "But I don't think you're dead, Justy. If the priest is still up there, the house didn't blow. You should only be bumped or bruised."

"Maybe like Andre does, we've gone unconscious and slipped into another dimension?" I asked tentatively, trying to find walls but touching only nothingness.

Of course, Max didn't know about Andre's dimension walking, or did he? He didn't question my statement. "Where is Andre? We were all together," I said, remembering more. The wretched man had actually apologized—because he'd known this was coming? "Andre!" I shouted.

I was starting to feel maybe just a little nervous. I stood up. Or thought myself up. Whatever. Max did the same, not releasing me. I wasn't arguing. I needed to know I wasn't alone in a blackness where nothing existed.

The best sex in my life, and it was all in my head. Maybe I should learn from that.

"Montoya?" Max called, helpfully. "Have you murdered Gloria again?"

"Keep it up," came a faint reply. "I'll find you just to kill you."

"Andre!" I jumped with relief—or I thought I did. "Are you okay? What happened?"

"Hell if I know," Andre said grumpily from a distance to our left. "I should have let Dane burn."

"Yeah, probably," Max agreed, speaking of Dane's body.

Since Max didn't hug me, I had a nasty feeling he meant that. So I punched the *essence* of his biceps. "Not after all the trouble we went through to bring you back. We're getting out of this. You have the opportunity to change the world, and I'll be...danged...if I let you give it up."

"I've been toasted again," Max grumbled. "I think Gloria sent us all to hell."

"Been here, done that," Andre said surprisingly, sounding closer. "Clancy, get between us. I'm not holding Vanderventer's hand."

This confusion had to stop sometime. "Not Vanderventer. Max, meet Andre. Andre, meet Max." I got to be grumpy, too, as I patted around, hunting for the invisible.

"Max?" Andre asked in amusement, grabbing my free hand. "Not Dane? Want to explain that one?"

This was weird. Body or not, I could tell the difference between Dane's manicured soft hand on my right and Andre's tough lean one on my left. Maybe memory of those hands was part of my essence.

"Don't laugh, Legrande," I said, wanting a level playing field so we could find our way out of here. "Your old boyhood chum is roasting with his mother in hell. And I'm guessing they're out to roast us back."

"If they can," Andre agreed. "You really sent Dane to hell?" He almost sounded impressed, if I disregarded the amusement.

"Don't laugh, Montoya," Max mimicked in irritation. "Acme's version of hell apparently has permeable boundaries."

"Dimensions," Andre corrected. "We've been blasted through one of the dimension boundaries. I thought that was only possible in the Zone."

They were literally talking around me. And for once, I had nothing to say. Nothingness felt real to me. Just dark. And hot. But not fiery and filled with lost souls. Dimension hell almost made sense.

Both Max and Andre had experience in walking through dimensional veils, although Andre had claimed he'd crossed time, which was how he made his occasional unreliable predictions.

"Do we go looking for mirrors?" Max asked.

That's how I'd found him after I'd sent him here the first time.

Before I could start worrying about my cat or the various people who might possibly miss me, Andre squeezed my hand. I wasn't dead yet. My hormones responded predictably, even after I'd just boffed Max. Guess head sex didn't last long. I started wondering if I could do the same with Andre.

"There's always a way out," Andre informed us. "It's just a matter of finding it."

"Party pooper," I muttered.

Andre chuckled as if he knew how I'd responded to holding his hand.

Max didn't laugh. They'd both been through war and various

kinds of hell, so they were entitled to their own way of dealing with life-sucks moments. Mine was apparently to think about sex.

Or get angry, but who would I get angry at besides myself?

"I don't think I can fling a flaming compact at Dane's head and visualize us out this time," I warned. "So how do you suggest we get out of here?"

"The compact was probably a one-off," Max agreed. "Not helping here."

He'd used the contact with the compact's mirror to enter Dane's body from the hellish dimension he'd inhabited at the time. Much too complicated to repeat, for sure.

"When we're out of here, I want to talk about Max being alive when Dane's body is out there," Andre muttered, apparently attempting to process what little he knew.

"Don't question us when you're our dimension walker," I retorted.

Andre had told me that Acme's chemicals had tossed him into other dimensions. He'd always found his way out. Maybe he could do so now.

Except—we'd been associating the dimensional phenomena with the Zone. We weren't in the Zone now. All bets were off.

"Don't see any mirrors into the world. Gloria probably didn't have any. Should we go to the light?" Andre suggested.

"I see a light at two o'clock," Max agreed.

"Got it. Let's go, boys and girls," Andre said.

Not liking the dark, I kept a firm grip on both their ethereal hands. I could see a bit of twinkle ahead, but it didn't pose much hope. One didn't exit space through stars, after all.

I couldn't see, but all my other senses were tingling. Andre's hand was tight around mine. Andre was not a hand holder, so I assumed the grip indicated he was as unhappy about our situation as I was. I hoped he wasn't as scared out of his wits as I was. One of us needed his thinking cap on.

I didn't think we were in Gloria's cellar anymore, Toto.

I felt a slow thump, thump, as if feeling a giant pulse. And now that I was more or less functioning, I thought I could smell the crap our witch doctors had been burning, along with hearing their chants and rattles.

"Not liking this, guys," I said, just to hear something besides the insides of my head as we walked. Or thought about walking. Or drifted like ghosts. Real hard to say.

"For good reason," Andre said. "They're probably splashing our bodies with holy water and rum and calling an ambulance. We need to get back or they'll be pumping us full of stuff that will really mess us up."

"You're jiving me, right?"

"Hell...heck...if I understand it," Andre said, belatedly covering up what we all feared. "But some part of us found each other, and that part needs to get back where we belong."

At least Andre was sounding bossy instead of talking in that weary, disjointed way he had when he's stressed and fading fast.

The bad part was that our dimension walker didn't recognize this dimension—but Max did.

"Don't suppose it would help if we shout or sing?" I said in discouragement. "I'm kind of missing that red ragey thing that makes it so easy to just whack someone."

I felt both men glare at me. I shrugged. If I was going to die or wander lost forever, I wanted them to recognize that I was more than a misfit lawyer. They both knew a little about me, but even I didn't know everything I could do.

"Maybe it's time you tried doing something useful instead of whacking someone," Max suggested. He was closest to understanding my dangerous abilities since I'd killed him with them. Well, not exactly, but close enough.

"You caught Tim without being red ragey," Andre said. He hadn't actually *seen* me do anything, but he'd seen the results.

"You're the dimension walker, Legrande. And Max found his own way out of hell," I said, feeling helpless after my bit of braggadocio. "What makes you think I'm of any use here? Is that light any closer?"

It didn't seem to be.

Seventeen

I TOOK a deep breath, smelled rat poison or incense or whatever Witchita Hagatha had been burning, and I tugged my companions to a halt. That I had the strength to stop two hunks who towered over me said something about this dimension.

I didn't hear medics or sirens. Yet. How long had we been out? Medics would make a special effort for a comatose senator.

"I don't understand one milligram of this," I warned. "I'm hot." I'd just had the steamiest orgasm of my life, but that wasn't what I meant. "I see nothing. I can't even see the two of you or my own hand. But I smell incense, and I think the rattling is louder."

"We're still connected to the world through our corporeal bodies," Andre said. He'd had some experience in dimension walking, so I listened. "But whatever makes us—*us*—is here, on the other side of the veil."

"We're really holding hands in Gloria's kitchen?" Max asked dryly.

"Shut up, Max. Let me think." I glared at the light that didn't seem to lead anywhere. "I do stuff by visualizing. How do I visualize our souls popping back where they belong?"

"Not easily. Keep moving while you're puzzling that one out." Andre tugged us on down the tunnel.

The tunnel, with a white light ahead. Not sounding good. Andre could still be responding to his suicidal tendencies. I'm all about staying alive.

"All right, we're mentally or metaphysically connected somehow," I decided, refusing to move. "If I can picture men as frogs—"

"Frogs?" Max inquired with interest. He hadn't been there for that episode.

"Shut up, Max," Andre mimicked me. He'd been there.

"Can we picture our bodies sitting up and talking?" I continued, ignoring the boys.

"Go with whatever you did to catch Tim," Andre suggested. "That didn't involve illogical rage. You're whacko when you lose your temper."

True. I didn't do a lot of thinking when my head was full of fury. "I don't want to diminish your opinion of me, but I failed to turn a turd into a frog the other day," I warned.

"But you did a really bang-up job with the gnomes," Andre countered. "How is that working for you?"

"Shut up, Andre," both Max and I said.

"Can either of you feel the walls of this tunnel?" I demanded, since my hands were otherwise occupied.

They obediently stopped and felt around.

"Okay, that's weird," Max said. "I don't *feel* anything, but I can't push through. It's as if nothing is there and maybe I'm nothing."

"Don't say it, Andre, or I'll send you back as a toad," I warned.

Andre snorted in amusement but obediently refrained from calling a senator a nothing. "That's how it is over here. Although usually, I see things, not just this black hole."

"It was worse where I was before," Max said. "It took a while before I could see and hear other people. I could sense the source of the heat and avoided it. And then I found Justy's mirrors."

I could hear the fear and disgust in his voice. Or non-voice. He had a right to be afraid. We were trapped ghosts with no visible way back and people were about to haul off our bodies. I was too freaked to do more than shiver.

"We don't have too long if they're hauling us off to hospitals," I said, thinking aloud. "The docs couldn't help when our friends went comatose, which is what I guess we are right now. But everyone in the Zone came back after Acme's generator was turned off. I don't think that works for us."

Especially since I figured *Saturn* had granted my wish that time, by bringing the Zonies back from la-la land, and the generator had nothing to do with it. I'd had to kill a mad scientist to earn a wish large enough to save a village.

There was nothing evil down here for me to kill.

As if in response to that thought, a haunting wail emerged from the direction of the light. I would have jumped out of my skin if I'd had any. The intensity climbed until the resulting explosion of noise bounced off invisible walls while we covered our invisible ears.

Above us, the maracas and chanting grew louder.

In the distance, beyond the light, I swore I saw a blue blob. It glowed briefly. The scent of incense became overpowering. The heat intensified.

And then Gloria's face melted in demonic laughter in a fiery ring between us and the light.

"Damn you, Gloria," I shouted.

To my astonishment, the laughter turned to screams of anguish.

In terror, I visualized Dane's chilly kitchen and the sanity of chanting witches and voodoo doctors.

"Miss Clancy moved!"

I was shuddering and my ears were still ringing from that ghostly wail, but I thought I recognized Father Morrison's soft voice rise in triumph.

"Yeah, another live one here." The maracas stopped shaking. "Hagatha, you saved a senator yet?" The voice was mocking.

Swell. Our priests were having a competition over our dubious souls.

Before opening my eyes to whatever havoc reigned, I took inventory of my body's bruises. I could damn well feel them now. I ached in every bone.

I was lying on an icy floor with cold drafts on my feet. I'd worry about catching pneumonia going from the heat of hell to Dane's icy kitchen, except I couldn't figure out if a heated soul worked the same as a cold body. Waaaay too much thinking involved. And I'd just proved that fear worked better than logic in this voodoo world.

My *essence* wriggled with the memory of orgasmic sex, but my body didn't. It just felt bruised from head to toe. Weird.

Dane's physical body had been burned, I remembered. I tentatively raised a hand to my aching head and pried my eyelids open.

I wanted to shut them again, but unholy fascination prevented it.

The professor looked even more primitive than I remembered. He was wearing face paint that resembled dried blood. His ratty hair was coming undone and the bones were rattling loose. He practically had his big bare feet in my face. They were painted crimson.

I eased up on one elbow to watch Hagatha rub unguents into...

Oh damn, she'd stripped Dane nearly naked. His charred clothes were piled in a stinking heap by the kitchen counter.

Dane was one muscled dude, even if his burns now glistened with grease and smelled of scorched herbs. He shifted, apparently feeling the cold floor beneath him. And I'd just had soul sex with him? My gaze drifted downward, but Hagatha had left a towel over his privates. Sweet of her.

I reached over and poked his ribs so he'd turn my way and wake seeing me instead of the witch's wrinkled visage.

His eyes opened and he almost smiled, until the priest sprinkled holy water over him. The curse he uttered wasn't heavenly. Or dignified. Yep, Max was still in there. Arrogant politician Dane would probably have just died of humiliation or threatened to sue someone.

I turned my head the other way. The prof was standing between me and Andre, which was why I got a big whiff of crimson toes.

Andre was fully dressed, darn it. Apparently they'd just stripped Dane to address his burns. Bruises didn't rate extra attention.

"Wake up, Legrande, or they'll start anointing you with chicken gizzards." I couldn't kick him. The prof was in the way. I had to drag myself into a sitting position and shove past knobby knees to poke him. I seemed to be dressed as well.

"Go away, Clancy," he muttered. "I'm trying to wish myself home."

I chuckled. "Good reaction but not happening."

I leaned my bruised—but solid—bones back against a kitchen cabinet and shoved away a feather Hagatha was trying to brush in my face. "I don't suppose anyone called ambulances or fire engines or anything sane like that?"

"No, why would we?" Father Morrison asked with honest innocence. "The authorities aren't likely to believe in exorcism. And it's probably best that they don't know the senator was involved in one."

Hearing my own words thrown back at me had my eyes rolling, but I accepted the stupidity, for now. "Get moving, Senator," I said grouchily. "It's not getting any better if you just keep lying there. Better hang onto your towel, though."

"Bathrobe," he ordered without opening his eyes. "Top of the stairs, to the right."

No one moved. With a sigh, I studied our exorcists. "Did you get rid of Gloria or will I be walking through a towering inferno if I use the stairs?"

I remembered seeing her in the nothingness and hearing cries of anguish, but I'd also seen blue blobs and had soul sex. I wasn't sure I hadn't been having the weirdest sex dream of my life.

Had I just visualized us to safety because I'd been terrified? I'd study on that later.

"The tree is now ash and we've seen no more of the demon," the priest reported. "It's difficult to say if all is well, but all appears normal, and the evil emanations seem to be gone."

Maybe I'd finally released Gloria from Zone limbo into a real hell. If it wasn't in a law book, I really didn't want to know.

"Fine, then." I stood and looked around.

Hell's cellar door had melted and it looked as if the patio and back door had been bombed. Blackened timbers had collapsed into a hole below the floor. I blinked, then looked at our exorcists. "This is normal?"

"The demon left and closed the door," the professor said with a shrug.

I poked Andre with my toe. "Up, Legrande. We need contractors before Hell's Mansion falls into the cellar."

That brought both my slacker boyfriends to a sitting position. Taking one more long gander at Dane's gorgeous body, I moseyed on out to the front rooms in search of clothing.

The swinging door into the hall had been blown off its hinges. A blackened stain in the shape of a pentagram marred the terrazzo tiles of the foyer. I had a clearer idea of why they hadn't called medics.

I craned my neck upward to search the ceiling three stories above me. I didn't see any exit holes from the tree's rocket launch. It must have burned up in the atmosphere—which stank of sulfur.

I jogged upstairs and located the messiest bedroom. Expensive clothes were scattered everywhere, as if Max/Dane had expected a servant to pick up after him—a luxury both men probably had experienced growing up. Fortunately, Max hadn't risked crisping anyone by employing them in this hell hole.

I found a plush navy robe and some slippers and carted them back down. I could feel the ache of bruises from being sucked through doors and into walls. I was still a little woozy, but mostly I wanted a giant pizza.

I met Hagatha packing up her boxes in the foyer. She glanced up at me with a puzzled frown and sniffed, as if I was the one who stank of rancid herbs.

"Very powerful vibes," she said, shaking her head. "You shouldn't need us. If you wish lessons, let me know. The coven would welcome you."

Oh yeah, just what I needed, a coven of witches in my life. I'd sooner call on Max's biker friends. I might, at that. Several of them were good carpenters. Witches...not so much, I bet.

"Thanks, I think," I told her. "I'll help you with those in a minute. We owe you big time if you got rid of the demon."

"She's gone," the witch said, bobbing her head affirmatively. "We trapped her and sent her back where she belongs. No worries."

I refrained from snorting. My life was one big long worry. I'd just seen Gloria in a ring of fire one dimension away. "Send the senator a fat bill. He can afford it. But if one word leaks out..."

She waved me off. "It won't or we'd lose all our D.C. business. You have no idea what evil can be summoned by a bunch of demented politicians."

I had no idea and didn't want one. Just the thought of heads of state calling up demons to do their dirty work sounded too probable to me. That would explain a... heck...of a lot.

I dropped the robe on Dane and joined Andre at the blackened hole where the back of the kitchen had been.

"The cellar was just below here," I said.

"Still is," he said, studying the gaping maw where a floor should have been. "But it looks like molten lava with barrels."

Gloria's rusted chemical drums had been solidified into the crud.

Father Morrison sprinkled the last of his holy water across the hole. It didn't steam. Whatever had melted was now solid rock. "We sealed the portal to hell," he said as if he did this every day.

Belting his robe, Dane came to stand beside us. I was overly aware of his height and breadth and nakedness. I told myself it had been Max down there in that hellish dimension, not Dane, but my long-neglected body wasn't convinced.

"Gloria experimented with Acme's age-defying cosmetics. She used to store them down there," he said. "Do I dare believe that it's safe to bring out workmen, or should I just demolish the place?"

He sounded rather hopeful about the latter.

In the kitchen behind us, the voodoo professor and priest were arguing the same thing, while I was worrying about chemicals and thin dimensional veils.

The argument was interrupted by the doorbell and Hagatha shouting, "Company! The nuns are here."

Andre and Dane both looked at me. I shrugged. "You said I could invite them."

I grabbed a tray of sandwiches from the still-standing counter and sashayed back to the foyer as if welcoming carolers to a party.

Andre followed with the punch bowl. Father Morrison carried a tray of cups.

Since no one else emerged from the kitchen, I assumed the senator had taken the back way upstairs to get dressed, and the professor had escaped through a window rather than face nuns.

A few minutes later, Hagatha's VW putt-putted to a rattle and departed, hopefully taking the prof with her.

The sisters smiled benevolently and with some degree of puzzlement at an empty foyer adorned only with a pentagram burn. Passing it off as a misguided Star of David probably wasn't a good idea.

"A slight mishap," I explained. "Come into the dining room. We had to send the rest of the party home. So sorry we didn't have time to call you."

I'd forgotten the chandelier above the table had torched the ceiling. We had no light to illuminate the snowy gloom. I wasn't about to see if the fireplace had gas logs.

The nuns fluttered about the elegant table and hors d'oeuvres as if they were at a true diplomatic party. With an adoring audience, Father Morrison was in his element.

When Dane entered in all his sartorial glory, the nuns positively beamed.

In the gloom, it was hard to tell that half his hair had been burned off, and he was hiding a limp as well. Damn, but the man was good.

Patting to see if more of my own hair had been singed, pulling out a few more clumps, I stepped back next to Andre while the nuns blew on their pitch pipe and began their serenade.

Andre caught my hand behind my back and held it as the horrible house filled with joyous song.

I swear I saw angels singing with them. I was in bliss.

"Want to blow up the Zone next?" Andre whispered in my ear.

Eighteen

ANDRE and I left Max writing big checks to the church and to the hallelujah-singing angels. The nuns were happily recommending contractors to repair the senator's newly exorcised hellhole. He still looked lonely, but wealthy politicians have lots of options. I couldn't be one of them, no matter how *interesting* today had been.

It was dinnertime. I was bruised, exhausted, and as hungry as if I'd actually just had sex. The chicken sandwiches hadn't appealed. Andre agreed a Chesty's run was called for, and we set our mutual vehicles on the road to home.

To spare my tires from Zone rot, I had intended to park my Miata behind my boarding house and walk down to the Zone. But when I entered the neighborhood, everything was dark except the blue neon glow of the buildings.

And the red glow of the manhole covers.

Urgency beat out caution. I parked in front of Chesty's beside Andre's Mercedes. Warily, we both climbed out and stared at the restaurant's blank windows.

"No electricity?" I suggested. "They all went home?" The utilities had promised me...

It was eerie not hearing the metallic thump of loud music and the shouts of a noisy crowd. They hadn't even cranked up the manual music. I glanced down the street and elbowed Andre.

The lights were on at Bill's Bar.

In sync, we strolled toward the only lights in town. I kept an eye on alleys, looking for blue blobs and mad utility men. The genuine garden gnome I'd seen before was still bathing in the steaming run-off of the gutter. He kicked his feet and winked at me.

Inanimate objects had a tendency to develop a life of their own in the Zone. That got me to thinking that I probably should bring the gnome statues back down here, *after* we halted the fight with MSI. Uniformed Nazis weren't in my immediate plans for the Zone's future, but I couldn't keep them stoned forever.

The bar blasted heat, light, and raucous noise when Andre opened the door. I almost backed off. But curiosity and hunger forced me inside.

The complaints began the instant we entered.

"The harbor exploded!"

"They shut down all the utilities!"

"They're fencing off the harbor!"

"They threw out the bums!"

Well, that last didn't sound like it ought to be a complaint, but I figured it came from one of the Do-Gooders. I elbowed up to the bar where blessed Bill produced beer and pizza.

It wasn't Bill's pizza. He only did burgers and fish fries. I could see carry-out boxes stacked up on the counter behind him. Someone had made a pizza run. The Zone, unfortunately, loved pizza and tried to eat delivery vehicles. We'd been blackballed from all delivery routes.

I dug into anchovies and let Andre field the questions. Most of the buildings were his. He'd been our ex-officio mayor for years.

As the list of unanswerable questions stacked up, Andre glanced at me while I dragged out gooey cheese. I finished chewing, then shrugged.

"This morning, I had everyone agreeing they'd only turn off the utilities between eight and noon tomorrow. I'll have to go back to my office for messages," I told him.

"Technology is your friend," Andre said dryly. "Ever hear of voice mail? Or on a really elementary basis, you could *call* Ned."

I glared over my pizza. Until I'd been promoted to real lawyer, I'd had only the most rudimentary of cell phones—and few friends to call me. My fancy new phone was still a toy as far as I was concerned. Besides, the Zone seldom ever let me call anyone but bad restaurants in faraway places.

My leather jacket was only slightly damaged from dousing Dane's flames. I retrieved my phone and showed it to Andre. No messages.

I punched in Ned's number. To my shock, the call not only went through, but he answered on the first ring.

"The city called and said they have to shut down Edgewater," he said excitedly. "I didn't know whether to disturb you. There isn't a thing we can do."

"Did they say why?" I looked questioningly at Bill. How had he kept his lights on?

As if reading my mind, the big lout lifted an empty fuel can. Generator. Smart move given the Zone's erratic black-outs.

"Some kind of explosion opened a huge sinkhole in the harbor this afternoon," Ned explained. "They fear the entire area is unstable."

Explosion. "What time did that happen?" I asked warily.

"Around three or four, maybe?"

Just when Gloria had been rocketing trees to the ceiling, the priests had blown her back to hell through the walls of Dane's kitchen, and I'd damned her again. Scary bad.

"No one mentioned condemnation," Ned continued, attempting to inject optimism into my gloom.

Sinkholes were bad enough. Hellish dimensional explosions... Lent a whole new layer to the problem, probably involving Paddy's quantum physics. I sighed.

"But we all know what the city wants," I said. "Did you call the Montoyas?"

"The lights are out up the hill, too. They called me. I explained all I knew. Do I come in to work tomorrow? Have they barricaded the street?"

"No barricades yet. If you can get here, come in. I doubt it will be a slow day." I hung up and contemplated Bill's fuel can.

"Generators all around?" Andre suggested before I could.

"Depends." I wasn't hungry any longer. I took a deep slurp of beer.

"On what?" Andre asked with interest.

"On whether closing one hell hole opened another, and if Gloria and Dane can ignite generator fuel tanks."

The noise continued around us as we sat in our own bubble of pissed-off silence. Andre sipped his beer and pondered the unpleasant possibilities. Paddy had mentioned something about physics and closing holes in one place might blast them open elsewhere. Is that what we'd done?

I suffered an acceleration of the foreboding that had sent me exploring my cellar last week. I'm not a coward, but I was developing a real fear of dark holes containing potential demons and bats.

I really didn't want to venture underground to investigate the "sinkhole," but at some point, someone had to see what was happening beneath the Zone.

"Is Acme running on generators?" Andre finally asked.

"Nope." Bill refilled our beers. "They're running normally. And we had surveyors scoping the street."

No one in the Zone complained about gutter saunas or roaming gnomes, but they noticed surveyors. I drank to that.

"You burning off your hair one clump at a time, Clancy?" Bill asked in concern.

I'd avoided looking in my mirror this morning. I might cover it tonight. "New hairdressing technique," I told him.

Rob, the lanky D-Ger, elbowed his way over to our section of the bar. "We've almost got the insurance building ready for habitation. We had to start moving in the homeless when the cops burned their camp, though. We'll help you fight eminent domain. The whole town will be homeless if they condemn it!"

No kidding, Sherlock. I kept that sentiment to myself and idly asked, "The gnomes don't bother you?"

He looked puzzled. "What gnomes? Those little statues your assistant carried off? No, why?"

Amazing. People really did see only what they could comprehend. "How about blue neon?" I asked.

Andre and Bill listened with about as much interest as if we were discussing golf. No one in the Zone played golf.

Rob shrugged. "Neon is bad for the environment, but it's festive."

I refrained from rolling my eyes. "You might be crazy or blind enough to belong here. I'll go after a court order to reinstate our utilities in the morning. Spread the word. We can fill the courthouse with silent protestors."

Police action after my college protest had left me painfully crippled. I'd lost a year of my life to hospitals. I wasn't happy about another protest, but I wasn't going in there alone. I may be stupid, but I'm not suicidal.

As Rob shoved a path back to his buddies to spread the news, I heard a male voice shout crudely, "Hey weirdo, didn't your mama teach you real men don't wear pink?"

Just what I needed, a flag-waving bigot looking for a fight. I massaged the bridge of my nose. I didn't even have to look to know who had just entered. My insatiable Saturn need for justice forced me to check over my shoulder anyway.

Tim had come in wearing a pink down-filled jacket. Ned was supposed to teach him how to dress better, but Tim had a creative thing happening that Ned didn't appreciate.

Neither did the hard hats in the corner, apparently.

"If this is what it's going to be like if we let in mundanes, do we really want to keep the Zone?" I muttered.

"Zap the heckler," Andre said callously.

"What if I'm only allowed twenty-five zaps and then the justice juice is gone?" I asked.

Andre shrugged. Not his problem, I got it.

Tim disappeared as we watched. Typical. I sighed and held up a plate of pizza, waving it in his direction. A minute later, the plate disappeared.

Noting that the drunken hardhat did no more than blink and return to his beer, I noticed Sarah sitting in a booth next to Ernesto. They were looking really cozy.

I wondered if I should warn her about the dangers of hanky panky in our twenty-seventh year, but I hadn't worked out the dynamics yet. Did babies born only in December—as I had—fall under Saturn's aegis? If so, we were safe for a few months. But if it included the whole year that Saturn was in sight...

I finished my beer and headed for home and my cat. Andre fell in step beside me.

"Can a court order really turn the utilities back on?" he asked.

"Probably not," I admitted. "For all we know, it truly is dangerous under these streets." I scuffed my toe on the hot blacktop. Was it hotter than last night? "But I don't want the bastards thinking we'll give in."

"I'll try talking to Paddy again," Andre said with a resigned sigh. "All our troubles always lead to Acme."

"Through Gloria," I pointed out. "Unless MacNeill has gone to the dark side, which is always possible."

"Hell exists and we're sitting on top of it?" he suggested, opening my car door.

"Some outer dimension of it, I guess. What are the chances that Gloria's barrels of anti-aging cosmetics contained Acme's new element and that's why the mansion exploded?"

Acme's mad scientist had been experimenting with a new element that had led to our last gaseous explosion. The stuff was potent if it could cure cancer and cross dimensions. Paddy was supposed to be restraining his new staff, limiting their experiments to cancer cures and not the explosive weapons—and cosmetics—of Gloria's regime. But the stuff seemed to be mind-altering.

"Can an element open a portal to hell?" I asked.

Andre whistled. "Pretty intense. So, if Acme is sitting on vats of the stuff—"

"And occasionally spilling it or setting it off in puffs of smoke—" I let the suggestion trail off as he had.

"I want to believe that chemically opening the gates of hell is preposterous," Andre admitted.

"And the world is flat, the sun revolves around the earth, and global climate change isn't happening. G'night, Andre." I shut the door and powered on the Miata's motor. Thankfully, the engine still worked, and the tires hadn't melted into the blacktop.

I parked behind the boarding house. The utilities had been turned off up here, too, but I noticed flickering light in my landlady's first floor apartment. I trotted around to the front, let myself in, and called down the hall to my landlady's apartment that I'd never traversed, "Mrs. Bodine, how are you faring?"

This first floor was chilly and dark but warmer than outside.

"Leo lit me a nice fire, dear, and I'm keeping your kitty warm. Come on back."

She stole my cat! So much for two locks, a landlady who claimed she couldn't climb stairs, and a guard cat.

I sauntered down the long hall to Mrs. Bodine's Victorian kitchen. She sat in a rocking chair in front of a fireplace, holding a very content Milo in her lap. I studied the flames with worry, but they were from genuine logs and not gas. No Dane or Gloria writhed angrily.

"It's a chilly night, but I don't think we'll have more snow," Mrs. Bodine said cheerily. "Isn't this cozy? Just like the old days."

Since her white, fifties appliances were about as ancient as her kitchen, I was thinking she'd never left the *old days,* but I liked Mrs. Bodine and would never use my sharp tongue on her. "Thank you for looking after Milo. I hadn't realized they'd shut off our utilities this far up the street. When did the power go out?"

"After you closed Gloria's portal, *aziz.* The pressure exploded through a weak point in the veil under the harbor. The pollution is making the dimensions more permeable."

I started, swung from the crackling fire, and stared at the woman in the rocking chair. Was I dreaming and my subconscious was summoning my fears? Mrs. Bodine had her eyes closed and her mouth hung open. A knot formed in my throat. "Themis?"

"Your friend is a very proficient medium, dear." The voice came from my landlady, but her lips scarcely moved. "I wanted to warn you that all our actions have consequences. Exorcising Gloria had to be done, but perhaps you went just a *little* far. Your nice boyfriend should be safe now though. I'm not so sure about your neighbors. There's more there than you can see. Be careful, *aziz.*"

I had ten thousand questions to ask my weird grandmother. My mind went blank. I hurriedly gathered my scrambled brains to ask, "*Where?* Where is the new portal?"

Mrs. Bodine snored.

Typical. Themis never lingered once she'd passed on her cheerful admonitions.

Sighing, I poked the logs to be certain no sparks leapt past the grate. Milo jumped down and trotted off to the stairs. If he'd had a tail, he probably would have flaunted it.

I had no idea if my grandmother existed in physical form or just went about stealing other people's bodies. If she could move Mrs. Bodine about, that explained a lot. Locks probably didn't stop Themis.

I just wished she'd linger longer. This Saturn's Daughter business was pretty damned confusing.

I trudged upstairs to my icy apartment, tried to make coffee on the gas stove, and realized we had no water. We had gas but no water? That was seriously messed up. Crap.

I glanced across the street at my office, saw lights over there, and remembered Sarah. I thought I'd left her at the bar with Ernesto to keep her warm.

Why did my office have lights? And did it have water?

It was early yet. I shrugged my jacket back on, left Milo slurping down his food, and crossed the hall to Leo Schwartz's door. Caution was me.

"Leo, you in there?"

He hollered something incomprehensible and appeared a few minutes later wearing a ragged Aran sweater and baggy cords. He looked good, and I had to quit thinking like that.

"There's a light in my office and Sarah is down at Bill's. Want to investigate?"

He shrugged and followed me down the stairs.

Outside, the clouds had cleared off and the stars twinkled frostily.

I'd heard the same eerie wail in my cellar as we'd heard under Hell's Mansion. I really didn't want to believe hell's portal had opened under my office and demons were sitting at my desk.

"Light's in the back," Schwartz said. "Should we go around that way?"

"If everyone else's utilities are off, there shouldn't be any light at all. I'm not sneaking into my own office." I unlocked the heavy front door and entered the icy chamber that was my reception area.

Laughter and applause erupted from the unused storage areas in back.

Nineteen

LAUGHTER and applause in an empty building is a lot scarier than one would think. Schwartz shoved his muscled arm in front of me to hold me back, then slipped silently through the lobby to the back hall.

I tiptoed after him. Maybe we should have thought about weapons, but in my experience, weapons usually caused more harm than good. Shooting the uniforms blocking Andre's building would have been bad. Turning them into gnomes... Not good but probably not deadly.

I was contemplating getting a baseball bat to keep handy, when Schwartz relaxed and let me catch up to him. Even I recognized the sound now—a television. We'd been afraid of a sound heard in every normal home across the country.

Given that we had no power and that I owned no television, it didn't make sense, but that was canned laughter. A child's voice chimed in. I didn't know any children.

For all that mattered, why was it warm in here when it was freezing everywhere else in town? I'd learned to regard heat with suspicion.

It had been a long, strange day. I didn't know how much more I could face, but if I couldn't take a hot shower, I might as well keep on pushing on.

I walked into an ordinary family room in what had once been my empty, cobwebbed storage area. Cora, my snake-wielding bestie, and Jane Claremont, my perennially bankrupt journalist friend, glanced up from a catalog they'd been perusing. They'd appropriated the couch Andre had left in one of the smaller offices. A floor lamp illuminated the wall. A toddler sat in a kid's car seat and giggled at a cartoon on a computer screen.

"Cozy," I said, leaning against the wall while Schwartz studied the computer setup and cartoon with interest. "Ned said we had no utilities."

"Utilities are working in the neighborhood behind here," Cora said with a shrug. "Frank hooked us up and turned us on. Don't ask questions."

Frank was Cora's boss and the shady owner of Discreet Detection. I never questioned him, but I raised an eyebrow at Jane. She lived in my old apartment a bus ride away from the Zone.

"I called to tell you that the state is going forward with the eminent domain plans," Jane said, "but somehow I ended up talking to Cora. One thing led to another..."

"I got your keys from Sarah," Cora said. She was blunt where Jane shied from speaking out. "I was freezing my tail off. Jane here's about to be booted from her place, and Frank said he knew a man who knew a man, and here we are."

I glanced at our resident cop, but he didn't seem concerned that Frank was stealing utilities. Schwartz wandered off to inspect the rest of the place—or in search of an operational bathroom. This side of the street was closer to sane neighborhoods. It made a crazy sense that we could hook up to their lines.

I collapsed on the sofa, raising a cloud of dust. The fabric was so old, I couldn't even tell the color. Probably a good thing since it seemed to be woven in a paisley design. "We could be sitting on a portal to hell," I said off-handedly.

"Yeah, well, if it's warm, I'll put a grate over it," Cora said, not believing me. "Maybe we can shove MacNeill and his henchmen down it and add fuel."

I snickered. It really had been that kind of day. "What happened with the apartment?" I'd let Jane take my old place last spring. It was a student slum, but the rent was low and the space large enough for a kid.

"Lost the fast food gig," she admitted. "And the newspaper is failing. They haven't paid me in months. I thought I'd take the eminent domain story to the *Post* and the *Sun-Times,* and see if either of them would let me freelance. I could get some good human interest as well as the news story."

I heard water flushing. We had working bathrooms! Glory hallelujah! How did one turn on water lines?

Leo wandered back a moment later and I pointed him at Jane. "Tell her the Zone is dangerous, and she can't live down here with a kid."

"What she said," Leo responded obligingly. "Although technically, the hill isn't in the Zone."

I beat the heel of my hand against my forehead. "Not helping,

Schwartz. Ask Sarah if you don't believe me. The cellar here is haunted."

And sociopath Sarah lived here and had murdered a man not yards from where we were sitting. And I had fascist gnomes guarding all the dark corners.

"This building has been here a hundred years. It won't go up in flames overnight," Cora said scornfully. "You fret too much, Clancy."

"Anyone home?" Andre called from the lobby as if he owned the place. Which, oh yeah, he did.

"Only us wannabe ghosts," I replied wearily. Maybe I should go back to my cat. My bed would be warm. But I had no hot water.

Entering, Andre arched his sleek dark eyebrows at the sight of our motley crew. "Don't suppose Frank could get the rest of the town hooked up?"

Frank had been monkeying with our *infrastructure* for so long, that wasn't as good a guess as it sounded.

"He's working on it. But the utility guys are likely to be back out in the morning, so we're laying low for now." Cora returned to scanning the catalog.

"Sleeping bags, anyone?" I asked, closing my eyes at the inevitable. "I've never counted the bathrooms. How many are working?"

"Hundred-year-old building, Clancy," Andre reminded me. "Three floors, three restrooms. No showers. No kitchen."

"How about the Morgan building where they're stashing the bums? Are they living with three toilets too?" Maybe I could move my guests in there.

"I think they're setting up Port-a-Potties," Jane said. "I've been writing up the homeless situation, too. Lots of good human interest."

I dragged myself out of the sofa, grabbed Andre's coat sleeve, and hauled him to the front and my office. "What is your father saying about his eminent domain research?" I asked where Jane couldn't hear. Having a reporter around made life difficult.

"He's consulting with the authorities you found for him and putting together a petition to the court fighting it. Since we're on the extreme edge of Baltimore's boundaries, they're also researching the city-county line. We'd be in a stronger position if Edgewater and the surrounding streets could be rezoned, but all the voting residents need to sign the request. I doubt that many of our people are even registered to vote."

I snorted. "Which ought to make it easy. You, me, and Julius can be the town."

"We'll probably want to expand as far as we can, so we might get Paddy and Pearl and the interns next door to sign. We can ask the streets behind here."

"But it's the state that controls eminent domain, right?" I asked. "So if those wheels are already in motion, we can't stop the demolition. We could be making a town from a hole in the ground. Maybe the state's right and we should all just pack up and move on." I couldn't let my preferences deny the safety of others. The idea of Jane and the Do-Gooders being polluted by Acme's chemicals gave me cold shivers. I really didn't like them being down here.

"I'm not packing it in so Acme can build a medical center to experiment with the drug that made my mother comatose for ten years," Andre said angrily.

He never got angry. I conceded the point.

"Okay, Dane owes us. Now that we've solved his little problem, let's have him twist some arms, starting with our utilities." I pulled out my toy phone and punched in Dane's number, while asking, "Can Julius take down MacNeill and stop Acme from supporting the med center? Paddy is no use."

That's how my office became Command Central. I might make a lousy superhero, but I knew how to lead a protest.

By Wednesday morning I had resorted to sleeping on Sarah's cot—she hadn't come in last night—with Milo as my blanket. Flushing toilets, a shouting kid, and a cat batting my nose didn't fully wake me up. Rubber wheels rolling around in the room beneath me finally got me stirring.

They'd dragged Katerina in?

The second story room was warm, so we still had gas connections. I rubbed my eyes, checked that I was still reasonably decent, and stumbled upright. My singed hair flopped in my eyes as I availed myself of the facilities, then splashed water in my face. Haircuts weren't happening soon.

I needed to kill someone so I could wish for a new nose, I thought in disgruntlement, peering at my protuberant proboscis in the faded mirror.

Of course, after yesterday's touch of hell, I wasn't in any hurry to sell my soul to Satan or Saturn or Gloria in return for a petite nose.

I rambled downstairs to find my hunky office assistant handing out clipboards and petitions to a steady stream of teenagers and... I wiped my eyes again. Bums? Why not? They were living here, too.

Katerina was working in one of the back offices, wheeling her chair back and forth as she yapped ninety-miles an hour at some poor peon on the phone. She'd acquired one of the doors from the cellar as a desk top. She'd had it mounted on a couple of small filing cabinets purloined from who knew where. Papers already littered the surface.

She waved at me and I moved on. Julius had said he'd filed the papers and got me a date with the judge about the utility problem. We'd agreed to start with demanding the return of the Zone's services. I should locate Julius and find out where and when I was to perform my courthouse Idiot-Who-Doesn't-Know-What-She's-Doing act.

I nearly fell on my face when I discovered Julius in the storage room with Jane and her kid. I'd never seen him outside the house. I should have known he'd never let Katerina go too far without him or Andre, but I'd thought all those years of treating Katerina had left him agoraphobic. What the...heck?

He held up a finger to tell me to wait, finished his phone call, made a note on a legal pad, and handed it to Jane, who typed it into her laptop.

"Eleven sharp, Judge Crater's office," he told me. "I have your brief here." He pulled papers off a printer that hadn't been there last night. "Go forth and get our services back."

Ah, utilities were the mother of all necessity or something like that. His house was as cold as mine.

"The utilities are a lost cause until we fix the sinkhole," I muttered, skimming through the petition. My visit to Dane's cellar had cured me of my interest in descending to the Zone's equivalent.

"We have men on that. At your request, the senator has twisted arms, and Acme will be joining our cause. The utilities will have to send workers to locate the sewer main break. They can't deny taxpayers the services for which we pay."

"Sewer main break?" Right. Give it a name the judge understands. *Hey, Judge, Acme blew a hole to hell*, probably wasn't a good starting point.

"You're our new spin doctor?" I asked Jane.

"Part time," she agreed. "I'll file objective news stories. Mr. Montoya says he has connections at the *Sun,* and they may be interested in me freelancing. I could be the Zone's press office."

"Oh, that's objective, for sure." I backed out. I left Milo guarding everyone else and headed for home and clean clothes. Showers were apparently still out of the question. Maybe I could take a couple of the vagrants to court with me so no one would notice if I smelled. Or maybe my stench would wake up the judge.

Across the street, Mrs. Bodine gave me her usual toothless chirpy greeting, apparently no worse for being occupied by my grandmother. She handed me a bucket of water she'd been heating over the fire. "Here, dear, Leo brought the water over from across the street. I'm heating another if you need it."

I accepted gratefully. I'd already bought her a quilted red satin jacket for her Christmas gift. Maybe I'd add a red sweat suit to go under it.

It would take half an hour to drive over to the courthouse, with light traffic, and it was already ten. I was about to have my first real day in court as a lawyer, and if we got into utilities versus sinkholes, we could end up debating the existence of hell. Oh goody.

How did I dress to represent insanity?

Attitude. I needed attitude. That whole dress-for-success thing was me trying to be a normal lawyer. It was time to admit that I wasn't normal and neither were my clients. But judges were, sort of.

So I went with semi-normal. It was cold, and I meant to take my bike because I could zip around obstacles—like traffic. Black leather bike pants were needed, but I topped them off with a perfectly spiffy gold angora turtleneck from the thrift store, a black blazer, and Max's biker jacket to keep out the cold. I pinned my most glamorous asset up in a loose topknot to pretend propriety and hide the missing hunks.

I wasn't large in all the right places, but I knew how to use what I had. I dragged on knee-high heeled boots and grabbed the cool briefcase Andre had given me for graduation, shoved in my petitions, and dashed off to court.

Security at the courthouse scrutinized me strangely, but I wasn't carrying anything more dangerous than pant buckles. I dashed down the hall and hit the judge's courtroom at one minute to eleven. Removing my leather jacket and helmet, I straightened my blazer, left my hair up, and strode toward the assigned room with Julius's petition in hand. A security guard redirected me to the judge's chambers. My eyebrows soared. So much for my day in court.

Ex-senator MacNeill, Dr. Abdul Bakir from the new medical

center, and another gray head, probably someone from the city, were waiting for me in the office.

"Gentlemen." I nodded politely, trying not to freak. "I hadn't realized we were holding a trial today. I'm merely submitting a petition to have our utilities returned."

"Where's Julius?" MacNeill asked in his hearty politician's voice. "We were hoping to have a word with him."

I hid my surprise. "Anything you wish to say to my partner, you can say to me."

The judge wandered in, frowning. "What's the ruckus in my courtroom, gentlemen? I thought this was just a private petition."

Uh oh. I glanced out the window. Signs waved from the pavement.

I may have mentioned last night that I needed a crowd, but I hadn't had time to organize one.

On the other side of the wall, in the courtroom, a joyous chorus arose. The nuns?

And were those maracas? I *had* said silent protest, hadn't I?

I placed my hands innocently behind my back and waited for the Zone's version of hell to break loose.

Twenty

JUDGE Crater was a goatee-wielding skinny crank of a man suffering from a chronic digestive disorder if the number of Rolaids he popped was any indication.

"I don't like holding a hearing here," he grumbled. "I need my courtroom."

He glared at me as if singing nuns and maracas were all my fault. I didn't point out the protest signs on the sidewalk. The newspapers would later.

I would have liked to believe that Max's inner rebel had hired the exorcists to exorcise a courtroom, but it was far more likely that the devil in Andre had done it. For all I knew, he had exorcists on retainer now.

"Good morning, Your Honor, I'm merely here with a request that the city rescind their order to shut off our utilities. I'm not sure why these other gentlemen are here." I handed over the papers Julius had prepared.

The judge frowned at my boots and leather pants, but I had my respectful face and a blazer on. No contempt there, judge, no sirree.

The unidentified suit removed papers from his own briefcase and laid them on the judge's desk. "We can't allow that, sir. The city is representing the various utilities and their workers. The area has been labeled hazardous, and we've asked the governor for emergency orders to demolish it. The EPA has already begun removing the polluted material on the harbor grounds currently owned by the city."

The choir's voices soared higher, and a drumbeat joined the maracas. The judge scowled and skimmed both our petitions.

"Those are taxpaying citizens in there," I argued, pointing to the courtroom. The nuns ought to add a favorable impression. "The city cannot rob us of our homes and businesses because it's found a potentially bigger, better landowner." I glanced at the medical center man. "One assumes you're not a nonprofit and the city will be collecting higher taxes from you than from average citizens."

He shrugged. "We'll pay our fair share and our employees will contribute payroll taxes."

Andre paid pitifully low property taxes and probably had some kind of poverty or historical credits against those. Because of our technology problems, most of the Zone operated on cash. As a result, any sales and income taxes were nearly nonexistent. I got that. But that was no reason that folks struggling to survive should be booted in the chin.

Greed was evil, right? Could I justify blasting greedmeisters with my Saturn talents?

The judge hit his intercom and yelled at security to hurry up and remove the nuns. That was a shame, but I couldn't turn him into a toad for being a prick. I wanted to open the door connected to the courtroom and see how guards removed angels.

As if responding to my wish, Andre entered the office through the courtroom side door. Past his shoulder, I caught a glimpse of three nuns leading a handful of D-Gers in a song praising God's bounty or some such. Cora glanced up and waved, then returned to enthusiastically beating a handheld drum while Dr. Voodoo kept a beat with his gourd. Had they carried them in in briefcases? Uniformed security watched uneasily.

The door shut before I could watch security heave out my friends.

"My job here isn't to rule on payroll taxes or the EPA," the judge reminded us sternly. "My only role today is to decide whether the city has the right to close down a district's utilities if that district has become hazardous to workers. The city does have such a right."

My stomach dropped, and I shivered. I was about to fail my pals.

He glared in my direction. "Bringing protestors will not sway my decision. You may tell Mr. Montoya that I rule on the law alone. Unless you can prove the property is not dangerous to the health of innocent bystanders and workers, your petition is denied."

I wanted to go all red ragey and curse the lot of them, for stupidity and cluelessness, if nothing else. Unfortunately, I understood law and logic and knew the judge was right.

I turned on smug MacNeill. "I thought Acme meant to support us in this. How can the city justify leaving on *your* utilities when you're sitting on vats of poison?"

Andre caught my arm as if to warn me not to lose my temper and turn anyone into a toadstool. I wasn't at that level yet. I had my lawyer hat on.

"Our chemicals have been properly contained and inspected," MacNeill said with a politician's smile. "We're here simply to offer the residents of Edgewater aid in finding new situations."

Andre tugged my arm, yanking me back down from my outrage

place.

The singing and maracas stopped in the other room. Sort of. I think someone was chanting a protest song as they were being led out. I had *nuns* standing up for my neighbors. I couldn't let them down.

I faced the judge and announced coldly, "You have not heard the last of this."

"Is that a threat?" the judge asked with a scowl.

"As they say in the westerns, that's not a threat, that's a promise that I will appeal by all legal means available, and I and my clients can be very creative." I turned on my high heeled boots and strode out, Andre beside me.

Oddly, I wasn't shaking with rage or disappointment. I had enough understanding of the judge's side of the law to know he had right on his side. We shouldn't be placing innocents in harm's way.

But the Zone had its purposes, and it needed to be protected, like wild animals and national forests, maybe. Hard to pitch that argument. Most people would rather shoot wolves and loot national forests of natural resources than protect them. It was difficult to convince people that existence was more important than money.

Which was apparently why I had been placed on this planet. Saturn's daughters could bring about justice in situations that didn't fit into courts of law.

"Okay, Saturn Daddy," I muttered under my breath. "How do I fix this?" Beating the judge with a tire iron and wishing him dead was not an acceptable alternative. Beating MacNeill... Nah, even I couldn't justify that. He'd actually done me a favor once. He wasn't totally evil. Yet.

News photographers snapped pictures of nuns being escorted from the courthouse. The PR possibilities of those images would get the public's attention, but that wasn't enough to solve the Zone's utility problem.

The photographers ignored Cora in her business suit. She fell in step with us as we strode down the steps.

"Now can we blow up Acme?" she asked cheerfully.

"That's one solution," Andre agreed, "But I think Clancy has already overruled putting people out of work."

"I should have let Gloria blow up the good senator," I said bitterly. "He's the one who sent the utilities checking infrastructure. He wants the Zone shut down as much as Acme does. The Zone needs to own its utilities. Wonder what it takes to get that?"

"Magic," Andre said, stopping on the sidewalk. "We've had a good run, but the end is in sight."

That was not what I wanted to hear.

"The fight has drawn your parents out of the house. That's a positive step forward," I reminded him. "We're not giving up yet."

"I can't run a business without utilities. Nancy Rose is moving her plants to your office, but they need her fancy plant lights. I'm all out of tricks," Andre said in resignation.

I stared at him in disbelief. Andre never gave up. He was a fighter. Then I remembered the fat check he'd been offered. He was fighting his amoral instincts. I was on my own here.

"Don't be a bigger jerkwad than necessary, Legrande. We've got to find out what's under the street before we give up," I warned. Not wanting to discuss our potential demises in hell, I stalked off to my bike.

I wasn't ready to die, especially for the damned Zone. But the Zone's inhabitants had stood beside me every step of the way, accepting all my dangerous peculiarities. I couldn't let them go homeless and jobless.

Maybe we could move underground, I thought grumpily as I cruised on home. Plenty of heat *under* the street. No water or electricity, though. Even if I found whatever had caused an explosion yesterday, I didn't know what I could do about it.

I'd been in some pretty bad places before, but this one seemed insurmountable. It was almost *Christmas,* damn it! They couldn't put people out of their homes and terminate their jobs over the holiday.

Once I reached Edgewater, I stopped in front of Tim's forlorn Christmas tree stand in the empty lot next to the florist shop. He'd sold quite a few over the weekend, but with no hope of festive lights, sales would be down. Or dead.

Not wanting to return to my office filled with unhappy people—and plants, apparently—I parked the Harley and walked over to a glowing manhole cover. I really couldn't blame the utility workers for not wanting to go down there.

Seeing both sides of an argument sucked and wreaked havoc with decision-making. Compromise seemed so puny compared to a glorious flag-waving cause, even if it was doomed.

The low roar of heavy equipment along the harbor provided depressing background noise.

A vagrant wandered over to join me, beer can in one hand,

cigarette in the other. Cigarettes had been banned in the Zone, but I wasn't arguing with anyone's choice of lifestyle. If he blew himself up on hazardous gas and waste, that was his problem. I just didn't want to go with him. I kept my distance.

"Used to sleep down there," the vagrant informed me. "Nothin' but sewer lines. All the rest of that crap is buried. They'd have to dig up the cables and pipes. They're being assholes."

I had to take a minute to work my way around that convoluted declaration. The utility lines *weren't* down there?

Of course they weren't. One couldn't expect utility workers to muck through sewage to connect an electric line. And running water pipes through sewage was a recipe for disaster. They had to dig up the streets to reach water lines. I glanced overhead. And power lines. We had buried power lines.

I'd been had.

I punched Andre's number into my phone and waited to see where the Zone would send me. Amazingly, it only took three tries to reach Andre. Maybe turning off the utilities had limited whatever interference polluted our phone signals.

A cacophony of voices provided background to his irritated greeting. He must be at my office.

"Have Frank and his friends hook us up to Acme or turn on our mains," I told him. "Let Acme foot our utility bills. It's only sewage we need to worry about."

"Are you down the hole, Clancy?" he asked in disgust.

"Not yet, Legrande." I hung up.

It made a crazy kind of sense. Chemicals had flooded the streets and harbor. Street runoff went into the sewers. Chemical sludge and gas could have been filling the pipes for a decade. I *sooo* preferred scientific explanations to hellish ones.

I looked around me. Edgewater was eerily silent with no businesses open. Even Bill's place looked deserted.

Another vagrant wandered up to bicker over the beer can. I moved on. I should have gone home, but I had no utilities, and my office would be a madhouse. I needed a place to think.

Unlike my former obedient self, I jaywalked across Edgewater in front of Chesty's. Even our street cop must have been toasting his toes elsewhere. He didn't appear to hand me a ticket. I took the side alley that led behind the restaurant, to the Dumpster lane between the buildings and the deserted harbor.

I watched bulldozers dump layers of pollution into trucks . Where did one carry polluted dirt? To another hazardous zone?

A utility crew was jackhammering pavement outside the chain link fence line. Looked like it was okay to risk the lives of workers if the EPA said so. I wondered if they got hazardous duty pay.

Shivering in the chilly wind, I leaned against a Dumpster in the shadows, hoping to go unnoticed.

I saw no signs of a sinkhole or explosion. But even Themis had admitted another portal had opened—in the sewer? Did I really want to locate it? To what purpose?

I still had hopes of negotiating a truce with Acme long enough to demand Zone representation before the city council so we could protest the medical center. I'd believe anything rather than climb down a fiery manhole.

Without my being aware of his approach, Frank materialized beside me, crossing his arms and leaning against the tin can, too. He wasn't much taller or wider than me. Dressed in rumpled gray slacks and shirt topped by a faded brown jacket and fedora, he blended right in with the shadows.

"Weird stuff happening," he said cryptically.

I arched a cynical eyebrow in his direction.

He shrugged. "Weirder than usual. Do-Gooders are trying to build a greenhouse garden over a manhole behind the insurance building."

"Locavore gardening. Makes sense to me. Use the natural heat." Crazy, but not weird.

"Plants are already growing in it."

Okay, that was weird. Plants took time and there hadn't been any.

Frank nodded toward the hard hats down the block. "Those pricks refused to pay their bar tab at Bill's. Bill threw them out, and they threw his generator into the harbor."

Episodes of violence had been erupting since we'd been gassed. They'd been particularly rude to Tim the other night. Maybe the utility workers had been down here long enough to absorb the pollution. I frowned more in puzzlement than disapproval. "Bill called the cops?"

"Leibowitz can't be found. Bill couldn't identify the perps. All hard hats look alike. It gets weirder. Tourists are flocking to those Jacuzzis, swearing the water is healing what ails them."

Jacuzzis? As in, more than one? People were actually traveling to the Zone for a spa treatment? "Who the heck came up with that?"

"I looked into it," Frank continued. "Some exec at MSI started it.

Another copied him."

MSI thought our hot water was really healing people? Acme's pink and green gas attack a few months ago had cured a lot of ills, while putting the ill into comas. Not precisely a fair trade. But greed drives drug companies to experiment when they shouldn't.

"Is anyone comatose yet?" I had to ask.

"Don't know. The tourists go home—after bashing gargoyles and trashing Dumpsters. Lots of aggression. Scene is really peculiar."

Aggression. Acme's new element had proven dangerous in more ways than one.

The crew we were watching must have hit a pipe. Water spewed in a geyser higher than the nearest building. The men stepped back and just watched.

A plain white van rattled down the alley. Within minutes, they were unloading—another hot tub.

"Okay, that's officially weird," I agreed. "If the city isn't allowing utility workers down here, what gives MSI the right to start businesses here?"

"You try to stop them," he said cynically. "Call the cops. See how far you get."

Out of fatalistic curiosity, I did. I got a sushi joint in Fairbanks Alaska. I tried a couple of more times with the same result. I debated whether creating geysers came under Saturn's law.

"They're killing themselves," Frank said unsympathetically through the wad of gum he was chewing.

Diverted, I looked up. Sure enough, one of the drivers clearing ground zero toppled from his dozer as it scooped up harbor mud. An ambulance marked with Medical Science Inc's logo immediately drove over the rough terrain to pick him up, as if it had been stationed there just for this purpose. As if it had happened more than once.

Maybe MSI was already collecting rats for their experiments.

The guys at the geyser didn't even look up.

"Looks like OSHA needs to step in," I said, debating angles.

"Could be interesting," he agreed. "Won't get Acme off our backs."

He had that right. Can't say that I liked the way Frank's mind worked, but he was nicely feeding my wrath. "Acme has money and power. We don't. How can we level the playing field?"

He thought about that as the ambulance lumbered away. "We either get rich, or Acme gets poor."

"Very helpful, Frank."

"Yeah, I thought so. Leo called and says your hard hat guy is on the prowl and you need to get home. I'm going in to fix the water main."

He slipped into the shadows as invisibly as Tim. Frank was creepy, but he was usually on our side as far as I could tell.

Hard hat guy—Kaminski, the utility worker who wouldn't turn into a gnome. The one I'd had arrested. Not someone I wanted shooting at me again.

"Wouldn't being bulletproof be a whole lot more practical than visualizing idiots to perdition?" I asked the universe while I checked my surroundings. If Kaminski was wearing his hard hat, he'd blend in perfectly around here.

I retreated down the alley to the main drag, halting before I left the shadows. Tall, dark and dangerous—minus the hard hat—leaned against my bike. Damn.

Twenty-one

HAVING learned I couldn't toadify Kaminski or visualize him into a statue, I intelligently avoided the menace—and my bike. I returned to Dumpster alley and set out in the direction of Acme, past the idiots setting up hot spring spas, and away from my home and office. I needed someone who knew how to *physically* intimidate without using the weapons the former frogs liked so much. I missed Max's biker buddies. Out of nostalgia, I dialed up Lance, one of late-Max's biker friends.

No sushi joint this time. Lance answered. "Tina! Moving into the governor's mansion yet?"

"Not quite. Still down here cleaning up his family's dirty work. I've got a man who wants me dead leaning on my bike. Any chance you're free to tell him to move on?"

"Buy me a beer?" he asked cheerfully.

"A whole case," I agreed. My spirits picked up just thinking of Max's rebel friends.

I had no idea if Kaminski would wait around long enough for Lance to show up. Didn't matter. I'd get to see the boys, and in the meantime, I'd taken a hankering to see Paddy. I'd be safe behind Acme's walls, and my need for a normal approach to our problems would be assuaged.

Our resident eccentric scientist should have been a thorn in Acme's side now that he was on the board of trustees and not quite crazy. He'd hated his mother's greedy chemical wars. Why wasn't he holding up his end of the bargain and stopping Acme's outrageous depredations?

I walked up to the chemical plant, knowing there were men inside who wanted me dead. Or on another planet. But unlike Krazy Kaminski, they wouldn't shoot at me. So I stopped at the guardhouse, showed my ID, and asked to see Paddy. I really liked entering lawfully for a change.

He had me buzzed in. I hoped no one was standing at a window aiming squirt guns of chemicals at me. Last time I'd been here, I'd turned their violent goons into frogs and impaled their demented head chemist—not that anyone but Andre actually knew that for certain.

Paddy met me in Acme's sterile lobby. New management hadn't

improved the plant facilities, but Paddy had cleaned himself up nicely. With his beard and hair trimmed, and wearing his white lab coat, he looked like any respectable scientist.

Since he'd been forced to act crazy for years to keep a toehold in his mother's monstrous chemical factory, Paddy knew better than anyone that the walls had ears here. He greeted me with an innocuous, "Good to see you, Tina. Come on back."

Instead of taking me to a quiet office, he led me to a lab with music blaring from a computer and gadgets humming. I wandered among the beakers, gazing in admiration at nothing I could understand. "Nice set-up," I said.

"Annoys the devil out of MacNeill that he doesn't know what I'm doing down here," Paddy admitted, checking a gauge and making notes on his tablet computer. "I take my work home with me and keep it off the network, so it's frustrating a lot of people."

"Which means they're probably not letting you see what they're doing either, doesn't it?" I might not get science or understand chemicals, but I knew people.

"They have to make reports to the board. As trustee, I get to read them." He almost smiled as he checked another gauge. "MacNeill has no idea at all what the reports mean."

"But MacNeill knows how to wield power and money. I take it you haven't been able to stop this devil pact with the clinic?" I leaned against a lab table and looked for cameras in the ceiling. New management or not, I trusted Acme as much as I would a viper crossed with a piranha. For all I knew, Acme was another of hell's dimensions.

"Can't say the clinic is all bad," Paddy admitted. "We cured cancer with the X-element. Experiments need to be done. Not totally sure that condemning the Zone is a bad thing, either. Andre will be reimbursed."

As I'd feared, Paddy was being assimilated by the Borg. He used to sarcastically call the *X-element* the Magic particle.

"Want me to start reciting a long list of chemicals meant to save lives that ended up killing or crippling people?" I asked. "How about the flip side of pink particles—the stuff that made seniors beat each other up for no reason? You don't think a can of that wouldn't explode the Middle East? *Chemicals* are the reason the Zone is what it is."

"And uranium is radioactive and can heat homes or blow up cities. I'm not ignorant, Clancy. The chemicals aren't at fault. People are."

"Guns don't shoot people, people do," I mimicked nastily. "Let's kill people then."

"What do you want, Clancy?" he asked wearily.

"I want Acme to back off, to leave us alone, to plant their nasty clinic somewhere other than on our backs. I'll let you deal with the guilt when you render half the population of Baltimore comatose with your experiments. We just want to get on with our lives."

"I'll see that you're all hired by the clinic," he said helpfully. "Perhaps we can arrange for apartment houses to be built up the road so you can still have a neighborhood."

"Boy, you really drank the Kool-Aid, didn't you?" Disappointed, I prepared to leave. "I guess it doesn't matter to you that the chemicals probably turned your mother and son into demons, and now they're probably working on you?"

He looked up, and I studied him carefully. I hoped the glitter in his eyes was the overheads. I'd always liked Paddy. Now, I had to be wary.

"Demons exist only in your head, Tina," he said sympathetically. "That's where Gloria's demons were. And Dane is turning out much better than I'd hoped. I don't agree with all his policies, but he's a fine senator."

That's because I'd sent the demon to hell, and Max inhabited Dane's body now. But no way was I explaining that to Dane's father.

"I'll cross you off my ally list then, Mr. Vanderventer. Thank you for seeing me." Putting on my lawyer face, I walked away.

Disappointed that I had no one on the inside to help my case, I hurried out. My memories of Acme's interiors were not pleasant, and wouldn't get better if they were sitting on a portal to hell.

Cursing, I checked my watch. I wanted to give Lance plenty of time to remove Kaminski. Since he hadn't called, I didn't go any farther into town than the security of Bill's Biker Bar, just a block down the road from the plant. I was feeling like a law-abiding citizen by not taking a tire iron to Kaminski's skull as I'd once done to a rapist.

Of course, the fact that I hadn't been able to turn him into a gnome kind of skewed my self-confidence.

Bill's was still warm and packed. He must have got his generator back. Realizing I hadn't had lunch, I ordered a fish fry—think crab cake without the crab—with my beer, and studied the crowd.

It was Monday and Acme was still operational. The usual lunchtime crew was here—workers from all the industrial plants up the road. Some of the D-Gers had set up shop in a corner and were enthusiastically discussing world peace or whatever turned them on. The half of the Zonies who weren't parked in my office were down here trying to get warm and fed. And even a few utility workers hung out.

I still didn't understand why utility workers would be down here if our utilities were shut off. Wasn't the point of shutting them off the safety of workers?

They looked at me. I looked at them. And a creepy sensation crawled down my spine.

When Bill delivered my plate, I waved him down to my level. "I sense hostility at nine o'clock."

He glanced down the bar and nodded. "They used to work security for Acme. They recognize you without fondness."

"More frogs," I said with a groan. "Next time, I'll send them to Antarctica."

"I'm going to pretend I didn't hear that." Bill returned to polishing his glassware.

Other than transforming into a gentle giant and losing his need to break other people's bones, Bill didn't seem to have attracted any of the more notorious Zone disabilities. He respected our individual weirdnesses and had our backs when we needed him. I wouldn't disturb him more than necessary.

Besides, my latest theory was that once I'd visualized a thug into an alternate life form, I couldn't transform them a second time. If I couldn't turn frogs into gnomes, could I transport them to another country? I still didn't have a Saturnian rule book.

My phone rang and I glanced at the ID. It just said *Terminator*. Either Schwarzenegger or my guy Lance. What were the odds?

"Find Kawinski?" I asked as I tuned in.

"Yeah, I think I persuaded him that you're a little angel, and he should leave you alone," Lance growled. "Real punk, that one."

"How many broken bones?"

"Just a kneecap. His skull is too hard. You owe me a beer."

"I owe you a case. I'm down at Bill's. You want it all at once or shall I set up a tab?"

"Sweet. I'll be right down." He whistled off.

I lifted a beer to my non-existent daddy. Sometimes, it didn't take superpowers to get the job done.

Lance was six-feet, two hundred pounds of heavy muscle, beer gut, leather and graying hair. People stared when he sauntered in. He didn't bother noticing. He made a beeline back to me and caught me up in a bear hug. "Babe! How do ye do?"

I pounded him on the back. "I do fine, lug. Put me down, and I'll do better." Especially since the utility thugs would soon realize I'd sent Lance after their buddy. Oh well. I liked Lance's simple, direct honesty.

I signaled Bill. "A case of beer for my friend here, anyway he wants it."

Lance and Bill exchanged male gestures and a foamy mug appeared on the bar in front of him.

An ambulance siren wailed on the street outside. One of the hardhats checked his phone. An instant later, they all lumbered out. Probably not a good sign for me. Lesson learned, Tina, if you can't do it yourself, find someone a little more subtle than Lance.

"You got any more jobs I can take care of for you, babe?" Lance asked through his foam mustache, not acknowledging the reason for the siren. "Me and the guys are running a little short since Max left."

The *guys* were the usual suspects—dopers, vets, slackers, and the chronically unemployed who had a hang-out biker club in the country. It would be fun to turn them loose on Acme, but not healthy for either side.

"No money here, either," I told him regretfully. "Looks like we may have to shut down."

Lance's gang had been Max's friends. They'd relied on his leadership a lot more than anyone let on. His loss had devastated them.

And then I had an evil thought. I held up my finger to indicate silence, pulled out my phone, and dialed Max/Dane.

After the fourth try, I got voice mail, of course. "I've got Lance down here. He and the boys are running a little short. Could you use a security detail?"

Lance snorted into his beer as I hung up. "Who's gonna hire us for security?"

"Senator Vanderventer," I said smugly. "He sent the Do-Gooders down here to improve the Zone. It's only fair we do something nice for him in return."

Lance thought my reply was pretty funny. I left him laughing and ordering a second beer. My job here was done.

As I sauntered back to my bike, I got cocky. Walking over a glowing manhole cover, I decided to study the situation. I took off a glove, wet my finger, and tapped it against the metal. When it didn't steam, I put my glove back on and tried to lift the thing, just to see what I could see. I couldn't even rattle the damned lid. Add one more bit of knowledge to my useless encyclopedia.

I kept a wary eye out for hard hats as I aimed for my bike, but they must have accompanied their pal to the hospital. Kaminski had carved his initials into the bike's leather seat before Lance popped his kneecaps. Rat bastard. I wouldn't have a single whole piece of leather left at this rate.

The wonky traffic lights were back on, I noticed as I cruised past Chesty's. They were actually a normal red and green, in honor of Christmas, I supposed. Except both stop and go lights were on at once.

Since there was no traffic, I didn't worry about mixed signals. I saw cars in Chesty's lot, so I swung in, hoping that meant Frank had worked his magic and we had what passes for electricity again.

Canned music was playing as I entered. Chesty's was never bright even when lights were working, so the dimness was no surprise. I saw only a few customers at the tables. The naked murals were standing around, smoking, not bothering to writhe for an empty house.

On stage, Sarah was practicing a pole dance routine. Her stubby legs would never rival Ginger Rogers, but her newly-glorious hair hid a lot of flaws. Her stiff, cone-shaped boobs poked out from the Lady Godiva tresses. She was wearing pasties.

I considered turning around and walking out, but she spotted me. Pulling on a long t-shirt, she clumped down the stairs in her awkward heels. "Tina! Ernesto said he'd try me on the stage. Isn't that cool?"

What was cool was that six months ago, she'd been an abused wife who had jumped at shadows, and now she had the nerve to stand in a spotlight. That's what the Zone did. And why I couldn't condemn it as Paddy wanted to do.

"If that's what you want," I said guardedly. "We've got lights back?" It still felt chilly in this barn of a room, but it would take time to heat.

"Frank's got people working on it. Your office is pretty crowded still. Ernesto said I could sleep in a storage room here, if I wanted. You don't mind?"

After she'd painted half my second floor Pepto-Bismol pink? I shrugged. "Do what's best for you but don't trust Ernesto."

She giggled. "He wanted to charge me rent and to dance, too. I told him it was a trade. He's sorta cute, isn't he?"

I used to work for him. No way in ten million years was dumpy, greasy, penny-pinching Ernesto anything but a douche bag. But I smiled optimistically. "He grows on you, I guess. Glad it's working out. I'd better get back to the office if everyone is still there."

I checked out the bar's arrow-slit of a window to be certain my bike wasn't surrounded by thugs. Reassured the coast was clear, I drove back to my office, where chaos reigned supreme.

My lopsided, fragrant Christmas tree sparkled with lights, and apparently tinfoil decorations, courtesy of Jane's kid and maybe Ned, who was currently helping a pink-coated Tim carry a palm tree out to an already over-full truck.

"Hey, Tina, can we set the rest of these palms in the window of your apartment until we know for sure the heat's staying on?" Tim called as he propped the door open with his heel.

I glanced up at my barren bay window across the street. "Milo won't eat them?"

"Won't hurt him if he does. Give me your keys." He held out his hand, and I flung the apartment keys at him.

I admired the twinkling lights lending cheer to my front office and let my chilled body regain some warmth while listening to signs of life all over my once-empty building. I wasn't a loner by any means. I loved the buzz of a hive.

Mostly, I was scared someone would take it all away from me. Again.

Even as I acknowledged that fear, a boom shook the office, and the Christmas tree swayed.

Twenty-two

THE porch of my boarding house across the street exploded. Leaping back from my office door, taking Ned back with me, I added my screams to his. Smoke and flame billowed from the Victorian's porch. Boards, bricks, and shattered flower pots incinerated into raining shrapnel. In the eruption of dust, I couldn't see Tim—not exactly unusual.

Recovering from the first shock, I ran out, sending frantic prayers to unseen entities for Tim's and Mrs. Bodine's safety.

The palm tree Tim had been carrying was reduced to ash and charred soil in the middle of the street. I frantically visualized dousing the fiery porch, but Saturn only produced justice, not general wishes.

"Damn you, Saturn, make them be alive," I muttered, sobbing and patting the street around the palm tree remains in search of Tim.

If Saturn damned himself, I couldn't tell.

Andre and Leo ran out of various buildings with fire extinguishers and hoses—far more practical than cursing planets.

I didn't find Tim until Cora ran into the street and tripped over him. She dropped to her knees, and I crawled carefully in her direction. Unlike Cora, I tended to blink out—go invisible—when I touched Tim, so I didn't really dare test him for a pulse.

"Tim? Blink on for me, please?" I pleaded.

Beneath the screams and sirens and crackling flames I thought I heard a moan. Cora started patting the ground, presumably in pursuit of his wrist. I thought I saw a flicker of pink.

"Tim, please, focus. We have to see you to help." I was choking on sobs. Tim was just an innocent kid. He'd had a hard enough life.

The keys I'd given him dropped to the ground. That couldn't be a good sign. A second later, a melted pink down jacket gradually materialized. Swallowing my cries, I poked around for the zipper, but it had melted, too.

Cora produced a knife and ripped the jacket open. The rest of Tim returned. Unconscious, he lay sprawled in the street on his back. We could see the outline of palm leaves etched in the soot and burns on his face. His untidy crop of brown hair was scorched. But it appeared the hated jacket was impervious to flame and had taken the brunt of the blast.

"Tim, can you hear me? I'll buy you more jackets in pink and purple if you'll just wake up," I pleaded.

Cora cut off the jacket sleeves. His clothing underneath seemed untouched. Knowing Tim, he'd just passed out in terror.

Across the street, the flames were almost out. The front porch was nothing more than charred posts and dripping shingles. One of the DGs, or maybe the interns from next door, helped Mrs. Bodine totter down the narrow alley between houses. Her wrinkled face crumpled in tears at sight of her porch.

And I was pretty damned certain it was all my fault.

Tim moaned and his seared eyelashes blinked. Once I knew he was alive, I went through the motions of reassuring him and myself, but my mind traveled on to criminal warfare. I was bringing down one demented frog. Or maybe a pack of them.

"If you were really fair, you'd let me wish them dead," I told Saturn. He didn't have to answer back. I already knew I couldn't do it. Saturn might not need evidence, but *I* did before I could damn anyone. Fact-finding mission coming up.

Andre was caught up in dealing with disaster or he might have recognized my rage. As it was, he merely glanced our way, ascertained that we had Tim in hand, and went back to shouting orders.

Fire engines arrived. Mrs. Bodine was led over to the house next door that our interns occupied when they weren't sleeping in hospital hallways. D-Gers arrived in groups carrying building materials and tarps and I'm not sure what all.

I should have been reassured. I wasn't. I needed heads to roll.

I hoped Dane's trust fund was paying for the materials because Acme was as much to blame for this warfare as I was. The frog-men had obviously been polluted by the green violence element—except Ned, who liked pink and scarfed up the good element.

I let Cora take Tim over to be examined by the baby docs. Milo had joined the crowd in the street. Bless my kitty! He always appeared when I needed him, if he could. I needed to know he was safe. I hugged him and whispered sweet words in his ear. He did not respond but studied the chaos around us as if I were merely his throne.

"You don't think you're needed to deal with terrorists?" I asked my cat.

Milo sniffed in disdain.

"Fine then, off you go." Reassured, I handed him back to Ned.

I'd once turned Ned into a frog, and he'd come out a better man.

If Kawinski was any example, his fellow frogs had *chosen* evil, while Ned had chosen good. Just watching Mrs. Bodine weep and Tim shiver built my case against vengeful frogs.

First, I had to verify that the explosion wasn't accidental. I was pretty damned certain it wasn't, but I had to be fair. This was not a situation that required immediate action. I had time to weigh the evidence for a change—not that Saturn seemed to require it but my overdeveloped conscience did.

I located one of the firemen rolling up his hose. I was still wearing black leather, so I couldn't precisely mimic Average Citizen, but I tried not to look too crazy as I approached.

"I've called the gas company," I said innocently. "Is there any danger of more leaks?"

"That was no gas leak," he said angrily. "That was some stupid bum planting a pipe bomb on an old lady's porch. We've called the cops."

I refrained from snorting. Despite their promises, the cops had been conspicuously absent lately. Acme must have sent them on paid holiday.

"I'll let the gas company know, thank you," I said politely. "And a cop lives there, so I assume that's who the prankster was after. They'll get him. Thank you for coming out so quickly."

Information for information was fair trade, even if I was half lying. The fireman nodded approval, I thanked him again, and using the fire engine to hide my actions from Andre, I slipped down the street.

I had utterly no idea how I'd figure out which of the utility workers were Kaminski's pals. Like Frank said, they all looked alike.

But the evil minions I'd turned into frogs had all been over six feet and well-muscled. I'd start there. Their time out as frogs apparently hadn't harmed them physically. Morally, they'd all been questionable at the time I'd zapped them. I could have killed them. Maybe I should have. But Ned had turned out okay. One in five ain't bad.

Unfortunately, that apparently left four willing to kill *me*. And who didn't care who got hurt in the process.

For the security of Tim and Mrs. Bodine and other innocents, I had to stop vengeful cretins. Lance obviously wasn't the answer if my enemies meant to up the ante every time I tried to teach them a lesson. Hardhats had access to detonators and explosives that I didn't. Like any war, escalating skirmishes didn't resolve the problem.

Maybe I should offer a peace pipe, but they'd tried to *kill* me twice now, and that wasn't counting the pre-frog attempts.

I took the back alleys where I could hide in shadow. The day was gray and getting darker, so I blended nicely, just as I used to do. Although these days, the Dumpsters tended to shift out of my way instead of blocking me. I hoped that was a sign of approval from the Zone.

I was starting to think of the Zone as a sentient beast with its own opinions.

The bulldozers were still running inside the chain link along the harbor, so it wasn't quitting time yet. Not that the utility guys I was after seemed to be working—they seemed to spend a lot of time in bars and beating up unsuspecting motorcycles. Of course, they could be part of the spa crews drilling holes in our parking lots.

Standing beside an abandoned gas station, I gazed down the long harbor alley. The chain link had been disintegrating for years, but it looked as if it had been deliberately removed to allow better access to the spas that dared to crop up closer to the water.

A vaguely carnival atmosphere had developed back here. It was *December,* but nuts were creating palm tree oases around steaming baths and heated tents. So that's who Tim had sold the palm trees to.

People in down jackets lined up to enter the tents. Others jostled about trying to peer inside, curious. There were probably carny barkers out on Edgewater extolling the virtues of miracle healing, but I wasn't interested in showing myself on the main drag just yet.

Even demented frogs wouldn't expect that pipe bomb to hit a moving target like me—they had been deliberately drawing me out. Which meant they were lurking, waiting for me to hunt them down.

If there were actually four of them, I was outnumbered. Even if Kaminski was in the hospital, three was too many when they had guns and size and I didn't. Without my visualization powers, I was at a severe disadvantage. But this Saturn justice kink in my head wouldn't let me risk any more of my friends.

My tire iron had been confiscated the last time I had taken out a menace to society. I needed a new weapon to focus my fury. Except the Zone didn't have guns and swords lying about for me to harvest. I found a splintered two by four in the trash beside one of the Dumpsters. It would have to do.

As I studied the harbor and the various crews of hard hats, another geyser spouted high above the buildings. How much water was down there? This couldn't all be from the mains. Was the harbor seeping under the town? I'd ponder the sinister implications after I took me down a few mean frogs.

I slipped through the alley shadows. The saunas had started down by Bill's, on the north end of the street near Acme. They were gradually working their way south, nearer our homes. Cradling my lumber, I focused on a group of hard hats working to channel the new geyser with pipes.

Two more utility vans raced toward the geyser from either end of the alley. I raised my eyebrows as the vans played chicken and nearly met in the middle. At the last second, one veered over the broken fence and into the harbor grounds.

Both trucks advertised saunas and spilled men in khaki overalls, one set with blue lettering, the other with red. As both teams raced for the gushing geyser, a brawl broke out between the blue and red. Guys in khaki swung fists and rolled through the trash and dirt, beating the crap out of each other.

I swear, it was a scene straight out of Dante's *Inferno*, not that I'd ever read it, but I'd seen pictures of paintings. Men writhing in the mud, fighting each other for no good reason, looked like a circle of hell to me. Too bad they weren't naked like in the painting.

The hard hats around the geyser merely continued working, siphoning heat from hell into pipes.

It sure looked as if our conclusions had been verified and that the portal to hell had opened in the Zone. If I were superstitious, I'd believe that the sins of avarice and wrath were escalating. Interesting twist of the devil's, using healing water to promote evil.

"The devil doesn't exist," I growled at invisible gods, counteracting my ever-vivid imagination. "And I don't believe in Hades either."

I was hoping Saturn was a good god, and this violence was a result of chemical pollution.

I was past Chesty's now. I could hear the grunts and blows as the two crews flailed at each other. These weren't professional fighters. They looked like ordinary working men smacking and kicking and having temper tantrums. I could buy them all a beer and they'd sit down and exchange jokes. But the Zone had affected them.

One of the hard hats working with the pipes glanced in my direction, as if he knew I was near. Or had been keeping watch, awaiting my arrival. I plastered my leather jacket against a Dumpster.

Walls that glow blue aren't good hiding places, but there was nothing else back here.

He sidled away from the group in my direction. Well, setting myself as bait was one way of hunting murderous frogs. I hefted my lumber mace, getting a feel for its weight.

Maybe it was my imagination, but I could swear Hard Hat's eyes glowed red.

I needed to know for certain that he meant me harm before I could return the favor. I could only hope damning him would work. If so, I had my wish reward ready.

Testing my theory, I burst from my hiding place, running into the open harbor ground where bulldozers loaded dirt into dump trucks. Like zombies, the drivers kept on trucking even though I was zigzagging across their turf like a demento.

My boots skidded in the sticky mud. Landing face-first in this crap could be a death sentence in itself. I slowed down. The dozers kept rolling. I ran toward the water and away from the sauna where Hard Hat had been glaring at me.

I heard the thud of heavy boots on my heels. Guess that answered one question—he was after me. Even though Saturn Daddy had heeled my bad leg, I wasn't the runner I'd been in school. And muscle man had a longer stride.

To verify that he wasn't simply chasing me off the grounds, I changed direction and raced for the nearest spa. The footsteps got closer. I shouted as I ran, but the tourists apparently thought a giant worker chasing a small, charred-hair woman was part of the entertainment. They watched, but no one interfered as Hard Hat bore down on me. I had no illusion that me and my wood weapon could bring down two hundred pounds of crazy unless I could turn him into a crab and crush him.

I checked over my shoulder and shuddered. His eyes really were red. Running faster, I visualized Hard Hat morphing into a scuttling crab.

His loud boot thumps continued, pounding closer. Shoot, darn.

The pop, pop, pop of an automatic weapon changed the game. My lumber sword couldn't fight bullets. I had been trying hard to play fair, and what did I get?

I almost welcomed the familiar red rage. I'd learned to wish for what I wanted before I sent a soul to perdition—Saturn Daddy liked to reward us for removing evil—but it's hard to think sensibly when my head is full of fury.

With all the creepy newcomers just standing around gaping as I was about to be massacred, I recalled the basic intent of my planned reward. I wished them back home where they belonged.

Then I veered toward an oncoming bulldozer. Hard Hat, as expected, still hadn't turned into a crab. I heard him smacking another cartridge into the automatic. I grabbed the handle outside the bulldozer cab and swung in.

As I did so, I caught a glimpse of the gunman in the side mirror, raising his arm to fire again. With an apology, I shoved the driver out of his seat and grabbed the controls.

It had been a long time since I'd driven a tractor and bushhog, but I figured the basics hadn't changed. I grabbed the motion control and blade joysticks and swung my weapon straight at Hard Hat.

Now who was running from whom?

Bulldozers only have three speeds: slow, slower, and stop. But they're big. And I wasn't feeling the guy's pain.

If he'd had a brain in his head, he would have veered off at an angle where I couldn't reach him. But apparently the devil's minions didn't have brains. Maybe zombies ate them. I pressed the blade down, let the engine out, and scooped him up.

He fired through the windshield at me and sealed his fate.

"Damn you to hell!" I screamed as the bullet winged my temple. Now I had two bullet wounds in me, bruises all over, and scorched hair. I could feel a warm trickle of blood down my cheek that fueled my rage. That shot had been too damned close for comfort.

Frigginfuckit—the guy didn't disappear but kept shooting. So much for Saturn's wrathful justice. For all I knew, Saturn had gone away after I'd cursed him over Tim's disappearance, and now I was really on my own.

Fear only escalated my fury. I ducked and drove straight for the harbor, not caring who got in my way—not that I could see anything while cowering behind the dashboard. Hard Hat kept shooting, apparently operating on the same red rage as I was. Zone madness had us both in its grips.

The treads sucked mud as I hit the water. I kept on trucking.

Hard Hat screamed in terror as I tipped the blade joystick. If he couldn't swim, all the better.

I couldn't hear the plop of his six feet of evil in the water over the roar of the engine, but I saw the splash. I ran the dozer treads out a little farther, just for fun, then put the machine in reverse and returned to shore.

My temple throbbed from the bullet crease. Suddenly shaking from the adrenaline crash, I wiped my head with the back of my hand and smeared blood on my fingers. I gasped for air and choked on pure terror. Murdering people wasn't exactly my way of life. I was trying very hard not to look behind me—mostly for fear the thug would rise up and walk on water, still shooting.

The dozer lumbered back to land. I expected an hysterical crowd and a line of police cars, at the very least. Or maybe the rest of the hard hats bearing down on me with AK47s. There had been a time in their former occupations when they'd done that.

Instead, as I parked the dozer and jumped down, I encountered weary men shutting down their machinery and packing up their lunchboxes and heading for their vehicles.

I stared in disbelief as the sauna guys folded their tents and loaded them into their vans. Tourists, looking puzzled, began wandering away.

I'd just murdered a man, but no one paid me the slightest attention.

Too wiped to care, I snatched a towel from one of the tents to staunch the bullet wound. Then I tramped back across the mud to Chesty's rear door. Behind me, I could hear the bulldozer driver rolling his machine away as if I hadn't just hijacked it and killed someone. Maybe I had turned as invisible as Tim.

I was pretty sure I'd just damned a man and sent him to hell. He'd been shooting at me, so I couldn't feel real guilty about what I'd done.

Standing beside Chesty's smelly Dumpster, I watched as the sauna vans began driving away.

I'd wished for the *creepy newcomers* to go back where they belonged. And from the looks of it, they were. Saturn Daddy—or Satan—had rewarded me for sending another demon to hell.

I gave up looking for logic and entered Chesty's in search of a bowl of soup and a biscuit.

Apparently, I didn't mind killing the devil's minions. Now, if only I could identify them *before* they hurt people, I might be useful.

Twenty-three

I WASHED up in Chesty's restroom, using paper towels to staunch the graze on my temple and hiding it with my messy hair. I took a seat at the bar and pondered becoming an alcoholic. Would that numb me from my red ragey need to murder people? Well, at least, so far, I'd only gone after ones who threatened me or people I cared about. I still preferred law books.

A college kid on a stool beside me was tapping away on his phone, obviously intending to text someone—without much success. I sipped my beer and considered warning him that his text would likely end up in China even if it went through. But reading his message, I sighed at his bad spelling of *haullicongenic experence* and refrained.

The Zone was a hallucinogenic experience all right. Tweeting about it to the world would make us a real tourist attraction guaranteed to get us shut down.

Maybe they'd even find the body in the harbor and think it was part of an amusement-park game. I got sent to jail for egging a provost's office, but I could murder a utility worker and no one cared? How did I work my head around that?

I watched a tourist video our dancing mural and another bash his beer bottle over a friend's head. I hadn't been specific enough in my red ragey wish. I'd only sent the newcomers on the harbor away.

Andre came up from behind me, slapped my shoulder in a seemingly genial gesture, and hauled me off the bar stool by my collar. "The place is quiet tonight. Why do I assume it's because of you?"

Quiet! I snorted at the sarcasm. The violence factor had grown exponentially since our gas attack a few weeks back.

He dragged me to our favorite booth in the corner. With Andre, it's difficult to tell hostility from friendliness, so I just took a seat across from him, sipped my beer, and continued pondering life's little mysteries.

"Katerina says according to Roman mythology, Saturn ripped the Furies out of his father's head. That doesn't exactly make them his daughters," Andre informed me.

He studied the way my hair flopped in my eyes but didn't look to see what I hid.

"Uranus's eye, to be perfectly correct." I studied a group of DGs in the corner getting royally drunk. I doubted that they'd ever touched a beer before entering the Zone. "Or his drops of blood, depending on the version you prefer. You don't think I've read Wikipedia too?"

"But the Furies are sent to punish sinners. Sound like anyone we know?" Andre signaled for his usual.

"I'm a lawyer, not a product of mythology," I replied stonily. "The planet Saturn has seven rings, nine unofficial moons, and fifty-three official moons. It takes twenty-seven years to orbit the sun. It's the lightest planet in the solar system consisting mostly of helium and hydrogen. And it's lopsided. Maybe I'm an unofficial moon."

He almost laughed. "The Furies are depicted with bat wings and snakes around their waists. That works better than a moon."

"Bats." I rolled my eyes in disgust. "There are only three Furies and there are a lot more Saturn's Daughters. Maybe even fifty-three. I just dumped a demon in the harbor with a bulldozer. Do not give me bats."

He whistled and glanced around. "You scared off all the customers in the process?"

"I wished all the creeps away." I was in a rage at the time. I didn't know precisely what I'd wished. I just knew everyone packed up and left, and that's what I'd wanted.

He nodded as if that made sense. "Sarah's still here. And Ernesto. You didn't wish hard enough."

This time, I laughed. Diane brought me another beer along with Andre's. "Jimmy made gumbo. Want some?" she asked.

"Not if the fish comes from the harbor," I said ungratefully, imagining dead bodies bobbing with scallops.

"He won't use anything that isn't trucked in. I'll bring you some rolls too. You might want to talk to Sarah. She's found a gun somewhere and has taken to threatening customers with it."

I sighed and pinched the bridge of my nose. It didn't ease the ache in my head. "I want a vacation," I said as Diane walked away. "How's Tim?"

"Shaken and bruised but fine," Andre said. "The DGs who aren't down here drinking are up there rebuilding Mrs. B's porch. It's the Zone, Clancy, not you. We're polluted, and it makes people crazy."

"If you tell me you're accepting MSI's offer, I'll reach across the table and punch you in your pretty face," I threatened, giving him the evil eye so he'd know I meant it.

"I'll buy a warehouse in Fell's Point, we can all live in it, and call it the Yellow Submarine," he suggested.

"*NO!* We are not going down without a fight." I shoved my beer across the table at him. "We do not let the bad guys win. Remember what Acme did to your mother."

"They cured her of cancer," he pointed out.

"And took away ten years of her life, turned Julius into a recluse, and you into a maniac. Maybe Katerina was meant to go to heaven, except chemicals changed Fate and allowed more demons in instead. I don't know what the hell I'm talking about, but Acme is *evil*. Or the new element is. And until scientists recognize the danger, they shouldn't be using it for medical research."

He knew all that, but Andre was nothing if not pragmatic. "They gave me until Friday to sell out. After that, they sue and try to take the lawyer fees out of the proceeds. And the longer the fight takes, the less they offer."

This was Wednesday night. So much for talking reason to the EPA.

One of the DGs began shouting. A couple more stood up to assist him outside. The loud one swung a beer bottle that flew wildly out of his hand, nearly missing Sarah who had just emerged from Ernesto's office. The bottle smacked a mural and splattered beer remains on Sarah's new fake fur and Godiva hair.

She pulled a gun, and I screamed a warning. Everyone ducked, a waiter tackled Sarah, and the bullet hit an overhead light, knocking it out.

Shades of the wild west. And I didn't want to be the sheriff.

Justice was becoming a fuzzy gray spot in my eye. I got up and walked out and left others to deal with it. I didn't even get my gumbo.

I thought I heard nuns singing Christmas carols as I strode up the hill, huddled inside my jacket. My breath smoked in the chill night air. The real wreaths on the street lamps smelled of pine, reminding me of my desire for a normal holiday with pretty lights and presents. My laugh emerged as a sarcastic bark.

I'd just killed a man and didn't deserve a normal Christmas, but there you have it. We can't always get what we want, but sometimes we get what we need. Obviously, I needed justice.

I dodged a purple bat swirling up from an open manhole. A tourist snapped a picture with his cell phone. Was he telling the world about his hallucinogenic experience in the Zone?

Andre's proclamation about selling by Friday had doomed what was left of my day. I trudged up the hill, admiring the spotlight on Mrs. B's front porch.

The DGs were finishing painting the once-blackened exterior in a bright blue with green trim to match the rest of the house. A bowl of punch and cookies had been set up on a folding table on the new porch, along with one of Tim's dilapidated Christmas trees.

There was still some good in the world, I had to remember, watching Cora scarf a cookie and genially elbow one of the painter boys.

"Can anyone join the party?" I asked as I reached the steps. I hadn't had any supper, and those cookies looked good.

Hanks handed me a paint brush and pointed at an unfinished corner. "Everyone's welcome as long as they work!"

Maybe the Zone needed more innocent idiots. I painted and I ate cookies but I couldn't forget that by Saturday, we might all be out on the street—and Andre would be moving on.

Thursday morning I woke up realizing that If I wanted to save the Zone, I couldn't do everything myself. I needed my own posse, by own Do-Good Inc. It's not that I hadn't been aware that I could do more with a little help from my friends. It was more that I didn't want to be responsible for anyone's actions but my own. But our problems were community wide, so the solution had to be also. Big duh, Tina.

I called Katerina and asked how she and Julius were progressing on getting the Zone recognized by the city council.

"They're all eager to talk to Julius, of course," Katerina said with an exasperated sigh, "but they believe he's playing Don Quixote for a condemned wasteland. Progress is not good."

Julius had a brilliant legal mind and had written textbooks still taught in schools today. He was a local legend who'd dropped out of sight for a decade. Of course every politician in the county wanted him on their side.

Which was why MacNeill had shown up in the judge's chamber yesterday. Duh, again, Tina.

"It's getting too late to go the city council route," I said, trying to think this through before breakfast. "Could we go straight to the governor? The state is responsible for eminent domain. The city has vested interest in the MSI clinic but the state doesn't. Mostly. Julius will need to speak to our state reps. I'll see if Dane can do the same."

"We've thought of that, but Julius hates using influence. And he's in a weird situation with Andre owning that property," Katerina admitted.

"Then I'll talk to Andre too. Let me think about this some more." I hung up and went to wash my head before I got in any deeper.

I still wasn't intellectually convinced that keeping the Zone open was a good idea. But emotionally, I knew I couldn't bear seeing it destroyed—even if Sarah sat outside picking off rats with her Walmart automatic. *Home* wasn't a rational decision.

After damning a bad guy yesterday, I was real reluctant to check my mirror for fear Daddy Saturn had rewarded me with horns or haloes beneath my shampoo-ad hair. I hated these physical reminders that I'd sent a soul to hell. Or wherever. But I'd postponed my ablutions long enough. I showered and peered nervously into the foggy glass. Nada—except for shaggier hair and the scrape from yesterday. It had scabbed over nicely.

Maybe sending the creeps home was all I got. I was more than happy with that.

I took scissors and whacked off the worst of the burned patches of hair that I could see in the mirror. I was looking pretty ragged by the time I was done. Maybe I could be a trend setter.

Grabbing a bagel, I ran across the street with tons of determination and no more plan in mind than I'd given Katerina.

Inside, my once empty lobby had turned into office heaven. I had copy machines and color printers and telephones and *people*. People everywhere. Jane was on the phone, sitting on the edge of Ned's desk. She waved as I entered. Do-Gooder Hanks had a crew on the floor making posters. Ned had a pencil clenched between his teeth as he typed on his keyboard and gestured in different directions to people standing in line at his desk. I had no idea what that was about.

Had Katerina set all this in motion without mentioning it to me? I didn't think Andre capable of this level of organization. He's more the lone wolf type. But Katerina was a different force to reckon with. I already had community action—now I just needed to refine their approach.

I hurried into my office and closed the door. I needed to get my head straight, and as much as I enjoyed a beehive, the activity wasn't conducive to clear thinking.

I reached for the phone before I realized—I had a desk phone. With blinking lights. I wondered if it worked or if I'd end up with raw shrimp from Alaska if I tried it.

I pulled out my smart phone instead. It had Dane on speed dial.

"This better be a booty call," he said with surliness, actually picking up the phone for a change.

"Only if there's no booty involved like last time," I said cheerily, hearing Max behind Dane's voice.

"I'm not going back to hell no matter how good the sex," he growled unhappily.

"I totally concur." Although the sex had been unreal, and I wouldn't mind trying it again. "So want to start this conversation over? How are you doing?"

"Hagatha's ointments work better than hospitals. I'm fine and I hate this place. What do you want, Justy?"

"How's the haunted house?" I asked, just to keep reminding him that he *owed* me.

"Cold and drafty and empty. I'm thinking of selling it to a funeral home. The kitchen is full of workmen cementing over hell, and your weirdoes are back there chanting and throwing in crucifixes or something. I'm thinking of siccing them on the Zone next."

"My, we are in a fine mood this morning. I take it Granny's not been back, so maybe sending your exorcists down here wouldn't be a bad thing." I contemplated the possibility. If they'd worked on Gloria, why not on Acme's hell hole? I added another item to my agenda.

"Offer them money and they'll follow you anywhere," Max conceded. "For all I know, Granny will do the same. What's wrong now, Justy? If you're not going to keep me warm, we've got to move on."

"You're such a sweet-talking charmer, Max. That's what I love about you." And I wasn't lying. Max's blunt honesty had always appealed. Dane's political charm didn't. "We need you to call the governor and tell him eminent domain is fine as long as it involves tearing down Acme and keeping the medical center out of a dangerously polluted environment."

If Acme was the evil down here, then they needed to tear down more than Andre's buildings.

Max actually fell silent, considering it. I waited.

"You might have a point," he agreed. "The city will resist. They want the money MSI will bring to the coffers. They'll pull the governor's strings. I'll have some people talk to the EPA and a few environmentalists. I can't technically get involved because it's a family business, but I think you're on to something."

Tearing down Acme was what he'd always wanted. He hated his family's business as much as I did. I had just hoped that they'd clean up their act with better management so people could keep their jobs. But it might be too late for that. The demons running Acme would be breeding zombies next.

"I don't like it," I admitted. "People need jobs and homes, but if they're losing them anyway, then it ought to be for the right reason."

"The family will scream bloody murder," he said with satisfaction. "Merry Christmas! Thank you for the gift."

He rang off. My Max was one sick whacko.

Twenty-four

Since I had no legal secretary, I typed up my own letters. I prepared a few and sent them to the printer. The machine was apparently now on my desk instead of Ned's. Wondering why I even had an assistant, I signed the letters and took them out to Ned to package up.

He added them to his empty inbox while gesturing to a dowdy, bespectacled female who had to be one of the Do-Gooders. "Third door on the left. Tell Tom you can do graphics."

I stepped in front of the next person in line, propped my palms on his desk, and got in Ned's face. "*What* are we doing here—besides working?"

"As you requested, Mrs. Montoya is planning her petition for recognition of the Zone district, and your partner is battling eminent domain. The DG's are helping out in return for housing vagrants in the Morgan building. We've got a protest march scheduled for one o'clock and Jane has TV crews lined up in front of the florist shop and uptown at city hall." He checked off a name on a list and gestured at the person behind me. "Big room on right. They'll tell you what to do."

Fine, battle lines drawn—with me smack dab in the middle. Andre versus his parents. The Zone versus Acme. Max/Dane versus both his fathers. I needed to plan my fights better.

"Tell Julius to take a good long look at MSI and their connections to city hall," I recommended.

"We've got detectives asking questions about MSI's missing CEO and security guards," Ned reminded me. "Now might not be a good time for investigating them."

"Tell the city that Graham Young had a penchant for Nazis and the lot of them are probably all practicing World War Three in a forest somewhere," I grumbled, before heading for the stairs.

It was probably time to produce a missing CEO, if possible. I had a few ideas, none of them safe. But I didn't have time for detailed planning. I had to act now.

The climb up four flights was invigorating but even the cold wind on the roof couldn't clear my head. I glared at the Graham Young gnome. He didn't appear to be shivering.

"The rest of the world doesn't see evil," I said to the statue, testing my theory. "They sort of see greed and perversion sometimes." The gnome didn't respond. I figured him for a greedy pervert. "But I saw evil in Granny's eyes when she died and evil in the frog's eyes before I heaved him into the harbor. That, or Acme's magic element."

From the roof's edge, I looked down the hill at the Zone in mid-morning mode. Trucks and beat-up old cars straggled down the street to Acme and the other industrial plants to the north. Morning fog still lay over the harbor area, and tentacles of gray crept up alleys to Edgewater. One of the spa vans was back, setting up shop where chain link used to be.

A bum wandered out of the Morgan building and kicked at a manhole. It didn't gleam as red as earlier in the week. Disappointed, he ambled to the Dumpster at Chesty's, probably looking for not-quite-empty liquor bottles. The Dumpster shifted, confusing him.

Street crews had dug holes in the pavement along Edgewater and left them surrounded by orange cones. Tim's bedraggled Christmas tree lot was empty, its inventory no doubt stolen now that the florist's door was boarded shut.

If I was the only person who could see evil blighting the streets, then I was the only damned person who could fight it head on. The others were merely treating the symptoms.

I tucked the gnome under my arm and proceeded back downstairs.

I set the statue on Ned's desk. "Call Dr. Abdul Bakir at MSI and have him meet me at the Morgan building at noon. Same with MacNeill and Paddy at Acme. If Andre and Julius are interested, tell them they're welcome to come. Representatives from OSHA and the EPA might be good. Tell Jane to stay far, far away, but if she has any reporters she hates, send them in. I believe in the south they call this a Come-to-Jesus meeting."

"You want me to call it that?" he asked, raising a plucked eyebrow.

"Sounds better than a meeting with the devil, doesn't it?"

He poked uneasily at the gnome with his pencil. "I like it here," he declared, irrelevantly.

Or not so irrelevantly if I followed the path of his thoughts. "Yeah, so do I. And no, I don't know if we're sitting on hell. I'm going with letting the EPA test the soil, okay?"

"My old pal Kaminski got his kneecaps broken the other day," Ned continued. "Sarah killed Harry. And now Ben is missing. That's three of the guys who were with me at Acme when Bergdorff went bananas. The plant manager is still gone."

Probably because he was now a perverted bull frog and with any luck, got run over by a big truck. Before he'd eaten the pink articles, Ned had been little better than his hired goon pals. These days...I got the point. Ned was afraid.

Crapola. I rubbed my brow and looked for some way of reassuring him, but really, I couldn't. It wasn't just me. Things simply happened in the Zone that didn't happen elsewhere. "I'll understand it if you need to look for a safer place to work. But everyone in the Zone likes you. No one liked your old pals. I think you're safe from us unless you pull a gun."

Ned hid his look of relief by straightening the pink handkerchief in his coat pocket. "I haven't been to the gun range in months, but I could start practicing again, if you need me to."

I opened my mouth, but nothing came out. Judging by his body language, Ned-the- former-tough-guy didn't want to commit any more violence. I could get with that. I wasn't partial to being shot at. Do unto others and all that...

I stuck the gnome under my arm and shook my head at his suggestion. This time, Ned didn't bother disguising his relief. "You get to be a good guy," I finally said, grasping a few of his fears. "I'm still learning, but I'll get there. Maybe. Meeting. Noon. Don't forget."

I left him pondering his to-do list. This was why we had to have the Zone. Yeah, we were freaks, but Ned had been a gun-wielding steroidal thug just like Kaminski and his pals, and now he was a teddy bear. Where else in this universe could that happen?

I studied the evil gnome under my arm with interest. Time for experiment number two.

Experiment number one had ended ignominiously with wailing shrieks, evil bats, and Super-heroes Milo and Tina fleeing the premises. I didn't want to go in any more tunnels, so I had to hope this next experiment would be more successful. And not quite so humiliating—for me, anyway—since I'd have to conduct it before an audience.

I admired the formerly gun-toting gnome that Tim had half-hidden under our lobby Christmas tree. This Nazi had apparently been holding out his automatic when I'd stoned him. Tim had neatly cracked off the gun and added a bowl of peppermints to the statue's outstretched arms. Then he'd painted him red and green and added a sparkly elf cap—presumably so I wouldn't notice that he'd ignored my order to leave the gnomes alone. Tim was weird, but I accepted that. He gave me some of my more creative ideas.

I carried my own personal elf across the street and up to my apartment. Concrete is heavy, and my wounded arm still ached. I set him on my counter and eyed him with suspicion. "How far do I push my luck?" I asked of no one in particular.

Milo leaped up to sniff the intruder. He tried scratching but the gnome didn't topple. Milo is not a small cat, nor a stupid one. He pushed his kitty shoulder against the concrete in an attempt to shove it over the edge. The concrete didn't budge.

"You don't like him either, right?" I asked. "What kind of fate does he deserve?"

Milo bobbed his head and jumped down, then trotted off to my bedroom. Out of curiosity, I followed him. Milo's presence really is that strong sometimes. I trusted him more than myself. Real lawyers didn't do what I was contemplating.

Milo walked across the top of my second-hand dresser. I'd broken the mirror back when Max had been appearing in it. Since I didn't like mirrors anymore, I'd left the glass as it was. I still scattered lipsticks and various cosmetics over the top. Milo swatted at a nasty red lipstick I'd picked up at a sale. The tube rolled to the floor, along with a sample bottle of blusher.

Remembering Tim's decorated elf, I grinned and claimed the red colors. "You're an artist, master."

Milo graciously dipped his head, then leaped over to my bed and curled up on the pillow, leaving me to do the dirty work.

I collected some eye shadow and other ornaments and proceeded to decorate my very own elf. Rouged lips and cheeks, purple eye shadow, blackened brows...I rubbed his styled gray hair with the green goop I once used to streak my hair for Halloween. For the grand—and I hoped—successful finale, I gathered up the spray can of pink gas I'd confiscated from Acme a few months back, threw it in my backpack along with the gnome, and headed out.

On my way down the hill, I stocked up on donuts and cookies at the minimart. I tested the heated streets but apparently snow turned them on and a dreary day didn't. The glow from the manholes had decreased substantially. Lines of people had started snaking down the alley again to the spa I'd seen going up earlier. I ought to figure out how they were advertising those things, but my to-do list already overflowed.

I liked to share the fun so I stopped and asked Cora and Sarah if they'd be interested in attending my meeting. Sarah wasn't smart enough to be suspicious and chose to stay at Chesty's. Cora, being a clever girl, said she'd be over a little later.

The Morgan building had changed substantially since I'd last visited. The Do-Gooders had set up a jolly family room in the front, complete with television, sofas, and card tables. The television was broadcasting a Russian news report and no one was watching. I could have told the DGs to save their money on electronics, but maybe the TV was someone's castoff.

There were actually kids playing a card game at the table. We had *kids* living on the harbor? So very not good. And living in a Zone building wasn't much better. Adults got to make choices. Kids didn't. They could be warped forever by the decisions of their elders.

I punched Max's button on my phone, and he answered on the second try, after a lobster plant in Maine. I hoped that was a good sign that the Zone favored me today. "Did Lance get in touch with you? I trust there've been no more exploding gas lines?"

"Yeah, the guys have set up a club in the guardhouse," he said with classic Max dryness. Apparently he'd had his morning caffeine fix and was feeling better. "The neighbors aren't happy about the parking lot of Harleys, but oddly, I feel better having them there. And Gloria seems to be gone. I owe you. And Andre," he added grudgingly.

"Have your PR people take pictures of the Harleys. You'll get the popular vote—Senator Dane employs local vets. Excellent promo. And yeah, I'm calling you for a favor. Your Do-Gooders didn't go home. They're down here turning one of Andre's buildings into a homeless shelter. I don't have a problem with that, but there are *kids* here. Kids, Max. That's just not right."

I could almost see him attempt to run his hand through Dane's gluey hair. Max hadn't wanted *me* near Acme. I knew he wouldn't want kids here.

"All right, I get it. Senator Dane lends a helping hand to the homeless," he said with a sigh of exasperation. "I'll put my staff on it and find an opening for them in shelters somewhere safer. Will you move in with me now?"

I chortled, warm and sexy, just the way he liked it. "I'm about to blow up a CEO, dude, what do you think?"

I hung up on his spluttering. I called Ned. "Send one or two gnomes down here, will you? This place needs more holiday décor."

I had plenty of time until my meeting, provided there was a meeting. The likelihood of any of my antagonists showing up because Ned had called them probably wasn't high.

I carried my backpack to the kitchen...the building now had a kitchen. Very nice. I admired the second hand cabinets and battered appliances that someone had been trying to connect. I wasn't certain how successful they'd been, and I prayed none of them involved gas.

I set the donuts and cookies down on a large trestle table. A kid instantly materialized to snatch one of the Christmas ones. I escaped before the parade started. I had intended to bribe my meeting with sweets but that was before I realized there were kids.

My arm aching from the first bullet wound, my head still not happy with yesterday's scratch, I looked for empty office space. There were people everywhere. Our vagrants had showered and been given clean clothes. Some still slept on sleeping bags in the upstairs offices. Others had rolled up their nests and gone out to forage for the day. A women's hostel had been set up on the third floor. Everyone from pregnant teens to elderly drunks gathered there.

The eager Do-Gooders were repairing bathrooms, cleaning up messes, breaking up fights. Rob Hanks sought me out to show me the library of discarded books they'd been gathering. One of the kids was curled up on an ancient beanbag chair that was popping its seams. She perused Robin Hood while munching one of my cookies. That could have been me a million years ago.

Andre found us as Rob showed me an unused storage area on the third floor, at the back of the building. The walls were lined with dilapidated shelves Rob had plans to turn into a food pantry. But for now, they'd been collecting cleaning equipment in there. It wouldn't take too much effort to make it my meeting room.

Tim arrived, bearing two more concrete statues, and huffing and puffing at the climb. He set them down on a three-legged table, carefully balancing it, and looked around. "Santa's warehouse," he declared. "The cops the district promised finally showed up this morning. They said they've been collecting toy donations. They could store them here."

"I like that," I agreed. "I don't suppose we could have Santa Claus on hand, too?" I envisioned him in Cookie Monster blue but knew that wasn't happening.

Andre relieved me of my backpack and nearly dropped it from the weight. I jerked it back. "I'm entitled to my secrets," I scolded.

He glanced at the gnomes Tim had carried in. Smart man, he knew who was in my backpack. But instead of arguing, he merely said, "I can find a Santa suit. Get one of the less intoxicated bums to wear it. And don't do anything rash until I'm back."

We only had another hour until my Come-to-Jesus meeting. Miracles could happen.

Tim and I wacked stone guns off his gnomes with hammers and carried the now-weaponless statues back downstairs. I produced a pack of markers from my backpack, set them and the gnomes in the front room, and let magic happen. Really, the Zone had nothing on me.

We returned upstairs to help the DGs clean out the storage room and brace the shelves. Hunky Lt. Schwartz and his fellow cops began arriving in their patrol cars. Schwartz only lived down here. His office was more uptown, but he could summon respect for his neighborhood. I admired the sight from the upper story windows. Cops. In the Zone. Beautiful. I watched fat Officer Leibowitz waddle hurriedly down the street to see what he was missing.

One of the guys in blue handed Leibowitz a sack full of toys to carry in, and I smiled naughtily. I seldom came down on the nice side.

I unloaded my rouged CEO gnome in the supply closet of the ladies' room. Ignoring my various wounds, I jogged back to my apartment. I found my music, an old DVD player and some DVDs left from my time with Max, and refilled my backpack. This time, Milo trotted after me. I probably ought to keep him out of the Zone, but his company was comforting. It also meant trouble was coming. Well, yeah, I was planning on that.

Back at the shelter, I plugged the DVD player into the TV in the front family room and slid in one of my favorite cowboy flicks. The Universe was still favoring me. It actually worked. Kids needed to learn about honesty and justice instead of the bloody murder and crime they see on regular television. I drew my own warped vision of justice from those old movies.

The kids happily colored their gnomes and watched shoot-'em-ups. Maybe not normal holiday fare, but we could start our own traditions.

I downloaded some Christmas songs into my tablet computer and set it up in the storage room upstairs, providing good cheer for the cop elves filling the shelves with their goodies. A couple of he-men scowled at the tinkly music, but that was okay. I was getting into the spirit and despite disaster looming on the horizon, I was feeling better already. Action, any action, was better than giving up with a whimper.

Milo took up a space behind some stuffed animals on a high shelf and went to sleep, blending nicely with the décor.

Andre arrived just as Leibowitz huffed and puffed in with the last load of toys. It was closing in on noon. I shoved Andre's Santa suit at our unjolly fat man. "Try this on. Let's see how you look."

Leibowitz started to argue but a few of his fellow officers ribbed him, and Rob Hanks—apparently enjoying the irony—led our dirty beat cop off to a dressing room.

Andre glanced around at the toy-laden shelves. Holiday music poured through my portable speakers. He angled his head and studied me in my red leather skirt and black tights. "MacNeill is not going to be swayed by sentimental crap and good legs."

"You're such a Grinch." I stood on my toes and pressed red lipstick to his cheek. "If I'm going to die, I'll go down singing."

That said, I warbled the hallelujah chorus and headed back downstairs to check on my gnomes in the front room. The kids had colored the ugly stone with red and green and black polka dots. I liked it. "Polka dots are the new Christmas," I said, nodding approval. "Next time you see Tim, tell him to help you make elf hats."

They ran off in search of Tim. Once they were out of the room, I put a plastic sack over the gnomes, pulled out my can of magic element, and squirted inside the bag. The green gas stayed contained inside the bag, and the resulting pink particles settled over the colored concrete. I had no way to know if the gas would have any effect, but I needed to try. Pink particles had presumably cured Ned of frogdom when he'd licked them. Maybe they'd made him a better person as well.

Of course, the gas had caused Bergdorff to leap out a window and others to go comatose, but I didn't think stone could inhale.

Nothing happened. Apparently the particles had to be ingested. I should have stuck to frogs.

I sighed in disappointment, but nothing ventured, nothing gained. It was almost noon, so I checked out the big front window. Two limos pulled up behind each other. Conspicuous consumption in the face of all this poverty was cruel, if not evil. It would serve them right if their tires melted.

The green gas in the bags had already dissipated. I yanked the plastic off the stone gnomes and jogged back upstairs to the storage room, working off the cookies I'd snatched. Upstairs, I smiled in delight at Leibowitz in his Santa gear. The beard was pretty ratty, and he wore it so I could see the string, but his beady eyes were so much more interesting nearly buried in snowy eyebrows. "Wait right here," I ordered.

I rushed off to the ladies' room, bagged my cosmetically enhanced CEO elf, and gave him a coat of chemical spray. Nothing happened here either except the can ran out of spray and the sparkly pink gave his red cheeks and green locks a cheery look. I tossed the can and bag in my backpack, lifted Graham Young and hauled him back to Santa's playroom.

"Sit," I told Leibowitz, pointing at a chair I'd hauled in earlier. "Let's see how you look with a kid on your lap."

He dropped his heavy weight on a derelict upholstered rocker. I added painted Graham to his lap and stepped back to admire the effect. "I like it." I took out my smart toy and snapped a photo.

Rob did the same. Happy to sit still for a while, Leibowitz mugged for the camera, not even looking at the ridiculous statue in his lap.

My luck was still holding. Dr. Abdul Bakir arrived first, with his entourage from Medical Science Inc.

Twenty-five

MSI'S good doctor scanned the toy room and Santa with vague disinterest. His gaze came back to rest on me and Andre. I heard Milo growl from the shelf, but he's protective. I had no reason to believe Bakir was evil. I couldn't even be certain he was guilty of more than cluelessness. I couldn't evaporate him just because I didn't like wealthy corporate doctors who thought they were God. That would make me worse than them.

I wondered if a lobotomy would help me get over my over-developed conscience.

The guys from the EPA and OSHA arrived right on Bakir's heels. Former senator MacNeill finally dragged himself out of his limo, still nattering on his phone, and found his way up to our crowded enclave. Paddy didn't arrive with him, but showed up a few minutes after my noon deadline. Leibowitz had fallen asleep in the corner and was snoring, with Graham Young on his lap. No one paid Santa any attention.

Cora slipped in with another batch of cookies. I gestured at the three-legged table. She set them out, then did her best to disappear into a dark corner. I was happy to have a friend to lend support while I made an ass of myself.

"Sorry for the accommodations, gentlemen, but this time, I thought you needed to see the place you're condemning." I could tell they weren't impressed. Rightfully, so, probably. "As long as you're all down here in the Zone, I want you to take time to have a good look at the harbor where the EPA is currently dredging out the polluted ground and hauling it off to who-knows-where. I particularly want you OSHA fellows to note the ambulances sitting on Ground Zero, waiting for the bulldozer drivers to topple over from toxic fumes."

Protests broke out around the room. Leibowitz ripped a loud snore, intruding on the anger. In the momentary, startled silence, I waved my hand for their attention. "You can make your own decisions after you look. I'm not an engineer or a safety inspector. Those are your chores. What I want you to understand is that you're ten years too late to save the Zone, and that this is no place for a medical facility."

I heard shouts in the street, followed by chants, and I sighed. As

Bakir began preaching about the wonders of modern science and the Great Medical Experiment, I checked out the window. The storage room overlooked an alley, not the street, but I spotted a familiar reporter scanning the back of the building below. Jane had called the media. This particular reporter was a sexist pig with reason to hold a grudge against me.

The chanting was probably Katerina's work. Andre would have told her about the meeting. Since there was no elevator, and she wasn't up to climbing stairs yet, I hadn't called on her. I lifted a quizzical eyebrow in Andre's direction. He smirked.

So the street out front was probably filled with media and protestors. Great. I would have to try not to blow up anything. With kids in the house, that had to be a priority anyway.

While Bakir prosed on, I tried visualizing Graham Young back to life. But I wasn't angry, and justice had been served when I'd stoned him.

How could I prove to these men of science that the Zone was warped and they needed to stay away? If tourists thought talking gargoyles were toys, it would take some convincing to persuade these pragmatists that they'd fallen through a rabbit hole.

I reached back to Milo's shelf, scratched behind his ear, and tried not to yawn at the eager doctor's speech. Milo offered a kitty snort, waited until I'd stepped out of his path, positioned himself, and leapt—on top of Bakir's head.

That shut up the verbose medical man. While Bakir struggled with his cat fur hat, I held up a hand again. "Gentlemen, I'm not disagreeing that medical science is a wonderful thing. I'm telling you that the Zone isn't where your clinic belongs, and Acme isn't a good partner. Senator MacNeill..." I smirked at him. "So good to see you here today. Would you kindly tell these gentlemen that Acme has had one scientist commit suicide, another who attempted to murder one of your stockholders, then disappeared, a squadron of security guards vanish, and most recently, a gas explosion that has turned untold numbers of Zone inhabitants comatose?"

The room fell oddly silent. Milo had gone to ground and found a position beside our sleeping Santa. The OSHA guys looked a little surprised at my announcement that Acme had accidents. Gee, ya'd think no one had told them.

MacNeill smiled genially. "Miss Clancy misunderstands. We had a small boiler problem a few months back, nothing to worry about. You know how these eccentric types are though. Bergdorff was convinced his experiment was ruined. The police report is on file."

Chants of "Hell, no, we won't go," filtered through the silence. The vagrant vets was my bet. I waited to see if I was the only one who might question the obvious.

"Comatose?" OSHA asked.

Yay for the good guys!

Paddy snorted and leaned against the cookie table. It wobbled. He crossed his arms and glared at me as if it was my fault. Paddy is a smart man.

"I'm the stockholder Ferguson tried to murder," he said before MacNeill could find a silver-tongued explanation. "Acme had a few personnel problems that have been corrected. The X-element with which we're experimenting has a great deal of scientific and medical potential. It has cured cancer. Now that Acme is under new management, we've instituted tighter safety measures."

"Too late for the Zone," I argued. "We're damaged, and bringing in innocents unaccustomed to the chemical environment will only cause more harm than good. You can build your medical facility elsewhere. I don't know how you dare expose anyone else to your dangerous fumes and spills. If anyone ought to be condemned, it's Acme. Take out the plant that caused the problem in the first place."

"We did that," both OSHA and EPA guys protested. "The old plant on the harbor was unsafe. The new one has been thoroughly inspected."

"Oh, so you know about the underground labs?" I asked with glee.

By their blank looks and Paddy's glare, I assumed they didn't. Talking to authority was almost as entertaining as egging a provost's office.

"Look, the little lady is trying to protect her turf. That's understandable," MacNeill said reassuringly.

Okay, red-ragey began to boil. *Little lady*, indeed! Andre smacked the top of my head as if he could see the steam emerging. He knew me a little too well.

"But we've agreed to pay a fair price for the property," MacNeill continued, obliviously revealing to Andre that it wasn't the medical facility buying him out. "We can make arrangements for the residents—"

"Throw the bastards out!" screamed a shrill rough voice from our snoring Santa's corner.

All heads swerved to Santa's lap. A full-sized Graham Young, CEO of Medical Science Inc, green hair, red lipstick and all, tumbled on the floor as Leibowitz woke and jerked with shock.

Looking a bit pale but unstoned, Young sat up, livid with rage and painted like a cartoon. He pounded his fists on the rough wood floor, then appeared startled at discovering he was in a storage room. Recovering, he glared at his shocked and staring audience. "What the *hell* are you people doing in here? Don't you know the bulldozers are coming?"

I wondered if I'd prevented him from wrecking the town last week—followed by one of those "oops, we got ahead of schedule" apologies that corporations often made after the destruction was done.

While I tried to keep a lid on my fury, everyone else gawked at the rouged ruin of a man. You might say that Young hadn't weathered well on my roof. His clothes were worse for wear and looked as shabby as if he'd slept in them—outdoors. The pigeon poop was a bit of a giveaway. His green hair was filthy and lank. And well, the red just didn't flatter his cheekbones. Pink particles from my gas canister fell off his shoulders like dandruff.

Paddy and Andre recovered first and had the sense to glare at me. The others simply watched in awe. Young stood up, ranting and raving when no one jumped at his orders. Catching sight of me, he lumbered in my direction, shaking his fist.

Milo slipped between Young's legs, causing him to stumble before he could swing. That brought me abruptly back to reality. I put the table between me and the angry elf.

Making certain my cat had escaped to high ground, I rapped the table with my knuckles to get their attention. "*This*, gentlemen," I announced, gesturing at our unbalanced CEO, "is why you don't want to introduce innocents to the Zone."

I was wicked with glee and wondering how I could zap more statues. Maybe I could start a parade. I had absolutely no idea what I'd done—other than to paint the scene with explicitness to a few engineering types who lacked imagination.

MacNeill caught the reeling gnome by the shoulders and shoved him to a chair. Reality must have been setting in for Young, too. After nearly toppling from the chair, he held a hand to his icky hair and studied his filthy clothes with horror.

"The pollution turns sane men mad," Andre said solemnly,

distracting from the comedy routine. "We can't predict how long it takes. Most of us living here have been inoculated against the worst of it, but it's not safe to bring in anyone else. You'd be wise to go back to forgetting our existence."

I needed a hypnotist to enforce that warning. *You are getting very sleepy, you are forgetting we exist...*

Perfectly sane scientists stared in horror at the crumpled CEO who had moments ago been a stone toy in Santa's lap. They probably didn't know if Graham was mad or they were. I knew that feeling.

Childish shouts of excitement tinged with fear and shock echoed up from the front room, reminding me that I'd gassed two other statues. Oops.

I turned to head downstairs when a roar rattled the windows and rumbled the foundation. Milo dashed between my legs, and I took off after him. The floor was still shaking beneath my feet, and screams echoed from inside and out, upstairs and down.

I raced for the children in the front room first. The two polka-dotted Nazis were flat on the floor with terrified kids scrambling all over them. The thugs tried to struggle to their knees while the kids used them for security from whatever had shaken the building. The former gnomes looked too stunned to be dangerous. They certainly hadn't rattled any foundations.

I glanced out the big plate window to a scene of chaos.

Sign-toting vagrants and Do-Gooders were shouting, running, and staring at a mushroom cloud by the harbor. In shock, I gazed a few seconds too long before registering that the cloud was steam, not a nuclear explosion. Gloria might be gone, but the hole she'd vented in the veil between dimensions had just ruptured.

"Get the kids out the back," I ordered the few adults who had run into the room. "Take them to high ground, as far from the harbor as possible." *Before any gas or polluted steam spread* went unsaid.

Leibowitz in his Santa suit lumbered downstairs, took one look out the window, and fled for the back door. At the sight of Santa, the crying immediately stopped. Stunned, the kids stared, then in excitement, ran after the man in the red suit as if he were the Pied Piper. The adults raced after them. Good deal. Cowardice had its purpose.

Andre had his phone out before he even set foot in the room. One look out the window, and he was shouting orders into the cell. Across the street, the patrons of Chesty's were fleeing for their cars. They were closer to the harbor and could probably feel the heat.

The gargoyles didn't shriek as they had the last time a gas cloud had enveloped us. Maybe they were only attuned to Acme. The steam was coming from the area of the former rusted-out plant on the water, not the new, EPA-approved, one to the north.

Graham Young stumbled in. At sight of his colorfully inked comrades on the floor, he started raving and ranting again. Fortunately, none of them carried guns or we'd have wholesale mayhem. I dodged as the painted demon CEO lunged in my direction.

Paddy entered and caught Young in a headlock before a brawl could ensue. Cheers for the home team!

The other shocked and grim figures of authority stumbled down to see what the excitement was about. Like good scientists, they studied the situation from a distance. Andre, Cora, and I knew better than to stand still while the harbor boiled.

My friends ran out the back, shouting into their phones, setting up phone trees, and evacuating buildings. I followed Milo, the trouble-stalking cat, out the front door.

I didn't really think Paddy could hold back a raving Young and his two polka-dotted fascists if they recovered enough of their senses to fight back, but without weapons, they couldn't cause too much harm. As I dashed after Milo down an alley next to Chesty's, I met Sarah staring at the chaos of fleeing figures in the wasteland along the water.

"Protect people, remember?" I shouted at her. "Not kill them. Run up and see if Mrs. Bodine and the others are okay."

I didn't think steam should cover the area as the gas had, but keeping Sarah from turning into a freaking chimp sounded like a good idea. She nodded and took off running. Good girl.

Bad cat. Milo dashed between momentarily paralyzed trash bins, leaped over the fallen chain link fence, and headed for the last remaining tent spa.

The blue blob was emerging from the tent. It stooped to pat Milo. I screeched to a halt and tried to take stock of the situation before I got myself into real trouble. I had to keep reminding myself that I was a lawyer, not Super Tina.

Men in bulldozers were intelligently retreating to the far end of the wasteland, leaving the geyser of steam alone. It didn't seem to be spreading, but I could hear it pop and sizzle as it hit the cold air. I didn't smell gas, but the real poisonous stuff was scentless.

The tourists who had been lined up for the spa simply stood there and gaped as if they were watching Old Faithful. Maybe the steam was that safe. Maybe it wasn't. I didn't plan on testing it to find out.

The tourists didn't seem to notice the blue blob, or thought he was part of the fantasy park for all I knew. I eased in his direction. He looked up, saw me coming, and returned to the tent. Milo sat outside, patiently waiting for me.

I'd forgotten the demented frogs and lingered out in the open too long. Bullets buzzed over my head, tearing into the tent canvas. I cursed and dove for Milo.

Tourists shrieked at the automatic gunfire. Smart ones hit the ground. The rest scattered. I had no idea which direction was best, so I rolled with my cat into the tent and out of sight. More bullets whizzed through the canvas, lower this time. I jerked and screamed as one seared my thigh.

Tents were obviously not good cover. Biting my tongue against the throbbing agony of the wound in my leg, I crawled—dragging myself more on one knee than the other—toward the curtain in back that I hoped held a sturdy hot tub.

I counted frogs in my head. After Sarah had killed one, there had been three left that I knew about. Kaminski was supposed to be laid up with a busted kneecap, and another one ought to be in the harbor, but there was at least one more roaming free.

Damning the thugs hadn't helped without bulldozer persuasion, but I flung a curse in the gunman's direction now, just in case it made a difference. "Damn you rotten frogs to hell!" I shouted. Another hail of bullets rang over my head in response.

Behind the curtain, a large round tub steamed. Whoever had been collecting money had abandoned his ticket table. The dressing booth was open with no one cowering inside. I wondered if the tub would protect me if I could get into it.

Milo sniffed around the bottom of the tub, but like most cats, he avoided the water. I didn't want my cat shot any more than myself.

Where had the blue blob gone? Somewhere safer?

When had my normal world gone from law books to blue blobs?

The ground rumbled again. More predictable screaming. Leg spilling blood and hurting like hell, I belly crawled behind the tub, to lift up the back of the tent and peer out. The steam geyser was impressively tall, forming vapor clouds that floated over the water. Cracks had begun to spread through the harbor mud from the cloud's source near the rusted-out chimneys of the old plant. Even as I watched, one stack bent, crumpled, and toppled in heaps of dust and ash, spraying the area with who-knew-what toxic waste.

I was glad the DGs had moved the vagrants to safer ground.

Milo stuck his head outside the canvas but retreated, returning to sniffing the tub. I'd quit calling him a bobcat and call him dawg shortly.

I didn't see the blue blob anywhere on the bleak muddy terrain between the tent and the water. Where had it gone and could I go too?

A *pow* like a bomb exploding shook the ground again, and the geyser abruptly spewed muddy, rust-colored water. A hail of bullets rained over my head just as I was considering grabbing my cat and running.

Before I could choose between demented landscape or guns, the ground cracked under me, and I slid in.

Twenty-six

I BLACKED out—again.

When I woke up, I was lying in dark nothingness—again.

Shades of Hell's Mansion haunted me. I couldn't see my hand in front of my face, provided I had hand or face. If I was in hell alone, I would freak, so I was aiming for reality. I dug my fingers into dirt I could crumble. Real.

The agony of my bullet-riddled thigh proved I had a body this time.

With that wake-up call, I breathed deeper. While waiting for my wildly racing pulse to slow, I clinically assessed the state of my health, then studied the ceiling in hopes of finding the rabbit hole I'd fallen through. Given the chaos I'd created, I prayed I'd simply crashed through cracking dirt and not a portal to hell.

I'd had a lot of hard experience and knew freaking wasn't a good choice. So I concentrated on sensations. I could hear water dripping. That seemed like a good sign. Hell wouldn't have water, would it?

My head hurt as if someone had coshed my skull with a steel bar. Or a rock. My back was definitely lying on rocks. I gingerly scooted my hip off a sharp one and let the shooting pain in my leg subside before moving again.

I couldn't hear or see Milo. Anxiously, I listened, but no kitty protests. I prayed he'd had the claws to stay above ground.

I lifted my hand and patted my face. I could feel skin. That seemed pretty promising too. If I was real, I could climb out of here.

A wailing shriek echoed off the stone walls around me. *Crap, crap, frigging crap*...I was down here with the Force. I expected red-eyed bats any minute.

Panicking, I sat up fast, and almost crumpled over in pain. Grabbing my leg, I carefully scooted backward and away from the direction of the ghostly wail.

My back hit a wall. I still couldn't see a thing. I patted around, discovering loose dirt and hot rocks, damned *hot* rocks. Hot enough to make a sauna. I groped around them anyway, burning my fingers but looking for a purchase upward—not that I could see any gaps above my head. I just knew that if I fell *down*, I needed to go *up* to escape.

My heart beat like a timpani again. I was stronger and less afraid when I had Max or Andre at my side. On my own, I wanted to shout in terror and weep, except I couldn't hear anything from above, and if I couldn't hear them, they wouldn't hear me. Besides I had this vague notion that loud noises might shake loose more debris.

Painfully, I pulled myself upright. I felt bruised and shaken, but I seemed to have all my body parts. Definitely not hell, I reassured myself, just underground somewhere.

Leaning my torso against a wall of dirt, I reached as high as I could but couldn't feel a ceiling. I groped along the wall on my right but it was blocked by that barrier of hot rock. Holding my right hand to the hot wall and reaching out with the left, I couldn't touch anything. I tapped my foot as far as I could reach without releasing the wall. The floor seemed solid. I just wasn't brave enough to let go.

It made sense that I must be directly below the place I'd fallen in, so I should try to climb back out where I knew there had to be an opening. Unfortunately, I saw no light above me, and I'm no rock climber. Even if I were, I'd need gloves to manage the rocks without third degree burns. I groped about for handholds but clumps of dirt fell off in my fingers.

If the ground shook again, I could be buried alive.

I tried to test for a slope under my feet but couldn't determine any. I might have stayed there for days, paralyzed in terror, except I caught a glimpse of Cookie Monster blue down the tunnel or whatever this was.

"Help?" I tentatively called, both hands now clinging to the wall at my back.

The blue hesitated.

"How do I get out?" I asked, praying I wasn't hallucinating. I was starting to hate irony.

You see me?

I didn't hear the words with my ears so much as inside my head. Wicked weird.

"Yes, you're blue. I followed you here," I said aloud, not knowing if mind-speak worked for me.

No one else sees me. I'm not really real.

"Okay, then how are you talking to me?" This was more entertaining than shivering in terror or dodging bullets. Even my leg quit shaking.

My own personal hallucination seemed to ponder my question.

I hear Others, it said slowly. *I learned your words. They are crude and not very effective. I am...projecting...those words that seem to relate to what you're asking.*

Okay, I must have hit my head when I went down. Was I dreaming? I shivered and remembered Andre's dream world, the one he said was another dimension beyond our own. Had I crossed the veil to where our comatose patients had once gone? No one had mentioned dirt tunnels or talking blue doughboys.

"Can you lead me out of here?" I asked.

If I could do that, I would leave. This is not a happy place.

I'd second that. At least, the Force had stopped wailing. "I saw you above ground. How did you do that?"

More hesitation. *I project images, I think. I try so very hard to see what is happening outside this dark wall.*

"The blue blob is just an image?" I asked warily. "That's not you?"

Blue blob? I thought I heard amusement, but that could just be me projecting.

"That's what I'm looking at right now—blue with sort of a round head and sort of a torso and sort of appendages. But pretty formless otherwise."

I am not very good at making myself look like you. Blue is this color? I like it. Sometimes, the bowl above is that color.

The bowl above? The *sky*. This was freaky. I swallowed and tried to wake myself up, but I was still feeling hot rocks and smelling...ozone. Could I hope this was all natural and not the dimensions caving in?

This was the polluted Zone, and I was talking to a blue blob. Forget natural.

"The sky isn't quite that color. How are you seeing it if you're trapped down here?"

The projection—the blue blob—helps me see outside. And the other things, the... wires... and pipes, I think you call them. They are not quite satisfactory but better than dark. I have only just learned to make this form. It is very hard.

"You speak well, so you must hear things well?"

Yes. Man has run pipes and wires, and I can hear through them better than I can see. There have been many pipes lately.

Pipes. That might be promising, if I wasn't crazy. "Can you show me a pipe?"

They are not safe, it said sadly. *The...element...that confines me is meant to imprison. The heat is corroding the element. It is mixing with your chemicals and earth. The pipes are taking these things away. This weakens my prison, for which I am... grateful. Is that the right word? But the pipes rattle and explode with gas. I cannot think this is safe for you.*

Pipes, gas, explode...Magic gas clouds, steaming geysers, chemical floods. Saunas. My brain was still working. It calculated likelihoods and admired the extent of my subconscious if I was dreaming up these explanations.

"What are you?" I had to ask.

More hesitation. The blue blob became a little less clear, and I got scared again. I kind of needed someone to talk to besides my head. I eased a little closer in its direction.

I am dangerous on my own world.

Again, I detected—or injected—a note of sadness to its thoughts.

"Dangerous?" I inquired warily.

I ask questions. I am curious. I play instead of work. I like pretty blues. This is all very bad where I come from.

I tried not to snort. "Yeah, they're bad here, too, but not dangerous. Not usually." A misfit in the Zone, how appropriate. "Where is your world?"

This time, it didn't speak but sent me images of a cloudy planet orbiting an orange sun. I'm not an astronomer. I hadn't a clue. I just knew it didn't look like Earth. No rings, so it didn't look like Saturn either. "How did you get here?"

Another image, this time of a ball of rock hurtling through space, approaching a planet that did look like the Earth I'd seen from space images. I winced at the impact as it hit rock and drove deep into the planet's core.

A meteorite. This thing had landed here in a meteorite, maybe back during the Jurassic for all I knew. Boy, this was one fancy dream. I could see Andre's fascination with other dimensions. Where else could I talk to a space alien? It wasn't all that strange to someone who had talked to an invisible grandmother through her shape-shifting chimp friend. Call me open-minded.

If this was my subconscious at work, I hoped to find clues in my weird dream that would help me get back to my world—kind of like Andre brought back knowledge of the future.

"I don't suppose there's any way I can release you from that rock?" I asked uncertainly. I really needed a scientist with me in this dream.

It erodes slowly, it said with a fatalistic tone. *I am able to do more now that the imprisoning element is being taken away.*

Siphoned off, sucked up, pumped into Acme's tanks—an element from outer space that could potentially cure cancer. Or bring hell closer.

I started easing along the wall, testing the ground, trying to get closer to the blue thing. Maybe there were pipes or cracks or something I could use to see the outside world. I didn't want to believe I was in hell. This was too real. My previous encounters had been ephemeral.

The rocks were definitely hot. I wish I'd run out of the office wearing my leather bike gloves.

Was I hearing chanting? Yells of protest? I halted and looked around some more, but I couldn't see anything. "Any ideas on how I can get back to my world?"

Must you go back? I like having company.

"Yeah, so do I, but my friends will worry. Did you have friends in your world?" I repeated my earlier search, running my hands up the walls to look for holds for climbing.

We do not have friends as you see them. We work. We produce. We rest. We work again.

"That doesn't sound very jolly. I'd be dangerous there too."

A sliver of blue neon suddenly illuminated the far wall. Gasping, I applied my back and hands to the wall and studied the opposite side of what had to be a tunnel. Or an old sewer.

I will make it pretty here for you, the voice offered generously.

Well, now I knew the source of the Zone's blue neon. Blob was decorating his world.

"Thank you, but I really need to go home or my cat will starve." Not likely, Milo was too smart to starve, but that was the best excuse I could conjure. It wasn't as if I was supporting a passel of kiddies or a dying mother or anything.

The freaky wail finally kicked in again. The shriek bounced off the tunnel walls, and the blue blob abruptly vanished. I couldn't blame him.

I bit my tongue to keep from screaming in accompaniment. I was glad to have the pale light so I could duck if the bats returned. Goose bumps dotted my arms beneath my coat, and my internal organs started to shiver. Probably not a good reaction considering the heat of this place. I tried to remember first aid courses on shock and blood loss. I could feel wetness dribbling down my leg.

"What is that noise?" I asked in a voice I hoped didn't sound terrified.

My friendly captor didn't reply instantly, and when he did, he seemed uncertain. *I do not know exactly. There are...beings...in another world close to yours. They are not happy. Some are very...angry. I do not like that place and do not go there.*

"Sensible," I concurred. Did he just confirm the existence of hell?

I couldn't keep calling the voice "it." He seemed male to me— young and immature, like Tim. Although I suppose space aliens might not have gender or even age for all I knew. I was *projecting*, giving a space alien Tim's familiar character.

The blue light stopped near the wall where I'd fallen through. I couldn't quite tell if the wall was a landslide of debris from my fall or if it had been there a while. I heard no sounds of frantic digging. No bulldozers.

Whereas, if I crept closer to where I'd seen the blue blob last, I thought I could hear voices. I edged along the wall, terrified the ground would give out from under me again. I should have studied more science. My mother had talked incessantly about the dangers of fracking and geothermal energy from radiation and other underground power, but I'd mostly tuned her out. I just had a notion that if the water and heat were being sucked from underground, that the dirt here could destabilize.

"Do you know who I mean when I talk about Andre?" I asked, just to hear the sound of my voice as I eased down the tunnel, listening.

It is very hard to distinguish one of you from the other, but I know you call each other by names. I have heard of Andre.

"Andre can see your blue form. If you can send it up there, maybe he'll follow you down too. You'll like talking with him." Just call me a silver-tongued devil.

Interesting. I am very tired. I will try to send the projection above for a brief period. Then, it is rest time.

We work, we produce, we rest, yeah, I got it. "Do you have a name?" I asked, hoping to keep him talking.

We do not have names. We just are.

I could sense his departure. I closed my eyes and sent a prayer to Saturn. Being buried alive didn't seem like a fair ending. I should have at least taken out a few more villains before I died.

If only I knew who the villain was in this picture, I could damn him and wish Saturn to get me out of here.

The temptation was strong to damn Graham Young and then wish for escape, but he wasn't any more evil than most of corporate culture as far as I was aware. And the evidence seemed to point at MacNeill more than Young on the eminent domain. Still, greed didn't make him guilty of crime much less evil.

Maybe I should curse my absurdly sensitive conscience.

One cautious, painful step at a time, I eased down the tunnel. Remembering escaping from beneath Hell's Mansion through sheer terror, I tried visualizing myself safely above ground. Nothing. I tried cursing Gloria again. Still nothing.

Maybe I needed to be more specific. I tried visualizing a hole above me. No light appeared. I pictured Andre digging at the rubble in the tent with shovels and backhoes. Didn't hear a sound.

I was running out of ideas in the face of failure.

The only thing that kept me moving away from the place where I'd entered was the tug of voices. I really needed to know that someone was looking for me.

The hideous shriek wailed louder. An enormous bat flew out of nowhere. And the floor fell out from under me. Again.

Twenty-seven

THE dirt carried me deeper into the earth on an avalanche of debris. Admittedly, I freaked. I cursed and tried to scramble up the slide while it was sliding. My wounded leg screamed in agony.

I really needed a villain to vent my rage on, but I only had myself. I was sort of avoiding damning myself. Being buried alive was probably better than eternal damnation. Probably. I hadn't reached maximum freak-out yet.

Visualization was safer...but I'd already proved that once I did it on someone, it didn't work again. So I'd resist visualizing myself out of this mess until I had no choice.

The air in this lower level was worse than outside, far worse. Sulfurous fumes gagged me, but I had to breathe. I remembered tales of miners dying from toxic gas below the earth. Mines couldn't be much more toxic than this polluted waste-ground I was buried under.

"Are you still there?" I called to my blue friend.

No answer. Did that mean he was resting? Or couldn't hear me?

I was alone, breathing toxic gas, and buried under the Zone. And now I couldn't hear anyone—not even the shriek.

I wanted to weep, but I was too frightened, too tired, and too angry. "All right, Saturn, what do I do now?"

Saturn, as always, didn't answer. "Themis, can you hear me? Want to send some help, please?"

Nothing. That was the rotten part of this blasted Saturn's Daughter job—I was on my own. If I knew where to turn in my badge, I would—or cut out the tattoo, which was all I had that resembled officialdom.

I dug my boot into the first layer of the slide and reached above me, burrowing my fingers into the loose dirt. It wasn't much of a handhold, but I could lean against the slanted fall of loose debris and lift the other leg to scoop a foothold for the other boot. It hurt, but not quite as much as I expected.

I didn't know what good it would do to reach the tunnel I'd just fallen out of, but the blue lights had been friendlier, and I'd heard voices up there. Down here was just nasty dangerous.

Of course, up there had been bats and wailing shrieks, but compared to sulfurous fumes, they didn't seem so bad any more.

By the third boot hold, I thought I could make out the weird blue glow above. That's when the loose gravel gave way, and I fell backward, hitting the cement below.

Cement, I thought groggily, before passing out.

"Clancy?"

I groaned and tried to wake, but my head pounded as if someone was beating sledgehammers on it. Multiple sledgehammers.

"Clancy, you'd better be down here or I'll put up a memorial saying *She gave her all and it wasn't much.*"

"Andre?" I rubbed dirt off my eyes and rubbed my sleeve over my nose. I must have been buried under an inch of crud.

"What the crap have you done now?" he asked grumpily.

"Dug a hole to hell?" I asked tentatively, still smelling sulfur and not entirely clear what had just happened. But I certainly wasn't cold. "Where are you and can you get me out?"

"Don't know. Still not seeing you." Andre's voice came closer.

"You're getting warmer," I said idiotically, leaning my head back against my rock pillow and staring upward, remembering something about a tunnel up there.

And then, Andre's *essence* was there. I frowned, trying to figure out how I knew that. I waved my arms around, but I couldn't feel him. "I can sense you, I think, but I can't see a blamed thing."

"I'm on the other side of the veil." His voice was right beside me. "I know you're there somewhere but I'm not seeing you yet."

"Oh swell," I muttered, wondering if I should sit up but lacking the energy. "Gives new meaning to the blind leading the blind."

"I'm not into philosophy. We need you out of there. They just threw Graham Young into the loony bin. His fascist idiots found a new gun supply, and they're shooting anything that crosses their path. Stoning them was probably not a good move."

"Nah, gassing and waking them up was the bad idea. I'd hoped stoning had taught them a lesson." I sighed. How did one learn what was possible without experimentation?

"Gassing them?"

I could hear him near my ear and had a sense that he was lying beside me. I waved my hand around and thought I brushed against...essence. "I could hold your hand when we were under Hell's

Mansion. Why can't I feel you now?"

"You're avoiding the question, Clancy. You gassed the gnomes?"

I could swear I felt his hand brushing dirt off my face. "Can you see me?" I demanded. "I can feel you now."

He chuckled low and sexy in my ear. "I found you. You gonna stop me from copping a feel?"

"Andre, you obnoxious twerp..." I tried smacking the hand toying with my chest but naturally, I didn't connect with anything.

"Am I making you mad enough yet, Clancy? Want to bounce us back upstairs?"

I swear, his hand parted my shirt buttons and slid beneath my bra. My nipples tightened just thinking about it. Except I was in the flesh this time, and he wasn't, so it was probably just my imagination.

"I tried getting mad. It didn't work. I need a bulldozer. And if you don't stop that, you're gonna lose an arm once they dig me out. Are you comatose again? Hitting the drugs?" That's one of the ways he slipped out of his body and into the ether—drugs. Exhaustion and emotional overload was another. And apparently being slammed by the Force in Max's kitchen. Over-achiever was our landlord.

Invisible kisses played along my ear and jaw and my hair practically stood on end. Even invisible, Andre was electrifying.

"I had a bulldozer. I was digging my way down to you when I think one of the thugs shot me," he admitted. "I'm probably comatose. Or the bulldozer ran over me and I'm dead. Nothing better to do here than to explore tunnels. And you, now."

I could almost feel his leer as he stroked my breasts to attention. I thought he planted a kiss along my jaw, then nibbled a nipple, but it was all sensation. Good sensation. Forget the bleeding leg. I wanted more. He'd been operating a bulldozer? To find me? I wish I'd seen that.

"Not quite as good as the real thing," he said with regret, caressing my breast. "If I get you out of here, will you go to bed with me?"

"Andre, you're a dirty low-down ratfink pig, and if you don't stop that, I'll damn you to perdition along with Dane." I didn't mean it, of course. His kisses and invisible hands were distracting me very nicely. He'd revved my hormones nearly as well as Max had.

"Not what your body is saying, sweetheart, but go ahead, get mad. Let off some steam. Maybe you'll move dirt."

I groaned as he cupped my breast and played erotic games.

"Maybe this is why monks are celibate," I muttered.

"Makes them more powerful when they pray?" Andre asked in amusement. "I'm all for that. Let's experiment."

He ran his invisible hand up my red leather skirt and found the elastic of my tights. I nearly rose off the rocks.

"Get mad, Tina," he whispered. "I don't think it matters if I can't pry off your clothes. I don't think clothes matter when I'm like this. I just need to touch you, and you'll let me in."

He did—he touched between my legs, and I did—I opened for him. Next thing I knew, the damned man was inside me somehow, rocking my socks, and the ground beneath us was shaking so hard, dirt fell on my face. The earth quaked. Literally.

I screamed in release, heard Andre's muttered moan of half shock, half pleasure as he achieved some kind of visceral orgasm, and then the sky fell. Dirt plumed everywhere, coating my face and clothes.

Stunned, I couldn't move, although no heavy weight pressed against me. I thought I felt Andre still inside me, but not as intense as before. And then he was gone, I was alone, and there was a great gaping hole in the ceiling on my right. I could see the blue bowl of the sky far, far above.

The second greatest orgasm of my life, and this time I was buried beneath the Zone. Crap. Did I only get laid when I was in deep doo-doo?

Dirt and gravel trickled from the ceiling, covering me with fine dust, but not so much that I couldn't struggle to a sitting position.

"This has gotta stop," I muttered under my breath, trying to shake the addled languor of great sex so I could return to reality. Other people got knocked unconscious and had concussions. I had paranormal wet dreams.

I was so shaken that I just buried my head in my hands and didn't attempt to find a way out of the hole that sex had opened. I'm sure there was a metaphor in there. The polluted air made me groggy, but I thought I detected a harbor stench now that I had a vent.

Had I dreamed the Cookie Monster Space Alien too?

Ultimately, the cops and firemen used heavy equipment to lower a line down the hole, and Schwartz swung in to haul me out. I snuggled against his rock hard body and clung to reality.

He dumped me unceremoniously on a canvas spread across the polluted mud. People crowded around as Schwartz unhooked himself from the line. I wasn't sure my head was fully recognizing faces yet. I picked out Cora and Tim in the crowd but not Andre.

Medics were on hand. I think I told them to get their fucking fingers out of my face. I pushed up when they started waving needles at me. I'd had more than my fair share of hospitals and had no intention of ever seeing the inside of another.

They examined my wounded thigh and puzzled over the scratch that had made such a bloody mess of my clothes. I didn't have the brain cells to puzzle over the lack of pain. I just wanted everyone to leave me alone. I wanted Andre. Where was he?

An idiot journalist shoved a microphone in my direction and risked eternal damnation. I recovered enough of my senses to stop my imprecation just in time. "I need to get out of here," I muttered.

"You need to go into the hospital for observation," a worried young medic argued. "There are dangerous fumes down there."

"Tell me about it." Fumes that made me dream about Andre had to be dangerous. "Where's Andre?" I asked, grabbing Schwartz's arm and hauling myself to my feet.

A bulldozer idled nearby. The tent I'd hidden in was now dust. There was a damned big hole where it used to be. Andre had dug half the harbor trying to reach me? Where was he now?

My head spun a bit once I was upright, so it took me a moment to realize no one had answered my question.

Once I did, my heart sank. I glanced at Cora. She had her garter snake out, writhing and frightening the news crews into standing back. They needed to learn the difference between harmless and poisonous reptiles, but I wasn't in the mood for enlightening them. Cora's expression told me I wouldn't like the answer to my question.

"Take me to Andre," I insisted. "Right now."

Medics protested. Reporters yelled questions. Tourists made helpful suggestions. Cops tried to hold back the crowd. I just hoped they were holding back lunatic gnomes as well, because I was starting to understand that Andre's visit hadn't been a dream.

Schwartz and Cora took my arms and elbowed their way through the masses. Night had descended while I was down under. Outside the jury-rigged spotlights over the tent, I caught a glimpse of the dark harbor and saw no steaming geysers, no blue blobs, and no gnomes with guns in hand. And no Andre.

We stumbled through the demolished fence and up the alley. Ernesto opened the back door of Chesty's, and the delicious aromas of marinara and garlic bread emanated from the kitchen. My stomach rumbled. Judging from the darkness, I'd missed half a day and several meals.

Ernesto lifted a hand in greeting, saw the crowd of tourists and reporters following us, and gestured for someone in the kitchen.

Sarah sauntered out, her Godiva hair barely concealing her pointy breasts. She waved a sign advertising free garlic bread.

The crowd behind us wavered. Schwartz chuckled and practically lifted me off my boots to hurry me past Chesty's back door and the aromas of dinner.

"Let's scoot before the mob knows what hit them." He steered us down the next alley, behind a protective Dumpster, out of sight of the masses.

We took the back way home. I wasn't too steady on my feet, but Cora and Schwartz were strong. And determined. I knew something was wrong.

I didn't know if I had the strength to deal with it.

They didn't even give me time to shower or change but dragged me up the stairs to Andre's home. All the lights were on. Milo, the wretched fiend, was sitting on the windowsill, waiting for me. He jumped down and followed us in.

My kitty was safe. I was starting to breathe. I knew Andre was alive. He'd just done the nasty with me, apparently. Maybe I could do the same for him.

Not with his mother and father in the same room, I realized after Schwartz hauled me back to Andre's crowded bedroom. I sighed and sank into the chair beside the bed.

I'd seen Andre still and comatose before. It was a pretty scary sight. He turned gray around the edges, and with his usual expressive face in repose, he looked dead. This time, he had a bloody bandage wrapped around his skull.

"We can't take him to the hospital," Julius said. "We don't even know what saline would do to him while he's in this state."

Comatose, beyond the dimensional veil, in the dream world that had held Katerina captive for a decade, was the state he meant. The outside world didn't understand that. I really didn't understand it. But I'd been there. I didn't know how it worked yet, but Andre had helped me. Somehow. I had to help him.

"Bring me some food, please?" I asked. "I'm about to pass out from hunger. And then leave me alone with him."

I heard protests but didn't listen. I didn't think "it's complicated," would explain.

But I'd talked to Andre when he'd been out like this. He'd told me he'd been shot. I hadn't been dreaming. He was over there in that other dimension, all right, the smug bastard.

I just had to bring him back.

Twenty-eight

I WAS filthy. I stank. I was probably leaving mud and blood rings on Andre's fancy chairs. But no one objected when I took his hand because he instantly seemed less gray. Andre had apparently come to my rescue—again. We seemed to be developing a pattern: I stuck my neck out exploring the insane in an effort to find solutions, and he yanked me back to safety when I went too far. This time, he'd taken a bullet for me while taking down the maniac gnomes and opening a hole to my hell.

Yeah, he'd also invaded my personal space and more than copped a feel, but that was half my fault.

I didn't know how I felt about that, but I wanted him here and present before I knocked his socks off. "Out, now," I told them. "Give me a few minutes alone."

They probably thought I could wave magic wands. I couldn't do a damned rational thing that I knew of. But once our audience had departed, I leaned over and whispered in Andre's ear.

"I'm going to rip your arm off, bastard." I closed my hand tightly around his.

I swear, the beast almost smiled.

"Or maybe I should rip off something a little less useful." I slid my filthy hand under the covers. I didn't know how I'd explain the mud stains to Katerina if she was stupid enough to do his laundry, but that wasn't my concern now.

They'd dressed him in pajamas. I snorted inelegantly and slid my hand beneath the elastic band. I could swear I felt his blood stirring.

"We have so many problems that I can't begin to count them on all your fingers and toes," I grumbled, clasping his penis in my muddy paw. "And you're gonna lounge around over there on the other side pretending to be a succubus? Or is that incubus? I'm not into that crap. I'm into this." I squeezed.

He groaned. He squirmed. And damned if he didn't get hard.

"Wake up now, Andre, or I'll leave you like this and let you explain to your mother." I curled all my fingers around him and there was plenty of room left to rub up and down. Hard. And fast.

"Geez, Clancy," he spluttered, jerking his hips. "You have no class."

I laughed. I laughed hysterically. I let him go and collapsed against his chest and when his arms circled me, I laughed some more.

Everyone rushed back in, and I kept laughing.

"She's hysterical. Get her out of here," Andre said above my head. But he was hanging on to me too hard for anyone to pry me loose.

"I hate you, Andre. You're a wicked bastard pig. And you're so going down one of these days." With that double entendre, I pulled myself loose. "I need a shower."

Ignoring the platter of sandwiches and cup of steaming coffee Julius and Katerina held, I walked straight into Andre's decadent shower and turned on the spray, then stripped.

My leg was nearly healed.

I stared at the once bleeding wound in disbelief, then ripped off the bandage on my arm. I couldn't even see a scar.

Cora brought me undies, jeans, a sweater, and my tote bag. I must have left the bag at the homeless shelter when I ran out. Handy, because she couldn't have got into my closet without my keys. Or carried Milo, who liked his sedan chair and had apparently returned to it.

I checked the mirror when I got out of the shower. The wounds were gone, but my hair hadn't miraculously repaired itself. I was starting to look like a homeless bum.

By the time I emerged from the bathroom, fully dressed, Andre was sitting up in bed, looking a little more ruddy, with Milo covering his lap.

"Chandelier, Andre, really?" I asked, commenting on his decor. "Marble? Is your toilet the Taj Mahal?" I grabbed a sandwich from the platter Julius swung under my nose.

"She's still hysterical. Better take her home." Andre sipped his coffee and ignored me.

"Pretty blue pjs, big boy," I said through a mouthful of tuna fish and basil. Katerina must have fixed these. Julius didn't know how to open a can. "I'm not going anywhere until I know you're here and not sucking around some other world."

He studiedly ignored me. "I'm accepting MSI's offer tomorrow. The Zone is too dangerous."

I staggered from the blow. All my work, for *nothing*? I wanted to send him back where he'd come from.

"Big bad Special Ops boy is afraid of a couple of lunatic gnomes with guns," I taunted, not letting him know my despair. My stomach knotted, and I wasn't hungry anymore.

Andre had once been my boss. I knew how tough he could be. He wasn't lying.

Milo leapt from the bed to curl around my ankles. I picked him up and stroked him to keep my anger level down, but I felt as if I was teetering on a precipice.

"He may be right this time, Tina," Katerina said worriedly. "If the ground under the harbor is so fragile that it's collapsing, it could do the same to the town."

I may have dreamed there was a space alien trapped in a meteorite under the Zone, but I knew for certain that our homes and friends were here, in the Zone. I couldn't give up.

I took a chair and put my bare feet up on his covers. Milo curled up on the bed to keep an eye on us. "Yes, the Zone is dangerous," I agreed with a semblance of calm. "Do you want to invite MSI and their patients to suffer in our place?"

"Their problem," Andre snarled. "I'm buying that warehouse over in Fells Point. I'll turn it into a condo and retail complex. Makes more sense than staying here."

I glanced up at Cora, who was regarding him worriedly. "If he does, we'll move in with him," I threatened. "I'll turn his customers to stone, and you can freak out the neighbors. Tim can go *boo* and before long, we'll have the place to ourselves. Not so bad for anyone except Andre, who'll have to make the mortgage payments on bankrupt businesses."

"You might want to try that here," Schwartz surprisingly suggested. "That foreign doctor was pretty freaked today. Someone needs to make it clear that Acme's magic element has violent side effects. MSI might change its mind."

Acme's magic may have healed my wounds—but it was also cracking open our community.

"I truly appreciate a rational man," I told him, practically inhaling my coffee. "But if the traitor here strikes an agreement," I kicked Andre's leg beneath the cover, "Acme will just take over instead of MSI. They've wanted us out all along."

"Let them have the place," Andre growled. "I'll laugh as it crumbles beneath their feet."

I was pretty worried he was right, and I was wrong, and I ought to just go home for the little while I had it. I'd never had a home so nice. Of course, I'd never talked to space aliens before either.

"Fine, then we'll all move up to Dane's mansion," I sneered instead of shutting up like I should. "I bet I'd look good in Ruxton. Dane could find me a place on his staff. With all that money, I'm betting I could find a place for everybody. You can go live in Fells Point by yourself."

A pop-pop-popping sound outside broke up the argument. In my despair, I was ready to blast anyone who crossed me.

Schwartz gestured for us to stand back while he put his back against the wall by the front window and peered out. "You've got uniformed men with guns pouring out of your place, Tina. Did you leave the gates to hell open?"

Oh crap. I wilted in my chair. "I don't suppose one of them is carrying Christmas ornaments?" I asked, too tired to care. I'd left the rest of the gnomes scattered about the office, unfettered. Mistake, apparently.

I could feel everyone gawking at me, but I forced myself to take another bite of my sandwich. If I had to fight stoned gnomes, I wasn't doing it on an empty stomach.

"A couple are wearing red caps," Schwartz said warily, glancing in my direction.

"I didn't do it." I held up my hands in innocence. "I swear, I did nothing. Not to that lot anyway. Maybe the lunatics found them. Maybe Paddy is experimenting with canned gas again. Are they coming this way? Do we need to open Andre's weapon chamber?"

Andre had a complete arsenal in a bomb shelter beneath the street.

Just as an experiment, I tried visualizing my stoned fascist gnomes into strolling down to Chesty's for pasta instead of terrorizing the neighborhood. That would be justice, wouldn't it?

"Nah, they're stumbling around, looking kind of lost mostly. I think the one with the assault rifle shot up the florist truck Tim left out front. Another freak is holding a holly branch and beating it over his head. And now they're all arguing and looking for their phones. I'll go out and see if I can play helpful cop."

It didn't sound as if they were heading for Chesty's. So much for that experiment. The gnomes hadn't responded to my visualization any better than the frogs. New theories needed. Maybe I needed to be in peril before I could visualize my enemies to Tahiti.

I raised a cautionary eyebrow at our normally taciturn lieutenant. "Give them a minute, see if they put their toys away."

Unlike Gloria's hellhounds, Graham Young's security guards hadn't spent years drinking in the pollution of Acme and Hell's Mansion. Chances were good they were just stupid, not evil. I had no evidence otherwise and didn't want to have to damn them. Not that damning had worked on Kaminski.

Andre threw off his covers and stalked to the window in his blue pajamas. Apparently gunfire had leveled any lingering arousal, but he was still a lithe muscular panther who shot my hormone level sky high, even if he was a selfish, amoral bastard that I had to take down.

"They're holstering their guns and phoning in for orders," Andre concluded. "Go out and give them Graham Young's new address in the psych ward." He turned and faced us. "Out. I'm getting dressed. Time's running out if I'm going to be a rich man."

He'd saved my life. I couldn't kill him, although beating him with a big stick had appeal.

Schwartz left to steer our would-be gunmen out of town. Looking bewildered and worried, Cora left with him. She sent a pleading look to me, but I was still too shaken to know right from wrong. I knew what I *wanted*. That didn't mean saving the Zone was right.

Something in that tunnel had healed my wounds—just as it had healed seriously wounded psyches like Andre's had been. And the mystery of the Zone had given second chances and stronger characters to people like Bill and Fred. The Zone wasn't all bad.

Which was when my imagination ran away with my logic, and I put together Gloria's barrels of chemicals and holes to hell and meteorites and confused space aliens and formed a crazed puzzle of them. All I had to do was remove Andre from the equation.

I finished my sandwich and came to my feet. "Sell out, Andre, and you're opening the gates to hell to MacNeill. I'm not letting that happen."

He glared and started unfastening his pajama buttons.

Milo and I followed his parents out, leaving him alone. They looked worried as I kept on going, but as Andre had said, time was running out.

Tomorrow was Friday, the last day of the offer to buy the Zone before eminent domain bulldozed us all. I needed a plan.

Twenty-nine

DON'T *turn creeps into inanimate or incoherent objects,* I wrote in my mental rule book as I hurried home with Milo hot on my heels. *You only get one chance to make them pay. Make it count.* There was probably a better word for croaking frogs than incoherent but my brain wasn't yet up to par. It was about to explode, in fact.

I was pretty certain I'd just verified that I could only visualize thugs out of my way once. After that, I was on my own. I could never turn Ned into a frog again, or even a gnome. I couldn't make the fascists or the ex-frogs stop shooting at me.

I wasn't even sure I could damn them, since I'd had to drop my last victim into the harbor and bulldoze over him before I got rid of him. Although I may have sent his soul to hell since I'd been rewarded with the saunas packing up and leaving. But my personal goal was survival, not being the devil's minion.

If my visualization didn't teach the baddies to be good, they'd wreak havoc forevermore, and there wouldn't be a blamed thing I could do about it except have them arrested like a normal citizen. That sucked, because here in the Zone, getting justice didn't happen often.

And based on the guards' spectacular return from gnomes and frogs, it looked like the visualization only lasted a little while—around the Zone, anyway. I didn't have time to experiment elsewhere.

Daddy Saturn was a piss poor parent if he left everything up to me to resolve. No wonder my mother had run away and his other daughters hid and skulked in dark corners of the earth. We were all paranoid and hiding because none of us knew what we were doing.

With Milo leaping ahead of me, I hurried upstairs to my place to start organizing my campaign to save the Zone in a day.

I nearly crashed to a halt when I opened my apartment door to find a computer tablet in the middle of the floor, flashing a red and pink exclamation point. I checked inside my tote bag where my tablet ought to be...and it was gone.

Someone had swiped it while I was underground?

Then left me a message. *Themis.* At the homeless shelter?

Cora had my keys, but she would have just said what she needed to say to my face. Sighing, I scooped up the tablet and collapsed onto my couch. Milo hurried off in search of food while I tapped the screen.

Whatever you're doing, aziz, don't let it happen again. I was a virgin when I had your mother scrolled across the screen.

A virgin. Right. I pinched the bridge of my nose and wondered if I shouldn't just go to bed and let the world take care of itself. Or lock myself up in the psych ward with Young.

Not wanting to think about virgin births, I dialed up Max.

"What's happening down there, Justy? The TV is reporting earthquakes with an epicenter in the harbor. I could feel the tremors up here."

"If you'll believe me, I'll tell you. Otherwise, it's too long a tale and I'm too tired." I got up and rummaged in my refrigerator for a beer, hummus, and chips. Sandwiches couldn't fill the empty place in my gut at Andre's threat to sell out.

"We had sex in hell, Justy. A priest exorcised a demon in my front room. What's not to believe?" he asked wryly.

I'd had sex with two men without body parts touching. Is that what Themis was warning me about? She really believed planetary forces control our bodies? I shuddered and concentrated on the here and now.

"Then believe Acme is literally sitting on a meteorite that's eating its way to hell. I'm not a chemist so don't ask me to explain, but the explosions today were probably a combination of Gloria's demon heat and the meteorite and Acme's chemical waste ground. We can't just blow it up, unfortunately. Whatever elements are in that rock can also save lives—and heal wounds," I added as all my spinning thoughts attempted to coagulate. "And cause violence. Or maybe Gloria does that. And I think Acme pumping the element out of the meteorite is causing fissures or fractals or whatever in the ground around the harbor."

"That almost makes sense," he agreed warily. "Almost, given what we've gone through."

I didn't mention space aliens. That could have been hallucination and wasn't necessary for this story, but if a living being was down there—that really crippled my alternatives.

"Acme has offered Andre a fortune to sell out," I continued, "presumably so they can build a medical clinic and experiment with the healing powers of pink particles."

"Almost following," he said with more doubt.

"Keep up because it's going down tomorrow if we don't stop them. You know your ex-dad better than anyone. How heavy is he into the pockets of the war machine?" I was talking of *Max's* dad, not Dane's. Mike MacNeill had been kicked out of office because of his shady weapon deals.

"Very heavy," Max agreed. "Mikey is a lobbyist and picks up funds out of war machine back pockets that I don't want to know about. Acme got the nerve gas contract because of his contacts. Is that what this is really about?"

"I have no proof. But ever since Acme gassed the zone with this element, we've had outbreaks of weird violence." Like Sarah carrying guns and shooting anything she came across. Tourists punching each other out for no reason. Goons shooting at me because they got divorced. Weird crap, but again, I didn't want to give Max too much. "When that gas was sprayed at them, it caused Gloria and her mad scientist to go berserk and attack anything in sight. Do you want to see what happens if we gas the Middle East with that stuff?"

He sighed. "I can't shut down Acme because it makes chemicals, Justy. What did you have in mind?"

"My bet is that your father really wants to turn the Zone into a munitions factory, that cancer research is simply a blind for testing chemical warfare. Persuade your mother and sister not to let him vote their shares. Let *Dane* persuade them," I amended. "Don't let Acme buy out Andre or continue with their pressure for eminent domain. You may lose credibility if word gets out that you're messing in the family business, but short of sending out witches and exorcists to expel your father, I'm not sure what else we can do."

He fell silent while I fretted about making the right decision. Max would be a good senator. I wanted him to have that power and position. I didn't want him to be humiliated by his ex-father and bad press over the family business. But Acme was sitting on evil, and world peace trumped any one person.

"I don't think it can be done overnight, Justy, I'm sorry. Better call in the exorcists and maybe the witches, because I'm afraid Mikey sold his soul to the devil a long time ago. I'll call and talk to them, but there's too much water under that bridge for me to hold out hope."

"Dane is still their shining star," I reminded him, needing some hope that if I failed, I had backup. "Don't think like rebel Max, think like smarmy Dane. Make promises. I'll call in everyone I can to help. Send Lance and the boys over tomorrow, too, because I'm likely to make a really big stink and may need someone protecting my back."

"What are you planning on doing?" he asked in alarm.

"I've just been to hell and back, big boy. I'm going to blow a crater straight to the devil's private den." I hung up and sent my calls to voice mail.

I spent the rest of the evening making calls. Cora helped. We needed to keep the innocents far, far away from whatever I was about to do.

Someday, I'd ask myself why *I* had to do it, but I figured it had something to do with justice and superpowers and maybe a personality disorder.

At one point, I heard a clatter outside and checked out my bay window. In the faint glare of Mrs. Bodine's porch light, I could just make out a large man in khaki uniform attempting to walk up the street with boards on his boots. It wasn't until I realized that he was carrying a sawed off shotgun with an evergreen branch stuck in the barrel that I worked it out—Tim's gnome from the florist shop. Tim had apparently done as promised and glued the statue to the table—and apparently the tree to the gun. Enterprising that our Nazi gnome somehow managed to break the table down so he wouldn't have to remove his boots. Once his stoned condition wore off, he'd figure out how to remove boards.

I fell asleep after midnight and had nightmares of virgin space alien babies and blue blobs wearing diapers and Andre's smirk.

In the morning, I dressed in boots and leather and stalked over to my office, ready for bear. The place was considerably quieter than it had been the day before. Katerina must have given up her petition in the face of Andre's threat to sell out. I missed the hectic office bustle. Sarah had said she was taking up residence with Ernesto. Jane had her kid watching a DVD of cartoons while she typed busily on her laptop. She glanced up and eyed me warily, but I had bigger things on my mind than arguing over her choice of jobs.

"We're about to be inundated by some very strange characters," I warned. "You might want to take Junior to the park. Or over to my rooms." I dangled my key. "I left Milo over there but he's likely to escape if you open the door."

She handed me some press releases from the printer and began gathering her kid's stuff without question. I really liked Jane. Had we lived in the same worlds, we could have lunched together. Maybe we would if I survived today.

"The MSI project manager maintains he's continuing with plans to build on Edgewater despite yesterday's earth tremors." Jane summarized the top release as I scanned it. "He says earthquakes happen everywhere, and the new building will be protected by the safest earthquake-prevention techniques available."

"He doesn't mention their CEO checking into a mental ward?" I asked meanly, wishing I'd been around when the green-haired, lipsticked fascist turd had been brought in.

"That's not the sort of thing one puts in a press release," she said, shutting down her laptop and hiding a grin. "I traded that snippet to a guy in the business news at the *Sun*. In return, he's helping me find names of people who protest eminent domain and will start raising a stink."

I looked at the next printout. Not a press release, just a portion of the morning's business page with the news that Graham Young, CEO of MSI had checked into a psychiatric unit after an inexplicable episode on the site of the company's new medical clinic. "*Inexplicable episode*, nice. Wonder if rich sheiks grant funds to men who are off their rockers? I probably should have put him in a dress."

"Not PC, Tina," she scolded. "You have no reason to believe all sheiks are bigots. Keep your argument to the evil you know."

I eyed her with interest. "Very good, Mama Jane. You'll bring your kid up right. I'm heading into the cellar. If I'm never seen again, tell Ned to send my friends to exorcise Acme."

She didn't look too alarmed. Jane didn't know my propensity for recklessness. She thought I was just a lawyer with a strange sense of humor.

"Better leave Ned a note if I'm moving over to your place for the day," she said imperturbably. "Call me if the devil materializes on Acme's roof."

Leaving a note was next on my list. As Jane moved her gear across the street and out of insanity central, I scribbled messages all over Ned's desk. *Give Schwartz the addresses of your divorced goon friends and have them arrested for shooting me and Andre yesterday*, was just one of the many epistles landing in his in-box.

Now, all I had to do was reach my objective without getting my head shot off. Or blown up, or whatever the Zone had planned for me today.

I didn't think it would do much good, but I shoved ear plugs into my ears to protect them from unearthly shrieks. I wished for a hard hat as I headed down my cellar stairs. Not that a hard hat would be of much use if a few tons of street descended on me.

After yesterday's earthquakes, I ought to rethink this little adventure. But a whole troop of goons with guns was on the loose and probably after my hide. I had no other way to explore underground without sliding through sinkholes and knocking myself silly. So the tunnel looked like my best alternative. I donned my motorcycle helmet and pretended I was going for a ride.

I'd felt braver when Sarah had been with me, but since she'd taken up toting weapons, I figured I was safer without her.

The cellar door was easier to open now that I didn't have to fight the lock. Shouldering the tote bag I'd brought for just this purpose, I pulled out a weapons-grade flashlight and kept the beam on the ground. The timbers above me had been there for centuries. If they chose me to fall on, it was for a purpose. I could believe in Fate or karma easier than heaven or hell.

It was winter outside but it was a nice spring down here. No bats flew out, thankfully. Maybe they'd all left by the holes down by the harbor. No Force shrieked. I was preparing a visualization just in case terror actually worked as well as fury for my weirdo abilities. If I could only visualize once, for a temporary length of time, it had to be effective and not release any more damnation-proof villains into the world.

The tunnel sloped downward in the direction of the water as I'd expected. Yesterday, in the harbor, I'd had *concrete* under me when I hit bottom. I figured that had to be an abandoned sewer or bunker, but I couldn't count on reaching it from here. I had to reconnoiter.

Humming naughty ditties to keep up my courage, I flashed the light back and forth. I'd worn my biker boots, so I wasn't particularly afraid of rats. I just didn't like surprises. I bypassed a couple of rock falls where the timbers had given away. Yesterday's tremors had probably de-stabilized half the territory.

"If I sacrifice myself for nothing, do I get to go to heaven, O Great Saturn?" I asked as my compass showed I was walking northeast—toward the harbor hazard zone.

Saturn, naturally, didn't answer.

The Civil War tunnel eventually ran smack into a sewer line. The odor wasn't as strong today as it had been the last time I'd ventured into my basement. I flashed my light around the barrier and located a grate in the top of the pipe. I scrambled up and peered inside.

The giant concrete culvert I was sitting on was filthy but not running water—probably because we'd cracked half the lines by now and it had been abandoned long ago. Deteriorating infrastructure didn't even half explain our problems.

I didn't know what was supposed to be connected to the grate but once I removed the rusted iron bars, the opening was large enough for me to lower myself through. So I did. I'd have to buy new boots if I survived.

Crouching, glad I wasn't large, I checked my compass and took the direction that should lead me closer to Acme. As I walked, the slope leveled off and the spring-like heat got warmer, so I assumed I was walking under the business end of Edgewater.

I heard a loud growl, sighed, and turned around to see Milo racing to catch up with me. "You can't leave well enough alone, can you?" I asked in exasperation.

He gave me a look that I interpreted as *neither can you,* then stalked ahead.

Idiotically, I felt better for his company. The walls here were dripping and nasty. I had no real idea what I was doing other than looking for an escape hatch and avoiding spies. Maybe I could clean the place up and make this a permanent shortcut to Chesty's.

"You can see the blue blob, can't you?" I asked Milo, just to fight my jitters.

He threw a look over his shoulder, then raced ahead.

"I need someone evil to damn," I told my kitty as we trudged through the muck. My back was starting to hurt from the stooped position. "If I damned someone, I could make a wish, and I could save the blob and push the meteorite into hell."

He snorted in kitty language.

"Okay, yeah, the meteorite could cure cancer. War machine versus miracle cures. Which do you vote for?"

He ignored me and waited patiently beneath a hole leading upward. Had I traveled far enough to be past Chesty's yet? I flashed my light on the ceiling and could see a ladder. So this was where the utility guys went when they dug into the streets. I swung my light forward, but the culvert narrowed and started going up. I really didn't want to end up inside Acme or any of the other industries on this end of the Zone.

I added my heavy cat to my tote and caught the lowest rung—above my head. I needed to find a gym and work out more. I nearly pulled my arms from my sockets attempting to walk up the side of the tunnel so I could reach the next rung.

With an oomph and a few kitty complaints, I finally got my feet on the rusty metal and climbed my way up. A manhole blocked the exit. Most people don't approach a sewer from underneath. Oh well.

I hadn't been able to lift one of the blasted iron doors when I'd been on the street. I took off my glove and tested this one now. Hot, as if it had been sitting in the sun, but not scorching. Hanging onto a rung, I tried shoving the metal open with my shoulder and one hand. As before, it resisted my puny efforts. I was dripping sweat inside my leather but that was the least of my worries.

I could hear voices above me. I didn't know exactly where I was. I could be coming up on a mob wanting to play whack-a-mole with my head, should I manage to pry the door off.

Milo growled and I gave him an evil eye. "Yeah, I know I don't know what I'm doing. No rule book, remember?"

But I had planned ahead enough to hope I'd loaded the street out there with friends and not foes. I'm insane, not stupid.

I removed the earplugs, pulled my smart toy out of my tote, and hit a number. It actually rang. Maybe the utility guys had fixed our crossed wires.

"Tina?" Schwartz asked on the other end.

I tried not to let him know how relieved I was to hear a human voice. "The one and only," I agreed. "Where are you?"

"Where do you think I am?" he demanded. "Edgewater is filled with kooks, so I'm covering Kooksville. Andre just arrived, looking seriously pissed. Where are you?"

"Did you arrest the gunmen who shot us yet?" I asked, resting against the ladder, probably not far from his feet if he only knew. Edgewater is short.

"The boys are bringing them in now. We'll need statements from you and Andre. Tell me that's not a voodoo priest building a fire over the sauna we pulled you out of yesterday."

"That's not a voodoo priest building a fire," I repeated obediently. "Are the witches there yet? And my biker friends?" I'd had a really busy evening.

His sigh of exasperation was deep and heartfelt. "I'm asking for a transfer."

"You may get it if this fails. Start tapping manhole covers until you find mine, please. I can't hang onto these rungs and my cat and push at the same time."

"Manhole—" He cut himself off, realizing it was a stupid question.

Schwartz was one very smart mundane. And he might not be a mundane much longer if he stayed in the Zone. I'd have to think about that.

He rattled my lid about the same time I heard the fireworks shooting off.

Thirty

I SAW daylight as Schwartz lifted the heavy manhole cover. I warily peered over the edge to be certain the popping sounds weren't guns.

Reassured that there were no guns in sight, I took the good lieutenant's hand so he could haul me into the street. I'd come out on the far north end of Edgewater, past Bill's bar and practically at Acme's gates. Nice. I was still alive but had learned nothing of what we were sitting on. Andre's deadline was making me a little frantic.

"Your doing?" Schwartz growled, gesturing at the bonfire on the shoreline.

Up here near the industrial park north of the Zone, only a large dirt lot separated the street from the water and the industrial park. The town began at the intersection to the south of us. My crazies were benignly occupying an empty lot.

"Shouldn't they wait until night?" he asked.

"The boys like a little excitement while they wait," I said with a shrug, studying the situation. The line of shiny Harleys along the curb easily explained the noise that resembled a Gatling gun. Firecrackers were the bikers' toys of choice, the louder, the better. "They didn't get enough fun in the war. Thanks for helping me out."

"What would you have done if I hadn't?" he growled, marching steadfastly toward the bonfire.

"I'd have had one of the witches curse you," I said cheerfully, following him. "When Senator Dane arrives, play nicey-nice and you may be promoted to personal bodyguard. Those bikers are his guys out there."

Schwartz rightfully shot me a look of disbelief. I get that a lot.

"Do you have any clue as to what you're doing here?" he asked with insulting dubiousness.

"I'm tired of fighting with Acme from the civil side, where they have all the power," I said with a shrug. "So I'm trying another route."

"Sic'ing Hell's Angels on them? That almost makes sense."

It did, in a warped sort of way. Except Lance and friends weren't Hell's Angels. Maybe I was, since I intended to give a few people hell before this day ended.

As we traipsed across the field, I checked over my shoulder and verified that no kids were streaming out of the DGs' homeless shelter to watch. Cora had warned them to clear out. Excellent.

It was too early for Bill's or Chesty's to be open. No lines waited at the remaining saunas. Yesterday's earthquakes had apparently scared off the tourists for the duration. Whatever in heck we did today should only hurt those responsible for the problem, knock wood. Of course, so far, it looked like only my people out there.

I hadn't invited the nuns this time. Those nice ladies didn't deserve glimpses of the devil or whatever we were about to raise. Father Morrison, however, met us at the remains of the chain link fencing near the contamination zone. I introduced him to Schwartz.

"I don't think it is *impossible* for evil to inhabit the ground," the good priest said solemnly as we progressed toward the hole Andre had created with his bulldozer yesterday, before he got shot.

"I have reason to believe that the same chemicals causing the hell hole in the Vanderventer mansion have also eaten through the ground here," I explained, looking for terms that a priest might believe. String theory wouldn't work on him. "When we closed up the hole in the mansion, another exploded on the harbor. Hot geysers have been the only result, until yesterday."

Hands behind his back, the priest listened gravely. "But you've seen no actual demons?"

"I'm not the demon expert," I pointed out. "I have no way of recognizing evil other than behavior, and that's a tough call, as you know yourself."

He nodded. "Well, I suppose exorcising a hell hole would be a trifle different than attempting to drive a demon from someone's soul. Couldn't you just close up the hole with explosives?"

Here's where I had to play verbal dodgeball. I couldn't talk about blue blobs or space aliens or even meteorites. My credibility was on the line. Where was a good courtroom when I needed one?

"We have excellent reason to believe that whatever is down there also holds miracle cures," I said, choosing the easiest route. "That's why I've called you in. If there is some way of exorcising the evil and leaving the good..." I let him extrapolate.

He lit up like a Christmas candle. "Heaven and hell, right here on earth," he exclaimed. "Is it possible?"

Milo leaped out of my tote and raced ahead, obviously bored with our chatter. Maybe he communicated with space aliens and could warn Blue Boy to hide.

Lance saw us approaching and nudged one of his buddies and before long they were all cheering and raising mugs of frothing... beer? Who knew? It steamed in the cold December air. Not absolutely necessary given the ground heat, but it looked good.

"Excellent Irish coffee," the priest explained in satisfaction. "Senator Vanderventer has been very thoughtful."

I was betting the boys were drinking something a little less fancy than whiskey and coffee, but I wouldn't disillusion the good father if he was getting along with bikers in ragged leathers and even more ragged beards.

Agatha's coven gathered around the bonfire, warming their fingers on hot mugs. Behind them, their cauldron bubbled in a battery-operated crockpot. Nice touch. The older witches eyed the bikers with wariness, but the younger ones seemed oblivious to a bunch of old guys. They were ogling Andre.

Damn, I'd hoped he'd keep his long nose out. Stupid of me.

I left the priest behind and crossed the rough turf to punch the smug expression off his handsome face. He wore a hat to hide the bandage on his head. He held up a cashmere-coated arm and blocked my blow.

"Have you sold us down the river yet, punk?" I demanded.

"What, and miss the floor show?" he asked, laughing at my puny attempt to hit him. "I have a meeting with MacNeill at ten. I can put it off until later if the spectacle takes longer."

I kicked his shin with my sewage-laden boot. The gabardine looked better muddy. "Make me do all the work and you come out smelling like roses and richer than ever. You're a skunk, Legrande." He may have saved my life, but we did that for each other.

It was the morality issues where we clashed. If money was the root of all evil, he risked his soul by selling out. I expected better of people I knew and respected.

Not wanting to damn Andre, I turned my back on him and went over to greet Doctor Voodoo. He was at least wearing clothes out here in the cold wind off the water, although they were little more than skanky rags covered in layers of herbal wreaths. He'd apparently brought a few of his students with him. They hadn't got into the naked, headless chicken shtick yet, but their jeans and hoodies were well decorated with pretty colors and weeds, and they carried an assortment of jungle-type instruments.

"You saw what happened last time we messed with a hell hole," I warned him. "You really want your students at risk?"

"As long as we walk this earth, we are at risk. They must learn how to fight evil," the prof said solemnly.

I turned to the kids and pointed at the hole surrounded by orange cones. "This ground gave away yesterday. The whole harbor area is permeated with fissures and the heat is crumbling the chemically-permeated ground. It could collapse under you at any minute. Your professor knows what he's getting into. I want to make sure you do as well. Backing off is a sign of intelligence."

They glanced at Doctor Voodoo, who scowled and waved them backward. They scattered. "You're no fun, Tina Lawyer. The battle against evil is not for the weak."

"This is a battle against geothermal fracking or some such crap. We can't close hell. But we can cut off its access to the Zone by making as big a stink as possible." I gestured at the cameras starting to gather a safe distance back along Edgewater, bless Jane's little heart. "We're going to show them that the Zone isn't safe for medical science."

The professor studied the journalists setting up their cameras, the witches stirring their brew and drawing pentagrams in the mud, and the priest setting up his altar, and he nodded. "There is real evil here, and you know it, don't you?"

"First smart thing I've heard you say. If you could define and pinpoint the source, I'd be appreciative, but you can't. Neither can I. So shutting off Acme's access to it is the best I can do. Your job is to keep evil from spreading should it escape in some way I can't fathom."

He crossed the clearing to talk with Agatha, showing he was as smart as I'd hoped. Gloria and Dane had been polluted by *something* besides chemicals. Somehow, evil was leaking into our existence.

Schwartz stationed several of his fellow cops at a distance, as if this were a normal mob scene. This was Friday, so workers were pouring into the plant on their normal shift. Cars slowed to check out the bizarre scene at the harbor, but the drivers had clocks to punch. I didn't think shutting down a meteorite would put them out of work, I hoped.

I just didn't know if a meteorite could be shut down.

A limo slid up to the curb, blocking the Harleys but far enough out of the street to allow the workers to drive by. I prayed that wasn't Max. I'd told him to contact MacNeill, but not at eight in the morning. I wanted the action over before the bigwigs arrived.

Ex-senator Mike MacNeill stepped from the limo, accompanied

by Dr. Bakir, MSI's corporate flunky. Apparently we hadn't scared the good doctor enough yesterday. Andre walked up the hill to greet them.

I stupidly wanted him down here helping me. But he'd joined the enemy and we were on a collision course.

A familiar lanky figure bicycled down Edgewater—Paddy. So that's how he was getting about these days. I hadn't seen or heard him around the boarding house lately, but then, neither of us spent much time at home. Or maybe he'd moved out. His apartment had been above mine, but I never heard him up there anymore. He parked his pedal-pusher beside the Harleys and ambled over to Andre and MacNeill.

I guess I'd have to get moving. I stopped to speak with Agatha first.

"You've really stirred the forces, haven't you?" she asked before I could speak. Today she was wearing a heavy wool coat over her apron, and a knit stocking cap to warm her ears. The heat from the ground should have made that much covering unnecessary, but I had no idea how old she was. Maybe she was frail and thin-skinned.

One of these days, I should have her teach me about evil forces. Not today. "You stir your cauldron, I stir mine," I agreed. "I'm hoping you and Pierre and the priest can block anything that escapes after I go down. The bikers only have muscle to stop the crowd. If there really are evil forces down there, I'll need your help."

"And what if the Evil Ones inhabit *you?*" she asked, giving me more insight into the supernatural than I wanted to know.

"Andre will probably shoot me," I said with a shrug.

I approached Lance, who had miraculously remembered my request—a mechanic's tool box. He'd stoned a lot of brain cells over the years and didn't have the world's most reliable thought processes. He propped his big scuffed boot on the box.

"Another case of beer at Bill's for you, dude," I told him, giving him a quick hug. "I like a man who listens."

"You got the boss riled pretty fierce," he warned. "I don't know whose arms you twisted to get us that cushy job, but it ain't gonna last long if we keep ignoring the senator's orders."

"If I come out of this okay, you won't have to worry about that. I've got the senator's number. If I don't come back out, then you can obey him all you can tolerate. I appreciate this." I grabbed the heavy box and hurried toward the roped off excavation before they could worry. Not that the gang was much given to worrying, but one never knew when they'd take it up. After all, Lance had just expressed concern about a job, which had to be a new first.

Before I could fully psych myself for meeting the shrieking Force, a Town Car pulled up to the curb behind MacNeill's limo. I had a prejudice against black Town Cars. The Vanderventer goons had preferred them when they were spying on me. I slipped under the tape and examined the best way into the hole.

"Justy!" a big voice bellowed.

Oh crap. Glancing over my shoulder and seeing Senator Vanderventer making an ass of himself by running toward me, I just took a deep breath, sat on my rear, and slid down the hatch, tool box firmly in hand. I'd explored caves all over the country. I hated them. Nothing lately had changed my mind about dark enclosed places. I shuddered just thinking about unleashing the Force's wail.

I'd simply have to hope that Lance and his guys took their bodyguard job seriously and would prevent Max from coming in after me. I stuffed the earplugs back in.

If Milo came down here ahead of me, I couldn't see him. Andre had bulldozed a really big hole in his efforts to reach me. The top was wide and deep. I could see a square concrete tunnel doorway—not the kind of sewer line I'd just traversed. Newer. Probably Acme's entry into the underground, and where I'd whacked my head yesterday after falling down the second rabbit hole.

I flipped on my flashlight beam while the senator argued with whomever was blocking his access above.

The newer concrete had been built into an old culvert, like the one I'd traversed to get down here. The old sewer had cracked and crumbled, possibly from the earthquakes and most certainly because Andre had driven a bulldozer through this section to reach me. While shouts and arguing ensued overhead—and a lot of weird chanting—I sauntered down the underground passage. This trip down the rabbit hole felt better with a light, cell phone, and tools in my hand—and with no Forces shrieking.

I tugged at the new concrete door. The door actually opened.

"Hey, Blue," I called into the darkness, popping out my ear plugs. "I've come visiting. Are you awake?"

The pretty blue neon lights lit up the ceiling for me again. Guess that answered that.

Blue? he asked with that mental tone I took as amusement.

The concrete tunnel behind the door went in two directions, one up the hill toward the industrial park, the other down to the harbor.

"On this planet, we have names for each other," I said out loud. "We're all unique individuals, and that's how we identify our uniqueness. You can choose a better name, if you like."

I didn't need my compass to know which direction was Acme. If they were pumping crap from underground, Acme was the direction I needed. I took the tunnel to my left.

I like Blue, he agreed genially inside my head. *There are a great many of your kind above. What is happening?*

"I'm trying to stop the bad things from reaching you." Always interpret in favor of the listener, I'd learned at my mother's knee. She'd advanced from tree-hugging protests to manipulating the wealthy by the time I'd gone off to college. It was only after I'd left home that she'd disappeared into the darkest Amazon.

I progressed pretty far through the tunnel while Blue pondered that, or how to word whatever question formed in whatever passed for a blob mind. It's not as if I conversed with space aliens on a regular basis.

The unique individuals *above are causing... disharmony... with the foul creatures below*, he finally said.

"Your verbal intelligence scores must be over the top," I said, nervously. I was pretty certain he wasn't saying *fowl*, as in chickens from hell. I feared *foul creatures* was his way of describing the denizens beyond the veil—demonic bats and uglies like Gloria. Being reminded how close I was to Gloria's dimension didn't ease my tension.

I scanned the roof of the tunnel looking for the conduits Blue had described yesterday. *Wires and pipes,* he'd said. I had to be closing in on Acme. Where were the pipes to hell?

Blue sat on my verbal intelligence remark for quite a while. Time was obviously irrelevant in his world. I had to wonder how long he'd been trapped down here.

Communication, he finally decided. *In my home, we communicate with images more than words. Words are very primitive in comparison.*

"True. We have images we can send with machines, but not mentally, as you do. So we need words." I had a sci-fi moment where I envisioned computer chips in everyone's brains communicating images instead of language. Not sure even images could translate what I was doing here.

Ah hah, my flashlight connected with a conduit and a big honking pipe that steamed and rattled. I wasn't an engineer and couldn't identify the purpose. Overhead, I could hear the hum of engines—pumps?

I swung my beam around to study the wall. Dangly wires. More pipe—conduits? The wires connecting to the ground wire in the rubble at my feet ran back toward where Acme ought to be. Underground electrical, possibly phone lines for all I knew. Maybe gas in the pipes. A lot of this stuff looked like the enormous machinery inside Acme that Andre and I had shut down in the fall—which had caused Bergdorff, the mad scientist, to flip off his rocker.

I was playing with fire to mess with any of this.

"Justine, if you touch anything down there, I'll kill you myself!" came a low roar from behind me. I'd so hoped Max would be cowardly Dane and stay out.

Milo reappeared and snaked his big body around my ankles, preventing me from moving too swiftly. "Whose side are you on, Maxie baby?" I called back. "Get your senatorial ass out of here. I'm more expendable than you are."

Max was a mechanic. He'd be great down here. Dane was a senator. He needed to do good on a level beyond my capability, so he didn't need to be getting blown up with Zone problems. I just didn't need this confusion right now.

I edged around Milo, flashing my light up and down the pipes, looking for valves or anything sensible I could turn off. I'd messed around with generators and bad wires while growing up and had a middling knowledge of how things shut on and off. If I could shut off the motor noise, I figured I'd accomplished something.

"I can knock him down and drag him out," Andre called helpfully. "But if he's who you say he is, then he's the mechanic, so maybe you ought to listen to him."

I sighed and closed my eyes for a moment. I'd wished for company. I really would have to watch what I wished for, even when I wasn't offing baddies. I was pretty rattled right about now and not thinking clearly enough for both of them.

"Oh swell, did the two of you shake hands and make friendly to gang up on me?" I called back, disguising my relief and fear. "Unless you came down to tell me MacNeill is turning off his stairway to hell, you'd better get your butts out of here." I found a pressure gauge. It was chugging on full blast. Not looking healthy.

I will stop them, Blue said cheerfully.

Oh great, a fourth party heard from, if I counted Milo. Before I could decide whether this was good or bad or even utter an epithet, the Pillsbury Blue Boy appeared between me and the tunnel entrance.

"What the f..." Max/Dane halted at a curve in the tunnel just within my sight. His tweed blazer over black polo and jeans and pricey athletic shoes weren't precisely what I would have chosen for sewer explorations, but presumably he had to keep up appearances in the outside world.

He could see Blue? I'd have to work that out some other time.

Andre wore his usual smirk as he examined the creature he'd seen before. He, too, was sartorially correct, although today he favored black silk. He'd sensibly removed the coat and hat for his tour of hell. The white bandage on his head stood out in the gloom.

He studied Big Blue. "Has potential, Clancy. You do this? Not very artistic."

I so wanted to ream him a new one—for so many good reasons.

The Force chose that moment to shriek and yowl as if someone had pulled its evil tail. If that was Cerberus guarding the gates, I hoped he was chained up, because I wasn't leaving until I'd turned off the magic pipeline.

I was bringing down Acme's evil if it was the last thing I did. Which it could very well be. I shoved in my earplugs and went back to hunting for valves.

"Hey, Blue, scare them back where they came from, if you can. I'm about to let all hell loose." I'd found a valve, and I reached for a wrench in Lance's toolbox.

Thirty-one

"JUSTY, that's not a shut-off valve!" Max shouted in Dane's rich politician's voice. "You'll blow the whole Zone to hell!"

He tried to dash past Blue, who was smart enough to feint back and forth in front of the good senator, blocking his path. A space alien tackle—cool—if I wasn't actually blowing us all to eternity.

I tried the wrench on the valve anyway. "Why should I trust you, Max? This is your family gold mine."

"What is this thing?" he asked again, backing up against the wall and trying to sidle around my imaginary friend.

While I wrenched at the valve, Max/Dane realized Blue had no real mass. Damn his intelligence. I hurriedly tugged on the valve, but it was rusted. I needed oil.

Max eased past the alien image and jumped me before I could reach for the tool box again. He used his whole body to whack my back up against the wall, grab my arm, and fling my wrench away. Maximum contact with the body of Dane—a man I'd sent to hell—kind of froze me in place. I *knew* that was Max inside there, but all I could see was Dane's furious expression—quite similar to the one he'd worn when the real Dane had pointed a gun at my head.

He held my wrists pinned so I couldn't punch him. I brought my knee up but he dodged.

"Your zombie is right, Clancy," Andre said, sauntering up to examine the pipes. "Shutting that valve will only allow pressure to build. For all we know, you could spray demons across the harbor if it blows."

"I'm not a zombie," Max growled. "Not any more than you are at least. And what is that blue puppet who's looking over my shoulder?"

The throbbing hum of the generator seemed louder, more ominous. I didn't notice the Force's wails any longer.

"Don't ask," I said hastily. "He probably won't hurt you unless you hurt me." Not that I knew if a trapped space alien with strong visual capacities could do anything at all, but I needed some leverage against two men bigger than I was. "Let me go, Max."

I tried the knee maneuver again, except Max and I used to wrestle in the old days. He knew all my tactics. He tightened his grip.

"This crap doesn't just pollute your head, it pollutes your souls," I warned him. "If the two of you are here to persuade me to sell the Zone to the war machine, you can go to hell."

Andre turned from his examination of the pipes long enough to send me a worried glare. "I think she means that literally. Either strangle her or tell her no war machines are involved."

"No war machines are involved," Max promised, "although strangling sounds good right about now. This tunnel could cave in on us at any moment. Or your raving maniacs could decide to come down here and shoot demons. Are you out of your mind, Justy?"

I pointed my chin at the pipes. "Those things are draining magic juice from a meteorite under our feet, and in the process, they're probably thinning the veil between here and hell. *You're* the one about to unleash demons if you let Acme continue."

Max with Dane's face turned to Andre. "I've seen hell. It exists in another dimension. What's she talking about?"

"Acme is your family's company—for both your personas. If anyone knows, you should." Andre shouted over the noise of the pipes and eerie wails. He studied the hole the conduits ran into and started down the ladder to follow them.

I didn't want to explore any more damned holes, and I certainly didn't want to take the direction to hell. I wanted to scream and kick and shout, but frustration had got me here and wouldn't get me out. I glanced at Blue, but he'd wandered toward the outside entrance. He'd said it was hard to take that form and that he was curious. He had no idea what we were talking about, no particular moral understanding of the battle we were fighting. He was more interested in the witch hunter entertainment outside. He was about as much use as Milo, who had disappeared down the tunnel looking for rodents, presumably.

"MacNeill swears that Acme is providing the chemical for the miracle cure MSI wants to experiment on," Max said, warily releasing my wrists.

"*Paddy* may be working on miracle cures," I agreed. "I'm sure MacNeill swears he isn't inventing violence in a can, but even Paddy has used it," I countered, torn between breaking these pipes and following Andre down the ladder. At least the infernal shrieking halted, although I felt it ominously hovering, just waiting for a reason to start again.

"Skeletons down here, Clancy," Andre practically sing-songed from below us. "Several nice skeletons you can fret over. And if I'm standing on a meteorite, it would take a semi of explosives to blow it out of the water."

Skeletons! Murder victims? Gassed victims of Acme's incompetence? Did I want to know?

I closed my eyes and muttered a few choice imprecations. Above us, the voodoo chanting was growing loud enough to hear over the hum of machinery. I could swear I heard a loudspeaker. I couldn't hear what it was saying. I bit my tongue on a *damn* and reluctantly followed when Max took the ladder down. The Hardy Boys and Nancy Drew visit the Mystery of Acme Hell.

"I'm not a forensics scientist, Legrande," I warned as I clambered down the ladder—this one wasn't rusty. But the underground cavern stank of sulfur, and the heat was oppressive. My flashlight barely cut the gloom. In comparison, the culvert had been a bed of roses. I couldn't see any bones. "Do you want me to bring cops this close to hell?"

Blue? I called inside my head. *Know anything about people down here?*

But Blue had wandered off on his own pursuits.

I had a posse with me. I shouldn't need Blue. I was simply looking for someone to agree with me. Bad Tina. With a sigh, I followed the beam of Andre's small but powerful flashlight.

He illuminated the slimy, dripping walls in ever-widening circles. The ground sparkled a muddy pink and green. No cement floor here. Still seeing no bones. I looked up and flashed my own light along a cement ceiling to see how safe we were. They must have installed supports to hold the tunnel above the meteorite instead of smothering it. Which told me exactly what? That the meteorite destroyed concrete? Not good for the supports, if so.

I stepped off the ladder onto the sparkly mud. The crud stuck to my soles.

"I don't think we want to be touching this stuff, boys," I warned, climbing back to the ladder. I still couldn't see what Max and Andre saw. I decided I liked it that way. I clung to the ladder and tried to think of a way to drag their asses back to safety.

"We can't leave these bones down here," Max protested, apparently studying the skeletons further down the dark tunnel. "They could be murder victims." He fished around on the ground.

Ewww yuck. I'd call him a grave robber but I assumed he was looking for ID. Or dog tags. Military training dies hard. I looked away when his light flashed across something vaguely gray and bone-shaped.

"Or they could be victims of another of Acme's industrial accidents. Or they killed each other after standing on violence-inducing green goo for too long. Get out of here before the two of you do the same." I flashed my light back and forth over the ground so they could see what I saw.

"It's just slime," Max argued, obviously intrigued by the cavern and studying the layout after he pocketed what he could find from the skeletons.

Men! They climb mountains because they're there. Testosterone-addled even in the face of clear danger. I was feeling lethal enough to turn valves and blow us all up. I wanted *solutions,* not more mysteries.

"What did you find?" I finally lowered myself to ask when he didn't say.

"Can't tell but it felt plastic. I'm thinking employee ID tags." Max continued looking around.

Andre studied the conduits piercing the meteor. "Giant straws?" he suggested. The pumping engines hummed steadily above our heads, draining the *element* out of the ground.

The irregular surface of green and pink spread as far as the eye could see. The meteor could have crashed here back after the earth became a planet for all I knew. It was the ground we walked on and probably the support of all the Zone and the entire industrial park. There was no pushing that sucker anywhere. That was one whopper of a meteorite. If our alien was trapped inside, we could never reach him. We might reach hell faster.

Speaking of hell... The weird shriek struck again, far more piercing down here. It worked to a climax that nearly split my eardrums, thrummed the air, and seemed to be approaching at high speed.

I practically flew up the ladder. Andre and Max followed. I collapsed on the concrete floor and covered my ears. The Force flowed up and around us, as if the shriek had mass. Both Andre and Max dropped down over me, which probably ought to have broken my spine except they propped their weights up on their elbows. That they sought to protect me would be really sweet, but I knew my guys. They were overdosing on competitiveness.

I'd fret over all that hot male proximity except I couldn't think through the shriek in my head. I twisted to see Andre and Max holding their ears but looking around with curiosity. No bats flapped.

The chanting above grew louder and more frantic. Drums pounded harder, and I was pretty sure I heard Lance and his crew adding their bellows.

"Not looking good, guys," I murmured, still stupidly holding my ears. It wasn't as if I was blocking out the din any better than my earplugs had. "Want to run, or see if I can send a meteorite to hell?"

"It's just a *noise*," literal Max protested. Really, he'd heard hell. He should know better.

"Always more fun to come," Andre said cynically. "We've already had flood, so I'm betting on fire this time."

"Let's not get Biblical at a time like this. Get off me, both of you. A shriek can't knock me down." Although the pain of it was laying me flat. I still had the urge to crawl away.

Where was Milo? *Blue?* I called tentatively inside my head. No reply. The blue neon that had illuminated the tunnel when I entered it was fading.

Could I damn a shriek to hell? Not if it came from there in the first place.

When both Andre and Max hesitated over moving, I used my elbows to start wiggling out from under them. The shriek had reached such proportions that if the world wasn't ending yet, I was sure it would shortly. A million and one voices had to synch to reach that hair-raising, chandelier-smashing level.

I was afraid the cement would start cracking from the sheer force of the sonic vibrations. How could I damn what I couldn't see?

"Noisy down here, isn't it?" a genial voice asked from the tunnel nearest the entrance.

How was I hearing anything? And then I realized the shriek was dying.

I glanced up and almost threw a *damn you to hell* right then and there.

Mike MacNeill had my cat in his arms, stroking Milo's head and studying us humped over in agony on the floor. He didn't even seem to notice the pain of the shriek. And what was Milo doing? Had he gone to fetch *MacNeill* the way he usually delivered Andre?

That wasn't right. The shriek dying so abruptly wasn't right.

And then I noticed the gun the ex-senator had hidden beneath my cat.

"What the hell are you doing down here?" Max/Dane asked, dragging himself upright and dusting himself off. Dane was taller than

MacNeill, younger and stronger, but that was still Max's father. It wasn't as if he'd physically attack his old man. But what a man crazy enough to come down here would do was anyone's guess. And that went for all three men.

The skeletons in the basement took on new meaning. Was my purpose in life to draw the evil-polluted crazies out of the Acme woodwork? It was certainly looking that way.

Andre and I remained on the floor. He grabbed my waist and hauled me behind him while he studied the situation. He still rubbed his ear with one hand.

"There are a lot of worried people above, wondering what you're doing that's causing all the racket. I told them I'd come get you, that we can work things out one way or another." MacNeill looked directly at me. "The state is stalling on the eminent domain now that someone has raised a complaint."

Oh goody. Julius had followed through despite everything. His connections were legion. And probably legendary. That explained MacNeill's presence. The devil was in danger of losing a boatload of moolah and an opportunity to expand Acme hell.

Milo bared his teeth and struggled against the arms clutching him. He was big for a cat, but he'd been leading a soft life lately. MacNeill grabbed the scruff of his neck and wouldn't let him go. One wrong move, and Milo was likely to expand into killer cat, but he seemed reluctant to do so for some reason. I heeded his caution.

The ground started to rumble again and the stench of sewer gas permeated the air. Andre glanced at the pressure gauges I'd been playing with and swore.

MacNeill didn't blink an eyelash. *And that's when I saw it*—the faintest outline of another image haloing him. That so wasn't right.

I hastily scrambled to my feet. Andre followed a little more slowly, positioning himself to one side so he could watch all parties.

"Do you see what I see?" I asked Max, elbowing him, keeping an eye on that flickering... what did I call it? Spirit? Ghost?

"I see a lying no-account," he muttered. "Want to hold a trial and ask him what he did with my mother's money?"

He meant his real mother—the actual Vanderventer heir. Max hadn't chosen to introduce me to his family while he was alive. Old story that. His mother had left the control of Acme to the man standing in front of us now.

MacNeill looked startled and stared at the Dane he could see. "I never did anything with Gloria's money. How could I?"

But I knew we were talking about *Max's* mother. So that's where the hatred came from. Sort of got it.

That outer layer of darkness around MacNeill really had me worried.

I'd learned my lesson about turning people into amphibians. I didn't want to make MacNeill invulnerable by visualizing him into something he could return from. But sending him to hell was a little drastic without a jury trial. I couldn't even get furious enough yet to curse him. I was puzzled by that ghostly image.

I was seeing ghostly images. Auras. *I had a new superpower.*

Oh crap.

"Dammit, Saturn, couldn't you just send me a nicely wrapped birthday gift?" I muttered under my breath. Andre looked startled, but Max/Dane and MacNeill were busy having a stare-off.

"Senator MacNeill," I said with wonderful lawyerly unctuousness, "do you know anything of the bodies below us?"

I peered past Dane's big shoulder to see Mikey's facial expression reveal shock, but the hand with the gun lifted steadily and with purpose—guided by a ghostly helper? In another lifetime, I wouldn't have noticed the dichotomy. These days, I was pretty attuned to the insane—like one hand not knowing what the other was doing.

"In the early days, right after the flood exposed the new element, we lost a few workers," he growled. "Exploration is a dangerous business."

Oh, right, yeah, too dangerous for anyone to retrieve the bodies. Still didn't have conclusive proof that Mikey had killed anyone. And I couldn't damn him for being an immoral ingrate or I'd have damned Andre long ago.

"Senator, have you ever been down in this tunnel before?" I prodded when he seemed too paralyzed to say more.

Max/Dane sent me an odd look but inched to one side, out of the path of my destruction. Smart boy.

Of course, he was finally playing hero by sidling closer to the demonically possessed man with the gun.

Demonically possessed. I had to play fast with that notion. Sarah's serial killer mother had said demons walked this earth, but how reliable is a sociopath? I was pretty sure Gloria hadn't been normal. Max was able to inhabit Dane's body, so why shouldn't demons move into his father—who had spent years hanging out at

Acme? Demons, evil, whatever. I'd only been working this shift a few months and still didn't have a rule book.

So, if a demon had killed the men below, could I blame MacNeill and damn him? I wanted to.

"Why would I come down in this hole?" MacNeill asked with a puzzled expression. But he was squeezing my cat's neck and fingering the trigger. "For all that matters, why are you down here?"

Why was Milo holding still for this? I'd seen him turn into a raging bobcat and stupidly try to take down a drunken killer. Milo was not ordinary. I had to believe he was still for a reason.

Was Milo keeping the demon image from completely taking over MacNeill? I was betting our lives on it.

As I stalled, the shriek returned at more piercing decibels—a siren call for minions? My mind was working overtime, so I had tuned out the noise. Maybe I shouldn't. Maybe I needed to damn the shriek to hell. What could it hurt?

Panic had worked to focus me before. In my mind, I built a warrant with every legal limitation I could summon, but a demon-infested ex-senator wasn't precisely a situation from the law books.

After I'd worked out all the parameters of what I was about to do, I staggered, held my head, and tried to look weak as I leaned against the wall. The gun barrel followed me, even if the demon eyes were fixated on Max/Dane. Evil controlled the gun?

I wish the meteorite's violent element will go away, letting Big Blue free, I told Saturn Daddy, improvising wildly. *And if you give me big boobs instead, I'll never play this game again,* I added, just because I was a lawyer and wanted all my bases covered.

Now, to the curse.

With the shriek piercing my skull, I called on all my Saturn willpower, shoved off the wall, and walked straight at MacNeill before Andre or Max could react. Polite visualizations weren't justice this time, I was pretty sure. I had to throw the book at him.

"DAMN THE DEMONS BACK TO THE DEPTHS TO WHICH THEY BELONG AND CLOSE THE PORTAL TO HELL OVER THEM!" I shouted my carefully rehearsed curse over the shriek.

And then, just for good measure, I kicked MacNeill's gun hand. Hard.

Milo yowled, did his blurry bigger-than-he-should-be act, and landed on MacNeill's face as he stumbled backward.

The gun went off, naturally. The bullet hit the ceiling and cracks crumbled the concrete. The shrieks escalated in fury, shaking loose gray dust like flour through a rusty sieve. The earth quaked and the floor beneath us rolled and groaned. Our flashlight beams barely cut through the dust cloud.

Andre grabbed my arm before I could fully register it all. "Out!" he shouted.

Wise idea, except my brain kept getting in the way. Wielding my Saturn power tended to leave me a wee bit confused and physically drained. I'd always used my power before in a red rage that left me in a state of shock. This time was different. I was still shaking—rightfully so given that the floor was rolling like a wave. But this time—I *felt* stronger, as if I really was a powerful person and not the meek mouse I'd always assumed.

I shook my head to clear the cobwebs. Power was dangerous unless wielded wisely. Had I done the right thing? I had to see results to know.

The ex-senator staggered around with a face full of cat fur. His gun skidded across the floor. Max grabbed Milo, bless his heart. I'd love him forever for that. He nearly collapsed under the weight of Mighty Cat, but Milo was apparently in a hurry to escape and went willingly, draping over Dane's big shoulder like a fur stole.

MacNeill fell to his knees, still screaming. I hadn't really noticed his screams amid the others but it was eerie and high-pitched now, kind of joining with the Force's shriek.

I pried off Andre's hand and shoved him toward the entrance. "Tell our voodoo priests to dance harder." I still didn't know if I'd exorcised the demon. I didn't feel so powerful that I wouldn't welcome a little help.

The cracked concrete floor couldn't hold much longer. I leaned over and tried to haul my victim back to his feet. Saving MacNeill's soul from damnation wouldn't do much good if he was buried under ten tons of tunnel.

Not that I knew I'd saved him yet. I just still had that problem with the death penalty for folks not legitimately convicted in a court of law.

Andre shot me a look of disgust, leaned over, and hauled a squalling MacNeill to his feet.

A cracking groan emerged from below us, as if the meteorite was shattering like the tunnel. I'd ordered Saturn to close the portal to hell. Stupidly, I hadn't really believed he would.

I had to believe now. A huge chunk of concrete fell from the ceiling, smashing not a yard from our heels, obliterating the gun— thank you, Daddy. Milo leaped off Dane and raced for the entrance.

Not as smart as my cat, Max grabbed his father's other arm.

"Blue, this is your chance!" I shouted, inhaling enough dust to make a garden gnome as we ran for the entrance. "Get out, get out, save yourself if you can!"

I had no way of knowing if he heard, if he could, or if I was just batshit nutso. I just wanted the poor creature to be safe. He gave no evidence of hearing me.

More tunnel ceiling dropped in a shower of concrete and dirt in our path. We scrambled over the hunks, hauling MacNeill, who seemed dazed and without any idea of what he was doing. I could hear chanting and singing and... gunfire? firecrackers?... above as we tumbled over the mountain of concrete, one step closer to escape.

The shriek crescendo reached a peak similar to that of Gloria and her tree going up in flame. I knew that noise. I grabbed both Max and Andre and held on as the vacuum whoosh of the hell hole closing hit us. *Again.*

The vacuum power yanked MacNeill out of our grasp, and he flew backward into a mountain of rubble, landing hard. I hung on to Andre and Max as best as I could, but we all collapsed into a heap on the floor, fighting the suction with our combined weights. Max and Andre each wrapped an arm around the nearest concrete debris and another around my waist.

This time, we weren't dragged across an entire mansion and slammed into a wall. The rubble may have saved our lives. Or our souls. I wasn't in any condition to work it out.

We huddled in a ball until the source of the vacuum blast was sealed off. Which, of course, was when we heard a more ominous rumble.

I'd really done it this time if the meteorite was being sucked into hell.

Thirty-two

WE all grabbed various parts of MacNeill and hauled him upright, then ran as fast as our bruised and battered legs would take us to the entrance. The rumbling grew louder.

We must have looked like gray ghosts when we emerged from the ground, into the sunlight. Even the witches backed off. Maybe they thought they'd raised the dead.

The earth cracked in a growing pattern behind us. I wanted to stop and kiss the ground and rejoice in the sky and breathe clean air. We didn't have time.

"Run!" I shouted, pointing in the direction of Milo racing across the field to Edgewater.

Andre was right on my heels, barking orders to his various employees, who began running for the street.

Leo already had part of his cop team herding tourists back to their cars as the dirt beneath our feet shook and the cracks widened in the harbor mud. The rest of his men dashed up to the industrial park to set off alarms and warn the workers to evacuate.

Taking their bodyguard status seriously, Lance and his boys grabbed a staggering Max/Dane and hurriedly hauled him toward the waiting cars. Max ordered them to get me, but I wasn't cooperating.

I dodged the boys and ran toward a bewildered Paddy. He stood at the front of the crowd with his bicycle, trying to sort out the unscientific action in his scientific head. I dragged him in his son's direction, and ran into the crowd, madly shouting, "Follow the cat!"

Milo had a habit of escaping unscathed and was as good a leader as any.

Intelligently, half the crowd obeyed and fled the crumbling, cracking harbor toward the safety of the pavement. The other half lingered in fascination as the hell hole belched gas, dust, and magic particles for all I knew.

Releasing Paddy now that I had him moving, I grabbed Hagatha's elbow and forced her to hurry despite her usual dithering. Her coven ran faster.

Slowly realizing the ground was falling out from beneath their feet, the rest of our audience began running for the hills or their cars.

The field shook and groaned, but this time, no water shot into the air.

The priest prayed aloud as he ran. Dr. Voodoo shooed his scattered students off the cracking dirt and kept them on our heels. I think they were dancing with happiness as they pounded their drums and shook their maracas and lithely scrambled for safety. A real live demon razing must have added to their curriculum knowledge.

The ground continued to crack and rumble as a sea of humanity fled up Edgewater. I feared if I looked over my shoulder, I'd turn into a pillar of salt. Or run into someone.

The news crews were torn between filming imminent disaster for the noon news and getting their padded rear ends to safety. When they finally panicked at whatever they saw behind me and ran up the side streets toward town, I knew it had to be bad. Still wasn't looking. The crashing, banging, cracking cacophony was scary enough.

I kept my eye on Milo. He maintained his pace so I could see him, but he was heading toward my office and home, exactly where I wanted to go.

Alarm sirens screamed at the plant. The gargoyles shrieked for a minute or two in accompaniment, then dropped into sullen silence. I glanced at the one on the florist's shop, and he shrugged at me.

Professor Nganga helped me haul a huffing and puffing Agatha up the steeper part of Edgewater. The blacktop seemed to be fine, for a change. The uproar behind us was dropping from train-rushing tornado volume to the steady pounding of hurricane-sized smashing ocean waves.

Miraculously, the air held only dust and a lingering stench of sulfur—no pink particles or poisonous green gas.

MacNeill's limo rolled to a stop beside us and the driver leaned out. "The senator said I should take you outta here. Hop in."

I opened the door and pushed Agatha inside. I gestured to Father Morrison to join her and lifted a questioning eyebrow at the professor, but apparently thinking about his students, he shook his head. A few more of the elderly witches trampled up, and I waved them inside. It was a limo. It could hold them.

The younger witches seemed to have partnered with the voodoo students, and they were all chattering excitedly and taking pictures of the devastation with their phones. With the invulnerability of youth, they had no interest in escaping the most exciting adventure of their lives. Only the elderly understood how senselessly life ended.

I could hear the Harleys roaring off in the wake of Max/Dane and his father's car. Nearing the crest of the hill, I was finally forced to look over my shoulder for Andre. He was walking backward, watching the destruction of the harbor.

And what a lovely obliteration my curse had caused. I watched in awe.

The entire contaminated zone—from Acme all the way down to the old chemical plant—was separating from solid ground and tumbling into the bay. I didn't think anyone would be fishing there anytime soon. Pillars, docks, rusted smokestacks, burned-out chemical tanks, all crumpled and spilled into the water with the cracking ground. Waves lapped against the blacktop where the Dumpsters used to dance.

The garbage cans had worked their way up the alleys to avoid rusting out their bottoms.

Clouds of dust settled over the landscape, but the blue neon buildings still gleamed through the gloom.

"Perhaps I should believe in the priest's God," the professor said thoughtfully. "It wouldn't hurt to have all the deities on our side."

"Yeah, I'm thinking we need all the good gods we can summon, because the bad ones are out to get us." I watched another chunk of real estate fall into the harbor, followed by a puff of smoke.

Acme and the other plants were on a hill, far enough above the devastation for their walls to be safe. But broken pipes hung off the side of the newly formed cliff. The pump to hell wouldn't be extracting meteorite anytime soon.

"Bye-bye, Blue," I said mournfully. Maybe the meteorite would protect him, but without his pipes and wires, he'd have a hard time spying on the Zone again.

I didn't intend to take credit for anything. Turning, I found my cat waiting patiently outside my office. Ned held the door open, but Milo wouldn't enter until I did. Checking to make sure that Andre wasn't breaking his neck walking backward, I hurried on with the professor and the students.

A crowd awaited us inside my lobby, standing around the blinking Christmas tree as if this were an office party. Katerina and Julius, looking worried, hugged me briefly, then harder when I told them Andre was right behind me. Cora and Sarah were pumping coffee from my giant urn and sharing with anyone who held out a hand.

They'd gathered most of the town up here to safety with their telephone calls, so Andre had a royal audience when he finally entered.

"Think Acme is still interested in buying out the Zone now?" I called from my perch on Ned's desk. I was still pumping adrenaline and my head hadn't completely processed the fact that Andre had almost sold us out, then walked through hell to save me. Well, he'd been Special Forces and suicidal in his past, so there was the crazy quotient to consider... but we'd had amazing sex and he'd scared me shitless, and I just couldn't handle the roiling emotions any longer.

The room got quiet as we awaited Andre's verdict.

My mouth was gritty with dust, and I was shaking like a leaf, so I sipped coffee and pretended nonchalance. My court of law was pretty weird, but I tried to stay in command of it.

Black silk wasn't pretty when covered in thick layers of grime. Even Andre's glossy black hair had dulled to the gray of old age, but there was nothing old about the fire in his eyes when he reached me.

He yanked me off the desk, spilling coffee everywhere. Before an audience of all our friends and neighbors, he kissed me.

I had no clue why. I'd been pretty damned obnoxious. But it was better than being strangled. Far, far better. Confusion cast aside, I fell into the contact with great enthusiasm, wrapping my arms around his neck and digging my fingers into his filthy hair and exchanging heated breath and lots of tongue. We both stank from sweaty fear but who cared? We celebrated being alive, bodies still intact.

He yanked me closer, and I would have been climbing his legs, except loud applause broke out, and I had to shove him away.

"I take it that means it's back to business as usual," I said, still shivering but for a different reason as we pulled apart.

"If they don't condemn the entire Zone," he agreed with a shrug. "We'd better let the city inspectors verify the town is stable before we return to work."

"So we'll still need representation on the city council," Katerina said, rolling up in her chair.

At Andre's reluctant nod, his mother gestured. "Back to our petitions, children! Where's Jane? We need a press release immediately. Ned, come with me—" She rolled off, leading her army of adoring slaves.

Julius stopped to examine us both. "The story, please, over dinner. Shall I expect more lawsuits?"

"MacNeill," I warned, coming back to ground with a hard thump. "And the skeletons. We should find out who went missing while working over there."

"Not now on the skeletons," Andre warned. "They're buried under a ton of debris and half the harbor. And your boyfriend walked off with the evidence. Find out about MacNeill."

Grasping that skeletons beat out civil lawsuits, Julius waited.

I called Jane in my apartment to tell her it was safe to return, then punched in Max/Dane's number. He picked up immediately.

"Justy, why aren't you in the damned limo? I need you and not batty witches to deal with this mess!"

"No, you need a doctor for Mikey and your PR person to deal with the explosion at Acme and a board meeting to put someone else in charge besides daddy dearest. And while you have him with you, you'd best start talking to Paddy for a change and pass the board meeting on to him while you quietly disappear into your mansion and have a fundraiser complete with nuns. If the media captured any photos of you with a voodoo priest, you'll never survive Christmas."

His sigh was loud and expletive laden. When he calmed down, he asked wearily, "Where are you? Is everyone okay?"

"I'm in my office and my partner is gearing up to sue anyone who moves and his wife is petitioning for a seat on the council and you'd just better lay real low. We have no idea what the damages are. Gloria's trust fund might be better put to work repairing..." I looked for a proper PC description of blowing up hell. "Repairing the Zone's infrastructure after today's devastating collapse of Civil War tunnels."

"Right." I could almost see him pinching the bridge of his nose as he adjusted his thinking. "Mikey is raving. We're at the psych unit now. Want to tell me what really happened?"

"You think I have a clue?" Shrugging at Julius and Andre, I took the phone to my office and closed the door to continue this conversation. "I think he was possessed. I can make up theories all day long, but if Gloria opened a hole to hell in her basement—and demons or whatever creepiness you want to believe infected her—then there's some chance the same thing happened to Mikey."

"But Gloria's dead and Mikey isn't. Not that I want him dead, but if he was responsible for those two skeletons..."

"No way of knowing that," I warned. "And how much do we lay on demons? We don't know if he's just plain nuts, or if Dane or Gloria shoved a couple of workmen down a hole. Or that two guys didn't die from messing with the meteorite, as Mikey seemed to believe. Let the legal system do its job. You walked away with the evidence. Any ID there?"

Max/Dane hesitated as if he'd forgotten and was digging about in his pockets. "They may once have been plasticized ID cards of some sort," he said, apparently finding them. "They're little more than illegible dust now."

"The skeletons just got blown to hell. Without them, we have no legal or scientific evidence to stand on. I believe in the meteorite. I believe Paddy and the scientists have found a new element inside that meteorite. I believe two people died, probably a decade ago, while messing with the meteorite. Those are the only real pieces of the puzzle that exist. All the rest... science fiction fantasy."

What, you want me to have a U.S. Senator tell the world that we exorcised a demon from MacNeill's soul and sent it back to hell, maybe with the help of voodoo priests and witches? And in gratitude, Saturn sank a meteorite at my request? Who do you think would end up in the psych ward then?

"Fantasy, right," the good senator said with resignation. "I'll just think in terms of disaster emergency teams and go from there. I'll get people down to inspect the damage."

"You're a smart man, Maxie, a lot smarter than Dane. You can go far if you just let go of the fantasy." I snuggled the phone next to my ear, knowing this was as close to a senator as I would get once we got past this bump in the road. I liked Max a lot, but his interests were now on the side of the establishment, which was too close to his cousin Dane for my comfort. He needed a wife raised for his senatorial lifestyle, and that ain't me, babe. "Let me know how MacNeill fares and if there's anything else I need to do."

"You have to start meeting and greeting power mongers if you're to be the Zone's attorney," the good senator declared. "Find your little black dress. The limo will pick you up Saturday night."

He hung up. Damn the man, no matter how I tried to brush him off, he refused to go. Like me, Max was a persistent mosquito. I'd have to find him a better target.

I returned to Andre and Julius, who solicitously steered me toward home and a shower without questioning me about my senatorial connection and his demented relation. Julius was kind like that. Andre asked if he could join me in the shower.

I almost said yes—until I remembered the tablet with Themis's warning.

Virgin babies, scary stuff. Not going there.

I took the stairs to my apartment with only my cat on my heels.

A piece of plaster with charcoal scratching lay on the carpeted hall in front of my door. I almost closed my eyes and walked over it, I was that drained.

But curiosity won out. I picked it up and carried it inside. While Milo licked himself clean in the window, I turned on a light and studied the chicken scratching.

You need a friend, aziz. I'm sending one. She is not as strong as you, but she is wise. The world is changing, and I cannot help.

With trepidation, I glanced at my tablet on the table. It could wait until after I'd showered. I needed to be prepared before I discovered what Themis's idea of a *friend* might be.

Over dinner at the Montoyas, Andre and I attempted to describe what we'd discovered under the harbor grounds—without explaining the supernatural. Even we didn't entirely understand hell holes and demonic possession. We could just hope that the sinking of the meteorite had ended that episode of Zone history.

"Will Acme be able to remain open?" Katerina asked. "They're still making other chemicals, aren't they?"

"We don't know how much of the element they've stored," Andre warned. "Paddy needs to pay more attention to business."

That was an old argument, and I let my mind drift back to the latest message I'd found waiting on my tablet—a Christmas card from Fat Chick saying she'd be in Baltimore over the holiday and asking if we could meet.

Fat Chick ran the Saturn's Daughters website. Themis had sent me the gift of a lifetime—a friend. I was both excited and terrified.

"We should have a Christmas party at the shelter!" Katerina was saying excitedly when I tuned back in. "It will be a wonderful way to bring the community together!"

Because so many of us had nowhere else to go. I brightened as the idea took root. "I can go shopping for the kids!" For something better than painted garden gnomes—another ugly blot on my escutcheon.

Plotting something pleasant for a change lifted my mood considerably. Who could worry about buried space aliens and meteorites churning up the harbor and armed garden gnomes while

planning Santa Claus and candy canes?
 Finally, I'd have a real Christmas!

Thirty-three

LEIBOWITZ refused to wear the Santa suit again, but Lieutenant Leo made a far more intelligent jolly old fellow. Schwartz handed out candy canes and new coats to one and all and didn't stomp off muttering when a toddler peed on the velvet suit.

"Leo's too good for us," Cora muttered, sipping the punch and wearing an elf costume. "He took the night shift all week so the guys with kids could have time off."

"Then he's flying down to visit his mother in Florida," I reminded her. "He's just normal. People like that exist. We just tend to forget it."

"For good reason," she grumbled, nodding at a khaki-costumed group in the corner of the festive lobby of the homeless shelter. "What are MSI's Nazis doing here besides frightening babies?"

I grinned and opened my box of elf hats. I was wearing reindeer antlers and a red nose. The spirit of Christmas should be on all of us. "Come on, I'll show you."

The uniformed security guards looked a little terrified at my approach—probably a lingering subconscious memory linking me to their time in concrete. This time, I wasn't making the mistake of letting my victims wander off and build up a hate against me. I'd made it my task to reform them—just a little. A little human compassion never hurt anyone.

I smiled and offered the box of red and green felt. "Join the party, gentlemen! There's enough punch and cookies for all."

They looked leery, then glanced to their fearless leader. Graham Young was dressed in a monk's brown homespun as he handed out gifts at Santa's feet. They hadn't been able to keep him in the psych ward just because he now thought he was a saint. Little kids clambered all over him, and he hadn't smacked one yet—close enough to sainthood, I supposed. I'd have to keep an eye on him too.

His security team reluctantly donned their caps. Cora tucked candy canes in their pockets. We swept away, stifling our giggles.

"I'm going to miss the weirdness," Cora admitted. "Where else could an arrogant CEO be turned into a gnome and then into the patron saint of the homeless?"

"We don't know that the Weird is gone," I warned. "Never get too confident." But I stopped to admire our handiwork anyway. With all the gifts handed out, Graham Young was climbing to his feet and talking to our eminent Do-Gooder, Rob Hanks. "I think Andre has agreed to sell the insurance building to the DG's, and it's Young's money financing the sale and renovations. Makes me believe in miracles again."

Or pink particles. If only Paddy could corner the market on Good!

Tim wandered up festooned in Christmas wreaths and ribbons but wearing clothes that fit and didn't scream pink—which clashed with red ribbons apparently. "Ned's dipping spiders in frosting again. He said he's taking them to some friends of his in jail. I thought he was one of the good guys."

"He is, young grasshopper, he is. Someday, you'll understand the many layers of good and evil." I hugged him and kissed his forehead, and he didn't disappear in embarrassment. "Thank you and Nancy Rose for the tree and wreaths. Is she still talking of retiring to Florida?"

"Nah, she thinks she's going to add a greenhouse so we can grow more of our own inventory. That federal grant thing she got from the disaster emergency fund is letting her fix up the apartment, too. She wants me to move in there and live with her and think about college. I don't need school to grow things, do I?"

"You need school if you plan to *sell* green things, and if you don't plan to sell them, then you'll need a job to pay for them, so, yeah, you need school, knucklehead. Go help Ned nab flies for his frosting feast and don't grow up too fast, okay?"

He shot me a weird look and dashed off to play.

"I think Santa needs to get lucky," Cora said, apropos of nothing as she watched Leo stiffly nod at a young mother babbling her problems to him. "And he deserves better than that skag." She sauntered off, all eye-popping swaying curves that Santa noticed for a change.

I grinned, glanced around, and found Sarah and Ernesto arguing over the punch bowl. Sarah arguing was actually a *good* thing, especially when she was no longer carrying weapons. Score another for the Zone and pink particles.

Mrs. Bodine had been persuaded to leave her apartment to join the party. She was wearing the red satin jumpsuit I'd bought her, and talking to Paddy. Our resident scientist was still wearing faded brown corduroy, with the added touch of a new tweed jacket with leather elbow patches. He caught me looking his direction and waved me over.

Paddy wasn't a hugger. Given what I'd learned of him over the past months, I thought he might suffer from some form of Asperger's. But he tweaked my red nose when I hugged him. I blamed it on someone spiking the punch when my eyes teared up at this gesture of affection.

"Not everyone at Acme hates me yet?" I asked.

"You're a burr under everyone's saddle, Clancy, of course you irritate," Paddy said. "But someone needs to remind us that we're not a majority of one."

"I love it when he talks smart like that," Mrs. Bodine said with a sigh. "If only I were a few years younger."

Maybe a few decades, but I politely refrained from bursting her bubble. "And are you seeing any of your family today, Mr. Vanderventer?" I asked with equal solemnity.

Paddy's eyes lit with what I suspected might be laughter. "Has the media arrived yet? I think the press conference is scheduled for noon."

"Press conference?—he didn't!" I exclaimed, glancing around for symptoms of media break-out.

"He did. Dane may be a publicity slut, but at least he's finally doing some good with his talents. He even has MacNeill eating out of his hand these days." Paddy studied a plate of sugar cookies one of the kids waved in his direction, selecting one frosted in a particularly hideous swirl of muddy color that no one else had wanted.

Ernesto's kitchen staff had been helping the shelter inhabitants bake all week. The results had been... interesting.

"He does?" I asked warily, still watching for journalists. And Dane, admittedly. "How is Senator MacNeill doing?" I politely didn't add "since his demon possession and resultant freak-out." I was practicing political correctness for the holidays.

"A little strange since his breakdown," Paddy said without concern. "We're keeping him out of the board offices, letting him work uptown. He's the one who talked Young into sponsoring the shelter. They've agreed the Zone isn't the best location for the medical center, even though the EPA gave Edgewater a clean bill of health and our infrastructure will be completely updated. Have you noticed that all our phone calls are going through now?"

That was the real reason for today's joy and celebration—the street was no longer an environmental hazard zone, just the harbor, and our manholes no longer glowed red. Andre could keep his property.

I wanted brass bands and fireworks to release the fizzing joy. We could keep our homes! The relief was so all encompassing that I wanted to hug everyone. Alcohol wasn't the cause for all the laughter and bright eyes around us—it was pure joy, everywhere I looked.

The swell of noise at the front door warned of Senator Vanderventer's arrival, or his advance entourage at least. I deliberately didn't watch but glanced toward the back instead—where Andre was working his way through the partying crowd, his dark gaze on me, making me remember that devastating kiss we'd shared. He had the power to light up my nights, if I'd let him.

Maybe it was time to let him, Saturn be damned, so to speak.

The bandage had been removed after his encounter with the meteorite. His thick hair fell over the scar—the medal for his heroics in rescuing me. For that, I allowed him to drop a possessive arm over my shoulders. He handed me a champagne glass that smelled as if it might contain something besides punch. I pinched his ribs.

"And what has the EPA decided to do about the harbor pollution?" I asked, just to prove I wasn't paying attention to the commotion at the entrance.

"The morons can't test for elements that don't exist, Clancy," Andre replied. "They're warning fishermen away because of the chemical contamination from the buildings that fell in. We have no idea what else is in there, but we won't be turning it into a beach anytime soon."

"I'm glad we have the shelter for the homeless then. And I won't miss that spooky stretch along the water in the least." I walked away from his arm and set the glass on a festive mantel adorned with empty stockings. We'd filled them with candy last night, but that hadn't lasted long.

I finally gave in to curiosity and turned to watch the senator make his grand entrance. Dane was looking good, less frazzled and more confident as he shook Graham Young's hand—while he held my gaze. Damn, but I *knew* he had the ability to rock my world. He'd done it more than once.

I waited for him to come to me, despite Andre's possessive arm over my shoulders.

I'd accompanied Dane to a party of D.C. bigwigs last week. I'd finally had my hair cut and styled into quirky spikes to keep it out of my face, and I'd worn my little black dress—with knee high leather boots and spiked heels. I think I made an impression. I didn't ask what kind.

Dane's smooth chestnut hair and politician's smile still grated my soul, but Max's naughtiness wrinkled the corners of the senator's eyes as he shook Paddy's hand and was introduced to Mrs. Bodine.

The senator lifted a grimy toddler in an elf cap to his shoulder and accepted a taste of a dirty candy cane. The media eagerly snapped pictures. He held the position until everyone got a good shot, then offered the kid a quarter and sent her back to her mother.

Andre rested his arm on the mantel next to me and watched the performance with his usual cynical sneer. "Still not liking your boyfriend, Clancy."

"He's not my boyfriend, Legrande. I'm swearing off boyfriends for the next year. I'm thinking of joining Agatha's coven."

I thought he might burst a gut holding in his laughter.

Dane marched over and held his hand out to Andre. The two shook with the same dishonest smarminess that got under my skin—except I knew both of them were good men in their own wicked ways, probably better than me.

They sauntered off to make the announcement of the grant for federal rehabilitation of the Zone and its environs, backed with a matching grant from Gloria's trust fund.

The banshee didn't shriek as they did it.

For New Year's Eve, Andre and I traveled across the harbor to Fell's Point to meet Anita Beaumonde—the Fat Chick in Canada. She was even prettier than her photo on her blog. She wore her gorgeous Viking red hair in an elaborate style decorated with gold sparkly ribbons and a slinky gown that revealed cleavage far better than anything I'd ever manage. The wheelchair didn't seem to hamper her much. Andre swung her chair around the dance floor and made everyone stand back and watch. Including me.

We exchanged cards and phone numbers and promised to stay in touch—all within the safety of the noisy bar where security could pass judgment on the drunks. I wasn't damning anyone tonight.

At the stroke of midnight, we blew horns and threw confetti and exchanged kisses like normal people. I was probably happier than I'd ever been in my life.

Later, when Anita had returned to her hotel, and Andre and I staggered toward the rooms we'd taken for the night, we stopped and exchanged a few more hormone-inducing New Year's Eve kisses. He was still my client. I still wasn't going to bed with him. But we were drunk and heading for a hotel. Anything could happen.

When we spun back to earth again, the dark warehouse in front of us was glowing neon blue, and I laughed with true joy. Blue lives on.

Author Bio

With several million books in print and *New York Times* and *USA Today's* bestseller lists under her belt, former CPA Patricia Rice is one of romance's hottest authors. Her emotionally-charged contemporary and historical romances have won numerous awards, including the *RT Book Reviews* Reviewers Choice and Career Achievement Awards. Her books have been honored as Romance Writers of America RITA® finalists in the historical, regency and contemporary categories.

A firm believer in happily-ever-after, Patricia Rice is married to her high school sweetheart and has two children. A native of Kentucky and New York, a past resident of North Carolina and Missouri, she currently resides in Southern California, and now does accounting only for herself. She is a member of Romance Writers of America, the Authors Guild, and Novelists, Inc.

For further information, visit Patricia's network:
http://www.patriciarice.com
http://www.facebook.com/OfficialPatriciaRice
https://twitter.com/Patricia_Rice
http://patriciarice.blogspot.com/
http://wordwenches.typepad.com/word_wenches/
http://patricia-rice.tumblr.com/

Made in the USA
Monee, IL
29 October 2020